OTHER BOOKS B'

Air-

Earth-

Winter Goose Publishing
45 Lafayette Road #114
North Hampton, NH 03862

wintergoosepublishing.com
Contact Information: info@wintergoosepublishing.com

Sea-Drawn

COPYRIGHT © 2018 by Laura Power

First Edition, November 2018

Cover Design by Winter Goose Publishing

ISBN: 978-1-941058-85-5

Published in the United States of America

SEA-DRAWN

Laura Power

Winter Goose
PUBLISHING
where words take flight
wintergoosepublishing.com

For Margaret Power
As indomitable and beloved as all these characters together

The Greenwood Court Challenge

It really wasn't the night for such a fool's errand, the tavern girls had warned her. Yet, with the moon high and the wind howling, Naya reckoned it wasn't a bad one for chasing dreams, as dangerous as they proved in times like these.

One night's warning before the storm breaks, Roanen had whispered, and now that night was half-leached already, filled as it had been with the difficulty of evading a paranoia-pressed mob of self-appointed townsguards. Yet if the Nomad's portent proved true, she wouldn't just be part of the warning, but part of the resistance, and the knowledge sent her fleeing onwards fast as a wolf.

Urgency thrummed through the narrow street, carried on the claustrophobia of a still-wary town that had only recently lifted itself from the shadow of Goblin rule. Now it was pulling its shutters on the whispers of an ephemeral, swiftly gathering fear. Of course the Authorities, those that remained, had dismissed the Nomad's stories, yet Naya was more inclined to believe the rumours of one who had walked with Dragons than the truths of those who cowered behind the city walls, and so Roanen's words had sent her breaking curfew and darting through the shrouded streets, fleeing the restless unease that clutched Arkh Loban.

She had to find out what it was they were facing, and her investigation could no longer wait for a more opportune time. The knowledge chilled her, yet the winds snaking in from the open plains kissed her heels in encouragement, sweeping their enchantment along her unfurling path and billowing her courage until her plans spread across the reaches of the desert and beyond.

With the starlight stretching expansively and dancing above her as she fled the entrapments of the city, Naya rode until the restless possibilities of the spilling sands snuffed the battering pressures of a fractious day. The open night swirled around her, voluminous with stardust and moon motes.

Would she be on time? Too late? What if—

But as she careened off the Travellers' Pass, ducking beneath the sheltering, secretive arms of the arboreal guardians of the Endless Forest, stumbling and almost falling in her haste as she jumped from Taiko's back, she glimpsed the shimmer of Fairy wings ahead, like the flash and glimmer of fireflies through the trees. Naya's face split into a grin. The Greenwood Court was gathering! Roanen had been right—it was time.

A twinge of guilt writhed as reality pressed in; she'd barely finished her nightshift and was due in again tomorrow morn. Flinging her doubts aside, Naya drew her courage around her like a cloak and, pushing her tangled hair from her face, slipped between the beckoning fingers of the trees. Her breath clouded in the wet chill, mingling with the ethereal mist shrouding the bank as she gasped to behold the fabled Moonstruck Lake shimmering beyond.

You are part of this now. She could almost hear the Water Nymph's voice curling around her in approval. *Those of the desert sands are needed here, as much as those of earth and wood, sea and sky.* The dewy touch of branching fingers urged her forward, and she crept towards the lakeside clearing until the trees parted and the moonlight smiled down unfettered upon a people unseen in the Realm for decades.

But she had no time to dwell on the implications further. Naya had invitations to write.

A Stranger Summons

The post-quest spark still lit her eyes, yet misgiving crawled along Amber's spine and curled nauseatingly in the pit of her stomach as she unfurled a different invitation: one as exasperatingly inescapable as it was now obstinately crumpled.

Her apprenticeship offer. She had received it not long after the Wolfren's disbanding of the Goblin horde, Slaygerin's self-sacrificial destruction of the Vetches, and her own near-fatal attempt which had destroyed the Venom-Spitter Samire. Yet, although the tangled threads of that conflict had only just been tied and cut, she found this new challenge filled her with more dread than the old one ever had.

She had got through that—she could get through this. She heard herself say the words in her head and tried desperately to believe them. *What we were part of won't die*, she reminded herself. *But neither will it be repeated. Be thankful for both.*

An impression of lava and shadow flourished into being, and a molten, ephemeral voice curled around her and the letter like health-infusing vapour. "Not what you were looking for?" the Genie urged.

Amber brandished the parchment dispiritedly, wishing she could stave off its intrusion into a reality she had so desperately hoped she could change after all she and her friends had been through. "No," she risked, awkward with embarrassment. "But I don't think I know what I'm looking for, now that things are normal again."

The Genie shrugged in his turn, managing to make it look like a subtle casting off of shackles rather than a manifestation of her confusion. "Or perhaps you just know you're not looking for normal." His fire-spark eyes glowed—some would say dangerously, but she'd never cared to listen. "Never settle for desires that don't satisfy. Never be ashamed to keep searching."

"You think my search isn't over?" Amber drank his words thirstily. "You think I'm still on a quest?"

His eyes sparked hypnotically. "That decision rests with you." And then he faded, leaving a void for her thoughts to fill.

She grinned and bit her lip as she considered. Okay then, she would find a way. She carved a fierce smile into the silence, feeling better, even though she had nothing left to deflect her attention from the step she now had to take. Nothing apart from her own thoughts—and maybe, now, they would be enough. But still, it felt weird to hold so much fear for something so normal. Maybe that was it, she risked admitting to herself. At least you were allowed to be scared of all that stuff. But being scared of this, they'll think you're just ridiculous.

Amber glared accusingly at the scrap of parchment, with its myriad instructions, read it again, and grimaced despairingly. "Apparently the magic really is fading from the Realm."

"Sen, but they tried to tell us that once before." Racxen's shadow appeared crouched at the window ledge. "And it seems to me the Realm is more full of magic than ever before."

Seeing him drop down lightly, Amber felt a joy bloom in her chest that for now eclipsed her doubts about the apprenticeship and that always made her know that the future would be faceable.

She let herself grin unashamedly. It felt ridiculously good to see him, and amazingly right. Despite what Ruby had well-meaningly prophecised, familiarity had only increased her excitement at seeing him; every day she grew to know him better, she found new reasons to admire and love him, and in turn enjoyed basking in his new discoveries. "Still feel the same?"

"No." Racxen encircled her gently in his arms, his reassuring smile betraying his word as he stepped closer, to hold her tighter than he had before only in dreams. "You mean even more to me now than ever."

"You ready, Am?"

Amber started guiltily, shaken out of her memory by the ever punctual, ever perky Ruby, who looked altogether too exuberant for the moment they were about to sign their lives away.

"I guess." Amber tried to inject some enthusiasm into her voice, but it felt like a betrayal. She refocused on the looming rec hall, the appointed registration centre for apprenticeships in medical and healing professions. At least this time she wasn't being carried here semi-conscious after—

"Amber, it can't be that bad if everyone's doing it," Ruby insisted. "You've already done a few months with Sarin anyway. I've signed up fully."

When her friend didn't answer, a note of frustration crept into Ruby's voice. "C'mon, Amber. You've got to grow up sometime."

"Mm," Amber answered distractedly, staring at the curling-edged parchment pinned unscrolled across the rec hall door: "Hall closed until further notice in preparation for the Greenwood Court Challenge."

Her heart skipped a beat and she turned back triumphantly to Ruby, her eyes fiercely agleam and her heart afire again. "Not today, though!"

Queenly Choices

"This summons," Laksha offered, the scroll clutched tightly in her steel-grey fist and glowing beneath the shivering light of the torch as dusk and decisions began both to gather. "Yer want me ter go, my lady?"

The Queen hesitated, contemplating sending her handmaiden. Possessed of the kind of restless charisma which on the tongue of the rest of her kin proved so dangerously beguiling, Laksha would establish herself as more than a match for any attendant at the Greenwood Court.

"Of course," Pearl promised with a knowing smile, as she swept a rich velvet cloak around her shoulders. "But at my side, for I would not miss this for another thousand years."

"But *you* haven't been summoned," the Prince complained weakly, clinging to his original premise as doggedly as he clutched his own parchment. "Good grief, Amber, the whole Realm doesn't revolve around you."

"Just give me this one night, Jasper, before everything sinks back to normal." Cheerfully ignoring him, Amber felt a shiver of the old excitement dance across her skin as she followed Racxen and Ruby. The once-familiar landscape shimmered enticingly exotic, painted with the silver brush of moonlight, and she slowed as a shadow-tangle of trees rose to greet them.

Normally, councils were held at the Fairy Ring. But this concerned the whole Realm, so everyone was gathering in a wilder setting: the Greenwood—rumoured to be the birthplace of sentience in the Realm. It sprawled slightly shrunkenly now, but the Wildwood Labyrinth, through Trickster's Gate at its centre, still stood in untarnished majesty, as it had through all the trials of the Realm. Knowing it lifted Amber's heart. The Realm was still huge, still thrumming with chances. These unknown boughs whispered with a collective rush of ancient arboreal tongues as she approached, breathing ageless secrets, murmuring soothing, subtle truths in languages every being of the Realm had once understood. Surely magic would find a place here, resting somewhere beneath the eaves. And, she found herself hoping silently, surely such spirit as resided therein would understand the reasons throbbing within her heart as to why she needed some kind of quest again, whether summoned to it or not.

They were getting closer now, Amber realised with a frisson of excitement, and with throngs of people gathering she pressed closer to her friends and zoned back into the conversation.

"So it's a challenge from whom? About what?" Ruby was asking Jasper again, struggling to make sense of it.

The Prince raised his eyes skyward.

"Perhaps if you told us what's going on, we'd stop asking you questions," Amber suggested with a grin. She could barely hear herself think above the jostling of murmured rumours rippling through the assembling crowds. "Could you not tell us now, before everyone arrives and the King sets the challenge?"

Jasper sighed, then spread his hands in acquiescence. "According to the announcement my father is about to make, Zaralathaar the Enchantress—our Water Nymph—is dying," he began, keeping his voice low. "So the leaders of this Realm, my father included, have called the Greenwood Court together for advice on how best to conjure sufficient magic to sustain the Fountain in her absence, so that the Realm is not left open to attack. But only one member came."

The news of Zaralathaar clutched around Amber's throat so strongly she had trouble following the others' responses.

"So? The Greenwood Court are the oldest, most magical denizens still living—and they are bound by a covenant of their own devising to assist the Realm's less magical inhabitants in exactly situations as these," Ruby reminded him, somewhat smug that she knew this. "Why are you worried?"

"Because I don't like the feeling that we are now beholden to a being who wields far greater power than anyone else left in the Realm," Jasper admitted. "I thought the Water Nymph was the last of the Greenwood Court. I didn't think anyone else would heed the call—and now I don't know what we have unearthed. It seems that now Zaralathaar is ageing, a new successor is emerging. From the forest, not the sea."

"But still from the Court," Ruby reminded. "So I assume it's a good thing?"

Jasper tugged a hand through his hair. "Difficult to ascertain. I certainly hope so. We don't seem to have much choice in the matter. We called the Court, and this being came—awoken from the depths of the Wildwood Labyrinth amidst the oldest forests of the Realm. He seems to share Zaralathaar's penchant for forcing us to solve our own problems, and only offering the vaguest assistance."

Amber managed to grin. "This is starting to feel like familiar ground. What does he think we should do?"

Jasper sighed. "He has directed us to an old legend regarding the restoration of magic to the Realm. If the Kelpie living in Moonstruck Lake can be summoned, and ridden for an entire lap of the Lake, magic will be returned to the Realm, and the balance restored sufficiently to protect the Fountain and everything the Water Nymph worked for."

Amber thought. "And Zaralathaar is in agreement with this?"

Jasper sighed. "She grows frail, Amber. We cannot force an elder to make such a journey. She has no idea, and I have not the heart to tell her. This is old magic. Dangerous. If one were being honest, one might rather call it sorcery. And yet magic is leaching from the Realm faster than anticipated, and the Moonstruck Lake Challenge is our last-ditch effort."

The friends considered it in silence.

"So, Moonstruck Lake? That everyone stays away from for fear the waters send you mad?"

"It would appear so."

"And the Kelpie? The ravenous creature more storm-energy than water-horse?"

"Indeed."

Amber grinned and squeezed Racxen's hand. "I think this might be your department."

Racxen grinned back, his eyes aglow as they watched potential challengers from every corner of the Realm arrive.

Unfathomable Depths

"Who are they?" Against the shifting hues of night Amber watched as the rough-skinned figures bedecked in grey fur seemed to float, solemn-eyed, beneath the trees, the shadowed contours of their gaunt faces stark against the softer darkness of the forest. A strange shiver rolled along her spine like the breaking of a midnight wave.

The Genie formed amongst deeper shadows, the outline of his form a swirling undercurrent. "Selkies."

The word tumbled into her consciousness like sea glass gleaming through near-unreachable depths; warning and alluring, washed through with the same chaotic promise of tumultuous renewal as a Renë tide.

"Seal People, from the North?" she recalled in a murmur. "You're going to tell me their presence is vital to this quest?"

"I don't think I need to," purred the Genie in an undertone. "Although the others seem not to have noticed."

"But why are they here?"

For once, the Genie did not have an immediate answer. "Why are any of us here? We come undaunted, to stand together against the inevitable. The Realm grows ever more fractured—we must never lose sight of the fact we are stronger together, in all our strange and wondrous diversity, than if we allow fear and uncertainty to split us apart." The Genie considered for a moment. "Being a people of the water, they share a powerful bond with Zaralathaar. Perhaps they come because her time grows near."

Amber shivered again, caught in an intoxicating chill. Jasper offered them not a second glance, but the Seal People drew Amber's attention more than any of the other people gathering. There was something hypnotic about their gaze. They seemed both haunted and strangely calm, as though soothed by something Amber couldn't be sure would ever lie along her plane of experience, let alone within her grasp. With their distant stares as soothing and as glittering with magic as the Icefields they had journeyed to make their journey, they gave the distinct impression that the great number of miles traversed during their migration had done nothing to shake off such an experience, nor diminish its meaning. And yet, for souls seemingly possessing so much, something felt missing. She couldn't help feeling like they might be the ones that required saving. They walked proudly and calmly, yes—but there seemed a desperation in the way they clasped the pelts draping their fine clothes, as though needing reassurance that they were still there.

Amber couldn't take her eyes off the group. She could vaguely remember Ruby having gone on about Selkies being as beautiful as the Sea Folk, but more powerful, more earthy and primal. Amber was pretty sure Ruby had been blushing by that point. But to her they looked unhappy. Dignified and resilient, sustained by some untouchable inner reserve, but unhappy. She had a fleeting memory of having seen a colony of seals so long ago when she had flown—*yes*, she told herself, *after all this time you cannot allow yourself to flinch*—over the coast; she had meant to fly out over the sea but had lost her nerve and traced the shore instead. There she had seen them, sending sea spray scattering in prismatic droplets as they hauled themselves out in the sun, fat and sleek and barking raucously, the epitome of happiness, and for a moment she wished more than anything that she would be able to one day see the Selkies like that.

Wrapped in her thoughts, Amber let the chatter of the others fade into a lull around her as Jasper broke away to push towards the front. The news of the Water Nymph squeezed hotly around her throat in his absence; Zaralathaar was the strongest, most impervious woman Amber had ever met, and she had automatically assigned to her the same immortality as the rocks and ocean the Water Nymph held sway over. Even the Prince bore her tremendous respect. She would leave a void in the Realm that none other could fill.

"She does not gather us to urge submission to her fate, but to remind us that the most precious time left is still in our keeping." Racxen's breath twined in her hair and her soul as he wrapped a comforting arm around her.

Amber leaned in against him and nodded fierce thanks. They owed it to the Water Nymph to try anything, and if she had but a short span left in this Realm she would leave it knowing its every inhabitant had pledged the best of their courage in fulfilling her last request. Amber could think of no one better to step forward to this challenge than Racxen, and whatever was best for Zaralathaar was best for the Realm right now—and must be held in far greater importance than her fears for a man who had never held her back from her dreams no matter how dangerous. Her own fears about no longer being needed—there was no point attempting the challenge when someone as attuned to animals as Racxen stood to triumph—she would have to learn to quash on her own.

"It's nearly time to call the summons. Go on." She kissed him firmly and grinned, her heart buoyant to realise that she was now pushing Racxen on as proudly as she had not so long ago urged Ruby forward at the presentation of the Gems. The knowledge eased her skittering heart. Zaralathaar might not need her, but Racxen and her friends still did. What they had survived, and pledged, and were building, bloomed in her chest, and formed a subtle armour which she knew would never fail her. She willed Racxen on, knowing what they were capable of both together and apart, and knowing she could stand on her own. He had supported her through all the trials of the past seasons. She was proud to lend him the same strength now and that had to start with being strong for herself. Providing support was more important now than taking centre stage.

"Who will attempt this challenge?" King Morgan's strident voice rang through her thoughts and chased off her fears into an expectant lull, charged with the thrill of anticipation. "Whence will step forth such a contestant for the feat?"

Jasper stepped forward smoothly: "From the Kingdom."

Racxen slipped from the shadows: "From the Tribe."

Yenna strode into the clearing, the Wolf Sister's golden eyes blazing beneath the night-deep scarf swept about her head: "From the Pack."

Night seemed to lift back a veil as a pale-skinned man cloaked in mottled fur stepped forward: "From the Clan."

The next moments passed in heraldic blur, until Amber let out a shuddering breath, trying to draw herself back to the present and anchor herself in a situation slipping already out of control. Everyone but her had a place, a purpose in this quest. It had all been decided without her, and soon it would all slide into motion completely independent of her intentions or actions. She itched for something to contribute, something to do—

something to battle the worrying sensation that this development rendered her utterly useless to her friends. Morosely, she took refuge amongst the darker shadows under the trees, instinctively seeking solitude and edging towards the Ring, the circle of toadstools that formed the seating for the Council.

"Welcome back, child." A deep, reassuringly familiar voice floated through the dusky twilight.

Amber's smile was tinged with melancholy. "I don't think you can call me a child anymore."

The King gestured lightly to the towering toadstools soaring into the farther gloom. "These are the oldest living things in the Realm. In their presence, we are both children." He paused, his ocean-grey eyes piercing the fog that she feared had gathered round her mind. "You have borne too great a burden of late. Let others take the load. You have your apprenticeship to focus on now; I would not take such an opportunity from you for all the gathering forces in the Realm."

Great. Even you don't understand.

Left alone, Amber listened with half an ear to the storm-shivered breeze. She thought she saw the ghost of a silhouette gusting amongst the cloud.

"Tell me your . . . you know. Wishes. Thoughts. Whatever." The Genie's grin lingered in the air.

Amber grinned back, then sighed fretfully as she let him guide her back towards the others. "Racxen's going after the Kelpie," she admitted in a mumble while they were still alone, knowing he'd see through any protestations that she was happy just to support. "He's got this covered, I know he has, and he doesn't even need me to help him with it. Is it really my path while he's saving the Realm to just knuckle down to my apprenticeship and pretend my soul's not gaping while I'm at it?"

The Genie twirled dramatically, fierce and free and flexible; the burning glance in his coal and ember eyes reassuringly dismissive. "Sometimes, to reveal the way," he promised conspiratorially, "you have to shift the path a little." He floated away, the angle at which he did so conveying the intriguing impression that he was bobbing away on the sea.

The sea? He knew the Kelpie haunted the lake, right? Following the Genie with her eyes until he dissipated amongst the dusk, Amber stared next towards the Selkie party hovering at the edge of vision, all grey furs and eerie light, only half hearing the Prince as he continued to explain the intricacies of magic—yet another skill she had no part in. The Seal People Ruby had deemed clumsy seemed to her to move with a magnetic grace. There was a wildness about their glance, a hauntedness—as if they were trying to seek their way home.

Six men there were, with their ghost-grey pelts draped across their chests like the tartans of a clan allegiance. Yet a seventh hovered in the background, wandering away into the shadows as if he no longer belonged with the others. Something twisted in Amber's own chest to see he alone bore no pelt. The knowledge shivered in her. No pelt. Nothing to help him get back to the sea.

The coal in her heart ignited. Nothing yet . . .

"Oh, no you don't," Jasper pre-empted warningly, but his hand grasped empty air as Amber slipped away between the darkening conifers.

"Ah, good, you're going after her," he acknowledged with relief as Yenna darted forwards, her flowing hair tossed behind her.

"Going with her, love of mine," her lilting echo corrected smoothly.

Once more, Jasper stood alone beneath the trees. "And so it starts again."

Conviction burned in Amber's blood, warming her as the wind moaned a tremulous warning, reminding her how far behind she had left the others. But it made sense that the man would have come here. If he actually was a Selkie, her mind goaded. Alternatives skittered dangerously, and she pushed them back with difficulty.

This section of the beach was quiet, solitary, old. Eerily so. The darkness pressed intrusively around her as if it couldn't quite believe someone was risking being out here. But she had to find him. There was no use expecting the Sea Maidens or Knights to be patrolling the shores tonight to rescue those in difficulty—they had congregated at Moonstruck Lake like everyone else. And the aura of loneliness that hung around the man felt desperate.

Hssh, hssh, the waves pleaded, with the urgency of a quickening breath, and her gaze drifted automatically to the shoreline—and stalled. How could she fear solitude, when there wavered the form of a man so much more alone than she? There, flickering and stumbling at the edge of vision—her heart clutched as she watched him stagger along the ocean's edge. She'd never seen someone look so lost. Worry rose like the tide—in his condition, there was no guarantee that he wasn't going to fall on his face and drown in inches of water.

Hshh! the sea warned, her feet slapping the crusted, tide-ridged sands as she fled towards him in the dark. *Hssh!*

She slowed instinctively as she neared. Something about his gait wasn't right. And that was before she saw his eyes.

Amber shivered, keeping her distance, although whether out of respect or caution she was no longer sure. Rraarl's stare had burned, but with fierceness born of hope and conviction. These eyes shone with but the ghost of a light: a strange, haunted light the direction of which she couldn't tell.

"Sir?" She didn't know what to say to him, only that she couldn't stay silent. He looked so out of place that she wanted to slip her cloak around his shoulders and guide him out of the shallows. She'd witnessed illness, of course, especially at Sarin's side, but she'd never seen someone look so desolate. "I know it's not my business, but you don't look well," she managed instead, her tongue awkward around her grave imposition.

"Many things are found a' th' edge." The man lurched erratically along the shoreline without so much as glancing at her.

His voice sounded like waves over gravel; she wasn't sure whether his words had even been directed at her, or just to himself. "Well, unless the sea's washed up some kind of magic bridle, I'm going to be no loss to the Greenwood Court," she offered quietly. "So, can I help you look for what you're after?"

"Many things mebbe found a' th' edge," he muttered again, the flow of his words as hypnotic as the pulse of tide upon sand. "Journey there, an' seek that which cannae be asked fur."

Amber took a breath and tried again. "Do you need to get home? The King can provide an escort to accompany you, if you want to leave before your friends? If you don't want to ask, I can."

The man lifted his face towards hers, with a weak bark of laughter. Yet, the sound was human enough to chase the spectre of danger from him and to prove that his derision was directed only towards himself, and so she stayed, undeterred, as he attempted to fix his watery eyes on her.

"Ye' sure it's me tryin' tae get haem?" The effort exhausted him, but the worry in his eyes didn't seem to be reserved for himself.

Amber stared at him unswervingly, realising his eyes had strayed to the wing stubs jutting beneath the now pointless slits in her shirt. "Mm," she managed noncommittally. He wasn't the only one who could evade questioning. She hadn't forgotten her wings, could never forget, but she had schooled herself well into not thinking about them.

"Perhaps, then, there is something I can get you, instead?" she reminded him, partly to change the subject, but mainly out of due concern. He looked so very weak. The grey formal attire that had lent an ethereal grace to the other Selkie men only seemed to accentuate his gaunt frame, clinging to his skin whether with the sea or sweat she didn't know. She wondered whether the man might consider eating one of Mugkafb's nectar sticks if she ran and got one. But that probably didn't constitute the healthiest food for a Selkie. Maybe she could scrounge some fish from the kitchen for him instead? Or was that idea as cringe-worthy as it sounded now she'd thought it through?

"Ah main stay. Ah main search. I am Hydd—as is mah path." The eyes that fixed on her then were as sallow as a Goblin's, yet his lilting voice reminded her of a Knight of the Sea, if more guttural:

"There is a place o' magic left
An' whit ye seek will there be foun'
But draw yer cloak tight an' stoke yer lantern
Fur there is bu' the lang way roon."

A thrill—of what, she didn't quite know—coursed along her spine at his words. A challenge, yes, lay within, but also a plea. She nodded fiercely, feeling his strange eyes upon her as she strode back through the sea of night. She would help him find his way back. She promised it by every drop of blood thrumming loudly through her heart. And, she let herself admit: in accepting this quest, in striving into the unknown again, she felt reassuringly as though her course had turned homewards, had realigned with the direction of her own compass again, no matter how many miles of unexplored terrain lay ahead.

Fluid Plans

The early morning chill roused Amber with an eager heart and a ready plan. She wasn't going to sit around and wait while Racxen went after the Kelpie. She had the Selkie's quest—or, at least, request—to unravel. The improbability of solving it swamped her mind, almost drowning her resolve, but visiting the Water Nymph seemed a good place to start. She might get berated for the intrusion but, despite Zaralathaar's legendary reputation for coldness, Amber knew—or at least hoped fervently—that beneath that protective façade the Water Nymph would not thank the Realm's inhabitants for leaving her in peace in her old age and failing health. After all, even at her weakest Zaralathaar was the most indomitable adversary Amber could imagine, and not only was she the elemental water guardian, she also knew what it was to be unable to return home to the sea. Surely, she of all people could help her help the Selkie.

If she were to stand any hope of convincing the Water Nymph, though, she'd need the entire route to settle her nerves and start formulating a plan, Amber reminded herself with a grimace of embarrassment. Yet finding the Enchantress's Fountain, which hovered capriciously outside the usual constraints and geographies of the Realm, demanded traversing such a course as encompassed the wildest and most circumspect of paths, so the prospect filled Amber with a kind of satiating hunger. Wandering the Realm had served her inadvertently well in the past and the meditative flow of landscape and stretch of sky always felt like they had a similarly expansive effect on her mind and senses. She found herself relishing the opportunity now.

And maybe there was something about wanting to prove, to both herself and the others, in particular Racxen, that she could still strike out on such quests by herself, too.

Shouldering a hastily thrown-together pack and drawing her cloak around her comfortably as she strode out into the crisp morning air, Amber let the route stretch before her, charting it in her mind with a touch as light as an artist who dare not grip the brush too tightly for fear of stemming the life in her grasp. Of course, she didn't have a route in the traditional sense, but she refused to let that frighten her, instead revelling in the freedom of anticipating what might come. To take the Wandering Way leading to the Fountain, devised by the Enchantress in the lull after the resolution of the Realm's most recent conflict had rendered the Way of Ice and Fire tamed for all, one had to traverse as many different environments as possible and when the Nymph deemed your travels sufficient, she opened the path. Amber harrumphed good-naturedly. The rumour sounded sufficiently perverse for it to appeal to Zaralathaar, and Amber couldn't deny that slowing down and paying real attention to her surroundings had proven decent preparation for her previous quests.

And so, to begin where she was, she took a leisurely trek across the spilling swathes of meadow. As she brushed through the long feathery grass, wildflowers flung back their heads, scattering the kind of scent that lingered at the back of her throat like the aftertaste of a favourite sweet, lodging in her memory as well as on her tongue.

As dawn simmered into noon, the bright open fields of Fairymead yielded peaceably to the shaded canopy of the Endless Forest, and Amber walked at ease amidst the contented sigh of wind rustling amidst the arms of the trees in a voiceless, ceaseless lullaby, whilst the birds, unseen, fluted comfortingly above her as they darted on their own quests. Above the uplifted arms of the forest, the sky drenched a promisingly even-hued wash of endless, unbesmirched blue, heralding the sort of day where you felt that even your own corner of the Realm stretched luxuriously for miles.

As the trees closed overhead to shield her from the beating sun, they also granted delicious cover for her dreams to stretch unseen and unjudged. She let herself revel in the unveiling of her path, enjoying these moments of discovery: the ground sloping into the bank of a lightly singing stream, tumbling and gleaming uncatchably in a shimmering invitation amidst arcs of silver reflection. She followed its flow on loose, free footsteps as the river curved down to a place of stillness where supple, willowy limbs dreamily trailed their fingers through the burnt sugar swirl of a deep brown tantalising pool, sticky and secret and intoxicating. Amber felt her senses relax and expand as she trod the mossy bankside. It was exactly the kind of place to begin a great adventure.

Amber let the site weave its spell, feeling the tug and pull it exerted on her heart and wondered at it. Here was a spot she would have to revisit. Perhaps some of her own answers would lie along these winding paths as yet untrodden, but for now she must continue for another.

Her heart quickened in recognition as further waterways began to seep from ever-dampening grass swathes. She knew their paths now, their criss-cross wanderings, as dearly as she knew her own palm-print, for Arraterr lay before her, sprawled and gleaming, its muddy waters burnished a proud bronze beneath the strength of the sun's unflinching gaze, grimy and glorious and teeming with the soup of life, tangled through with magic and memories.

A grin curled unconsciously on Amber's lips even after all this time. To some it might have looked messily redundant, incomprehensively wild; abandoned even—and that would be the aim to those unwelcome, in order to protect the communities within—but for allies and for Amber the murky depths held the greatest of wonders.

The air smelled not quite stagnant, but hot and heavy, hanging low in readiness, shaping itself even now anew amidst the swirls of mud that swept and burbled and burst as if following some ancient, long-foretold design whispered by the midgecloud wisps that gathered, whirring ancient knowledge across the marshes. She was part of this now; its secrets and its sharings; the half-unseen and longed-for; the boundary and the blur; the whole impossible, unforgettable memory of it.

But where she was going would be wilder still. And so she followed like a friend the resolute, slow-moving river that had once swept her and Mugkafb along on another adventure so long ago now, as its strength forged through the changing landscape, keeping her company and gifting her courage with its steady presence even beyond Arraterr's furthest border.

Amber looked back, flooded with fondness. This was one of the reasons she loved Racxen. Being with him didn't mean changing. It meant remembering her favourite self and finding it easier to return there. And this self ran with the jubilant riverlets, basked in the strange joy of the solemn, sacred waterways, and revelled in where they took her—even as they led her away now to a place at once familiar and formidable: the Fountain basin.

A Maiden's Legacy

Ice clung to cracks in the aged rock, and meltwater dripped as steadily as solemn tears through the gaping fissure that had once heralded the start of the Way of Ice and Fire. Amber missed achingly the rich, life-giving mists drenching the heat of Arraterr, the cool, moss-scented calm of the Endless Forest beyond, and the meadowsweet fields between, for now that her journey to the Fountain was at an end, the air in the chamber beyond hung still and stretched, no longer thrumming with the potent magic Amber had become accustomed to meeting at the Fountain. In times gone by, it had itched along her skin, intrusive and tempting, worrying and exciting in equal measure. Now the Realm as well as the basin felt emptier without it.

It took her several quickened heartbeats to realise the other difference: the once-glistening orbs that used to spin past as though alive, shimmering with contained energy, now floated listlessly, as glassy and passive as dead fish caught helpless in a current.

Fear instead now needled along Amber's spine. If the bubbles weren't working, she really was on her own. There no longer remained the slightest hope of even observing scenes of distress, let alone jumping in and trying to save anyone.

Amber felt her mouth dry. She'd never really dared consider how destructive the leaching of magic from the Realm would truly be, once it gathered pace. Yet here was proof. Irrefutable, palpable, and hateful proof, just as the Nymph had warned.

And what of the Nymph herself? Amber felt ice clutch at her chest. She'd come to have her fears refuted, not realised. The Nymph really must be dying. What if she were already too late? She took the stairwell at a clattering run, the cavernous basin shrinking into a claustrophobic implosion with the realisation of its emptiness. Why were the walls not flinging back the echoes of the Enchantress's chastisement as well as those of her unguarded footsteps? Why was Zaralathaar not sweeping imperially along some forbidden corridor accessible only to herself and berating from afar the Fairy's impetuousness as severely as her stupidity?

"My reign has not yet ended, child."

At the familiar harsh-ringing tones, Amber didn't know whether to jump out of her skin or rush forward in relief. Instead, she muddled through an awkward bow and counted herself lucky to have at least one last meeting with the Nymph, even though judging from historical evidence its entirety might well consist of sustained and unmitigated rebuke.

"You are in luck," noted the Enchantress cuttingly. "I am preoccupied with greater matters than your own ill-timed anxiety." Her gaze softened and drifted before Amber could entertain the possibility that it might have had anything to do with her at all. "The sea draws me, calls me home. That time rushes with all the inevitability of the final storm tossed upon a crushing tide, and I can no longer resist until my task is complete."

Amber swallowed hard, feeling as though the Water Nymph's words were dragging her inexorably out to sea and ever farther from the diminishing safety of the once-certain shore. "They tell me another is to take your place."

Zaralathaar regarded her quietly, her gaze easing the frigid silence of the chamber. "I must ask you to accept this, as I have asked so much of you in the past."

Amber's heart sputtered. "It was you who taught me to presume more than I could once have dared attempt," she managed wretchedly. "And yet my soul rails against this suggestion more strenuously than anything else you have asked of me which I once cried was impossible."

Zaralathaar sighed, with the sound of the ageless sea rolling in to ease even the most careworn of souls. "I am glad, now more than ever, that you repeatedly prove equal to the impossibilities I ask of you." The Enchantress's voice quietened, like a storm newly eased, and her gaze grew distant, her eyes more watery and less focused than Amber remembered, her flowing gown now drooping as though its fabric swamped her. It felt to Amber as though the changes in her demeanour and appearance depicted a slow return to Zaralathaar's namesake element. As though one day she might melt back into the sea entirely.

"You once approached me believing me to hold all the wisdom of the Realm's long years," the Nymph murmured at last, her moist eyes glittering like ice. "Yet now you see me for what I really am."

Amber refused to let herself be surprised that the Nymph's fate-laden tones were still as devoid of compassion as they were of self-pity. "Yes," she agreed, her voice firm. "The one I will always turn to, whether you like it or not."

The Nymph smiled sadly. "Have I not earned my right to wait for the end in peace, instead of being bombarded by ceaseless prattling?"

"I don't know," Amber half grinned in response. "Have you privately stopped wanting to save the Realm you publicly insist you want to be rid of? 'Wait for the end,'" she added hastily, before the Nymph could conjure a suitably scathing response, "are the words of one who has given up hope. You have not. You just doubt the commitment of those around you to do what you know has to be done."

"Not the commitment," corrected the Nymph archly, the ghost of a smile brushing her lips at the Fairy's impertinent truth. "Merely the competence." She paused. "You have no idea, child, what it is like to endure waiting impotently, while forces you once controlled conspire to endanger those it was once your duty to protect. I have outstayed my usefulness. It is my duty to retire and retreat. What else would you have me do? Stay to watch the structure I put my entire life into break and my ability to protect these people fail?"

"That is not your only option," Amber returned, eyes flashing even as she wondered light-headedly whence she had gathered the confidence to contradict Lady Zaralathaar in this manner. "I am willing to wager—as I only ever have once before, and that was also with you—that your own brand of enchantment, water magic, will be the last to fall, will still be standing once all other forms have drained away, and will be what saves us, this time. The Kelpie is not, I believe my Lady, the only elemental figure deserving of our attention."

Zaralathaar's eyes narrowed, but Amber continued. "Not everything has to be in defence of the entire Realm to be worth fighting for. I found a man I know nothing about, who needs my help."

The Nymph lifted her eyes skywards. "Of course you did."

Amber's courage surged high enough to ignore that. "I thought I needed to ask you how his plight fitted with our own, in order to understand his situation well enough to help, and to fire my courage that I was doing the right thing while everyone else was working to a larger goal, but I know now that I do not. Even if he were the only one to benefit from my intervention, I would assure it a hundredfold no matter the cost to myself. However much or little he chooses to tell me, whatever else is threatening to plunge the Realm into the coming storm, whether he is part of what unravels or not: his own need and value remain undiminished and will never be reliant upon any relation to ourselves. I know you have had to conduct yourself differently, because your authority has weighted you with responsibilities greater than my own, but I will not disown my heart's belief: that to sustain one life is worth as much exertion as sustaining a nation. I will pledge my effort to him, whether it helps us or not. It helps him, and that is enough for me, and I will defend it against anyone."

Her speech made, Amber breathed cautiously now. "What can you tell me of Selkies?"

"They hold great power, but it is contained within their skin," Zaralathaar surmised, with a rather direct look. "They slough it and slip it back on to share the Realms of land and sea. But their pelt is their soul, worn on the outside. It is a precarious arrangement, and so they keep mainly to the northern Icefields and other isolated places bereft of civilisation to guard against the basest injustice a Selkie can suffer—the theft of their pelt. Without it, they cannot return to the sea, or to themselves. I wish they had stayed out of this Kelpie business."

A convulsive chill possessed Amber's skin. "The man I met, he was a Selkie. And he—"

"Had no skin? It seems he has made himself known to the right person." The Enchantress's emotions sounded to Amber even more carefully locked away in that dispassionate voice than usual. Amber gathered her thoughts, and her poise, carefully. She felt unaccountably shaken, as though she had set into motion something greater than even the Enchantress's foresight could predict. But she knew in her heart that her decision was not one she could revoke. This quest might be small, and conducted in shadow, and irrelevant to all but one man, but by the four seasons she was going to see it done.

That ancient gaze settled upon her more calmly and surely than ever, Amber felt, and she dared not consider whether that might indicate the lateness of the Water Nymph's hour. Tears prickled at the thought that at least it might show some trust on the old Princess's behalf that this young interloper might live to see her pledge fulfilled, even if she didn't. Amber gulped wretchedly, feeling, as she snuffled away tears, as though the Nymph had control of even the saltwater brimming behind her own eyes.

"You must have known, my child," Zaralathaar murmured, as softly as oncoming snow. "I am an old woman, and I am aging still. One day soon my bones will be more hollow than yours even, and away I shall fly. But you have known me, and shall remember what I taught you, and that is all I ask and enough for you to give."

Amber breathed more steadily, held within that gaze the Fairy suspected could bear more than all the Realm's oceans combined. Their vision ebbed and flowed together, until Amber knew she had the strength, and the Nymph the peace of spirit, to look forward again, wherever their paths might lead.

As she turned to leave, the Nymph's eyes bore into her back, testing once more, but this time as an equal. "You did not come because you needed my advice?"

Amber shrugged, steadier now she had decided her own path, and her soul lighter because of what they had shared. "No. I came because I need you."

A flicker of uncertainty passed across the Nymph's face so quickly Amber wasn't sure whether she had imagined it. "That was not past tense."

Amber grinned shakily. "I don't think it ever will be. And I will come to you again, my Lady, when my quest is done. I might not be able to save everyone, as you once warned me, but I will risk my all to save even one." She drew a steadying breath, buoyant and breathless with the knowledge that to reunite Hydd with his pelt would be to help him return home. She wished more than anything that moment that she could, through doing so, somehow afford Zaralathaar the same release before the end.

"And hopefully two," she whispered in a private pledge as she slipped out into the labyrinthine passageways leading back to the sunlight, quiet as a cavern echo drifting into an uncertain future.

Seeking the Edge

Clouds of mist drifted atop the shimmering surface of the Glade Pool, mingling with the deep, restorative forest aroma drenching the sanctuary to cleanse the air and touch the ground with magic as they hovered above waters as green and vibrant as the swathes of grass bejewelling the bank.

The atmosphere cleared Racxen's head as he lingered, skulking with relish through the forest's expanses, absorbing the environment and letting it calm his senses left over-wrought by the dissonant clamour of the Night Council. His shadow skulked behind him, relaxed and free and in its element, his sole companion; but for now he needed no other, with Amber in his heart and purpose in his soul. He must ride the Kelpie. For her, for his brother, for the Realm. And to do so, he'd need to first accustom himself to tracking in such an environment as this, where every scent lay slippery and changeable, as misleading as the distorted reflections flickering uncatchable atop that lake-sheen glimmer.

An authentic smile slipped unguarded across his features as he considered the challenge, senses open to the night and its subtleties, his confidence rising in response. For, whilst everyone else in the Realm seemed to be preoccupied with how they were going to ride it, Racxen knew better than anyone that, equally important and just as hard, someone had first to find the elusive beast.

At first he had questioned his ability. There were better riders, in Loban for example, he knew that. So, as instinctively as a thought, he had asked the Genie what his odds were.

"You're the pathfinder," the Genie had reminded, gossamer-light and just as beguiling. "You tell me."

The prospect thrilled him; the chance to prove the most integral part of himself as vital and relevant in this new age as when it had been him alone in what had felt like an endless dark, struggling to support his brother and serve the Tribe. His eyes gleamed in the dappled light as he thought of all he had accomplished since then; how much had changed and to whom it was due. Now, seasons hence, he knew what he was capable of, and he had a chance to pit his skills in the service of those he loved best. Find the Kelpie first. Worry about riding it later.

His guard down as he contemplated the intricacies of tracking, let alone approaching, the creature, Racxen barely registered the flash of grey through a deepening night that betrayed the Goblin's spring.

Forcing his head back, she drew the blackened, rusted knife. Although one hand grasped like death as the Arraheng struggled and struck out with his claws, the other froze, its blade momentarily still. "Something changed," she spat, her voice dangerously quiet, loaded with venom.

"It is not with me that my soul now lies," Racxen managed to gasp amidst the Goblin's frenzied confusion, peace flooding.

Realisation of the presence of a magic she would never know flickered in the Pedlar's eyes. But then a serpent smile flickered. "Bad choice of words, son. Her doom awaits at Trickster's Gate."

"No," Racxen barked, his weakening struggles redoubled in sudden terror of what she meant, cursing himself frantically. "No!"

He loosed himself and sprang, but she was already away—and the path the Goblin took could lead only one place: Fairymead.

Racxen's anguished cry echoed through the trees as he ran.

"You are of the light and open air; he is of the dark enclosed. Yet yer want to be part of his world, don't yer?"

The Goblins' voices slithered through the darkness in pursuit, gaining on her. "There is still so much you cannot know about his world. About this world. Let's see how long yer last, down here in the dark."

At least you're doing a better job of keeping your mouth shut than last time, Amber tried to reassure herself, attempting to read the solid chill of the tunnel walls with her fingers as she kept their protection behind her, sweat inching down her back as the approaching Goblins showed scant sign of giving up. The Water Nymph's power must be waning fast, she realised in despair, for them to be haunting such sacred ground as these tunnels, woven out from the Fountain basin.

Amber's mind raced. The Fountain basin, like most caverns, criss-crossed the network of tunnels that laced the backbone of the Realm. Any winglet knew that. But which section was she in now? Knowing could mean the difference between life and death, but spend more than moments in the presence of a Goblin, and all orientation stripped itself from you.

As she hurried along as silently as she could, daylight sprang like a leak up ahead, illuminating two options: flee into the light or face the dark. Amber eyed both warily. Would it be safer to run across open land, which held no chance of hiding, or risk the passageway prising itself through deepest shadow, from which there might be no escape? It was the only choice left in her power. She thought she might have glimpsed the shimmer of water within, winking through as though in private support.

Darting forwards, she fled into the shadows of the tunnel, jumping into the water without a thought for what it could conceal.

She barely had a moment to listen for the Goblin's pursuit, before she felt the water surge and billow as though rallying around her. As she pulled hand over hand through the glittering water to put as much distance behind her as possible, the rocky ceiling descended as if to hide her, darkening the passage further. She had to breathe carefully now, kissing the surface to suck the low air before thrusting beneath. Specks of light, like tiny deep-sea creatures, bobbed and jostled in the current, illuminating the depths fleetingly with pulsing flashes.

Wishing she had one of the Sea Folk to guide her, Amber tugged more slowly through the water as it deepened, the light-creatures dissipating into the fathoms below. Kicking the tendrils of panic away as she trod water, Amber stopped suspended and ducked her head under to peer myopically through the sediment to try in vain to judge which way she should take. The water licked and jostled at her, cold and intrusive and impatient now that she had stopped. What if there was no way forward? What if she had to go back? It was so dark beneath she couldn't tell if the passage went any further. She ducked under again, reaching out her arms to try to feel for a gap beneath the sinking ceiling, groping through a drowning darkness.

Something so smooth and firm she didn't know whether it was skin or scale or something else skimmed her hand, and the remnants of her breath fled in a bubble of panic. She forced herself to look once more and was rewarded with a glimpse of a similar bubble of air escape in the wake of whatever it was that was streaking shadow-like through the inky water. It needed air too—the way had to be clear.

Gulping a final breath, Amber thrust beneath the ink and powered after the trailing stream of bubbles.

The trail of bubbles banked sharply and burst above her as chill light filtered welcomingly through the far surface, shivering invitingly above her, faint yet joyful after the deep, disorientating dark, and she surged towards it in relief, gratefully sucking in air as her vision adjusted to the damp gloom. The low ceiling peeled away from the water, rising to form a high cavern. Flat, grey-hued rocks worn smooth—she counted seven—protruded evenly from the water, and she wriggled onto the nearest one, beaching herself like a seal.

She would've liked to sweep the water from her skin, wring out her clothes and hair, and try to get herself warmer. Or at least dryer. Yet in this place, such action or noise would have felt intrusive. She'd never found herself somewhere so still. In the low, melancholy light, she felt as though something were poised waiting, as silent as a held breath, as if she'd inadvertently disturbed a deeper sadness than she could fully understand.

Amber cast her gaze cautiously, feeling inexplicably as though she ought to make amends for an accidental transgression. From her vantage point, she could see patches of what had to be fabric floating loose and drifting further; they must have been swept into the water by her splashing. At least she could rescue them. Carefully, she reached out and gathered them up.

She stared at the collection, a new chill creeping along her drying skin. Mottled and water-stained, they felt worryingly fur-like. With a strange foreboding, she spread them out, placing each one next to its fellows. But there were so few. The material wasn't enough to make anything of value, surely? And yet she gently picked them all up again, nestling them against her chest as she considered. There was something wrenchingly sorrowful about the tiny scraps. She felt as if she were in the presence of something broken, something that needed mending—something that she wasn't sure was within her power to heal.

The water before her swirled and Amber flinched violently as she beheld a silent audience: a ring of deeper-than-human eyes watched her awkward progress in solemnity from sleek, seal-like faces. Seal-like, apart from the patchiness of their fur, as if—

She looked back to the water. There should have been seven faces watching her—seven Selkies for seven seas.

But only six pairs of seal-like eyes stared back at her.

Amber dropped the pieces as though they were crawling with maggots. Those pitiful remnants she'd unknowingly gathered were all that now remained of the only link that could ever enable the missing Selkie to return to their sea home and their true self—a link that had been severed in the vilest way possible. A Selkie's skin was indistinguishable from their soul, and something—someone, her own skin crawled to realise it had to have been, because why would any natural predator rend a skin with no flesh?—had torn it to pitiful, dissociated shreds, and cast a lonely, damaged soul to the shore.

Reverently, she picked the pieces back up, laid them carefully out over the rocks in the manner she had seen Ruby plan a dress-making pattern. If she could reunite them, could she heal a shattered spirit?

She crouched, considering, the cold forgotten. There was probably enough to make the head-piece, and tailor it into some kind of cloak, but there was nothing amongst the pieces suitable for the tail, nor for the lighter underbelly, so how . . .?

She turned as ripples parted close to the makeshift shore, and a Selkie lifted his muzzle, something long and sharp and white clenched in his jaws.

Amber retrieved it carefully, his wiry whiskers brushing her skin as she did so. A rush of communication tingled through her at his touch. The sense of the unknown; the vastness of his need and the extent of the request overwhelmed her. Yet, her overriding impression was one of calmness, of resilience, and of faith. Amber smiled in wonder. Mayhap some of that had passed into her, for she felt an uncanny rightness about accepting his offering. Examining the gift, she couldn't tell whether it had been made out of bone, or tusk, or something altogether stranger, but it was definitely a needle.

Amber's hand hovered, as she shivered in the damp air now laced with magic and charged with expectation. Maybe she couldn't sew wounds, like Sarin, or dresses, like Ruby. But by all the magic that still remained in the Realm, she was going to stitch this soul back together.

Amber wedged herself between the rocks, picked up the first two scraps and brandished the needle warily. "This would be so much easier if Ruby were here," she muttered to her clumsy fingers. Yet she cast her doubts into the far shadows and let the slow-rocking sea lend her its ancient rhythm as she sucked a breath and started.

Leaving the cave, Amber felt as though she were returning to a changed Realm, filled with possibilities again. The magic of what she had begun tangled in the dusk sky, weaving a web of promise. As the cool air greeted her, her plans stretched to fit the spacious night. Something buzzed through Amber light as air and bright as moonbeams. She'd stitch his skin back together. She'd work on it day and night. He'd be a proper Selkie again— he'd be able to return to the Sea.

Nightfall and her determination had settled fully by the time Amber turned the key in the lock, closed the door on any doubts, and spread forth the pieces. The needle and scraps lay glowing on her dresser, drawing her eyes like a promise, tantalising and terrifying in equal measure, flooding her room with the scent of a storm-flung sea, and looking every bit as hypnotically beguiling.

She started it. There was no going back now. And yet, she barely dared touch something so sacred. What if she ruined it?

The first moments of shaping it felt charged with ecstasy, stretching with every possibility her mind, freed, could let itself alight upon. The pelt, or the potential of it at least, took form swiftly beneath her hands, and she trembled with a surge of power to feel the magic that had been conjured between her fingers. The needle flew so fast she needn't think consciously about placement or pattern. It took shape as if of its own volition, as though blood not thread were binding it.

Hours later, fingers cramped and mind exhausted, Amber found herself shaking to contemplate continuing it. Starting had been exhilarating—and terrifying. What if that could never be reproduced? What if it couldn't be maintained?

What had she been thinking, agreeing to something that clearly required the kind of preternatural skill she would never in a thousand seasons attain?

Vapour curled at the edge of vision, like the manifestation of a thought. "All our lives, we yearn for something we cannot name," the Genie reminded passionately, his eyes burning coals amidst cloud. "When you finally find it, don't fear it—follow it."

Amber grimaced shakily and released her doubt, safe in the identity of her audience. "If I do it, my mind will always be questioning whether I made the right choice."

The Genie grinned expansively. "If you do it, your heart will have the answers to ease your soul." He twirled sedately, as if his motion slowed the ticking of time sufficiently to facilitate such a momentous decision. "And yet the magnitude of this can neither be distorted nor dismissed. This could take many turnings of season."

"That long?" Amber blurted in dismay.

"A detour is not a turn-off," the Genie reminded. "Sometimes being forced to take the indirect route improves the outcome. Extending the map, allowing you to gather more fuel, will enrich the journey." The words faded. Their message did not.

"A pelt is the armour and clothing of a soul," the Genie advised softly. "It requires a soul to be put into it. Nothing less. Nothing more. It takes all you've got," he confirmed, his voice as expansive as the star-flecked night outside. "But you've got all it takes."

Amber nodded slowly, inner fire kindling in her eyes at the voicing of the challenge, letting her answer settle in her heart. The Genie swelled with pride to witness it. "Start from where you are, and you'll find your way," he advised gently, sensible of the crashing waves of emotion drenching his young companion. "Footsteps guided by courage have a strange knack of finding their path."

Amber let his words swell her heart. "Yet it may come to nothing," she admitted, the prospect sickeningly painful in the face of the alternative that she had only just begun to dare consider.

The Genie bobbed, accepting yet unswayable. "Or it may catalyse the best thing that will ever happen to you."

"You can't know that it will."

"Knowing isn't what makes it happen," the Genie urged, twirling a flourish through the expectant air. "It's the possibility, and your willingness to act on it, increase it, do everything to make it as much as it can be."

Amber half-smiled fractiously, her eyes restlessly distant as she contemplated it, anxious with anticipation, remembering her promise to Hydd. "I don't want to let him down. But the pelt holds a wildness, a magic, that feels so much greater than myself that I dare not trust I can contain it, and then we'll both be lost."

"Or you'll find yourself a new way of navigating that will never leave you."

Amber met his gaze and grinned, gratitude buoying that he trusted her ability, but she no longer had to see it reflected in those healing pools to know: she didn't just have to do this. She could do this. The Genie knew it. More importantly, so did she.

Amber's heart flushed with the realisation. "I would give my soul for Hydd's to return," she promised. She knew in her heart that she could only ever have given that answer, but now she knew also that it was not the tremulous response it would have been those seasons ago, more of misplaced hope than true faith in herself. This time, she had a better idea of what she was capable of—how far she could go to make something happen. Just as well, if last time was anything to judge by . . .

"Not would," warned the Genie. "Will. But it will be returned seven-fold."

"Returned?" Amber grinned back, heart and soul and plans buzzing. "I'll retrieve it myself. If I can learn to sew his skin, I can certainly learn to inhabit my own."

"In that case," the Genie bowed, wreathing a lingering smile, "I will get out of your way."

Cascade

"I'm not restless, or obsessive," Amber grumbled that night at Jasper's questioning. "I'm just looking for something you can't give me, and I'm not about to give up my search."

"Hm." The Prince stopped in his tracks. Whatever he had been about to say slipped from his tongue as he eyed her suspiciously: cross-legged, still holding the needle, and inpatient for him to be gone. "What happened earlier? I thought you were supposed to be revising."

Amber returned his gaze, steady and impenetrable, as if whatever had passed through the darkening hours had crafted her a refuge from such doubt. "I am," she promised brightly, with the ghost of a grin. "Revising my future." She pulled the pelt into the moonlight and waited for his response.

Jasper stared. He couldn't help it. "What in the name of all that's magic is that?"

Amber sighed, suddenly exhausted. "It once was a pelt," she admitted. "It will be again. Eventually." Even voicing it threatened to overwhelm her.

Jasper felt sick. "Goblin's teeth, Amber, did that belong to a Selkie? What are you doing with it?" The thing had been mutilated. It felt dangerous even to be in the room with it.

Amber gathered it up protectively. "Look, the violence wrought upon it is disgusting, not the pelt itself," she warned. "It needs mending. Healing, even. How can I prove to a lost and shattered psyche that it is intrinsically worthy of restoration, if I do not show the same belief and generosity of spirit? How do I help a traumatised soul believe that their spirit can prevail over any circumstance, if I cannot overcome my own trials?

"I have to prove through my own example, limited and lesser as I might denounce it in the face of all that others have suffered, that which may not be believed through words alone: that the only option isn't to resign yourself to a future of feeling squashed and battered and trapped, no matter what has gone before. These patches are held together not by scars, but stitches. They are actions of healing. Proof of survival. If I let myself believe such healing isn't worth taking the risk on, who else is going to fight for a nameless, homeless soul, once the Realm-wide challenge for the Kelpie takes hold?"

The Prince spread his hands helplessly. "Amber, I'm not saying it's not admirable. I'm just recognising that it's not very feasible." He grimaced; whether doubtful of the properties of the pelt itself or of her own abilities, Amber wasn't sure she wanted to clarify.

"Perhaps you're over-thinking this. You do know it's just fur, right? It can't hear you." Yet Jasper lowered his voice, all the same. "And a Selkie has already stepped forward for the Greenwood Court Challenge," he reminded awkwardly.

"And he's the only one who matters, is he?" Amber retorted, more out of habit than need. She didn't require his approval and he knew it. But she couldn't let herself balk at defending Hydd from a friend, if she was to have any hope of protecting him from the enemy.

Jasper sighed. "I'm the Prince, if you remember? Some things have to matter more to me than others, because they matter more to the Kingdom whether you want to admit it or not," he countered. "I know you've always been a 'pursue your dreams' type, Amber," he added. "But this is serious."

"So am I," Amber promised unexpectedly quietly, dissipating his crossness with her tone. "I know you're not free to see the Realm in certain ways, and I mourn that. But it makes it even more important that someone else ensures that they are. I don't want to cut myself off from that ability. Especially when it might prove causal to the one way I can best help.

"So, I will not just pursue my dreams," Amber promised, letting herself grin. "I will dance with them in the shallows, and let their waves engulf me, and I will loose them like arrows and see how far they let me fly. Jasper, this can't just have skill. It won't work like that. It has to have soul."

The Prince spread his hands helplessly. "I hope so. I truly do." Watching her, steadfast yet unschooled, Jasper felt the ground slither beneath him. "But you won't get it all done, Amber," he warned. "You can't master everything."

Amber shrugged, her confidence knitted close amidst the subtle strands she had already sewn in gathering proof that the unbelievable was transforming into the undeniable. The moonlight cut a bright swathe through the night, turning the window into a silver portal, and she wasn't quite ready to return through it yet. "I don't need to master everything," she argued, mumbling through a mouthful of pins. "I just need to master what matters. I need to master this."

"There you are."

Amber sat bolt upright, acutely aware of the late hour and the half-made pelt still sprawled around her. She hadn't seen Ruby's mother for a long time, and with a sickening flood of realisation knew why she was suddenly seeing her now. "Aunt Sapphire. I'd forgotten you were on the apprenticeship committee." Ruby's mother was more of a workaholic than anyone Amber knew. Most of the time, it was admirable. But right now she couldn't deal with it. Amber managed a smile she didn't feel.

Her aunt did not return the courtesy. "Focussing on your little hobby, I see," she admonished. "While the Realm is falling apart."

Amber fought the urge to bundle the pelt hastily into a drawer. "Helping a little is still helping."

"If you wanted to help so much, you would have chosen your apprenticeship," her aunt dismissed. "You are not just the last person to do so, but the only." She eyed the pelt with distaste and mistrust. "It's time to pack away such things, Amber. This is a nothingness. A hobby, a trifle. You'll never be taken seriously, never be respected, if you don't knuckle down and get a job. Not the few months here and there you're doing at the moment—a proper job. It's time you grew up."

Although she bristled at the insults, Amber kept her response clipped. This was Ruby's mother, after all. Although the woman had always frightened her. "It's a big decision, that's all," she promised. "I just need a little more time to decide." It sounded pitiful even to her. But not as pitiful as signing up for forty years of hollow days and sleepless nights.

Sapphire folded her arms, unconvinced. "I don't have time for this, Amber. People used to talk of your bravery, after everything you did. Yet now the girl who helped save the Realm dares not agree to what everyone must." Sapphire's voice dropped low and spiteful. "It's just a job, Amber. Nobody likes them, but everyone has them. Everyone deals with them. You can't just lurch from one distraction to another. You'll never be tolerated, let alone respected, if you can't even manage the barest minimum for our society."

"I worked with Sarin in the rec hall for several months," Amber responded firmly, cautious of how close she was to bursting into tears but unable to bear keeping silent. "I'm proud of the hours I've put in. But I need to look after myself as well. It takes too much out of me to sustain it for the rest of my life. So, I'm figuring out what else to do."

"Of course, my apologies." Sapphire's voice grew dangerously quiet. "What else are you experienced in?"

Amber's blood chilled. "Nothing."

Sapphire's eyes narrowed. "So what choice do you have? Do you want to become a burden? Do you want to rely on others—when you don't even have your own family? I know how much prestige your father put on you being able to look after yourself. Would you want him to see you like this? Refusing to work?"

"I'm not refusing to work! I just—"

"Think you deserve better than everyone else?"

"No! I want better for everyone—"

Sapphire laughed scornfully. "You don't even have a job, and you think you know what's best for anyone?"

Amber bit back a retort that wouldn't help and focussed on not breaking into pieces in front of her aunt.

"I've seen your work record, such as it is," Sapphire admitted, trying a different tack. "You've done quite a few months with Sarin, if you add them together. She might take you on as a health apprentice, if you're lucky. She speaks highly of you. You're very good at your job. It would be selfish to not sign up."

Something curled up miserably inside Amber. She couldn't deny it. What kind of person would she be if she didn't help others? But, could she not find a way to help that didn't hurt her quite so much? The words were too hard to form in front of Sapphire. "She interviewed and accepted me weeks ago. I'm grateful."

"I don't think you are, or you would have signed up by now. The Realm is falling to wrack and ruin, and you think it's the time to shirk your responsibilities? You cannot refuse an apprenticeship. There is no option here, Amber."

"So you keep telling me. And yet here you are, in my home after dark, demanding a decision as though I've still one to make."

"I'm sorry," Sapphire mocked, losing patience. "You're waiting until you can be the one person in the Realm with an easy job? You think you're so hard done by. You make me sick. You don't know real hardship. This is the easiest you're ever going to have it."

"I don't expect it to be easy," Amber growled, rapidly losing patience in her turn. "I've held hands with the dying when there was nothing else that could be done. Don't talk to me about enduring hardship or taking the easy option. I can do the job and do it well. But I come home every night and I can't even think. I can't do anything but cry and drag myself through a routine that ends the same the next day. I can't."

"Then you are the problem, not the job," Sapphire prescribed coldly. "You're oversensitive and a job will stamp that out of you. People accepted your silliness and shirkiness, after you saved them. But sooner or later, you have to come back to the real world. You have to pay your dues, the same as everyone else."

Something fired within Amber. "I work hard. I'm proud of what I've done. It's not the end of the Realm to not want to do it for the rest of my life."

"You selfish, selfish girl. The rest of us make do. And what about your mother, working every hour morning and night for a pittance and never taking any time to enjoy herself? Do you think she enjoyed her job?"

"I wanted her to!" Amber pleaded, distraught. Her aunt had gone too far this time. "I tried to help her. I would have given anything for her to be happy."

Sapphire's voice grew dangerously quiet. "I don't often say this, Amber. But what would your mother think?"

Tears lanced Amber's eyes. A sudden cruel pain crushed her chest. "She told me everyone hated their job; she told me that work was tough, and painful, and that that was life. And she was telling me what she knew, in an attempt to protect me. To prepare me."

"So." Sapphire's smile was bright and brittle. "Sign here please."

Amber wrote her pledge to Sarin between the neat, compressing lines, and her aunt swept out of the room.

Amber gulped a painful, steadying breath. "But my mother is no longer here," she murmured to the neutral, listening night. "And I have the chance to learn different—because I still am." She could breathe more freely now. "Mother would tell me to take the safer path—I know she would. But I know, equally, the fierce pride she would proclaim eventually, when she saw me strike out upon the one less sure."

Her voice couldn't have sounded shakier, but she'd lived two lives for long enough—she could fight a little longer. She told herself it again and again, and she tried to believe it.

But the tears she'd held back until Sapphire had left wouldn't stop falling.

Night Visions

No amount of Selkie magic could delay the apprenticeship, Amber had to admit the next morning as she reported to Sarin and began her first shift. Anguished as she was over the separation from her newfound purpose, she nevertheless managed to convince herself that it sped the days. Knowing she had the pelt to return to freed her soul to apply her energies fully to every task Sarin set her during the day, and she revelled in the pride she felt when she made a difference to her patients. Still, each night she breathed a sigh of relief to come home, having felt torn apart until she could hold fur and needle in joyous reunion again.

She bore it for several weeks, resigned to knowing this was now her quest as surely as hunting the Kelpie was Racxen's, and reconciled to their closeness being reduced to leaving footprints for each other in heartfelt pilgrimage destined not to meet. Yet as the weeks grew, and responsibilities pushed later and later, Amber felt as though her heart and mind were being rack-wrenched. The times when she truly made a difference were hardly on Sarin's scale, whereas the pelt had been committed to her alone.

The days crushed into her. The need to finish the pelt clung to Amber like a fever, harrying her through the slipping hours until she could return, relieved, to the stirring sanctuary of the night, convinced she was going quite mad, for they were never enough. She itched to make a difference—yet surely, she tried to assuage the guilt that bit and worried at her, there was more than one way to save a life. Was it wrong to want to pursue the way she was best at?

Throwing a despairing glance to the clock, Amber decided she had to make tonight different from the other nights. And so, she disregarded the desk, spread the pattern across the floor, and unwrapped the most precious of packages from her rucksack. The skin lay before her, softly gleaming. It was growing all the time, thrillingly, and yet it looked eerily body-like. For a moment bile rose: she had someone's skin lying on her floor. But she fought it back. She also had someone's only chance in her hands, so she'd better make a fine job of it.

Racing towards Fairymead, in his haste Racxen thought not of courting the Kelpie's presence. He wouldn't have let a pack of Venom-spitters stop him. And yet, with love and fear and urgency coursing their wild, clear cry through his veins, a call he'd never heard before slammed into him with all the force of breaking wave. Its echo throbbed through every fibre of his being. The Kelpie—it had to be.

He had to get to Amber. But what if, some intuitive thread woven through his mind cautioned, its cry spoke somehow a message or warning for them—for her? And, knowing Amber, she'd hate to think he'd left a creature, however eldritch, calling and crying without being answered. So he slowed both his breath and his careening descent and advanced, hushed and watchful and ready, into the spill of shadow beneath the silhouette tangle of the trees.

The heavy, forest-damp air bloomed, fecund, ripe, focusing his senses. A nightful of noises unfurled themselves softly, like petals amidst the aftermath of rain. The Arraheng reminded himself to heed their wisdom, to quieten his racing thoughts and open himself to the messages surrounding him in their stillness for, unmoored by the sudden, momentary call of the Kelpie's voice, every inch of the Realm was straining to recapture it. Reclaim it.

Racxen faltered. Was it really anyone's place to attempt such a thing? A flash in the dark, that's all it was. The luminous, transcendent blue of ice pierced through by moonlight, and he was spinning to locate it again. He would have thrown himself through briar and bramble to find it, even should it mean losing himself. Hooves slammed like a heart seized by shuddering ecstasy. But where?

As its presence closed, he felt, then heard, a chthonic thrumming like pipes. It was as though the Kelpie's call were blowing the storm-rush and sea-thrash through his veins, scouring his mind, ripping all else out of his memory and filling the gaping, clamouring void with ecstatic, unfettered wildness.

The briefest glimpse bloomed—a lightning-seared vision amidst an aching, treasured darkness. There was no room for his own self amidst this clamour of sea-drawn hooves and the pounding of salt-flushed blood.

For a euphoric moment Racxen felt and saw as the Kelpie did—and all was exquisite, electric intensity. The night was his, the storm was his. The thunder screamed his name and the rain turned into tongues dancing worship on his skin. And then the Kelpie ran on, tearing its temporary convergence from the Arraheng, who collapsed blindly with a wrenching yell, unfeeling. His mind was shuttered to the anxious chatter of the rushes, bereft of the all-encompassing union that had filled him so completely, leaving a cavernous, desperate emptiness. His lips parted in a grievous moan. He tasted silt.

Blearily pushing himself onto his elbows, Racxen's vision protestingly returned to reality. He'd stumbled to the bank of Moonstruck Lake itself and feared himself forsaken. In truth, numb to the balmy embrace of the soothing loam, he'd let himself dismiss its touch as soil.

You are of the earth, he reminded himself. *Return to it. Let it heal you.* Rolling over weakly, he let the clinging mud reaffirm his own skin, his own boundaries, his own connection to the Realm, terrified that without its containment his soul would spill and smear, could never re-gather itself, could never function.

The stars were spinning. Overhead, the trees craned anxiously. His breath slowed, steadied by the eternal embrace of the earth. *You have more than that*, he reminded himself, struggling to rein his heart to steadiness as it strained and shied against the loss of the Kelpie. *You have this. You have enough—and enough is everything.*

Peeling himself free from the healing mud clinging as sticky and yearning as Kelpie skin, Racxen turned once more towards the protective, obscuring knot of trees, beyond which lay Fairymead. He felt the eldritch lure of the Kelpie tighten around his mind, a gulf of longing wrenched wide clamouring to be filled by the promise stampeding through his veins.

"You can snatch my feet from solid ground," he murmured. "You can lure me into the deeps. You can make me question earth and air, and fire and stars. But there is one course that not even you can ever drag me from: the path between my heart and hers."

A cry, as mesmeric and alluring as the wild, heart-soaring keening of a hawk—a Dragon, even—rent the sky into savage and sublime dimensions.

The sound rooted the Arraheng where he stood, stunned by sudden realisation.

I have Amber, Racxen reminded himself repentantly, as the echoes of that harsh, pleading cry fell away unanswered. *To journey through the dark with. To come back for. The Kelpie has no one. Suppose the yearning we feel is its own? Perhaps that is why it comes.*

He felt his heartbeat slow, come back to his own self, to its own rhythm. And he was glad, and walked in silence and solace the way home, more determined than ever to not just find the Kelpie, but to help it.

Treading Water

Amber woke to crushing darkness, and the inescapable slipping of time. *Decide. De-cide*, goaded the clock's relentless ticking. Her probation at the rec hall would be over within days and a crossroads more frightening than she'd dare admit in waking hours loomed: commit to a suffocating claustrophobia or cast away from all known shores. Staring at the curtains, Amber shoved off the bedcovers, planted her toes deeply into the cool of the carpet, and threw back the drapes to release the sliver of moonlight twisting restlessly beyond. It didn't reveal a solution, but her Realm felt instantly less oppressive now that it stretched to the reaches of the star-touched night instead of being hemmed by four walls. Even though as her gaze fell on the pelt, her blood ran cold. In her sleep-deprived haste, she'd done it wrong.

Amber bit back her panic, and forced herself to think. Doing it alone was no longer working. And, at this time of night, there was only one place she could face visiting.

She'd have to unpick it. All that work. She was the very worst person the Selkies could have chosen. And she had the audacity to want to do this fulltime? Amber sighed. She'd come here to make use of the space, of the quiet and endless oak-benched banquet tables where she could spread her project and focus but, ensconced in the high-halled shelter of the castle, she sat, staring out, and cried with the rain.

"You do know this doesn't make you a bad person?" Jasper tried, materialising with a pile of research and a flickering candle, eyeing the misassembled fur and finding a spare corner of the table to divest himself of his books. "It doesn't even mean you're bad at this. It just means you're learning. And that you care that it's not going as well as you'd like—which just means that you care about it and want to do well. It's the lot of an apprentice. No-one begins as a master."

Amber wiped a hand across her face. "You're right," she managed. "Sorry," she admitted, embarrassed now. "And thank you."

The Prince waved away her apology. "I know Racxen's been away chasing after the Kelpie, but don't you dare convince yourself that no-one else sees you," he reminded. Jasper slid onto the bench next to Amber and nudged a bowl of soup in her direction, noting her hollowed, burning eyes and pale-shadowed complexion against the flickering warmth of the candle that staved off the lengthening shadows of gathering night outside. "You do know what they say about Fairies being able to survive on air alone is Goblinchat, right?" he added, worriedly watchful. "You know, Tanzan should try an apprenticeship in the castle kitchens. This soup's really rather good."

Amber half-grinned, wryly grateful, and gave the contents a token prod to show willingness. But her eyes strayed, and to the Prince the absentminded swirls of her spoon through the broth looked more like divination attempts than an effort at eating. He stifled his sigh as quietly as he could and resolved to listen. Her smile was apologetic now, as well as guilty. Jasper's heart slumped in testimony.

"You know, this project of yours is supposed to be sustaining you," he advised, with more tact than he was usually known for, Amber had to admit. "If it's depleting you, maybe it's time to reconsider it."

Or not, Amber growled in her head. "It's not my quest that's depleting me," she promised vehemently, with a spirit Jasper was relieved to see hadn't been lost. "It's the rest of what I—what we all—have to contend with," she added bleakly.

The Prince nodded, for once quietly accepting. And yet something akin to Yenna's fire glimmered in his green eyes. "Don't tell anyone I said it," he murmured conspiratorially with a rare smile. "But best stick with the project, then. In the absence of heroes to tell you, take it from me." Amber's eyes settled on him in silent thanks. "But what if I can't manage both?" she risked voicing. "How do I know which one I'm supposed to pursue, truly?"

"You already know that you can't manage both equally, I trust I can say without offending you," Jasper responded, watching her gravely. "Splitting your efforts cannot be effective as committing to one to the exclusion of the other. Leaving the apprenticeship to focus on the pelt would be no less difficult—probably more so, actually," he recognised. "And yet those efforts would fill you with energy instead of despair."

"But what if I can't do it?" Amber warned wretchedly. "What if it rips me apart?"

The Prince waved a dismissive hand. "What if it makes you whole?" he countered.

He stroked the pelt thoughtfully. "I would remove your obstacles as well as your doubt, if I were able," the Prince offered awkwardly, feeling inadequate. "But perhaps it comes down to: can you contemplate giving this up?"

Amber threw him the look that comment deserved.

Jasper arched an eyebrow triumphantly. "Then you have your answer."

Amber opened her mouth, to protest that it wasn't that simple.

"Sometimes, Amber, the thing is not to change your mind, but to change your circumstance," he reminded pointedly. "And to not beat yourself up about it." Jasper looked to the horizon, through windows older than he. "Simply make a choice as to what you will and will not do. Choose your priorities, make your sacrifices. And then the decision will have made itself."

Amber nodded carefully, feeling lighter already. Yet her eyes swam with the enormity of what lay before her. "I want to believe that it can be different now. After everything I've been through," she murmured. "But the situation is still the same."

Jasper smiled, on certain ground now. "*You* are different. You take chances and make choices you once would never have dared to. You know what you are worth, and what you are capable of. You know what you want, and how much you're willing to work for it. So *everything* is different."

Amber let the prospect settle, as possibilities reached and shifted, taking solid form in the waiting night. "What we went through, those seasons ago," she agreed quietly, reverently. "My mind was stretched, as were my wings. I may have lost the latter, but I have no intention of letting the former diminish. I can't fold either back up, neat and small, ever again, after so gloriously extending them. It's time to tell Sarin. In the morning, I'll hand in my notice."

Jasper lay a hand on her shoulder. "Oft-times, leaving takes more strength than staying. I'm proud of you Amber—as you should be of yourself."

She hugged him gratefully, and bundled the pelt up to go. She had one more person she wanted to tell.

The water gleamed, knife bright and just as sharp, beneath the moon. *Shortcuts are stupid. And he doesn't even know you're coming.* Amber's heart hammered, her breath as short as her nerves as she stole towards Moonstruck Lake. The eldritch coils of darkness almost alive crouched tense and flighty around its banks.

She'd thought on some level that coming here would bring her closer to Racxen; that, like the vigils of maidens of old, somehow her proximity could guard him from danger, and his presence could linger to protect her. Yet, although treading the path he had walked soothed her, she couldn't deny that this could be turning into a dangerous detour. The lake was a long way from Arraterr, and yet it was to here her heart had gravitated, had most expected to find him. She could no longer attribute her strung-out nerves to simply missing him, for she couldn't shake the pressured sense of time slipping irretrievably, and a claustrophobic need to ascertain for definite whether summoning the Kelpie would be safe for Racxen, but she knew it wasn't a choice she could make for him.

She had to admit, this place held a rare magnetism—although there drifted a curious sense of aftertaste, like smoke drifting in the air when fireworks had already dissipated. The spilled silver ink of the moon lingered tantalisingly atop the age-deep water's surface, and dark tongues lapped fretfully at the banks, as though testing the boundaries they would soon breach.

A strange opacity slid across the surface as her gaze strayed across to the centre, seeming solid in its enchantment, as though if only she were to try to walk across it she would find all her answers. Amber shivered, convulsed with fear for those who had pledged their efforts to the water horse within. The beast had not yet been conjured and yet, even now, the waters clung like a drowning weight.

Feeling as nauseatingly ashamed and depleted as when she had fought to leave the Goblin Market empty handed, with effort Amber stepped away from the edge. It took as great a strength to bear some voids as to breach them, she reminded herself grimly. She would take the long way round.

She fought to steady herself against the clutching grasp of the lake while, as if sensing her intention of leaving, its cloying scent closed around her in a suffocating rush, stagnant and stewing and sucking. Instinctively, Amber breathed instead the scent of the pelt still gathered protectively in her arms—and the salt-lifted tang cut through the confusion in her mind.

Racxen found Amber at the lip of Moonstruck Lake, crouched Gargoyle-like in strength and about to leave, staring distantly into the vast depths of thundercloud grey and pouring her restlessness into the receptive waters.

The anguish wrought by leaving the Kelpie dissipated from him in sluicing waves; eclipsed in this moment of seeing her safe. Yet her gaze hovered anxiously, remote, as if her soul had crossed the water to avoid the questions chasing her. Her eyes sought refuge amongst the scattered reflections.

Racxen's relief at seeing her felt crushed with the weight of a pain he would have faced Goblins to heal for her. What had he left her to bear alone in his absence? And so, he approached quietly, although he ached to hold her, fearing that to reach out before she felt ready might prove as disorientating and insensitive as waking a sleepwalker. They had spent weeks apart. He knew he couldn't just make it go away.

Sure of purpose now, Amber prised herself from the ground. It had been a mistake to come here. Her presence would not keep Racxen safe, and she didn't need the Lake. Her own quest lay beyond such trappings—to wilder waters yet. She allowed herself one final glance to the shadows under the trees, willing them to keep safe the one she loved who walked with such ease amongst them.

But then the shadows shifted into an unforgettable silhouette, and Racxen slipped into her vision like a dream.

"Amber!" His eyes shone like marshlight at midnight as he ran to her, and she threw her arms around him like she would never let go. Kissing her gently, he rested his forehead against hers, and Amber felt her constricting fears fall away as surely as when he had spliced the stemstranglers from her neck all those seasons ago.

"You're safe," she whispered as though in prayer, burying her face against his chest as tears slid down her face. There rushed so many things to tell him, to ask—and yet, just for now, she knew all would be solved, all could be surmounted, if only they could have these moments together first.

"Engo ro fash, Amber. I'm here. I'll always come back for you. Whatever it is, we'll get through it," Racxen promised ardently, wrapping her in his arms and stroking her hair, trying to banish her fears and sorrows.

"Whatever it is? You could have been killed by the Kelpie!"

Relief flooded dizzingly. "That?" Racxen blurted. "I was scared something had happened to you—"

Amber threw her arms around him, sobbing and laughing at the same time. "Nothing I can't find my way through, knowing you're safe. Well," she acknowledged with a grin, squeezing him even more tightly, "safe enough by your reckoning. I'd hardly want you to abandon the adventure of a lifetime because of a little danger." She realised she'd eased the strength of her embrace, as though fearing it would somehow hold him back.

But, gently and insistently, Racxen wrapped her even closer in his own arms. "You know I didn't just sign up for the massive, frightening, life-changing adventures?" he nudged, his smile as broad as it was warm. "I signed up for all that stuff with the Venom-spitters and Kelpie, too."

Snuggled in his arms, Amber tightened her own half of the hug comfortably again, a huge weight sloughing off her arms.

"Well. In that case."

A tender silence wrapped around them, honouring the time each had spent apart and what they had faced, which could now be shared and surmounted. A reaffirmation of everything that was theirs, no matter the time or distance between. As they kissed, and touched, she could finally trust that he truly was here, that they were safe in each other's arms. Amber felt her strength returning from somewhere deep inside, felt her heart work loose from the knot it had tied itself into in his absence. "I thought I'd lose you to the Kelpie," she admitted, sending the fear fleeing with its voicing. "I was so scared."

Racxen grinned shakily. "You really thought the second-most alluring creature in the Realm could keep me from you, no matter how powerful it proved? You're my compass out into the storm, Amber. And my safe harbour on my return." He stepped back slightly so she could see the sincerity in his gaze, and she never wanted him to stop looking at her like that.

"I meant lose you as in you being killed by it. Are you saying the Kelpie isn't a predator?" Her grin spilled over, giddy with relief. Racxen's safety meant more to her even than his love now, with the former confirmed, her soul felt free to bask in the latter, to dance with new words that wove her soul with his. His compass. His harbour. She kissed him deeply, twining her fingers into his hair, melting into his embrace. The lure of the Kelpie was legendary. If he wanted it, she would send him gladly. He deserved his soul to fly to the stars. But she wanted to take him there too. Go there together.

"It only captures. Bewitches. I didn't know until this day. But it didn't know I've given myself fully to one of the air, instead of the storm." Racxen could barely gasp the words amidst urgent kisses as Amber's legs buckled at his words and together they sank to the ground, clinging to one another, grinning and breathless, the Realm narrowing into a sensory rush of sunlight and brilliance, exhilaration and union, as all else faded.

All else, apart from a threat spat by a Goblin. "I have counsel I must offer, before we . . . go further. And it is not the Kelpie I came to warn you of, but an older foe," Racxen managed raggedly, even as he wished he could let himself fall into these moments with her. Releasing an unsteady breath, he bowed his forehead against hers, meeting her elated grin with his own. With every sense attuned to her closeness, to her body pressed against his, to her breath pulsing at his ear, to her hands imprinting her joy across his back as she pulled him to her, he let his eyes drift shut as he savoured these moments, feeling the racing of their pounding hearts ease as the kisses they shared grew soothing and steadying.

"Goblins?" Speaking the word dripped ice along her spine, but Amber let herself luxuriate in the fact that Racxen kept himself crouched close. Every inch of his toned body tensed as though in protection. Amber grinned in embarrassment, sure he could read her thoughts. "I share those thoughts." Racxen kissed her softly, his own eyes glowing warmly, forbidding shame. "I honour them." A final deep, melting, merging kiss. A promise for later, for all time. "And I will follow them to the letter when we have our chance. But I would forsake even that ecstasy to keep you safe so, first I must tell you this. You're right about the Goblins."

Drawing courage from Amber's gaze holding him safe, Racxen began. "Familiarising myself with the Kelpie's haunts brought me into strange territory, so perhaps it was not surprising that I ran into the Pedlar. When she cornered me with threats of claiming back the souldebt I pledged to Thanatos, I warned her, in an attempt to throw her off the scent, that my soul was no longer in my keeping. I've never spoken of you to her—I would not sully your name by speaking it to Goblin ears, and had I realised she could connect my words with you I would have kept my silence even to my doom—but she must have received word from a source outside of her kin, for she knew to whom my soul belongs. Amber, I'm so sorry." Guilt strangled him unbearably, and he pulled away in shame.

Amber sat up with him, pushed her forehead to his, mingled her breath with his own in the silent, accepting space between. "I might not have your history with them," she acknowledged gently. "But, after the events of last season, I know Goblins: I know their ways of making you feel how, whatever they do, like it's your fault. And the important thing is: I know that it's not, Racxen. None of it is. We didn't let them defeat us last time and we're not going to let them now."

Meeting the fierce, sure heat of her gaze, Racxen nodded silently, overcome. Robbed of words once more, this time he surrendered them willingly to the strength of love flowing between them. Resting his head against hers, Racxen let his doubts spill away into a wonder-filled smile. Amber was right. The Goblins knew nothing of the magic they wielded together. And, although against the devastating potential of the Kelpie's influence they couldn't promise to prove unstoppable, however far apart the quest sent them, he knew they would prove unbreakable. Racxen let his thoughts linger a moment in this sanctuary. He knew he'd have to leave so soon again, and the knowledge twisted more painfully than the debt the Goblins still chased, but his breath refused to hasten, for it drew a clean pain, this, not a rancorous one like theirs. And they still had these moments, just the two of them together. Here and now.

It was the Arraheng's turn to grin in embarrassment. Some tracker he was proving to be, if he could not stick to his original path. "The vengeance the Goblins threatened is strange as well as sinister," he cautioned. "Does 'Trickster's Gate' hold meaning for you? For they warned that doom shall fall there. It's just the old crossroads to the wildwood, sen?"

"Yeah—where Jasper said the Oak Prince came from." The knowledge sat strangely with Amber.

"But what can he want with you?" Racxen frowned in confusion. "What can he possibly claim you've done to have angered him so grievously?"

Amber untangled their embrace and showed him the half-sewn pelt. Swiftly, she updated him.

Admiration and horror caught on Racxen's breath. "So the Goblins stole the skin for the Oak Prince? And with being summoned to the Greenwood Court, he hasn't had a chance to make it his yet?"

Amber sighed. "And now I've stolen it back from the Goblins, because I need to reunite it with Hydd."

Racxen stared at her, speechless. "There's more, though," Amber admitted. "I don't just have to remake the pelt. I need to find the pieces, first—and doing so will take a journey beyond all known territory: to the Icefields." Even saying it sent a frisson across her skin. And it wasn't with fear that she was shivering.

Racxen grinned. "If this is how it makes you feel, you have to go. Plus, it'll keep you away from the Oak Prince for a bit."

Amber nuzzled into his shoulder appreciatively, her eyes sparking off his. "Might take longer than taming the Kelpie, though, at this rate," she murmured.

Racxen chuckled acceptingly. "Well, I'd track you down quicker, and give my heart to you far more readily." He kissed her softly. "And I'd trail you far longer, so take as much time as you need."

Amber's smile spread. Still, ever since they had met, she had prided herself on her independence, and knew it was one of the things Racxen had been attracted to within her. What would he think of her if she couldn't support herself now?

"It sounds tempting; to run back into adventure," she admitted awkwardly. "But what if my path leads me to a place I'm not proud of? I've no way of knowing how long this will take. What if I end up with no money and no prospects, still clinging obstinately to a dream I should have stopped pursuing seasons back?"

Racxen grinned. "Honestly? I would investigate this place with you, side by side, and shine torches in all its corners so that its shadows fled, and if it was to be your dwelling, it would be mine also, and my pride in you would never be shaken. We would live with what means we had; my trust in your choices would remain steadfast, and my regard for you would only increase. Arraheng do not as a general rule keep many possessions," he admitted. "We always had to move on quickly; we lived and travelled lightly. But what is mine would be yours, and you would always have a place with us, whether in our caves or 'round our fires. Turn up with nothing, and I'd show you how much you still had."

His promise rendered her speechless. "I have a bit of money saved from those months with Sarin," Amber managed, struggling to return to their original subject with Racxen so meltingly understanding, so distractingly close.

"But Fairy communities work differently; you know how to track, to forage, to find shelter, to protect each other, to teach the youngsters—I can't even do one of those, so I have to find something to make up for all the other things I lack."

Racxen's voice was shimmeringly close to her ear, and deliciously unsteadier than before. "The only thing you lack," he reminded her, as sternly as warmly, "is the ability to see yourself as the rest of us do. You've risked yourself to save others. You've braved ridicule and changed opinion. You've seen the best in others when they feared not look for it themselves.

"I might not have the Sea Folk's gift of prophecy," he admitted, wrapping her in his arms, "but I promise I'll be your shadow whatever you choose. I wish I could bear the weight you are under to choose the apprenticeship, but I know the resources you need are already at your command."

She squeezed his hand thankfully and lay back in his arms, letting her weight sink into his strong chest and shoulders. "Careful. I'm starting to feel like this choice might be the right one."

"In the quiet reaches of the night, when your thoughts turn towards it every time your mind drifts: you'll know it," Racxen promised. "That look on your face when you talk about sewing the skin—if what gave you it was within my grasp, I'd track across the entire Realm to bring it to you. If you know where you can find it, it's a rendezvous worth keeping, no matter how long it takes. You owe it to yourself."

Deep in her gut, relief welled at his words. "And you'll always have my blessing to do the same. Even if it terrifies me," she admitted. "Although I've never met an animal yet that doesn't love you, so perhaps I shouldn't panic about the Kelpie."

"That's the spirit." Racxen grinned, the breath of his whisper as intimate as a kiss. "And remember: these trials will not last forever, while our love will. I know your journey will take you further than I have ever tracked, but I would scour the entire Realm to return to your side. When you are ready, I will find you. Kelpie or none."

Inches from his lips and drenched in the fullness of his gaze, Amber breathed Racxen's words and scent deeply, soaking up the sanctity of his embrace. "My soul longs to show you I'm ready now," she admitted in a murmur, grinning. "And yet, even as delay increases desire, my desire must yield to my duty."

"With all my heart, I would see them both fulfilled," Racxen promised softly. "But in the time and manner of your choosing. I did not come to delay you, Amber, but to buoy your heart before you leave, and see you depart with eased mind, if it is within my power. Your heart will lead you true—trust yourself to heed its voice and follow its course. No quest will feel so right, however hard the path may prove, as the one of your authentic choosing. That one's worth chasing. And I'll never stand in the way of it."

"I know," Amber whispered, kissing him softly, sealingly. "And you'll always be the greatest part of it, I promise. You're my best adventure, as well as my deepest love."

"Likewise." Racxen clung to her fiercely, even while a chill more penetrative than the Northern freeze clutched at him in turn, to know that he would have to relinquish his protective embrace around her and wait, in faith and burning hope, contending alone with the knowledge that she would be journeying further than he could ever hope to track fast enough to genuinely aid her.

To keep tremor from tender whisper as perception-narrowing fear encroached like hoarfrost through his mind, he let his gaze brush the grace-touched eye of the moon as instinctively as a nictitating membrane slipping across the vision of a hawk. He saw how the place lived in her eyes already; the skydancer lights, the wild clean swathes of sweeping mirror ice, and he knew he could not let his own terrors mar the possibility of such ecstasy for her. And so, willing the moon to watch over Amber when he could not, he pushed his anguish aside and focused fully on the moments throbbing beneath his fingertips; her heartbeat against his chest, the heat of her breath at his lips, the warmth sparking in the gaze that she shared with him alone.

"You should go before dawn," he managed huskily.

"That gives us tonight," Amber promised. She sank into his kisses, revelled in his touch; felt her soul merge with his until she knew the memory would soar with her, to warm her in the wilds and beacon-guide her home whence no trail would remain.

And after, as Racxen pulled his cloak across them both and she nestled against his chest, she drowsed on a dangerous shore and felt invincible.

Down to the Woods

Hand in the letter and find another pelt piece: two plans worth rising before dawn for, Amber resolved as she padded home, her spirit dancing radiant in the glow of shared memory and the night shining as luminously now as if she had remained by Racxen's side. As she slipped into the bedroom that had felt claustrophobic when she had borne her fears alone, she felt it rendered anew a sanctuary of possibilities and found herself breathlessly considering her future once more, contemplating her next move with a spreading, determined grin.

She still had time. She could forge time. Working on the pelt amongst the constrictions of her apprenticeship had seemed to expand the moments available; had revealed their true elasticity, as well as augmented her energy. Now, she knew if she could claim but a short time, it would make all the difference. She wouldn't let this chance dwindle to naught. She had kept the fire burning thus far—now she had to trust it had gathered enough momentum to burst free from the confinement of the apprenticeship. Surely, it was time enough now for a trial that, if effectively and boldly wrought, would later allow her to afford the greater leap.

With a moon-brilliant vision of the future spreading through the window silver-touched and unencumbered, Amber slept at ease.

And so, while the trailing mists of night still dusted the first breaths of morning, she hastily packed her haversack, snatched up the scrawled note crouched atop her dresser, and padded through the waiting dawn.

The familiar gateway to the rec hall loomed, the comfortingly solid rendered just for now foreboding, but the gleaming wash of dew that lingered reminded her that just as dawn still held sway and heralded new possibilities, so did her dream.

It's real now, Amber urged herself. *You cannot fear what is of your free choosing and remains within your control. This is your time.*

Beneath the Greenwood Court summons still nailed to the rec hall door, she pinned her own explanation: her plea for one month's leniency to attempt to save a man's life. Bile-flavoured guilt rose as she stepped away, but she forced herself to remember that Sarin, of all people, knew the lengths a journey of healing, however unorthodox, could draw one to and the demands it entailed. She knew she was lucky that Jasper had agreed to field enquiry until the month had passed and provide guarantee that she had not simply fled under pressure. To be honest, she'd rather brave the ravages of the wild and the fury of the woodland wight than face questioning at home and she had a niggling feeling that she owed Jasper an assurance of his own having left him to it, because she was by no means sure that he believed her himself. Yet he believed in her enough to wave away such ineffective attempts as she had offered to explain, and he'd dismissed her apologies arrogantly enough to make her trust that they were genuinely uncalled for. So she'd hugged him before he could annoy her any further and left it at that.

Her steps lightened as doubts and worries sloughed from her soul like an old skin now that she'd shed the heart-weight of the letter and its decision. Amber sped from the rec hall grounds, padding the dew-rinsed meadows until she'd reached Ruby's home. She let herself in with the oldest secret she had been granted and replaced the key silently. Amber's heart squeezed itself against her throat as she let her gaze wander through rooms she often felt she knew better than her own.

She had rehearsed this part of her plan in her mind as often as her response to Sarin, and so her heart beat steadily even as her hand tremored, while she dipped into her pack, counted out her savings, and quietly stashed them in a dish on the dresser.

She felt her pulse slow with her breath as she let the crumpled paper go. These weighted, ephemeral notes she had earned through sleepless nights and pressured days, and to release them after so long dizzied her suddenly, but she reminded herself that what she'd used had flown in the service of survival and dreams—and as for what she had left, if she were fated not to return from the greater danger she now willingly walked into, there could be no one she'd rather bequeath it to. Her own future was unravelling faster than Selkie sewing thread, and let it, for she would learn to manage somehow—but Ruby had plans, potential. This money would set her up in Loban or wherever she chose to begin her apprenticeship. And, as she wouldn't be here when Ruby found it, her best friend couldn't exactly argue the matter.

As she stepped once more into the clean, chill air outside, a clutch of emotions tangled around Amber's throat. She felt indescribably proud and yet, the painful truth was, it had been borne alone, when it had taken so much out of her that she suddenly wished that instead of having to have been accomplished in solitude it could have been celebrated. Or at least witnessed.

Still, her footprints behind her left testimony enough as she pressed on in high spirits, conviction humming in her veins and recent-wrought memories riding the soothing swell of the clear morning while she decided which way to go.

Taking no particular route save the one that suggested itself irresistibly via some inner compass and the assumption that a Selkie pelt might find sanctuary amidst a terrestrial grandeur equal to the sea, Amber drifted from the streaming sunlight of the meadows to the nurturing shade of the forest edge.

Enjoying the sublime, elevating solemnity of the Realm's most ancient arboreal inhabitants, watching appreciatively as the trees arched their long limbs gracefully above her as though stretching themselves awake after a long sleep, at first Amber felt herself similarly, luxuriously stretched, as though leaving a cocoon and becoming birthed in the sensations of the forest. And yet the further she wandered, the deeper she could feel a festering unease taking hold of her, without being able to discern its root. Perhaps it was the awareness, drilled into her as a winglet, that any canopy, however beautifully woven, held intrinsic danger for a Fairy by creating a barrier against the open sky. But she told herself this without believing it. A sense of intrusion, of malice even, hung in the air like smog. Exactly how far had she meandered into this thicket, her senses smudged by stillness?

"If you go down to the woods today
You'd better not go alone . . ."

Amber's eyes flitted warily, as her skin prickled. Had those words been her own thoughts? A chill crept. Or were they something stranger?

"It's lovely down in the woods today
But safer to stay at home . . ."

Amber gritted her teeth and stumbled backwards, the forest beginning to spin as her vision bled and blurred.

"If you go down to the woods today
You'd better go in disguise.
If you go down to the woods today
You're in for—"

"Goblins' teeth, Jasper, seriously!" Amber shoved him away irritably as she collided back-first into him, her pulse scudding out of control. "Even for you, that rhyme was too weird."

"Rhyme?" The Prince looked worryingly serious. "Amber, not all of us wander beneath ancient boughs talking to ourselves. I haven't breathed a word. I came looking for you because this section of the forest isn't safe anymore."

Amber growled in frustration. "You think?"

Jasper ignored her outburst—some things never changed, Amber noted dryly. Instead, he was watching her gravely. "You've heard him, haven't you?"

The knowledge squirmed inescapably in Amber's gut. If the Prince of Fairymead dare not speak this figure's name, whom in the Realm had she just exposed herself to?

Jasper's hands were gentle against her cheek and forehead. "Did anything happen to you? Can you form your thoughts effectively?"

"I'm forming one effectively right now! Jasper, what is wrong? You're scaring me far more than that . . . voice . . . did. Tell me what you know."

"Well, I suppose we have to give him the benefit of the doubt, because he's part of the Greenwood Court, but from what I've found so far he demands further investigation." Jasper had the grace to look uncertain. "I'd planned on researching this Oak Prince as soon as I'd found you safe. Apart from common consensus that he is a particularly powerful forest spirit who was once assumed responsible for the living and dying of the forests, so far I've only really learned that he is not in the habit of suffering others to live." Jasper eyed his companion dubiously. "Although this appears incongruous with the evidence."

"Evidence, or assumption?" Amber glared back at him. "You don't tend to be great at first impressions. Why do you automatically expect this Prince to be dangerous? I might have been unnerved by what he said, but frankly no more than I have been about these accursed apprenticeships everyone's been pressuring me over."

"Mere assumption? Notwithstanding a particularly lurid assertion that if his branches touch your forehead, you go insane?" Jasper retorted. He wasn't sure whether her resulting expression was as a result of this revelation or his inept timing. He pressed his lips into a thin line and carried on regardless. "And we may have been through a lot together, but so help me, Amber, I will not tolerate insubordination."

Amber growled helplessly. "I never meant to run into this 'spirit'," she warned, fearing her emotions might overwhelm her if she couldn't voice them before they spilled. "I only came out here because the apprenticeship is suffocating me. I just wanted to clear my head. With the pelt, I know what to do. With this, I just—"

Jasper's temper quelled instantly. "You always take on more than your due, Amber. You need to be gentler with yourself," he warned more calmly, if as firmly. "I will research the being you encountered and try to decipher whether he is friend or foe or something in between. Although I don't hold much hope for the former, so be on your guard. But mayhap this has turned out for the best."

"How?" she challenged, unconvinced. "How did I get away with seeing him, then? Why did he allow me to continue unmolested?"

Jasper had the grace to look distinctly queasy. "Amber, you don't have wings. You don't have claws. You don't have a body of stone, carved out of the fires of torture. You don't have an ethereal beauty accentuated by the scars of your sacrifice. He thought you were a nobody. On the plus side, when it comes to him this gives you a disguise that even Yenna would envy." He grinned crookedly. "And, possibly, a quest that she will in time, too. Clearly, the Goblins haven't dared tell the Oak Prince of the theft—

and for now, he obviously believes you to be the last person in the Realm capable of finding the pieces. Carry on."

Amber stared in mute astonishment as he walked off, partly stunned that he had so brazenly left her to the devices of a psychosis-inducing wood wight, but mainly proud that he'd demonstrated his belief that she was perfectly capable of handling it alone. So she strode on undaunted with her head held a little higher.

Amber trod Jasper's warning into the soft earth as she journeyed further, refusing to skirt the waiting jaws of the deeper forest, for she could no more turn away from the woodland than she could from the quest itself. Forest-stalker or none, the pelt had to be sewn—and, first, the pieces had to be found. Standing solitary and uncertain at the threshold of the tanglewood, she hardly dared think such things for fear the Oak Prince could sense them.

> "Be engulfed or be enveloped
> By leaves and branches, sea and spray
> Which labyrinth will prove safe passage?
> You dare not enter, yet you stay . . ."

Too late. If he had meant to sway her path with intimidating words, he'd failed, Amber promised herself. Yet the voice sounded curious—creepily so—but not outright aggressive. Perhaps she really was insignificant enough to not be viewed as a threat.

Then she shivered with unease. The soft shrivelight that had filtered through the canopy was shifting into daggered shadows, branches twisting and clenching overhead and all around her. The forest grew so distorted that Amber had no way of retreating, let alone advancing.

"Why don't you show yourself?" she retorted, more out of irritation than fear now. She couldn't risk him realising her true intentions. If she could get him talking about himself, perhaps it would stall him from questioning why she had ventured so far.

"I have no skin with which to do so. I am not fit to be seen," the figure intoned mournfully. "I must borrow the cloak of the forest, the voice of the leaves, the strength of the branches. And they are so much less now than they used to be, so I must do what I must to sustain them, to re-establish them. And into all this, you have blindly entered. To do so indicates recklessness as to what may come after."

So much for hoping to find a piece of pelt unnoticed. "It indicates a determination to exercise my right to take any path I choose without fear of molestation," Amber retorted firmly. "I've simply come to the forest to find somewhere quiet to think my apprenticeship over—I mean no intrusion or offence." The Oak Prince's voice set her teeth on edge. Every time it spoke it shifted, as though its owner had stolen it and was trying to grapple it into submission. An unsettling, trapping undercurrent groped towards her, and uncertainty shivered with recognition in the waiting moments between the words. She did not know these woods. She knew neither the way through nor which direction to escape. How could she defend herself against someone who hid behind the façade of such chameleonic shades?

"You wish to avoid molestation, and yet you walk through my wood?" The voice descended swiftly, enveloping her with a predatory softness. "None come into the forests now who do not wish to see it cut down; diminished into so much produce. I could do the same to you. Plants are fed on blood and bone."

Well, that clarified things somewhat, Amber bristled to herself as she drew her defences around herself with reaffirmed conviction. Yet perhaps she had a chance to throw the Oak Prince off the scent. She had to stay calm, avoid arousing suspicion.

"Then I hope that the Moon Lake Challenge works," Amber offered courteously, and truthfully. "I suppose once sufficient magic is returned to the Realm, you will be back to full strength—and so will your forest. I look forward to that day."

"You think that will be enough?" screamed the apparition, with the force of rending branches. "You expect me to subsist gratefully in a meagre portion of all I once had? You will learn that ways once open to you have been closed. You think you are a creature of the elements. You have voided that right. The woods are mine—and that which is threatened is defended most dearly. Next time you feel like wandering through, you will pay with your life."

Amber quailed, suddenly aware of how alone she was and how closely the trees were now pressing. "What? Why?"

"'What? Why?'" the apparition mocked gleefully. "Prey does not ask questions of a predator. Prey quakes in the knowledge of absolute truth."

Amber breathed hard against her hammering heart. "Sir, you mistake me. I have never hurt these woods. I have never sullied their streams with rubbish, I have never burned their clearings. Why do you take against me?"

Gleaming eyes narrowed dangerously. "The question is: what can I take from you? I see someone has already had their pleasure with your wings. It is time you all, like myself, are restricted to your rightful places. You have reduced me to a shadow of my former glory. You have hemmed my range and destroyed my home, even as you seek to trespass ever further across what is left pristine in these beleaguered lands. Well, no more. You, wingless one, have no place left. It is the natural order of things: those that have no place perish. Perish and are consumed."

All at once she felt festering tendrils of malignance spread oil-like and sickening towards her from amongst the once-vibrant, iridescent tangle of green that used to speak instead the untameable richness of wild secrets. Amber felt a wave of despair threaten, nauseatingly strong, at the realisation that these sentient forests had fallen to the clutches of the wood wight. What hope stood she, when such stalwart wildwood hearts as theirs could not stand against his eldritch threats?

"Perhaps you know more than you tell." His words stroked lightly, urging confession, offering clemency before the first onslaught. Amber shuddered and bit her tongue. He would not draw her secret from her. She gasped and wretched as his mind stabbed at hers, applying an invasive, malicious pressure as though sensing that Amber's focus had drifted to her quest, and in response launching a tyrannical spatter-attack on every aspect of her soul he could grasp to drive it forth from hiding. Frantically Amber kept snapping her attention away, viscerally shaken at his intrusion—but where could she safely send her thoughts, with the forest closing in ever closer?

"Perhaps you are more than you seem." A chthonic power resonated within the growl of his gale-force voice in anger at her resistance. All thought bled from her as the Oak Prince redoubled his psychic assault, and

Amber's confidence leaked from her mental wounds as the apparition felt his way through her mind, sending out snaking, sneaking antennae, tentative and repugnant as the explorative eyestalks of a slug. Nausea wrestled with panic as the voice slipped across her consciousness, investigative, probing, too soft and insidious to fully slam defences against even as she clutched wildly for safer visions to form an inner sanctuary that could not be breached.

The Kelpie. She let the idea of it fill her mind, expand into the furthest reaches of her soul. Its image reared and thrashed, drawing all attention, holding even the Oak Prince ensnared. She folded her defences tight around herself and felt the tendrils of his consciousness scud off her body like the whips of the Goblins lashing at Seb's spinning wheels, unable to gain purchase.

Crushing pressure pounded against her ears and behind her eyes as the apparition pressed home his demand for answer, rendering the forest air suddenly suffocatingly thin, leeching the available oxygen away into his leaves to force her to speak. By the seasons, not even the Goblins employed such torture. Much more of this and neither her tongue nor her soul would remain her own.

"I'm beginning to think you fear me," she managed. "Why else are you seeking to control me?"

Relief stabbed fiercely as pride forced the Oak Prince to relinquish his grasp momentarily and reconsider his approach.

"What are you trying to keep me from?" Amber pressed. "What threat can my involvement in it be to you?"

It seemed to work, earning her mind an easeful silence which Amber clung to victoriously.

"Stray again if you dare, but you won't find my forest unguarded," the wight hissed warningly. "The Shadow-Armed Witness sees all."

Grimly, Amber clung to her silence, fighting to gather her scattered wits as the oppressive weight of the Oak Prince's presence fell back and sun motes drifted peaceably where previously had lurked shadows.

Amber breathed carefully, and considered. Amber chewed her lip, attempting to pierce the dense fog of vegetation and confusion with her gaze. For now, she gave silent thanks for the wild freedom of the Kelpie. It was thanks to that creature she could keep her own liberty for a little longer. But what of this 'Shadow-Armed Witness'?

She curtailed that thought wryly. One all-consuming quest at a time. Later, she would focus on identifying that new foe. But for now, she had to prioritise finding a swatch of pelt. Preferably in a different environment.

Touching the Edge

"Are ye sure she'd want ye tae follow her, lass?"

"That's not my accursed question," Ruby warned, teeth clenched against the wet clinging cold. The notes she brandished accusingly gleamed like fish eyes: chill and glassy, dangerously distant, and as dead as ties already severed, rendering their previous owner as vulnerable as a pelt-less Selkie, perilously close to irretrievable in their absence, floundering at the mercy of a still-thrashing sea.

"Where would Amber be going where she wouldn't need these?" she demanded, eyes glittering as sharply as the sternest of seas. "How far is this quest for the pelt going to take her? Tell me where she's gone!"

"I dinnae ken," Hydd insisted, turning away wretchedly. "If I'd had a thought where tae swatch I'd ne'er hae let her involve hersel'."

"Where to look for what?" Ruby skittered along the shoreline keeping resolute step with him, her dress clinging slimily to her legs like seaweed. The Selkie man looked so broken that she almost couldn't bear to argue with him.

Almost.

"You can't just take that." She changed the subject severely, jabbing a reproachful finger the way of the Gem hanging around his neck. "It belongs to my friend. Well, it's not hers, it's her boyfriend's, but—well, it's complicated." Ruby drew herself up, endeavouring to look as stern and regal as the water tugging at her dress and the wind blousing her hair would allow, and clung to her original premise despite the somewhat arresting appearance of this pale stranger. "And you can't keep it, either."

"Ah did'nae mean tae keep it." Hydd's voice shivered weakly, and he stumbled. "I was tryin' tae find someaine tae gie it back tae. Aiblins someaine like ye."

"Oh." Ruby's heart went out to him, although she studiously ignored the last bit. "What happened?"

"Ah foun' it close tae shore, an' it gae me hope that abody main help. But ah' cannae ask fur what ah need."

Ruby's jaw set as she struggled to cling to her patience. "Goblin's teeth, when will you speak plainly? This is about what I need, now. I need you to tell me where Amber is."

Hydd fixed a haunted, hounded gaze upon her, and Ruby returned hers steadily, unmoveable as the meadows.

"Right's right, no matter th' state o' th' tide," Hydd managed weakly. Sweat poured like seawater from his skin with the effort of speaking. "She's goan to th' lava tunnels." The words themselves seemed poison to him, Ruby noted in alarm. His lips were bluing as he spoke.

"Enough," she insisted in curtailment. "I don't pretend to understand this, but I won't ask anymore. Yet you do realise I have to go after her. I wish you would talk to the King, or someone."

Hydd's smile rose softly, like the moon over water. "Ah'd rather trust the word o' a lass who walks the shores at night o'er that o' a man who shuts himself away behin' staine."

The silence settled expectantly, lulled amidst the rocking of the sea.

Ruby let the spilling moonlight illuminate the path ahead, even as it swept and swirled with the waves. "This is my word, then. I'll keep the Gem safe. I'll return it to the one to whom it was given." She turned star-wisdom eyes to him, newly sure. "But you're not a well man. There is something you're not saying. I'm going to do you the courtesy of expecting that if it were in your power to do so, you would reveal it. But I cannot trust you until you do."

It felt to Ruby like even the surf itself stilled then, craving response. "I—it—" He chewed the words until they choked him, and Ruby couldn't help but reach a steadying hand to his to dissuade further effort. The pain he'd gone through in the attempt clenched around her heart.

He gasped at her touch, seal eyes flooding gratitude at being torn from torturous enchantment. Ruby held his fevered gaze, taking his measure evenly. She smiled calmly, even as she shivered in the night's chill. "Thank ye truly." His breath flowed evenly again, and yet a shadow crossed his face, like the rippling of a darkening tide. "Bu' ah fear fur whit main happen if ye involve yesel'."

The light that shone in Ruby's eyes, that he saw and wondered at, was not of the sea but it spilled as surely as a lantern across stormy waters.

"Both your encouragement and your dissuasion are irrelevant," she assured him gaily. "I have known Amber long enough not to need to ask her opinion, and I have known you little enough not to be under any obligation to pay attention to yours." The truth of her words strengthened her conviction, rendering her courageous before this queer, troublesomely enticing stranger and buoying her, she warned herself wryly, curiously light and untroubled in the necessity of what she must do.

To Hydd it seemed not curious at all. He found himself marvelling at her beacon nature even as she caught him staring and winked confidently.

"Yet remember, Selkie," she cautioned, both softly and serious now. "I know you have not revealed your whole self."

A smile brushed Hydd's lips despite himself. A smile both sad and yet whiskered with hope. "Ah will, lass. Ah tryst ye—although ah fear it main tak' an age longer than ye' deserve tae bide."

Ruby grinned back and she walked undaunted into the impressionistic night, a shimmering vision dancing at the sea's edge until the soft darkness claimed her. "Share your full self, Hydd," she promised in turn, "and I will grant you my full answer."

And he realised that for her he would walk these shores each night, even were they never again to lead him back home; for to walk beside her meant he knew he could forge peace from any path.

Inside the Cauldron

"Save your strength and hold your tongue, I'm leaving," Amber muttered pre-emptively to the moss-clung air swirling strange forms that had been trailing her jealously to ensure her departure. Now that she'd glimpsed the dark twists of tunnel burrowing into the forest-clad mountainside that rose in welcome before her, Amber darted readily towards them, eager to be out of the Oak Prince's jurisdiction and rid of his influence. The cavern mouth gaped and beckoned, spilling a logic of its own which she was only too relieved to heed, and as she slipped inside her fears slid momentarily away, sloughed by the chill calm of leaving her sight in the sunlight and returning to the soothing embrace of earth and stone.

Padding between the narrowing walls, eyes straining eagerly for any telltale signs to indicate a swatch of fur, Amber felt full of hope, as though she could almost be a drop of life-giving blood pulsing along an ancient artery. Yet, as she pressed further, she was forced to admit the initial calming chill was fast evaporating into a scratching dryness and airless heat. Her stifled breath echoed back on itself, shallow against the rock. The heat pulsed like a breath against her neck, threatening and nauseating even when she held still. An ancient complex of lava tubes carved thousands of years ago at the birth of the Realm traced in subterranean network across the lands; Amber knew this. But with the lands dormant, lava no longer flowed and the tunnels dripped with permeating glacial water that formed the ice chambers beloved of Zaralathaar. There was no reason for such torrid temperatures. Except for habitation. The edge of the thick darkness beyond curled ominously as she contemplated who might be hiding down here.

But she'd rather face that darkness and aid Hydd, than flee back and face the Oak Prince. So, with her heart fluttering, Amber breathed against the fear and padded on. She had to find the pelt pieces before the Oak Prince got wind of her quest. And caves held water, didn't they? Of course they were as sensible a place to look for pieces of Selkie pelt as they would be to trail the Kelpie. Let the wight think she was after the latter even as she sought the former.

On she kept, stumbling as the bone-smooth, warped-worn passageways led her deeper, struggling to catch her breath and rein the panic skittering ever more insistently in her gut as the temperature continued to rise. This had all made sense out in the daylight. Here, however, she was at liberty to feel even more furious with herself than the Prince would be when he found out that she had once again got herself lost and endangered with nothing to show for it, cause or none.

Plus, she let herself admit now that she was alone with her thoughts, it would probably have been a great deal more sensible to have asked Racxen for his help, considering the setting.

And yet… possibility and potential swirled in the potent darkness. Yes, Racxen had helped her stop fearing the darkness and opened her eyes more fully to its wonders—but she'd been blundering into forbidden passageways and reaping the benefits long before she'd stumbled into his life. Heart lifted by the reminder, Amber continued in a state of vigilance instead of fear. She had found Racxen by risking such an exploration, after all.

Dark twist after darker turn urged her forward with the lure of unspoken promise: that just a little further could be the gem she sought. Except it wasn't going to be a Gem, shining and obvious, to be plucked free pristinely, her mind goaded. It was going to be sable amongst shadow. It was going to mean scrabbling amongst cave-sludge. Or, more likely, snatching a burnt offering from the scalding dark.

Urgency snapped at her heat-itched heels. So much for her wish of finding water. Could she really hope to find a piece of Selkie skin down here?

Amber grimaced. Surely there could be no crueller place to hide a scrap of water-pelt than in such hell-heated depths. It'd be worse than throwing someone's wings into the ocean to spatter and sink. She couldn't run the risk of leaving part of Hydd's soul here, curling in pitiful defence against the scorching heat like a dying spider until all moisture leached and with it all vestiges of life and spirit. No matter how small the sliver, she had to find it. And, if she didn't use her break from the apprenticeship for this, what would have been the point of fighting for it?

She inched forward with renewed resolve. The tunnel staggered downwards and the billowing heat cuffed her soundly, left her gasping as she stumbled on. As sharply as when she'd been fleeing through the lava tunnels towards the samire's lair, the grievous ache for her wings pierced her now. At least they would have provided some semblance of heat protection. Having never had the chance to experience it, she had billowed it into near legendary proportions in her mind, she bad-temperedly admitted to herself, so it was probably just as well that she would never have the chance to find out how wrong she would probably have been about it.

Out of all the things to miss them for, a part of her mind mused—almost, after all this time, detachedly, she congratulated herself dryly. Although, if she was being honest, it wasn't detachment, more an overwhelming, tired sadness that most of the time smothered the anger.

There, she'd said it. She was still angry about losing her flight. About having cast away her wings.

She wrapped the end of her sash around one hand and leant against the scalding rock to steady herself. *I might feel anger,* she admitted. What drove her to reunite Hydd with the pelt, if not outrage at his torture? *But I'll always choose action instead.*

She breathed her thoughts in and out, letting them go unfettered and unable to harm her as they swirled away into the hot darkness of her surroundings, and continued.

An invading scent stewed warningly on the crushing heat of the next turning. Sweat prickled on her skin. Fear boiled in her chest as a thicker shadow solidified amidst the fluid dark of the broadening tunnel, allowing her to glimpse its origin: a gargantuan pot, iron and rusted, crouched swollen before her.

She could hardly turn back now, Amber attempted to reason with herself, drawn as she was by a macabre allure she could barely fathom. With the contents simmering belchingly, the keeper of the cauldron would not be far away—

"D' yer not get sufficient warnings when you were a child to keep yer away from the cooking pot?" The Goblin's eyes gleamed as if molten, reflecting the broiling concoction he was prowling towards. "Yer purport ter be revolted, and yet it is from us you learn most, girl. An' there's more ter learn than yer yet know, standin' at a precipice steeper than yer last. So here we are again."

All power of prediction and interpretation spun from Amber's mind. She'd never considered she'd see a Goblin again, much less encounter one in confined quarters, taunting her. She couldn't afford to process that now though. She couldn't afford to let him distract her with such riddles when she had first to navigate the viscerally obvious dangers of the next few moments.

"Surprised we're still here?" the Goblin goaded in the face of her mute shock. "Did yer not think we'd go lookin' fer another leader?" He paused, the silence stretching insidiously beyond comfortable boundaries. "The Oak Prince's magic is jus' our kind."

Tearing her focus from the hideous stew swirling in the grotesquely distended metal stomach of the cauldron, Amber forced herself to meet the Goblin's stare. "And what are you conjuring for him here?"

His gaze flickered. "Ain't imagination a curse?"

Options congealed into fears, but she refused to shy from seizing them. "Whether you tell me or not I'm walking out of here with it and ruining whatever you had planned."

"Walking out of here with it? Walking out of here at all? Ha! Yer got delusions of grandeur bigger'n us, girl! Does it look like the kind of thing yer want to be handling? The kind of thing yer'd want to be remembering?"

Amber's vision shuddered. An overwhelmingly nauseating sensation washed over her of blood and skin and fear and pounding heart; of disorientation and loss; of a blindness that she couldn't place and couldn't return from. Yet reliving it acquainted her with new possibilities, sent them skimming unburned atop the roiling Goblin-lava stew and tearing her focus back to the present.

Clarity swarmed in Amber's gaze, and narrowed into her answer. "It's the kind of thing I'd want to remember surviving." *It's the kind of thing I'd want to help someone survive,* she managed to bite back.

"Pretty words, girl," the Goblin taunted. "But decomposition's a vital function—and fer things older than the skin flayed off a Selkie's back. Someone's got ter oversee it. Someone less sensitive than yer good self, I'd wager. I'm just providing a service. Yer'd thrust your hand into the fire ter stop me, would yer?"

Precisely. With gut-deep certainty, Amber knew she had to. Her vision swam with heat and fear as she gauged when to act. How many pieces was he boiling up in there?

She flung her feverish gaze across the grotto's paraphernalia; the Goblinwares scattered in careless threat across the dual curves of the tunnel sides. A cold chill wrapped protectively around her as one pitiful bundle drew her eye. She kept her glance light, the most perilous of plans forming.

"You meet wagers, right?" She didn't even have to ask it. The Goblin's eyes shone with an ancient lust at her suggestion.

"If I can retrieve that skin using nothing that does not belong to me, I will keep it and leave here freely."

Those eyes travelled her licentiously. "If yer can't, yer flesh will strip itself from your bones and flavour the contents of this cauldron."

Amber's stomach twisted as she watched the steaming stew. "Doubtlessly."

The Goblin performed a mocking bow. "Until then, the floor is yours."

Amber clenched her jaw, and stalked over to the bundle. "I don't know how you got your filthy hands on these," she warned, snatching up a paired bundle of dried Fairy wings. "But I'm taking back what's mine—and I've a use for them yet."

Before the Goblin could lunge for her, she had wrapped the wings around one hand up to her shoulder, and thrust it deep into the boiling mixture.

As the rising waves of heat seared her face, panic lanced. Any moment she would be dealt debilitating proof that dead wings were as useless in this endeavour as they would be grasped in flight.

And yet what had for so long lain crisp and dead and severed now curled as softly as skin around her own into an unthinkable armour, and from within the makeshift gauntlet her hand closed around the drowned whispers of pelt.

She snatched them forth in a flare of triumph, the next moments blurring as fast as her gulping breath as the adrenalin of what she had done lent her speed fit to flee even the Goblin, her footsteps slapping down the corridors of stone and beating the memory into the ground, leaving it trampled and herself free as she darted into a twisting side tunnel and crouched hastily beneath the borrowed concealment of the first filthy, friendly corner she could squash herself into.

Amidst as many frantically scraped together moments as she dared risk before the footsteps of her pursuer bore down on her, she scrabbled at her smarting, trembling arm and its sickening encasement.

She breathed her thanks. Although the heat had flared her skin into an angry red to rival the lava-glow filtering through from the hell-lit chamber where stalked the Goblin, her wings had gifted her a final service: against all things they had remained intact, borne the brunt of the heat, and peeled off smoothly leaving no blisters.

To slough them off again left her shuddering, even before the full force of the afterburn smacked into her. She needed to plunge into the frigid seas. She needed the gusting winds of the shore to tear away the sensation that her blood itself were boiling. Yet she might as well have wished for the moon, for all the help it could do.

The Goblin's footsteps, pounding through the tunnel, shook her into focus, and she berated herself swiftly. Her Realm was reeling, yes—but she was still breathing and her heart still beating, and she'd die chasing after the moon before she'd let herself fall prey to a cumulative despair deadlier than any individual foe she could face. She had to get the pelt out of here.

She tensed and trembled as she raced her mind through options. Stay hidden? Hide better? Fight? Flee?

More footsteps splintered through the dark, their echoes assailing her from all angles. The Goblin must have summoned further assailants—from deeper inside the mountain.

The fear and fire threatened to strip away all coherent thought. No. Find a way through. Her sole anchor was the scrap of pelt. She hadn't snatched it from the Goblin's festering stew only to abandon it here. She clutched the sodden, acrid-smelling sliver protectively. Where her fingers touched it, a breath of ice seeped through as if from the Icefields themselves.

Amber stared at it in reverence. Retaining the fey charms it was famed for, the piece was no longer smouldering stickily. It lay cool and wet in her hand, as though somehow still alive, and as soothing against her skin as a Selkie's gaze upon her soul.

On impulse, she bound her hand with it. A fierce, clean cold bloomed in response, winnowing clarity from deafening panic and enabling her to differentiate the advancing echoes her mind in its initial terror had mistaken for an inescapable horde. Now that she could think clearly, she pieced together the revelation that might just guide her steps out of here: there weren't dozens of Goblins chasing her. There was simply the one, creating a foul-minded illusion. Trying to panic her and flush her out—and it wouldn't work.

She whispered her gratitude to the pelt. Where had the Goblin got his claws around the remnants of the Selkie's skin? These were lava tunnels; they had never seen water. Fear reached its claws towards her chest through the heat. Wouldn't that mean every hounded path she could take here would eventually just plunge to a lava pit?

Her Realm shuddered as she struggled to narrow her focus—if there was no exit, she insisted to herself, there would be nothing to gain from the Goblin spooking her into running blind. Which meant, conversely, if she could keep her mind and sense, she could find her way out...

If, she thought tensely. With nothing to retrieve her attention and anchor it safely from the fell bewitchment of the rhythmic pounding rattling in Goblin-thrall through the tunnels behind her, she panicked that her heart would have no choice but to respond in kind until it burst out of her chest.

So, focus on the solid rock that's safely beneath your feet, she reminded herself. *For continue you must.* The thrall seemed to seize at her limbs; running felt as impossible as flying now. So, if you cannot run, crawl. She heard the Genie's words from memory as if he had spoken them anew. And so, steadying her breath and creeping methodically forward, feeling her way with the touch that thanks to the pelt the Goblin hadn't managed to dissolve in his boiling cauldron, Amber felt the new sound before she heard it—a music deep and strange and stirring, cutting through the thrall's paralysing confusion like a sunbeam through shadow. Before racing ahead in urgent melody, it seemed to radiate, forming a pulse to indicate the way, as sure and steady as a heartbeat.

Heartbeat, or hoofbeat? An ungoblinlike thrill traced Amber's spine, like the touch of a familiar hand brushing in secret reassurance. Han!

Just thinking of the Centaur felt like a rebellion in this crushing, twisted labyrinth, and her heart burned with hope far fiercer and deeper than the cauldron's stew had scalded. The music sent tendrils reaching towards her as tender and unstoppable as the first green shoots of Renë, guiding her towards the light and air. Feeling her way like a bud through deepest soil, she climbed blind and certain towards the unseen exit.

Deeper than Skin

Don't move. Ruby desperately tried to focus, dragging her recollections together even as they tried to burrow away from her, and thought fast before her mind could sink back into a sickening, merciful nothingness. The Goblins were still here, and they were still talking. Ruby listened, feigning an unconsciousness that would become real again any moment.

"If that wingless wretch finds all the pieces, we're done fer! No skin fer the master means no place fer us."

"Stop yer whimpering. We still got the Kelpie fer insurance, right? Once they realise what he can do, it'll be too late. We just need one hand ter reach out close enough—"

The second Goblin laughed mercilessly. "An' they still think the Oak Prince is bound by the covenant. That he'll set their defence, and leave! That he'll be as weak as that water witch! He's had a taste o' freedom. He's never going back."

"An' yer think he'll spare us, when he stays?"

"He'll spare us alright. He plays by the old rules. The blood rules, same as us. Enough blood as penance, an' we're at his right hand watching the Realm fall."

"An' fall it will. That skinless sea-whelp is cursed ter silence. Who else is gonna tell?"

Ruby felt their eyes on her. She willed her pain away into the rock, kept her breathing imperceptibly shallow.

"What's she gonna do? Risk her pretty face? We'll report back, an' deal with her after."

As she waited for their footsteps to fade, Ruby focused on remembering the truth she had to tell: about the Oak Prince, the pelt, and even the Kelpie. But first, she had to save herself. In the silence, Ruby risked opening blood-crusted eyes. Everything ached sickeningly, pulsing as though her sputtering heart were leeching new waves of pain with every beat. She clutched a hand to her head and the darkness around her lurched and leered, guttering candlelight spilling drunken shadows as chains clanked and rattled. Spattering candlewax hissed as it hit the floor beside her. Chains, she could understand. But they'd left her with candlelight?

She scrunched up her stinging eyes in confusion, and caught the shriek in her throat before it could betray her. The chains binding her dripped from above like the limbs of a monstrous spider. But they weren't attached to the ceiling—instead, they hung from a massive suspended candelabra, filthy as the stagnant air and as rusted as the decaying stench loitering in the corners, branched with row upon row of fat grotesquely contorted candles dribbling an obscene amount of scalding molten wax. All of which had branched chains looped around them. The deep ache of her wrenched arms and the swelling bite of the rope swarming into her bound wrists snarled a stark warning, but she could escape. If she wrenched clear of the entire thing—upsetting the carefully balanced candles and spilling their disfiguring cargo of scalding wax onto her wounded body and unprotected face.

Something curled up inside Ruby at the realisation but, she contemplated her fate, something else started to burn inside her. The Goblins thought this would stop her. That they could control her—that she wouldn't risk this for her friend.

Ruby gritted her perfectly white teeth and chewed on a painted lip. All that stood between her and Amber was the key, the door, and the burning wax.

Clearly Goblins still had a lot to learn. Ruby sealed her resolve and threw herself sideways. Amidst the clatter of chains the sting of scalding wax slapped at her legs, her arms—and burned her face as though consuming it. She dared not open her mouth to bellow the pain away, but she truly couldn't open her eyes: her lids felt seized as though by skin-melting glue. Ruby's panicked wail stabbed through pursed lips into the furthest corners of the chamber as she stumbled blindly out into the tunnel. Where was the water she'd passed earlier: where Amber had found the Pelt?

Forcing her breath to slow and quieten, Ruby heard the river's urgent song lift. Skidding and slipping as she followed, she threw herself into its embrace.

Sleek flowing fur swirled around her with the waters, and she felt the pain in her face diminish and the light return beneath her closed lids at the touch of soft, webbed hands.

As a chillingly familiar, wrenchingly pained cry splintered from a far chamber, Amber plunged back the way she'd come. How could Ruby be here?

Discarding the guiding lure of the Centaur's pipes as she frantically tried to locate her friend amidst a cursed storm of scattering, disorientating footsteps, the only thing she could cling to as she stumbled further, hearing nothing but her own terror-clutched breathing, was the faint and desperate hope that this was all just a Goblin-spun trap.

"Ain't yer heard the stories?" a nail-across-stone voice sneered. "None survive our lairs."

But the outline of the Goblin glowed with the exit he was blocking. Ruby had got out. She must have. She was alone with the Goblin, but Ruby was safe elsewhere, and falling foul of a Goblin plot was worth knowing that, at least. Exhausted and alone, Amber warned herself to suck a last energising gulp of breath before she turned.

"None that are left to attempt it abandoned, you mean."

As Amber spun round in relief towards the beacon-like voice, a vision seared into her soul that would remain forever burnished in her memory: Ruby standing her ground, her face shadowed in the mire of this place so that only her silhouette remained, but her entire being as trembling and luminous, as awe-inspiring and exultant, as a flame at the tunnel entrance.

Amber's heart set fire in response, and she barraged into the distracted Goblin. He sprawled, spun, and snatched at her leg, sending her slamming backwards.

"Didn't think far enough ahead, missy," he snarled.

As her head snapped back Amber, with grim satisfaction, distortedly glimpsed Ruby flicker out of view and away through the tunnel. "You can't get her. 'S far enough for me," she growled thickly against her swelling bitten tongue.

The Goblin laughed softly. "Oh, I don't know, girl. You two, yer should be careful o' debts."

Something dangerous ran chill in his words. What had he meant? He wasn't even bothering to rush at her again. Why? His coldness crept into her, and for a wild moment Amber wanted more to insist he gave his answer than she wanted to run free from here. But countering flames of the kind he could neither banish nor summon—of friendship, of love—rushed sure and enlivening in suspicion's wake, scattering the shadows of doubt and drawing Amber's thoughts back into her control. "I can endure anything for my friends," she promised warningly. "A debt is nothing. And that's another thing Ruby's right about. You Goblins know nothing of Fairies."

She strode right past him, towards the ice-lit glow of the exit-leading tunnel.

Hours later, the cleansing chill of the ice chamber seeped beneath Ruby's skin, achingly soothing as she finally left the filthy heat of the earlier tunnel. The stark light filtering through the glistening shards refused to let her deny a reminder she dare not just now face but, alone in clearest view beneath a light more unyielding than any other in the Realm, she had no need to hide; so mayhap, given time and testament, she could feel the same outside. The possibility gleamed tantalizingly, but too sharply against her raw soul for now, so she tucked its ephemeral insistence away for later and drew more immediate concerns cloak-close around her.

With the shock and cold vying in intensity and danger, she knew she had to find her way out soon. The drip of glacial water spattered behind her like footsteps, and shuddering with distaste Ruby kept her eyes firmly ahead as she crept past bone-white icicles clinging to rocks like fingers. Never mind her skin, this was going to have ruined her shoes.

Awareness of a presence somewhere ahead prickled, ice-like, and she inched forwards slower than the dripping meltwater.

"Amber?" Ruby nearly fell over in her surprise as she rounded the corner. "What are you—?"

"Still doing in the chamber? I could ask you the same question," Amber answered with a wry grin, not looking up from her work. She gestured helplessly at the pitiful bundle of mismatched fabric patches resolutely sewn now going half sodden at her feet from the damp, and blew vigorously on her raw hands. "They need skins. They need skins to return to the water, and that man I found is a Selkie whose skin has been destroyed, and I'm trying to find the pieces and so far I've only found one myself but of the ones the seals gave me half of them look like they're still missing and this thrice-be-damned needle—" she cursed violently and flung the bundle down with a frustrated sob. "Sorry," she murmured to the pieces, and scooped them together apologetically.

Then she stopped, and peered keenly at Ruby, her voice as soft as her gaze was sharp as the ground fell from her Realm. "I saw you leave. I thought that meant you got away. Do you want to talk about what—?"

"Happened? I discovered that Goblins," Ruby proclaimed grandly, "would not know a heroine from a halfwit even if they tied her up, dragged her underground, and set up some weirdo burning candelabra thing from which she had to escape, risking permanent disfigurement in the process. I think the result makes me look like a Sea Maiden—and, let's face it: I was always pretty enough. Don't you dare apologise. I'm not ugly enough to leave you there."

Amber wordlessly pulled her close, stroking her tangled hair and kissing her cheek firmly. "Well, the Goblin wants me beholden to you, and you demand different, so I know who I'm listening to. But, well, you know."

"What I know," Ruby grinned through her snuffles, eyeing the half-patched pelt over Amber's shoulder. "Is that you need my help again, if you'll let me. After all, you've got to sew that man a coat to conjure with. And you're not going to believe what I heard from the Goblins."

Tales and Tendrils

The twin hands of loneliness and guilt clutched around Amber's throat, weighing suffocatingly now that Ruby had left and it was just her and the pelt again. And the knowledge, dearly bought by Ruby, that there were more pieces to find before she could fix the pelt, and that the Oak Prince wanted it for his own skin... Amber groaned in misery. She shouldn't have stayed here alone, but she couldn't sew any more pieces tonight; shock had stamped out all creativity. This quest had already exacted too much of her friends. What right did she have to continue it so stubbornly? She felt like punishing herself. She deserved to be down here.

Despairingly, Amber leant back against the ice, feeling it seep through her cloak. The depth of cold both dulled her pain and sharpened her senses, narrowing the many incomprehensively complex choices before her into the simplest one: stay and sink into eternal stillness amidst the bleak swathes of grey monotone, or heed the urgency of its bite and drive herself onwards, to warmth and life.

She breathed deeply, and tore herself away from a danger more insidious and immediate than the others she was facing for, if she was already having trouble forgiving herself for inadvertently endangering Ruby, how could she countenance leaving her friendless? She knew, deep within herself, that Ruby, in her boundless generosity of character, would forgive her for inadvertently endangering her. But she would never forgive herself if she wasn't around to support her in every way after.

Amber laid a sash-wrapped hand against a frozen gnarl in gratitude and decision, pushed herself to her feet and slushed through the chamber, trying with increasing difficulty to orientate herself through ever-merging ice tunnels and suddenly becoming gripped by a realisation colder and more dangerous even than her surroundings: Ruby had learnt the way out having escaped her captor. She, in contrast, hadn't learnt it and was now growing lost.

She stopped, in an absolute silence, and the terror seized her, ice-dangerous, threatening to drown her. She wanted to do anything just to break its hold, but to do so would be to throw down the one precious, tenuous thread that remained within her grasp and retained the ability to get her out of here: her clear mind.

Before you run, stop. Before you act, think. You can work this out. In this moment, you are safe.

In this moment—you can hear...

She stopped, flushed with an eclipsing wonder as the inimitable melody from before slipped beneath the defences raised by her encounter with the Goblin.

Unthreateningly unobtrusive and impossible to ignore; as enchanting and transformative as the strand of living magic winding through birdsong in reinhabited forest after a Realm-shaking storm, it sang into the chambers and onwards as a guide through the site of such trauma and onwards into transformation, and Amber set her course by it anew and scrambled across the once-trapping ice that roused her now with urgency, warning her with its bite that she must tally here no longer.

Dusk-glow shimmered above and strong sure arms reached for her as encouragingly as the beckoning music, forcing the twisting clutches of memory to renounce their crushing hold and relinquish their captive to the woods outside and into a peacefulness deeper and more far-reaching than the tunnels' dragging depths, as Han forsook the pipes and entwined his hands around hers, pulling her away as if leading her from a nightmare.

"Thanks," Amber grinned in relief, hugging the Centaur tightly. She breathed the live earth on his scent gratefully and felt it infuse her own lungs with a new strength, entwining now with his.

Twilight danced around them, soft and spacious and alive after the crushing confines of the tunnels.

"Haven't had to play like that for a while," Han admitted in a gasp, the same blazing, confident smile at his lips nonetheless and his eyes flashing as restless and unquenchable as ever. "I'm sorry and I thank you," Amber promised. "I shouldn't let my guilt thwart my actions."

"Your actions are needed as ever before, and are put to far better use than misplaced guilt," Han reassured easily. In the presence of her friend Amber felt her soul soar; the Centaur was all ecstatic fire and impossible joy; uncatchable and untameable, but never unapproachable. The forest could have no better guardian.

"Your Prince isn't taking the intruder beneath these boughs seriously," Han surmised quietly, now that he sensed Amber might feel safe enough to broach what was worrying her. "But I know that's not enough to torment you. What happened in those tunnels?"

Falteringly, Amber risked voicing what had happened to Ruby; a pain far more terrible than any of her fears for herself.

"The stream sang of Selkie intervention," Han disclosed, after he had heard her gravely. "Their healing surpasses my own, which you have borne witness to, and which eased your soul seeing it," he reminded gently. "Let hearing of it, by even greater healers, do so again."

Amber nodded shakily, committing herself solidly to his words. Helping Ruby was her best reason for keeping herself safe, now.

"I used to know these woods like my own skin," Han murmured, his gentle voice gathering a hoof's edge of toughness, drawing her out of her internal trappings and into the outside Realm again where she could help, instead of becoming caught in the endless struggles of her own mind. "Now a splinter is festering. The trees are listening to a voice older and wilder than my own. For the Goblins to be disposing of the pelt suggests they know of the Selkie skin's power—and it is the Oak Prince, not the Kelpie, who has shown himself to hunger for such power." Han slipped into silence, his strong features carved in thought. "Strange fate it is that that we stand to lose that which thanks to the Oak Prince we are now being taught to fear."

"You think he wants us to dread the Kelpie, in order for us to help him get rid of it?" Amber didn't think she'd ever seen the Centaur look scared, but this was probably as close as he let himself get.

"We need to find the creature to be sure," Han advised. "I don't think we should allow such a 'Prince' to close our minds. After all, the wearer of the pelt you hold could be considered just as strange, and yet you have braved the cauldron to protect him. Perhaps both the Kelpie and the Selkies are fighting the Oak Prince, in their own ways."

Amber nodded in relief, suddenly aware of the voices of the forest surrounding them as if newly awoken from a fell enchantment; a tumbling, sonorous wisdom singing out what should be shared instead of kept secret. Han was right. Whilst she had been with the Oak Prince, a part of her mind had been closed off to the severance he had wrought from all that sustained her spirit. She had still, against all things, managed to act according to her own spirit, but a chill brushed Amber's spine to remember how insidiously the apparition's words had come to her. She had wanted so badly to protect her friends that she had contemplated warnings from the unwisest of sources. She should have known better, especially in the wake of the Goblin situation.

"You have borne no hatred towards the waterhorse," Han reminded in reassurance. "And hearing's not the same as listening to the Oak Prince. Let that awareness be your guard, not your guilt. After all, could the Oak Prince really hope to succeed in his foul quest, after we've been cleansed in mud and fire?" The Centaur grinned in reassurance, his flanks plastered with the stuff. "Now let's get you home, before you embark on your own quest—as if you aren't sufficiently embroiled in it already."

Amber tugged a hand through slime-strewn hair and grimaced. "Even the King thinks I should be focussing on the apprenticeship, and leaving quests to others this time," she admitted uncomfortably.

The Centaur tossed back his head with a wink of understanding, his manner inviting her to retrieve what she'd feared lost. "Just for now, let yourself stop running anywhere. You offer help so freely, but there is equal strength in accepting it also. Let us walk together. After all, there's avoiding, which you fear they will accuse you of, and then there's escaping, which is what you are really doing," the Centaur argued unfazed, his eyes agleam. "Escaping is the bravest act of all. It is proactive, destiny-grasping, life-changing. For there are times when the healthiest—and most difficult—thing to do, is gather your strength and walk away."

"I can barely stand, let alone walk," Amber murmured thickly, embarrassed.

The Centaur bowed a foreleg. "I never asked you to."

She leant gladly into his waiting arms and felt herself rise peeled from the earth and yet wrapped in its scent, folded tight and safe amongst the heat of skin and fur whilst the mesmeric four-beat rhythm of his steps lulled her, healed her in a way she wasn't even sure she could explain but in a way that thrilled her soul. The Centaur had been her refuge in this way before, not all that many seasons ago. So much had changed since then. She had felt she had grown so much stronger—but now she wondered suddenly whether she would ever reach a point where she wouldn't need what he so freely offered.

"Strength to accept help from friends is strength indeed," he whispered in a promise. "It is growth, not regression. There doesn't have to be a name for it, nor a price on it," he reminded, his eyes steady upon paths unseen by others as he carried her surely. "I am what they cannot kill. And I will always come to you."

"I'm lucky to know you, Han," she mumbled drowsily, the Centaur and his boreal charges working a healing magic far deeper than any possessed by the Oak Prince. "I won't let that wight take your forest."

"Ah, come now," Han soothed. "I could find a forest in a sapling pushing obstinately through a barren patch of earth if I had to. There's magic in the shortest moments, in the most fleeting snatches of experience. The Realm could be razed to dust, but I'd find my way to them, and to you, and I will always bear you home—wherever your soul tells you that is."

As he walked, Han sang the songs of healing that had sustained Racxen and had sustained Amber on her flight to the Glade Pool with him those seasons ago; sang until the soothing, lilting notes had chased away the heat and torment of that savage darkness and replaced them with an equine sensitivity and steadiness, and a friend's company.

Amidst the yielding softness of the dark, Amber felt herself hovering next to sleep, lulled by the Centaur's unique gait as the wood, the undergrowth, the moss-scented rich air of the undergrowth and the healing moments of the present grew over the hellish escapades of earlier.

"You're not going to question me about why I was here?" The knowledge soothed Amber surprisingly, as she felt her strength sewing itself back together.

"Some quests need a wild place; a wooded place," the Centaur observed. "Somewhere to call and seek a reply; to peer beneath the boughs and peel back the veil. A place to get lost and found; to ask questions and invite answers. Especially when considering what to discard, and what to delay, and what to pursue."

"Listening to the Oak Prince, the apprenticeship, and the pelt—in that order," Amber grinned as she decided with the sudden clarity of reflecting it back before such a close friend. She breathed carefully, letting herself contemplate the future, fluid and without fear in the expansive evening air. "I guess I need to be prepared to give certain things up, in order to become who I want to be."

Han smiled in support. "Aye, but this is more like casting certain things away, in order to make space for what's most important. And that's a whole lot easier."

Amber grinned. Beholding Han's half-equine silhouette, impossible and undeniable before her, it did feel a whole lot easier. She would do it. Make the pelt her priority. Even though she feared she'd never find a reason big enough to withstand the evisceration of the general public.

Han nudged back a pelt scrap spilling from her haversack, like he was tucking her thoughts back under her control again. "Your own reason is more than adequate," he reminded her. "And with a conviction as powerful as that which brought you thus far, you have no need for the contrary opinions of others."

Amber grinned concedingly. "You don't think, as they do, that I'm just avoiding reality?"

"I think you're changing your reality, as well as Hydd's," Han grinned back. "That scares them even more, because they know that in your new reality there will be no place for things they have been beaten into believing inescapable."

"Things like the apprenticeship?"

"It's my belief that you could forge a genuine and positive impact through the apprenticeship," Han mused honestly. "But it is my equally steadfast conviction that you should only when you feel such a connection in your heart, such a yearning in your soul, as renders all other guidance unnecessary and brings you the answer that seeks no further question. The apprenticeship is not the only way, and I would fight against any who would seek to turn your steps towards a path you do not wish to commit to, and walk beside you along the one of your own carving."

Amber felt the weight she had been carrying in her heart shift and her own strength gather in response.

"I commit to completing the pelt, and to making it my priority," she promised. "And to carving the time to do so. Somehow." She grinned, overwhelmed, but relishing the prospect.

"You can do anything, but doing all things is more difficult," Han grinned back in acceptance as well as encouragement. "Choose your chase wisely. It might be long, but the right one will replenish and reward you as much as it receives from you."

Amber nodded, and breathed the possibilities carefully, letting herself contemplate them freely in the expansive evening air; feeling for all the Realm like just for now, rocked in the arms of the Centaur, these moments were conjuring the time she needed to make the right choice.

"I can't keep it all up," Amber accepted. "Fixing the pelt and resisting the Oak Prince have both taken my energy, but it's the apprenticeship that is really drowning me. All three are vital, worthy causes—but I don't have the energy enough for all of them."

"Perhaps not," acquiesced the Centaur. "Yet, if you had, you wouldn't now be making the choice that will ultimately save not just you, but many others. Your path will take unimaginable energy—but when you are truly yourself, you free up all the energy you need."

"True," she grinned peaceably. It was all starting to feel real and possible.

"You know what you need. You know what to do. You have the resources within you to work for it and wait for it. Those are the roads to your full potential" the Centaur advised, his voice an unsnuffable flame amidst the darkness of doubt. "Have faith in these truths," he grinned, "and there will be no end to what you are capable of, what you will accomplish. And so—" Han shuddered restlessly, his eyes warm with understanding, hot as fireflies sparking the night as he drew himself up, and tossed back his head in defiance of the wavering night breezing from outside that threatened to disturb the sanctuary of the forest within. "I believe you have arrived at your answer."

Relish curled on Amber's tongue. "I believe I have: I will fix the pelt and counter the Oak Prince—and until I have done so I will set aside the apprenticeship." The finality of voicing it quenched the shivering flames of anxiety that had been scorching her soul. She could do it. She knew she could. "To forsake the pelt would be to forsake Hydd, and I could never have countenanced that—but I need to know, deep in myself, that I am justified in not spreading myself too thinly; that committing fully to the pelt is as important as the work I could complete with Sarin. And I do know, now. In the future, I will learn to save lives with Sarin—but here is my opportunity to save a life now. I trust that in protecting the Selkie, I can aid in the fight against the Oak Prince better than I could by running after a Kelpie I have no chance of catching—but, whether it aids the wider quest or not, to save even one life is a quest greater than any other; one I would gladly risk my own for even should both the sacrifice and saving remain unseen."

Han said not a word in response, but his eyes blazed like fireflies, and his embrace bloomed even warmer.

"All right, you've convinced me," grinned Amber sleepily. "Don't let me forget it in the morning." She knew she wouldn't. The Realm had shifted with her perception and she couldn't change it back. She'd never want to. Here and now, she promised herself, she'd never have to.

"It'd take more than the Oak Prince—or yours, for that matter—to prevent me from reminding you," the Centaur promised. "You've shown such courage against the former. Remember that, when you stand in explanation before the latter."

Amber nodded, and yawned against his chest, comforted. As her thoughts blurred and blended, swirled and swept by the hypnotic beat of hooves, she let her mind drift with the ever expanding forest, caressing the fur scrap thoughtfully between her fingers in the absentminded hope that her touch might somehow comfort its estranged owner. She drew hope from the stitched pelt; each piece once torn through with suffering knitted now amidst its fellows in a mantle of protection far greater than the sorrows it had sensed. The idea gave her strength, for it felt as though the Selkie's suffering had somehow begun to ease. But it would take far more on her part to reverse the remaining injury now, for as cunning as the Goblins were, they could be no match for the cruel whim of the Oak Prince. The only option that could explain the presence of the fur in their lair was that it had suited him for some reason to manoeuvre it there, into that fiery pit.

Amber stiffened, a chill creeping along her spine despite Han's responsively reassuring touch. What if there were other pieces missing? Other pieces cursed and cast, scattered the breadth of the Realm, preventing Hydd from healing—from becoming whole again?

She tied an edge of the stitched pieces like a talisman resolutely around her wrist, anchoring both her connection with, and her pledge to, its true bearer. She would find every piece. And that would only be possible if she delayed the apprenticeship, so delay the apprenticeship she would. The scope of her quest had exploded, and so, she promised here and now, her response would be just as exponential. She felt the truth of Han's words surge inside her. By distancing herself from draining influences, she could free up all the energy she needed.

And she could feel it surging within her even now. With no indication of, and no known limit to, the span of her quest now that it had expanded to accommodate the necessity of scouring the whole Realm to return the pelt to its own entirety, things had not only grown massive, they had grown simpler, too. Rescuing Hydd now required more, and so more she would commit. She would no longer allow anything to delay, let alone prevent, her from devoting herself fully to what she must, from hereon in, accomplish no matter the personal cost.

That lonely, icy shiver threatened for a moment, but she decided to test her newfound strength by quelling such tremblings with her thoughts. If she could tackle the beginning, the ending would take care of itself. If she were brave enough to try, life would help her succeed. She'd always tried to tell herself those words. Now, she'd live by them.

"It has to be the Oak Prince who ripped the pelt asunder and threw its pieces to the winds," she voiced to the Centaur. "But I found in the tunnels that the Goblins now have hold of pieces—so the remainder could be anywhere."

Han let the Fairy's voice anchor him gratefully. An abomination, the voice amidst the leaves had hissed at him earlier. Or suggested, in truth, which was even worse because it meant that the rest of its owner's foul work had been wrought by his own mind.

But with the girl in his arms a rousing, soothing light against the darkness pressing at his back, Han found the strength to chew over the twisted Dryad's warning and spit it back with the disgust it deserved.

"Anywhere including, if this cruelty has been wrought by the Oak Prince as we suspect and not the Goblins as he wishes us to believe, the forest itself," the Centaur proposed, turning his attention back to the Fairy who had for him banished the spectre of the Oak Prince's fell influence.

Held as if in a soothing enchantment somewhere between dreaming and waking, Amber felt the stirring of Centaur magic ploughed up from the leaf mulch by his hooves. She wondered, not for the first time, if she would be able to still access this strength she felt welling inside her in his presence once she left. Left again, as she must, for the sake of all of them, and journeyed so far without him.

"I will be your strength, whene'er you have need of me," Han promised in a murmur. "You realign me with my own and, if it is in my power, it is my honour to reconnect you with yours." The warmth of his smile flooded the forest, his hooves clopping gently in hypnotic rhythm as they journeyed beneath the hushed, dusk-dewed boughs.

Recognition, reassurance and relief mingled, lightening like fireflies. Amber grinned, warmed right through. "I don't believe anything is beyond your power."

Han's smile blazed in return. "Right back at you."

With her spirit realigned, options started to make soul-sense to Amber again. "So, the forest?"

Mindful of the vast gravity of what had to be accomplished, Han ventured his suggestions carefully. "I get the impression the Oak Prince expects you to be too frightened to venture back into the deep, dark woods. After all, they are his stronghold. Or so," he added, murmuring strengthening whispers to the twisting arboreal roots basking in the moonlight as they slithered exposed above the ground, "he wishes it to be believed."

With the stars rocking above her and the branches swaying in and out of vision as though it might have been their own limbs bearing her as though through a forest in a story, Amber shook her head. "He's forgotten something," she promised, finding her courage in every fibre of the moment. "I've met stranger and far more wondrous characters beneath these eaves."

The Centaur's grin flashed in the twilight, and the gait beneath her rocked her jauntily as she gladly felt his spirits lift.

"Although he's right about me being scared," she admitted with a grin of her own.

"Finding it hard to navigate the dark isn't shameful," Han reminded gently.

"Racxen's of the darkness as well as of the earth, though," Amber acknowledged uncomfortably. "I wanted to be better at this part, for his sake."

Han flicked his tail, as though clearing a way through her doubts. "The possibilities which are opening up before you, and which you are opening yourself to, add to the whole of you, but they don't block the routes you used to take. The paths your heart yearns for are the right ones to take, whether they lead beneath twilit eaves or across sunlit meadows. Being your best self is your greatest gift; it's as much benefit to Racxen, to all those you love—to the Realm itself—as it is to you. Remember what you have accomplished and who you have become. You are of the Sea and the Earth as well as the Sky; you are as much at home amidst the soft chill darkness as you are beneath the streaming heat of the sunlight. Nowhere is off limits, if your heart sings you there. So, where draws you?"

Amber let his words swirl into her soul and forge a way. "The deserts Yenna introduced me to," she began, letting herself touch a yearning ache somewhere deep in her chest and letting it talk to her, letting it find its resolution. "The dew-tasting woods I have walked with you," she admitted next. "The hot pools drifting with fragrant steam, shimmering in the twilight that Racxen opened my eyes to. And..." she grinned self-consciously, honestly. "The Icefields I have never been to, but which my spirit seems to have lodged itself in none the less."

Han fidgeted coltishly. "Then you have your map!"

Amber blew a steadying breath, trying on for size the realisation. "And my plan."

The Centaur's eyes glowed like fireflies in the dark. "That's a lot of territory to traverse, for we don't know how many pieces."

Amber grinned. "You don't sound too worried."

His tail swished with relish through the still air. "This is getting bigger than the pelt. And I have no doubt you can handle it."

Amber laughed, feeling freer than in ages. "You make it seem simple."

"Perhaps not simple, but clear," Han acknowledged, his eyes agleam. "Some forms seem too vast, at first. It takes courage and vision to see the path winding through."

Amber sighed peaceably. "And a friend to foster faith for the first step."

They walked in companionable silence—or, at least, Han walked, and Amber rocked restfully in silence, soaking up the strange, stirring swell of the Centaur's song. He seemed to have chosen melodies specific to healing for, as she walked, she could feel her hands reawaken to full sensation.

She grinned wonderingly, shooting a glance at Han, who was flicking his tail in a pleased sort of way but endeavouring to pretend that he was as surprised as she was.

"Can I ask you something?" she blurted, knowing this particular question would be safer with the Centaur than anyone else.

Han flashed that grin. "There's a reason I live in the forest. My answers might not have a place in society."

Amber smiled sleepily back. "We're not exactly in society. And I'm very comfortable betwixt and between, thank you."

Han's voice continued the melody, lest the memory of the Goblin cauldron should rise in the telling. "A good place for questions. Offer me yours."

Safe beneath the healing drone of his voice, her words slipped forth without fear. "Mending, recreating the pelt; I love it," she started. "It makes me feel like I've never felt before. It's filling a void I never knew I had. And yet, I feel so hungry with it. It's almost painful. It scares me. I've never felt this…. ravenous before."

"That's not a kind of hunger to be feared, born of lack," the Centaur promised, his voice a fierce, warm whisper sparking like a firefly amidst the listening shadows. "It's an awakening to be embraced of an appetite distinctly yours. Its presence is proof that something sustaining lies within your grasp, if you have the courage to reach for it."

Amber let herself breathe the idea in, feel it swell within her, staying with it and letting it swirl and settle and bring her strength for what lay ahead. "I pledged to sew the skin and heal the soul; to that I hold, whatever it takes from me. If the remaining pieces are out there, I will find them and bring them home."

"When you are prepared to give your all, what you receive in return will prove immeasurable," Han advised. Then he grimaced empathically. "Even when it is also fated to be impossible to foresee."

Amber grinned in response. She was too buoyed now to be dissuaded. "I have a feeling that when your tongue and your soul are saying the same thing it frees up all the energy you need," she promised.

"That's the spirit," the Centaur snorted approvingly. Yet his manner grew uncharacteristically solemn as he considered all that lay unknown before the young Fairy. "It is no shortcut that opens before you, Amber," he warned, wishing he could walk it instead; hoping he could protect her from those darknesses that might stain her footsteps. "Deviating from a calculated path grants no measure of ease in effort or time—no measure of ease at all, in fact, save for the one our spirit yearns most for: the telling that your choice is the right one and the ease of heart you can only find when your soul and purpose align. The latter will sustain you, when the former feels certain to overwhelm."

"I understand." A strange, releasing dizziness tingled over Amber. "My choice is made," she admitted. "It is with the pelt that my path lies truly, and I will not return to the apprenticeship until I have wrapped its fullness around Hydd's shoulders."

Han squeezed her tight, and her heart swelled with his pride. "I know that much of this course is yours alone, Amber, and that it will twine inevitably with the influence of the Oak Prince, which is a frightening reality. But reality isn't just out there, in the moments we overcome fear and carve our destiny. It's in here, too—in the moments that cannot be torn from us, the memories that cannot be taken. Those memories forge the deep comfort of knowing that no matter what, you are held in the hearts of all who love you. Even when they are far away, if you cry out when you need someone, someone will be there. Perhaps even someone you have not yet crossed paths with—and yet, they will save you. We will move Realm and stars to come to you and be there. And you will always have us. Amidst the Goblinchat and twisting trails, we will balm his lies with our stories and take you to happier places than can be found in his version of the Realm. And, whichever crossroads he takes you to, we will keep the paths you have chosen for yourself open for you, for as long as you have need. That is my oath, as solemn and true as any I've spoken at Council. Right here and now is what we can be sure of, hold on to, if we choose to."

Amber hugged him unrestrainedly, her spirit lightening and lifting. Beneath the twilight boughs, she believed him. And later, beneath the glaring, unforgiving stain of artificial light, she would remember it.

Salt Water Soul Retrieval

"E'en the harshest tide main turn, an' turn it will." As always, the Selkie man seemed to be talking half to himself, his eyes fixed for support upon the sea scattered with a sheen of stars skimming atop the nightdepths far below, the eve-lights of Fairymead twinkling behind belying his route as Amber and Han approached, walking side by side now as the end of tonight's journey approached.

"Hydd?" Amber stared, wonderstruck. "It was you who healed Ruby? She felt a furred touch, and webbed hands."

He shook his head miserably. "I had tae send another. I could nae skin-change."

Amber's voice was gentle. "But you sent someone. You healed her."

Pale lips parted in an exhausted, grateful smile. "I ha'e dain whit I can. But your part, I feel, will be greater. O' this I hae nae jealousy, only admiration. An' hope."

He withdrew quickly, slipping like a silken shadow away to the shore-steps leading below, to resume his vigil.

Emotion caught in Amber's throat, and again moments later as she recognised where she was standing now that Han had stopped.

"You knew that when I said home, I always mean to Ruby's, even now," Amber murmured to the Centaur. The squat, rounded dwelling seemed to welcome her like a friend crouched beckoning to share a secret. And yet, Amber's footsteps seemed to sink into the earth—to go further seemed to mean to trespass, when she couldn't bring an answer.

"Ruby doesn't seek a solution," Han reminded gently. "She seeks only support."

"I know," Amber blurted wretchedly. "But she should have been spared this."

"I agree," Han soothed. "And yet her quest is of her own brave choosing, not of your forcing. You did not make this happen, nor can you take from her the course she will steer out of it. Good will come of this, not by the circumstance itself, but by Ruby's weaving of her response to it.

Your quest is aligned with the Selkie; Racxen's with the Kelpie. To whom does Ruby grant her allegiance? For I feel hers may encompass both, as well as extend beyond all our borders. Far she will journey, Amber—but none ever journey too far to be reached by a friend."

Ruby stared into a mouldering, uncertain darkness, her grief as raw as the pain. Her Realm had shrunken very small, and she had made herself very small in response until there remained only tiny snatches of herself that she knew how to hold on to. One snatch was digging into her wrist as an obstinate reminder; she had retied her friendship plait from Amber earlier, with the foresight of knowing she might need it later. And another, of course, was her Gem. She clutched it now, in the hope that its physicality, as well as its mysticism, would hold her. But all slipped tenuous and insecure in that horrible, cloistered darkness where no one knew she was hidden.

Through the fading light of her return from those tear-watered tunnels she had borne the trauma and coped by keeping mobile, and she could claim this rightfully as a hard-won victory; but now she lay, alone in the dark, and the night inside her room was vast, and as terrifying as the shattered dream traded for an unchartered future, and she dared not shut her eyes for fear of being engulfed by an abyss that roared at her whenever she blinked, let alone slept. The room was swimming as the Realm was swimming, awash with greater unknowns than she trusted she could cope with, and the covers she clung to couldn't stop her from falling.

Incongruously, through the ragings of the night there floated the sweet wet scent of tea. Like a petal flung upon the sea now bobbing to shore, its intrusion slipped so surprisingly into Ruby's experience that it anchored her in a Realm of sensation instead of superstition, and tugged her momentarily out of her besieged head. She fixed on it in grateful confusion. Before she could retract her attention and retreat beneath the covers and into the pretence of sleep, the benevolent reach of a candle peeked behind the ajar door, and a colourful mug wobbled in and set itself on the dresser. And now Amber, warm in the candlelight, was perched on the bed, stroking her hair, and suddenly she didn't need to turn her face away any more.

Ruby managed a grin. Mayhap no one had known; but one had guessed, having shared her childhood secrets.

"I didn't keep that up long, did I?" she yawned exhaustedly as she hugged Amber. "I know I'm lucky it's not more extensive; I know Hydd and the water saved me; I know it's not like losing your wings, but—"

"–But your pain is real and huge and I'm so sorry." Amber's heart felt like it was wringing itself in shame, that Ruby felt she had to quantify and justify her hurt – a hurt that Amber's own heart was strangling itself with, having had a part in it. With desperation akin to madness she wanted to plead with her friend, to explain her actions and beg forgiveness. But instead, she gave herself a swift mental shake, banished notions of drama and anguish from her mind, stirred the tea until her hands stopped shaking, and warned her voice to steady itself as she offered the cup calmly. "There is more than one way of hurting. But there are innumerable ways of healing, too," she reminded, in her warmest whisper. As Ruby locked eyes with her, both challenging and grateful, she saw her friend as she'd always seen her. "Even in pitch black, scalded and covered in snot, you're the most beautiful girl I'll ever know," she couldn't help adding.

Ruby humphed noncommittally and hauled herself up, and took the mug with a small smile. The heat warned her fingers, but now she had company she clutched it gratefully. "Well, the snot will wipe off," she managed to giggle, lunging for Amber's sleeve. "The scalding's a bit more of a problem."

"No-one can look upon your soul and see anything other than beauty," Amber promised. "The strength of your spirit blinds the eyes to all else. It is a more powerful and truer glamour than the paint on anyone else's face. You are stunning, Ruby—and you will see it again too, in time."

Ruby was silent, but Amber read this quietening unperturbed for it was between them a sacred and familiar one, fostering a trust beyond any uncertainty. A holding silence, an inviting silence, granting healing instead of fear, it meant Ruby was chewing the idea instead of spitting it back as she would have had it come from anyone else.

Honouring her best friend's choice and giving her time with her thoughts, Amber peaceably cleaned Ruby's face with the untouched water and cloth from the dresser. It gave her hand pause to realise that she had set it out this morning, when the dawn light had greeted her as usual, giving no indication of what was to come. Yet Amber gathered her thoughts around her calmly. The dawn would rise again tomorrow, and see Ruby as indomitable as ever.

"Let in the light?" she checked, as Ruby's breath grew steady and soothed. Leaning in comfortingly as she reached across, she drew back the curtains, spilling moonsilver.

Ruby drew a relieved, shuddering breath in response. Now she could see better, and with her face rinsed from tears, it didn't all feel quite so claustrophobic.

"I'm going mad," she snuffled, ashamed, pushing her hair back more neatly.

"You're not," Amber promised, her whisper fierce and warm as the candle. "You've had a horrifying experience, and your mind hasn't realised it's over. But we're going to help it, okay? And we're going to give it time. And you're going to heal, at whatever pace and in whatever way is yours, and I'm going to stay with you."

Ruby nodded mutely. Holding her gaze to stop her falling through the night, Amber began singing to her friend: a lullaby from when they were winglets, which Ruby had sung to her through those times when Amber had feared that the gifts the song spoke of could never again be realised— the same one that somehow, through she who sang it, had despite Amber's abject terrors sewn seeds of hope, and urged a nigh unreachable soul to strive and flourish again. Amber hoped she could send it back now, in lived gratitude and proof, to reach healing tendrils around the one who had sent it out in so much faith through such a trial-burdened time before, and see it renew her in turn.

"I'll have to get Jasper in here. He's best for regiment and routine," Amber suggested to make Ruby smile, when her friend's cheek was soft against her shoulder and her breathing had eased into a steady ebb and flow. "But we've started here and now, and that's enough for us and anyone."

Ruby sucked an energising sniff of breath, wiping her face and steadying herself. "I might be leaning towards a less regimented man, in fact," she managed to grin, arching an eyebrow to her best friend. "One whose lineage is far less certain. And whose company is becoming far more beguiling. Plus, Jasper's heart is for Yenna, and I love her too dearly myself to try anything silly." She drew another soothing breath, grateful to Amber for helping her turn her thoughts from herself. "What in the Realm am I going to do, once I've got through the next few days leaning on you and I have to stand on my own feet again?" she admitted.

Amber snorted emphatically. "Ruby, we're friends for life. The whole gamut of it: from when we were winglets, to when we're both older than the Water Nymph. Being your friend is more energising than any situation can be exhausting. I'm not going anywhere."

Resting her head peaceably against Amber's shoulder, reassured, Ruby considered the situation more boldly. "Right, then. What shall we do first?"

Amber released a thoughtful breath. "Well, you've always been the best seamstress in the Realm," she reminded, lightly enough for the idea to rest instead of intrude.

She left the bundle shining on the floor, and went to make more hot nectar tea.

When she returned, Ruby was bent over the pattern, making all kinds of alterations, her fingers flying and her hair pushed back; for now unselfconscious and complete.

Spilling a relieved smile, Amber smuggled the cup silently onto the dresser, and settled down beside Ruby, picking up a needle and gathering more pieces. She stifled a yelp as she stabbed her finger yet again. "See, maybe I'm the wrong person for this. You're so much better at patterns and things."

Ruby grinned as she cast an appraising eye over the collection of motley scraps, sprawled there as if in anticipation of their growth, like nothing she had seen before. "Something tells me that this is the kind of creation a pattern should neither rely on nor contain." She grinned, and then arched a brow. "I know what you're doing, Amber."

Amber grinned back. "I don't care if you know, so long as you want to."

For the first time since the accident—no, not the accident, Amber corrected herself savagely, anger jostling aggressively against the euphemised memory of the Goblin: the assault—she saw something that wasn't gouged from that trauma itch along Ruby's skin and shiver in her eyes. Something uncatchable and unconquerable. "The wax didn't catch my fingers, did it?" Ruby challenged gleefully. "Give it here."

Worm-Words and Wyrd

"She's sleeping," Amber promised Han, finding the Centaur waiting outside, his solid shadow guarding against the bewitching confusion of mould-mist spreading like a virus across the dew-touched grass with the advancement of the Oak Prince. Relief flooded to find him, yet she bore her own shield now also, in the form of the night she'd spent with Ruby. They had worked together, fingers and ideas flying until Ruby had decided, as though reformed by the stitching, to gift the half-worked image back to Amber in thanks with the promise that while the opportunity had reawakened her heart she would find her own quest, and wouldn't hear of taking over one she knew would prove to be in the perfect hands with Amber, seamstress or not.

"I wanted to make sure she was okay before I left," Amber explained, tasting the words carefully, "because the journey before me is longer than any I have yet taken. I must journey to the Icefields."

Han, as she'd trusted, didn't dismiss her conviction. Instead, his eyes shone like fireflies in the soft darkness cast beneath sheltering eaves as he offered his plan, his dancing-brook voice brushing away the fetid whispers that had festered beneath the trees in the wake of the Dryad spectre as cleanly as if they had been only so much leaf mould, as her Centaur friend's hand touched her brow in healing and apology. "Then I should have got here sooner; forgive me. The trees told me of your presence, but much is changing in this wood, since the Oak Prince attempted his conquest of the forest. I will not leave your side until we are somewhere safer—and I know where that will be."

He must have felt her hand tense within his, for he squeezed hers reassuringly. "Come, we have a little time before he suspects. I have no doubt you can survive anything he throws at you. I would just rather you not walk into it alone, if walk into it you must."

Amber nodded gratefully, and unclenched her other hand's grasp slightly around the pelt pieces she was still clutching protectively to her chest.

"I didn't know there was a way to the ice through the forest," she admitted with a grin, relishing the thought of such a night journey.

Han smiled back, in the delight of a secret knowledge soon to be revealed, as they started through the mist-clung forest together anew. "Don't forget that you are a being of all elements. We go to the sea, for there is a soul there beyond the Oak Prince's snaring, whose counsel is wiser than my own and whom you have not yet met, and she will aid you when the rest of us are out of reach. She will take you to the Icefields."

Amber shivered in readiness and awe, feeling strangely washed with an unerring sense that she would be equal to whatever she might face, instead of succumbing to the vice-like terrors of old. The sensation replaced the last gnawing vestiges of unease with a deeper, unshakeable security.

She half wondered why she dared let herself feel thus, caught still in the shifting sands of a constantly twisting fate. Yet, as she walked with Han, Amber felt the air ignite anew with a strengthening comfort. This was her norm now, she promised herself. It had been for some time; wrought by her own spirit and choices and by accepting the support of her friends as much as she had always offered her own. She was not bound to the standards of a predator, and she would not allow her life to be diminished by the shadow of one. Moments of wonder beneath these boughs far outnumbered those spent in desperation facing down the Oak Prince, and their memory would replace the flashbacks. Starting now.

So fully did this realisation fill her and so companionably did the journey pass by, that it felt as though no time at all had slipped beneath the smooth tangles of greenwood before open ground was spilling encouragingly before them, heralding their arrival upon the wildest shore Amber had ever seen.

Before they could step from the yoke of shadows cast by the last branches, a skin-prickling shadow dropped across their path. "You want these forests to survive forever, horse-man—but you will not live to see them," the Oak Prince rattled, with the menace of a deadwood tremor.

"Perhaps it is not my own survival I am concerned about." Han let out a hiss of his own as he nudged Amber protectively aside, turning his equine bulk to block her from the wight's attentions.

Yet Amber had stood up to the wight too often alone to stand back now, and stepped in front smartly. "You see now that you couldn't stop me before," she cast in bristling warning to the spectre. "And I am here better defended than ever. Save yourself the embarrassment you were unable to thrust upon me and go lick your wounds until you are ready."

Han tossed his head in spirited approval. "Your reach is shorter than your claim, wood-wight," he agreed with alacrity. "Follow us if you wish, and find out why."

"Going to the ocean will break you," dismissed the Oak Prince. "You won't stand glimpsing the being who has borne your suffering when it threatened to drown you. It was taken by another—and she bears it still."

"Then I will bear her witness in turn, and be grateful." Amber threw the promise solidly, and the spectre disapparated. But his words scalded her stomach, more frightening than the vanished wight. Who had taken the greater portion of her suffering when her parents died, and when her wings were lost? How could she dare meet such a being?

"He couldn't even speak her name," Han noted airily, thrilled with their success and hopeful. "He dare not meet her. If he faced his traumas as she helps us to, he might well not be the danger he is now to us. But we shall leave him to the forest, and journey onwards, as for you she will hold no fear, for her heart is as great as her mighty frame."

Amber stalled. "The one he speaks of is the one I'm asking to take me to the Icefields?"

The Centaur smiled. "She has borne what is too heavy for you. Bearing you is a much smaller thing."

Amber desperately hoped so. As she scrambled down the sloped bank of the beach with the Centaur's hoofsteps soft on the powder sand behind her, the great sigh of the sea slipped into view to ease her heart and allow her to relish the meditative aspect of their progress as they padded the shorescape, threading between salt-scented, weed-encrusted tide pools gleaming with the power of the moon.

As she neared the sea, she found the edge of the shore strewn with such jagged stone that it felt as though the Realm were already breaking into pieces. Amber, however, had never felt more whole. The wild shoreline lay, sky-clad and sprawling, as far as the eye could see, a new desolate note upon the sea murmuring in aching promise of a reward hard-won. Amber grinned breathlessly, knowledge crystallising like ice until she knew exactly where she was headed: far beyond even the sea, to the northernmost point of the Realm.

"This is where I must leave for the Icefields?"

"There is no 'must': the choice is ever yours," reassured the Centaur. "Yet should she appear, she will offer you an unparalleled boon."

"How will I see her?" whispered Amber.

"Simply make the decision to try," Han promised gently, scanning the crest-topped grey of the sea. "The more you awaken yourself to the Realm's wonders, the better inoculated you become against life's inevitable sorrows. The former will outlive the latter in your memory, and all will be as it should be." The Centaur's voice held a flame that could not be quenched. "You need go on alone from here, Amber. And yet my spirit walks with you, as ever it will. You need not be anything other than that which you are. Never think yourself unworthy, or unequal. You will bring back the whole Realm with you when you return—and return you will, I promise. The more fearlessly you walk the path, the further the shadows shrink back."

Amber nodded, newly afire, as she enfolded him in a final hug before watching him retire respectfully. Han was right. She'd traverse this and return stronger. Her skin wasn't torn. Her eyes were not bleeding. And she had a rendezvous to keep, on a cold and distant shore.

Song Weaver's Symphony

Her resolve restored with the new tide the next morning, Amber stared out from the stony shore across the starkest ocean she'd ever witnessed, a gale thrashing and jostling against her rocky scrap of relative safety, rendering her once-solid plan tenuous. "The Song Weaver," Amber reminded to anchor herself, trying out the name now that she was alone. "She'll know where to find the missing pieces, and she'll be here soon."

"Aye." Hydd stood before her so wrapped in furs that she had missed him at first. Even now, she could barely focus on him amidst the writhing greys of the storm.

"Are you allowed to be here?" She grinned, hugging him gratefully.

"Ye ken how this works," Hydd admitted. "I cannae act in my own interest on this matter—but while you're thrang looking after others, someaine needs to watch after ye. Someaine who kens this place, if not the void beyond."

The ice-cut wind howled, lifting instead of drowning his words as it wailed in a song lonely yet unapologetic, and Amber suddenly felt painfully relieved that out here it never fell silent, so they said. All day, all night, the wind railed and writhed, and Selkies such as Hydd lived amongst it still, accepting its strange song and neither shunning nor stoppering it up. Amber had slept in their shelters this night past; nestled within an igloo-like stone circle, the domed structure of which had seemed to magnify the constant song until it soothed a soporific balm upon her senses and swept her into slumber.

Having woken refreshed, she drew quiet sustenance from the knowledge that the Selkies had found a way to thrive amidst the unique and, at first, unsettling sound—and she hoped that somehow, she could too. Even if Jasper had thought her unhinged to come willingly to such a haunting place. Haunting's different to haunted, she'd retorted, and Jasper had sighed and acquiesced to her plea for directions, and admonished his own pleas for her safe return.

Now, to seek her guide for the trials beyond, she stood at the threshold of the emptiest place she had ever encountered. She wasn't sure she could enter without disappearing. But it drew her, even as it warned her. Ancient as it was, it spoke of renewal. And of Hydd's rebirth, she hoped. Dare she hope also for her own reawakening? Something bristled on the ice-touched breath lifting from the sea, and tingled against her skin.

Braced against the gale she stood, on the last stretch of this land before the long sea journey to the frozen north and the birthplace of the Selkies, showered with the shrieks of gulls and awash with the slapping scent of the coldest sea. The ocean beyond stretched unfettered: scouringly cleansing and barrenly accommodating, as foreboding and fortuitous to behold as staring into a mirror.

"Ah lived mah first years here," the Selkie smiled, a gesture of both melancholy and triumph. Amber had the feeling he was more concerned with finding what she needed to heal than acquiring the rest of his pelt. "Th' only ones who can survive beyond, in such a cavernous void as this vast, frigid brine, are the Whails – an' the Song Weaver is the queen o' these. Our folk say: give your sorrows to the Whails, an' they will weave them intae song.

"There are some hurts that cut tay deeply fur the strongest hearts tae bear. When your throat scratches wi' the words clawing tae git out but you cannae squeeze them frae where they hae lodged in yer heart; when you fear that the knot in your chest will crush your lungs because ye cannae find a way tae remove it wi'out cutting out everything ye are; when ye cannae understand whit's happened let alone begin tae process it—wade into the surf, and gie it tae the Whails. When it is tay heavy, they will lift ye with their stoatin warm hearts; when its been tay lang, they will swim tirelessly beside ye tae share your burden, and when it is time tae relinquish some o' the pain, they will bear it past the point all others could so that ye don't hae tae. They will be your voice, when yours is crushed, an' your heart, when yours is numb, fur nae only will they bear your sorrow, but they will help ye slowly shift it."

He smiled, sun across snow. "Ye must sift what ye seek frae mi words, for I must leave soon. Bu' she is findin' her way tae ye right now," Hydd promised, peace and wonder swelling in his quiet voice. "We shall grant her some of the boundless patience she ha' bestown upon us."

Amber nodded eagerly. Breathing steadily in the painfully clean air, she found she could bear the waiting harmoniously.

"Th' Song Weaver ha' borne witness since first th' Realm rose frae the brine," Hydd explained. "At your first meeting, her song will be o' mourning—as much fur ye as fur those whom, or that which, ye fear be lost. The Whail will work on your song thereafter, an' each time ye meet will sing it back so ye can hear how it has subtly changed; flowin' like the tide o' your emotions. She will contain it, wi'out shuttin' it off, an' ye can pick up the song whene'er ye need. There is nae rush, fur the Whail is too ancient an' auld tae attempt tae hasten such things. She knows it will last a lifetime an' will ebb an' crash afore it eases again, til it is finally transformed intae a song o' remembrance an' recovery. She will always have space in her heart an', while she bears the sorrows of all who need her tae, when the time comes she will sing again o' their joy—an' yours."

At his words, these final few steps she must take to the water's edge grew laden with promise and potential, and as the Selkie withdrew respectfully, Amber approached the shoreline alone and in reverence.

The sea lay hushed and calmed now, rocking slowly. And yet Amber's nerves railed in contrast, for it felt suddenly in a rushing sensation of falling that there was nothing she could do that could touch the magnitude of Ruby's sacrifice.

She struggled to drag the frigid air in and out of her lungs. She had long ago come to terms, quietly and determinedly, with what her quests might exact from herself. But from her best friend? She felt sick with guilt and confusion, and terror. Maybe, by sewing the pelt together, she could help Ruby stitch her life back together. Mayhap, though, she needed to tie up some old, frayed threads in her own life so that she could be her strongest self for Ruby. Especially now that everything was jostling within her, so muddled that she didn't know what she was thinking, so that in addition to her pain on behalf of her friend, Ruby's sacrifice had stirred long-buried sweeps of emotion, roiling again more tumultuously than they had for years since that fateful day her parents had died amidst the Sea

Battle. After all these years, the sudden crash of feeling threatened to sweep her off her feet into a drowning depth.

And yet her steps had brought her here, to the side of the real sea, more tangible and changeable and faceable than the one thrashing in her mind, and she clung to what the Selkie had reminded: that this was a sea she did not have to face unaided. She couldn't go around it, she couldn't avoid it. The only way was through—but she would not be alone.

Her tears broke like the breaking of an unstoppable wave whose path could no longer be denied. The relief carried her for a moment—and yet, beyond that, what good would releasing them do? Would it really ease the burden, to scream it to the sea?

In answer, seven of her tears added themselves to the ocean, springing from the rivulets coursing their tracks down her ravaged face. Although their voice was as nothing to the great roar that resounded eternally across the shore, a booming, sonorous response echoed from deep below.

And it was not, this time, around the sleek head of a Selkie that the glittering depths parted. A bow-headed hulk, barnacle-encrusted and pitted with great streaking grooves like wrinkles bearing testament to a truly ancient life, breached the surface, sending great rumbling crests of waves sluicing from her pocked skin.

A shrewd, wizened eye glistened beneath, as if younger than its withered casing; balancing sagacity with a brimming enthusiasm for the joyous gift of life.

"Song-Weaver?" Amber croaked, awed. "Let me call the Selkie for you."

Yet the leviathan's gleaming eyes shone into the Fairy's own, and bade her stay.

The Whail began to sing; a haunting, throaty tremor that thrummed in Amber's blood as strongly as the air would if she could skin-breathe, as other Fairies spoke of experiencing at the apex of flight. The effect was so powerful Amber half feared that aspects of her own self would drift apart in an effort to join with the chant. Yet the more closely she listened, the better she could discern its intention. The Whail was containing, instead of creating, the chaos: contouring with her great voice as if, were Amber to break apart, the song would catch her and knit her back together.

Shivers danced along her spine as she realised what the Whail was doing. Having gathered all the cries she had picked up on her travels which had gone unanswered, she was now singing those souls home. Not just Amber's, but all of them.

Amber's throat constricted in recognition. The Oak Prince would have had her believe that such cries now fell upon deaf ears; that only he could be safely listened to. Yet in the gentlest way possible, the Whail was proving the opposite, for her warbling, tide-strong tribute rose now in mournful triumph.

"You're singing for my parents." Voicing it almost choked her, but she had to set free the words, as the remembrance burst forth with all the crushing release of water sprung from a dam. Instinctively, she thought of Racxen. "And she's singing for the Tribe who passed before you," she murmured reverently, wondering if she could do the song justice later in her retelling of it to him.

Amber felt the tears start to slide unstoppably. All the suffering feared to have gone unseen, all the stories no longer told for dread that they were alive only in one's own mind, all the words for years unspoken for the pain: the Whail was still remembering, carrying everything too heavy to be endured...

The weight that lifted almost felled her, and her tears of grief melded into gratitude. She had to tell Racxen. She had to tell them all—

Around her swelled a great uplifting bubble of wordless song and a feeling so intense washed over Amber that she couldn't tell whether she was happy or sad, only that she was being heard and heeded. She floated in the bosom of whailsong, supported and sustained by the nurturing, all-encompassing voice and presence of a being vast and wise enough to not only contain her suffering, but provide the space and tools to begin transforming it...

Amber's vision wobbled like the sea's surface, but as she smeared the water from her eyes she was no longer gulping as if drowning, but drawing slow, steady draughts with the smoothing steadiness of the ocean's sway.

With the exhausted clarity that comes after tears, she murmured her heartfelt thanks to the Whail. Just because the song had made her cry, hadn't meant it wasn't exactly what she needed to hear.

She squinted earnestly. Now she had wiped her eyes she could see clearly the Whail for herself, not just what she had at first represented. She could discern the scars tracing her wrinkled, majestically glistening skin, and gaze into the soul-shone eye that invited her question. A sea-borne thrill frissoned across Amber's skin. She was ready to traverse the sea, and seek the pelt upon the Icefields of the North. If the Whail wished.

"Will you bear me, Song Weaver?" Amber whispered. "One more time?" She stared in awe, a strange feeling rising within her.

The deep-sunk eye sparkled, both readying and rewarding her for braving the outside Realm once more. Beneath her gaze, Amber had the prophetic sense of being guided into calmer waters after a storm, of being swept and then steadied as though her feet were being gently nudged into the shallows where she could stand. But Amber knew the waters she must traverse were not only fathoms deep, but crushingly frigid. What lay ahead?

"Do what you must," thrummed the Whail peaceably, in a low, melodic rumble. "And then come to me, and we shall do as you wish."

Emanating a stoic peace, she eased herself below the grey sea again, meeting Amber's gaze a final time before that great bulk slipped beneath the surface, her serene countenance radiating her trust both that the Fairy would be true to herself, and that such a compass would guide her well.

Amber watched reverently as the waters closed over the Whail, sealing both the way for now and the promise that she could return. She grinned resolutely and drew a steadying breath. Time for a decision, and then a return...

Between Earth, Sea, Wood and Sky

"You asked whether it was possible," the Water Nymph reminded her coldly. "Not whether it would be easy. You picked up the needle, you maddening girl. Now you have to conjure greater time and skill than you yet possess."

Amber's mind swam slightly as she tried to cling to the conviction she had conjured after her meeting with the Whail. "So, it is possible," she translated doggedly. She just had to find the resources. Or, rather, decide what she was willing to sacrifice. And yet, as the Nymph had reminded her, because there is always a sacrifice—there is always a solution.

If she was serious about this, she was going to have to brave Sarin Thornswen, Amber acknowledged, wrestling esoteric knowledge into grindingly awkward practicality. But Sarin wasn't the only master offering apprenticeships.

Zaralathaar read it on her face, and spread her hands simply, her fervour abating. "You know exactly what to do. What remains uncertain is whether you are willing to bear out the consequences. It is frightening, is it not?" the Nymph murmured. "When there is nowhere left to hide?"

Amber shivered uncertainly. "It feels empty," she admitted.
The Nymph smiled a private smile. "That's not emptiness, child. That's space. To breathe. To grow. To reclaim as you see fit."

Amber lay in bed, the night buzzing around her stretched with possibilities finally awakened after laying dormant for so long, knowing she could not rest when so much relied upon the next few steps. The ticking of the clock became a claustrophobic, pressing reminder squeezing against her temples.

She had to speak to Sarin. She knew that. But she had to decide within herself so securely that nothing the Matron said could sway her from her course. Right now echoes of the Oak Prince's voice repeated through her head, amplified by the dark silence. Here alone she could almost hear him hiss in derision, questioning what she could do.

Curse that voice, for one, she retorted grimly before the familiar anxiety could threaten.

She didn't have to listen to it. And she knew how to silence it: she must act. She swung her legs out from under the duvet and pushed herself off the bed, fumbling for her writing paper even before she considered turning on the light. If she were to die a year hence, what good would spending this year trapped prove? She cast her mind back over the past year and all she had been through, over all she had endured with the strengthening support of her friends. *I can meet the next horizon*, she promised herself. *Because in returning from the last one I came back stronger.*

As her pen hovered over the page, her thoughts trembled for a moment. What if she did it? What if she abandoned her apprenticeship, sewed the pelt, returned it to Hydd—and everything didn't magically change? She'd still find everything waiting, snapping at her heels and sneering at her from the shadows. She'd still have to earn a living slogging through something that drained her spirit and sapped her soul. Her options wouldn't have changed.

She chewed the pen thoughtfully. She didn't believe that, any more. And she'd prove it. In the deepest and most sacred of darknesses, Amber grinned. Her stomach scrunched into a knot, but for the first time in a long while she knew what to do about it. She'd wished for it for so long.

"I no longer make wishes," she promised herself with satisfaction, her face splitting into a determined grin as she signed off the letter with a gleeful flourish. "I make plans."

Grabbing her cloak from the pile on the floor, she swept it around her shoulders and slipped out of the door.

Outside, the meadow-scented silence swelled nurturingly and her possibilities broadened in response. Amber's grin stretched accordingly.

Rain fluttered down, soothing her fraught nerves as she hastened on through the secret night towards the rec hall. Drawing a steadying breath, she knocked on Sarin's office door. Time to claim her rendezvous with life. Time to hand in her notice for good.

Walking out, Amber felt as light as air. Almost skimming the meadows as she returned, bursting into a run out of pure joy, she felt the closest she had felt for a long time to flying. Such was the heaviness of the weight now lifted from her, that she imagined she could almost float away. Not float, she reminded herself, buzzing. Soar. This is my own doing. The knowledge almost made her forget what she couldn't do, so much there was that she felt she could accomplish now.

"I can do this," she whispered to the knowing trees who jostled with the joyful sharing of her secret. With no one else to tell right now, she spoke to them gleefully. "I can so do this."

She turned the key in the lock, slipping inside her tiny hut which, Ruby had warned her when she had first voiced her hopes for abandoning the apprenticeship, would likely prove the only home she'd ever be able to afford without a full working wage. Returning to it now, with the Realm newly expanded, it felt perfect.

Brandishing the needle she had earlier thrown down in despair, Amber licked a new thread and slipped it through carefully. Smoothing the skin, she began again.

Time sped needle-quick and just as fluid, as though lending its support through the silent, sacred reaches of the night, until a familiar knocking at the door scattered the spell into an exultant realisation that she had managed to maintain her focus and effort for the entire night, and achieved a not inconsiderable amount of progress on the pelt.

"I saw your light was on, and wanted to check whether you'd done anything foolhardy," Jasper noted archly. A grin played over his pale features. "And if not, why not."

Grimacing at Amber's somewhat unhinged exuberance as she hugged him, spilling over with her announcement about resigning, the Prince absorbed her news and tried to stifle his sigh. The irrefutable weight of what she had committed herself to vied with the stubborn kernel of conviction her soul insisted on nurturing pearl-like amidst the gathering grit and grime as Amber met his disbelieving gaze steadily, less annoyed at him than rendered untouchable by the strength of her own conviction.

"All this for Hydd? That name means 'sea tide'. A name that might draw or drown," the Prince rebuked finally with affection. "What have you got yourself caught up in? I thought this would be done in a week. I didn't know you'd quit outright."

"It takes what it takes—I don't see you riding the Kelpie yet, either," Amber protested, in not a dissimilar tone. "And enough of the melodrama; I walked into this willingly. I'm fine with the Selkie, you and Racxen are both seeking the Kelpie—I don't suppose you've had any spare time to arm me against the last piece in the puzzle: our woodland wight?"

"I've been poring over every text in the Kingdom and beyond that bears reference to the Oak Prince," Jasper promised, waving a hand in vague attempt to capture the vastness of the endeavour. "We'll get answers, but it will take time. Something tells me that this," he mused, glancing at the pelt shimmering chimera-like with potential in Amber's arms, "will reward your effort better."

Amber grinned her thanks. "Something told you? Or someone?"

"Yenna," the Prince agreed unashamedly, with a rare smile. "She is convinced that returning this man's skin has a significance greater than the obvious. She is farsighted even for one of the Wolfren—and she knows something of skins, and souls, and secrets. She suspects your involvement with the pelt is what has ensnared the Oak Prince's interest—and believes that something else you are destined to do will prove key to his fall."

"Something else?" Her mind faltered, overwhelmed. And yet Amber nodded thoughtfully and allowed herself a private smile, letting her mind slip back to her first meeting with the Wolf Sister. She knew Yenna's attitude towards destiny, and offered a silent thank you for her veiled encouragement to forge her own path and have faith in herself, however shadowed the future might yet seem. She drew a steadying breath to ease the warning shiver that traced her spine at the suggestion that her involvement in the Realm's latest trials would not end with the completion and return of the pelt, even should she manage that gargantuan task.

She knew Yenna would be even now scouting for information across the breadth of her range, but she suddenly wished the Wolf Sister were closer here, with her desert-balanced intensity and a surety born of surviving in two skins.

"It appears to all rest in your hands once more," Jasper murmured softly, recognising the doubt slipping across his companion's face.

Amber shuddered. "Don't remind me."

Jasper's smile rested on her, his bemusement hidden better than it once had been. "It wasn't a rebuke," he promised seriously. "It was spoken in faith. A reminder of what you accomplished last time."

Amber gulped and offered a grateful nod, overwhelmed, as she helplessly attempted to wriggle everything she couldn't express into a shrug.

In recognition, the Prince nodded solemnly, only marginally less awkward. "So, let me get this straight," he managed finally, in what he fondly hoped was a soothing, yet take-charge sort of voice. "You were fine with running off to the Fountain when it contradicted a direct order, never mind threatening your life, and yet this you're having doubts over?"

Amber grimaced. "Clearly, acting stubbornly and thoughtlessly wasn't something I had to learn from scratch."

Jasper examined the patches that she was carrying as kindly as he could. "As opposed, clearly, to sewing," he couldn't help adding with a grin. "You've taken a huge step by withdrawing from the apprenticeship," he appeased quickly, and honestly, as he recalled the anxieties she had spilled moments ago. "It's only natural to feel trepidation in the face of the sacrifice it will entail—to cut yourself off from the financial security and the social familiarity the apprenticeship would provide are levels of sacrifice, and ones you are not so familiar with making as the more obvious bodily ones you seem to throw yourself into with no self-regard. There will be time for the latter presently, and you will know exactly where you stand, but I hope your doubts will fade before then."

Amber grinned back. "When you put it like that." She folded the pelt protectively. "Might be time to go out and face the future. It's morning. They'll have found my letter."

Jasper looked to the lifting dawn. "You've worked out how to keep the Oak Prince out of your head. Don't let other haters worm their way in." He was silent for a moment before he continued.

"I've never had an issue with pride, Amber," he divulged quietly. "You never have to hide yours from me."

Appreciating his words, Amber squeezed his shoulder as she stepped through the doorway. "I did not drag myself through every trial thus far to allow myself to be swayed by opinions I no longer need," she promised. "The coat will be finished, no matter what they say. I just hope in trying to stitch it back together, I am not torn apart, and that there is still a place in this Realm for me after. But if I do not find a place, I will carve one, rather than crush my soul into something I would never want it to fit."

"If you can refashion someone's skin, I dare say nothing will be beyond your scope," Jasper rejoined. "There are occasions, Amber, when if I didn't know better I might judge you to be something approaching wise."

With as withering a look as she could muster before bursting out laughing, she gathered her courage as carefully as she would the pelt, and took off at a run towards the rec hall.

"You're delaying your apprenticeship?" Sardonyx's voice ruined any hope of her choice being recognised, let alone respected. Of course he's been put in charge of apprenticeship recruitment, Amber despaired silently, struggling to rein her thoughts as dismissive laughter rippled through the assembled workers. She supposed at least it was better than him working with patients. All the doubts that had worm-ravaged her conviction started squirming again—this time in front of an audience. But she drew her decision cocoon-like around her, and a lightness graced her now. She didn't have to explain herself to him.

"You can't keep this nonsense up forever." Sardonyx wasn't moving. He hadn't even opened the envelope containing the letter that was soaked more in sweat than ink.

"It won't be forever," Amber threw the promise over her shoulder as she gathered up her courage, walking away with her plan buzzing in her mind, throbbing through her veins and sparking beneath her steps. She grinned into the empty air, and didn't care who saw. "Just for however long as it takes."

Amber opened her eyes tentatively, every sense woken, every nerve waiting. The predawn had never felt so charged. That first heady disclosure had carried her through the whirlwind heat of last night but here, beneath the uninvested eye of a new and unknowing dawn, was where her choice would truly be made. Here, where there was nothing to stop her just avoiding everything, and frittering the time away, and skittering around the edge of her promise without anyone to check that she was approaching, engaging, creating.

She lay, just breathing, barely even moving. This is the day, she promised herself. This is the start of carving your new life. This is when you make it reality.

Her heart scudded. Her veins buzzed. It felt weird, being flushed with this certainty, floating above all the doubts and paralyses of old. It felt right. She felt right. And that felt weird. Grinning unrestrainedly, she sat up, swung her legs out of bed, the clean chill of the morning urging her on. She almost felt guilty at how joyful she felt, but there was so much riding on this, she promised herself, that she was completely entitled, and likely even required, to conjure and kindle every motivating and sustaining ritual and rhythm possible, and so she sprang out of bed and threw open the curtains with glee, almost dancing through her movements and not caring if anyone saw.

And yet: this was not the time to fling energy away needlessly, she knew. So she let herself, after that first well-earned flurry of physical glee, allow the feeling to billow its warmth into her, to fill her like the cleanest air, and to let herself just feel it in its fullness; without needing to rush off and risk dissipating it by showing the entire Realm and exposing herself to the expectation and judgement of others. Just for the moment, this feeling was completely hers and hers alone. She let herself revel in it without excuse or apology.

Embarrassment twisted momentarily that it felt so alien to not have the crushing expectation of the apprenticeship pressing in on her—but then, it was almost as unsettling to realise that feeling like this, so free and alive, had become nearly as unfamiliar to her, since the pressure enforced by the apprenticeship had intruded so unyieldingly on the changes she had been starting to work on, full of hope and diligence, in the aftermath of their first quest.

But she was done beating herself up for the delay. After all, everything she had been through and learned and become had brought her to this point and this place. She resolved to cast away the suffering and stalling of before, and pay heed only to the revelation it had wrought as a catalyst for change.

Amber pushed open the dew-touched window and welcomed in the expectant chill of the new day. The Realm outside lay still, poised and waiting beneath her gaze.

Okay. She steeled herself with a grin, looking back to the pelt, which was curled up as though sleeping. She'd actually done it, she reminded herself in wonderment. Started it, her mind corrected worriedly. And only just, at that.

Her room had never felt so quiet. No routine. Nothing to wake up for. No-one to make sure she did what she'd said she would. The silence pressed anxiously, craning to see if she had made a mistake. Amber stroked the pelt meditatively. Racxen's words swelled in her heart along with the Prince's counsel and buoyed her own determination.

Pushing through her nerves, she gently retrieved the pelt, which draped more heavily in her arms than its size would imply, as relaxed as a cradled seal pup. Amber sat down purposefully at her dresser, smoothed out the half-finished skin pieces, and resolved not to leave the room until she had something distinctly resembling a seal looking back at her.

Noon saw Amber sprawled across the floor, pelt pieces scattered in joyful chaos around her, hands streaked with cloth chalk and cramped from sewing and eyes gleaming with an exuberant, burning focus. She had no time for the clock as methodically she examined each piece; noting the lay of the fur and matching the subtle mottling in the fur scraps with their neighbours, before first pinning, then tacking and stitching, each precious addition.

Pushing herself to her feet to stare out of the window and reconnect herself with the outside, Amber grinned wryly as she watched dusk settle its soothing feathers atop the Realm and comfort its inhabitants into slumber. Stretching tired muscles, she returned readily to her task, fired with the flow of its progress and the fullness with which it enveloped her.

But the next time she looked up, the clock hands reproachfully jabbed towards 2am.

The loss of time unhinged her, and a wave of panic broke. She couldn't do this, not like this. The deepest enthusiasm in the world wasn't going to carry her through, unless she could find a way to back it up by skill far greater than her own at present. She gathered her thoughts. There was more than one way to become an apprentice, after all.

She pushed herself unsteadily to numbed feet and considered the pelt. While she couldn't finish the skin tonight, neither could she leave it lying here like some piece of discarded rubbish. It needed respect; it needed reverence. Wondering if she were going slightly mad, Amber tugged her favourite dress off its hanger and folded the skin up carefully into it to protect it, and tucked the bundle into the lowest drawer of her dresser where she kept her most prized possessions: her poi ribbons, archery certificates, Ruby's bracelets, Tanzan's trinkets from far-flung places she'd never been and whence his spirit had never entirely returned. She nestled the remaining pieces inside the folds, like snuggled hatchlings, even as she bristled to think what Jasper would make of such sentimentality, in the hope it would mean the skin could know itself regarded as the most precious and sacred of things.

"At this time of night?" Mistress Garnet watched her imperiously, her dark hair scraped back into a bun as tight as a pincushion and her eyes gleaming like buttons.

Amber's breath stumbled. It was common knowledge that the master seamstress kept the time of owls, but there was no denying the imposition of visiting her at such a late hour. And yet she of all people, surely, would value an explanation over an apology with regards to the thing that now beat its wings inside Amber's heart. Mistress Garnet, it was clear, had caught and claimed the same bird, and nurtured it so completely that not only had that bird flown free, but it had also granted her its feathers. And so Amber unravelled her thread of narrative with honesty and hope, and waited quietly for the verdict.

The seamstress's gaze fell on Amber's red-raw fingers and she tsked protectively, ushering her inside.

"Let the lesson begin, mistress Amazonite."

Night insects flanking the path hummed their disapproval as several hours later Amber padded homewards. Her head ached from squinting and her fingers were thoroughly cramped, but she could see the path to the pelt's completion forming in her mind, and the realisation that it was truly possible put a bounce in her steps.

Her mind was full of new tools, but they lightened, instead of added to, her load. Her entire Realm seemed to expand now that she had set in motion the previously unimaginable, and she forged into the darkness ahead strengthened indomitably by the blazing light shining within. Maybe she could forge a new future with these new skills? And maybe, she amended with a self-conscious grin, she could finally do so without feeling required to apologise.

The prospect of such an alternative traineeship rose tentatively, but shied from the surface of her mind like a Kelpie. She let it approach and skitter as it would, unwilling to risk challenging it before it had chance to solidify and protect itself against the ravages of reality. For now, the possibility was enough.

The night air rustled warmly around her. It still felt strange to complete the journey without some nameless panic pressing at her shoulders—odder still to reconcile that she was allowed to not feel frightened. Maybe things really were changing.

After all, they were with Racxen, the night whispered in intimate reminder. Even as friends, they had got each other through times that had seemed unliveable, so what could either not face now, knowing the other was beside them? Yes, with him gone to track the Kelpie she missed him, painfully so; so much sometimes she wondered if it were altogether normal and worried what he would think if he knew. But out of everyone in the Realm, they had found each other and declared it beneath the Renë sun and amidst the quietest reaches of the night—and kept to it in actions greater than the deepest words. Wherever they each were, whatever they each were doing, she had an extra heart warming her chest, and an extra soul to watch over her.

And so, as the shadow of her home loomed from the darkness to welcome her back, she felt a warmth flood her chest, for she didn't have to wait for Racxen in order to feel good. Nor would he want her to. Her choices, her quests, formed the compass that he strengthened but which was entirely her own—and she had realigned herself with it tonight. She'd love telling him about it later, but he'd want her to start on it now. And she had no intention of stopping herself.

Now that she felt secure in herself, she felt safe alone. So it was with vigilant focus rather than fear that she reacted late into the night when she felt, rather than heard, the Oak Prince emerge amidst the steady silence of her room whilst she worked on the pelt. Not emerge, she corrected, combating immediately the old, threatening panic that it was somehow her fault. Intrude. He had no right to be here.

She glanced to her clock, its uninterruptible hands stabilising, and urged her own continue their steady path in and out; as healing as breath and just as vital for the one with whom the skin taking shape between her fingers would be reunited.

Steeling herself for the onslaught, before the wood-wight's words could crowd into her head Amber corralled her own in a pledge to herself: although the speed of the dissipated hours and the rush of their enthrallment left her breathless, she would never allow herself to be frightened by what she herself had conjured, which had proven so complete a fit with her soul. Neither would she allow herself to be cowed into abandoning it by its antithesis, billowing and threatening as it now was.

"I wondered when you'd come slinking round," she murmured evenly to the drifting shadow, not deviating from her task. The realisation that his presence could no longer sway her from her endeavour, filled as she was with such strong, sustaining purpose, fired her soul. "I'll take your arrival as an indication that I'm nearing my goal."

"You'll never finish in time." A warning hiss shivered in the dark. "You are scrabbling fever-gripped and alone in the dark," the voice scorned. "Such desire is as toxic as the Kelpie. It exhausts and disappoints—eventually it kills. I will be there when it does."

"Maybe yours kills," Amber countered, hiding her fingers, scraped raw, beneath a turn of the pelt. "Mine drives and sustains. It frightens you because you cannot control it, and thus, cannot control me. Because I have this, I will never need you. And you cannot handle that."

"This need in you can never be satisfied," the wight tried again, wheedling. "But all others, I can provide for. Why do you not yield?"

"I would rather draw sustenance from my desires alone, than settle for any satisfaction you could grant," Amber warned.

A laugh shivered through the gloaming before the presence faded, and she tried to shake the tremor out of her hand before continuing, struggling to keep in mind that the remaining darkness was not predatory and could not harm her.

He must be riled, to be pursuing her so, Amber reminded herself as an anchor amidst the storm of fear his attention had stirred. She let her concentration on the pelt's task form her defences, feeling her focus flow in and out with the needle to secure all that healed and sustained, noting the stitch-steps of the sewn journey as steadily as Rraarl counted the links of his chain.

In the holding quiet, Amber considered what she knew about the Kelpie. The Oak Prince could have been out hounding the contestants of the challenge, but instead he was here, harassing a seamstress. Why did he care so much? Perhaps the pelt had a part to play in protecting the Kelpie as well as the Selkie. After all, the Kelpie was as much a part of the water as the Selkies were. Perhaps they were linked in greater ways than she could now guess at.

Amber's thoughts raced with the needle, but she dared not let their echoes reach her face in case the Oak Prince were to come back. She grimaced. If not only Hydd's wellbeing, but also the safety of the Kelpie, were bound to her completing the pelt, it was more imperative than ever that she hold her nerve and maintain her momentum, as intrusive as the wight was evermore intensely becoming. Amber shivered. Such defiance could prove as dangerous as anything Yenna might be planning. But how could she attempt anything less, knowing what was at stake?

Amber's thoughts strayed to Racxen, out there in the storm with the Kelpie. As worried as she was for him, she was glad he was out there with it. Perhaps it was right to fear the creature but, if it was in their power to do so, surely it must be equally right to save it.

Even if her own power seemed to pale against everyone else's in this quest. She sighed, caught in angst for a moment that threatened to overwhelm. But the needle glowed brilliant white against the floor, so she picked it back up, squeezed out the tears from her eyes because she couldn't afford for her vision to blur now, and she sat sewing for the rest of the night until in the morning the skin was a little more completed and a young man's journey a little closer to its end.

Amber woke to restless shadows amidst a fretful, drifting half-light, unsure what had woken her. She felt so alone that the curtained gloom could have been a hole she was falling through. What time was it?

"Evening!" Ruby introduced herself, as brazen as Sarin Thornswen and more welcome. The earthy, comforting scent of mushrooms cooking in cream and accompanied by still-warm bread wafted into Amber's soul as Ruby padded through carrying a steaming bowl of soup and a fat, precariously balanced roll.

Amber's mouth watered embarrassingly. She was suddenly and painfully reminded that she'd forgotten to eat last night. Had she worked all night and slept all day?

"Well, you might not be able to afford the bakery, but you can still afford the bread," Ruby promised, her voice muffled as she took a first mouthful agreeably. "I haven't seen you for two days."

Amber's word of thanks threatened to choke her. Knowing she was the reason Ruby had been so savagely hurt was so sickening that she almost couldn't bear it.

"Look," Ruby offered, as sure as Amber had ever heard her as she swiped another swatch of bread. "The only way the Goblins will keep causing me pain is if what happened leads to one of their infernal debts between us. I need you as my friend, Amber. An equal. I need you to not fall into their trap."

Amber took the plate gratefully in response and enfolded her friend, gently and tightly, into a long hug, before kissing her fiercely on her healed cheek. "By my Gem, I promise," she invoked, her whisper shaking and earnest.

They both grinned, recalling all the similar pledges, both silly and soothing, pledged with equal fervour in days long gone by when the Realm had seemed young and they had felt small. Those days may have gone, but their friendship had stood the test all of them. And it would bloom deeper through this one, too.

"So, how fares the quest?" Ruby offered, her eyes sparkling as she comfortably changed the subject.

"A uniquely pleasurable frustration," Amber admitted with a wry grin.

Ruby chewed a painted lip. "This is a wonderful thing you're doing for another," she started carefully. "But what is its effect on you?"

Amber shrugged honestly. "It's like I'm consumed by fever," she admitted. "But it's a fever that keeps me well."

"That keeps you well?" Ruby suggested carefully. "Or means more to you than keeping well?"

Amber grimaced in acknowledgment. "Maybe I don't care which," she admitted.

Ruby chose her next words carefully, although they overflowed with love. "Maybe you should—both for your sake, and the pelt's. If you want this to become your reality, instead of just your relief, you need to approach this wholeheartedly. Then it will release you, instead of ruin you, and a prophecy of your own making will come true instead of the Oak Prince's poisonous spore-words."

"You're wiser than Pearl and Morgan together," Amber admitted, raising her hands in confession, her gratitude spilling into a restful smile as she gazed at Ruby. "I'll not let making the pelt cut me off from the outside Realm," she promised, stretching her aching fingers. "I'll let it awaken me to its wonders, and help me experience them twice instead."

"That's the you I know, Am," Ruby soothed approvingly, her fierce gaze softening into a smile of her own once more. "I know it's scary—it's a one-time-only chance. Of course it's overwhelming—but it's exactly those kinds of memories that can sustain you through anything, if later you have to return to what you have fled. This could be the making of you, Am. It won't consume you. It'll create you."

Tears brimmed Amber's eyes, until all she could do was squeeze Ruby's hand in silent thanks. Ruby squeezed back, understanding. "Dreams need space," she offered soothingly, withdrawing. "But they also need fellowship, so I'll see you in the morning. You're not on your own, and you're not confined to this room, either. The sunlight holds gifts not afforded to the night, Am. I know Racxen holds your affinity to light and air as sacred as he considers his own to dark and earth, and a Selkie isn't exactly going to demand you shut yourself away from sky and sea, is he?"

Amber's throat clenched to realise the gentle, insistent truth in her friend's words, and how blinded to their message she'd become through the urgency of the quest. She hadn't realised how savage to herself she'd become in her efforts for another. She needed to look after herself instead, in order to have her best self to offer.

"It's nothing you don't know—I could have been a Genie," Ruby winked, understanding. "Remember—this isn't the apprenticeship. This one's the adventure. Let the solitude hone and sustain your craft, and it won't strip anything away. Plus, I know Beryl and that lot would try to tell you that once you have the time, the urgency will go, so prove them wrong—further it. Let it be all in can be, and it might just become everything you need. See how far you can take it. And then let it take you further. But first: sleep."

"And then: completion," Amber agreed, a deep smile of peace spilling across her face as she held her friend's gaze. "Thanks, Rube," she whispered fervently, tears squeezing suddenly as her friend enveloped her in a last, sure hug. "I'll make it up to you, I promise."

"You're welcome," Ruby replied simply. "And you will, but you don't need to."

She slipped out of the room quietly, a floating flame amidst the shadows of the night. After watching her safely to her door, Amber wriggled back under the blankets again. The darkness seemed to press, close and comforting, as though it were waiting, hushed, for the morning. Amber's soul fizzed as she stroked the bundle of fur. Completion, and the pelt, nestled close.

Amber woke suddenly, but it wasn't stifling. It felt as though she had won extra time. For her. For the pelt. She sprang out of bed, soul buzzing, the long-before dawn darkness swimming urgent and expansive.

All her experience needed to go into this. And even more so: all those experiences that in the enchantment of this moment flooded back to her in a sweeping, glorious rush. So, she sewed the clean, sparkling air that had carried her as she had flown through an endless sky, and the dancing light that bore glad witness above the meadows in Renë. The sea-fresh spray that had drummed the shoreline of the mystical Silent Sound as she'd communed with Maidens and Knights of the Sea. The wonder and joy, the wild abandon and tender care, of her nights with Racxen, and the dew-touched dawns waking tangled in his arms. The soul-tending times in company of friends, and the crisp, sun-brushed mornings when she had run with the birds atop the sea cliffs, and called out to Rraarl below when it felt like no one else in the Realm was awake. Every moment that had left her recharged and alive she streamed into her sewing, so that her fingers flew with her mind and her plans, and the pelt wriggled with a vitality previously unreached.

As she brought her best memories to the pelt, in the privacy of this most sacred night, she found herself reliving everything they had gifted again, as she felt herself become a channel for the creation of something partly her and so much more: something awe-inspiring and unknowable in its fullness.

She wasn't afraid. She was found. This quest couldn't deplete her, no matter how long she spent on it. Feeling so charged, so alight and alive, it no longer scared her to feel the hours slip away or to realise her time was blurring into a strange kind of otherness. This was her, at her ultimate.

"Do you still think that this is healthy?" the omnipresent echoes mocked, uncounted hours later.

"Shut up," Amber retorted steadily, keeping her mind focused on the unbroken flow of even stitches, rising and dipping as ceaselessly as the ocean's tidal breaths, even as the threads clung tightly together as though aiding her work like tiny hopeful hands holding broken pieces and making them whole once more. "This doesn't concern you." Then she shrugged, her eyes agleam with something he couldn't snatch. "Or, rather: I'm glad it concerns you—but save your energy, for mine is beyond your influence."

The winds shivered with wrath at her impertinence. "That is not an answer."

"I've no intention of giving you an answer. The only thing you deserve is a command. That I give you freely: leave me."

He did so—so quickly that Amber worried whether she had hallucinated the whole thing.

Still, there was the bundle on her lap that needed finishing, and she had no doubts left to fade.

Hours later, Amber clung to the final pieces, feeling lightheaded and half-starved beneath the inconstant moonlight, barely able to hold the needle any longer. Itching sweat slicked her cramping fingers as she realised: it wasn't going to be enough. She needed more pieces. Everything she could give hadn't been enough—

She pushed out of the door, took the path through the meadow at a run. She hadn't run out of options yet.

Yet at the broach of the wild woodland atop the crest of the hill, Amber stalled on instinct.

After the enclosed sanctuary of her room, wherein she had conjured magic and created something even more, the space outside her door suddenly felt cavernously lonely.

"While you must take the path beneath the trees," purred the ever-encroaching Oak Prince, with a deathly satisfaction.

"Only should she choose so freely." The Centaur voice she'd recognise anywhere glowed firefly luminous and uncatchable, disdaining the fickle darkness. "And not necessarily alone."

Warmth blazed within Amber, and she clutched the skin close, as if doing so could imbue it with the courage that seemed always to envelop Han. Danger was certain, but fear was a choice she discarded.

"Are you sure it is not the completion itself, yet curtailed, which you should be fearing?" the Oak Prince throated. "Such reckless ecstasy is doomed to diminish should it ever be satisfied. Violent passions are fated to ignite equally fiery endings. And end this will, wingless one—in a death of fire and powder, upon battle-ashened sands."

"Instead of diminishings and endings," the Centaur urged, shivering more with passion than with fear, as he stepped from beneath the sheltering boughs with all the authority of some wildwood God. "I shall talk of vanquishings, and validations. For the woman who stands between us will make it so, instead of listening to foul prophecies that deserve no heed."

The forest seemed to bristle in response, caught between the primal forces of antithetical energies. Amber shivered at the sudden change. Soon would come a point at which her only option would be to run—and she knew to whom.

"You cannot stop me," the Oak Prince spat towards the Centaur.

"Yet I can slow you," Han promised, his more-than-human form solid against the shifting shadows beneath the canopy, his bay coat glowing warm as flame against the chill litch-light of the Oak Prince. "You might be able to break this Forest's spirits to your dominion—but they answer my call willingly."

Before the wight could gather response, the Centaur reared up, stirring a great dervish of leaves as though summoning the Realm to its senses once more, even as the Oak Prince flung his half of the forest into fetid-green frenzy against the roan defences of the Centaur.

"To the sea!" Han cried, as though the whole forest urged it, and his words possessed Amber's soul of wings. His voice billowed like the spreading of wings of his own to slow her pursuer, willing her on as amidst the leaf-flurried hurricane she fled to the far safety of the sea.

Finally the branches overhead relinquished their hold on the sky, and the great dark curve of ocean welcomed her as the shoreline spread like spilled quicksilver beneath bright stars. Her heart scudding in relief, Amber padded across the surf-damp sands, searching the glimmering swell for a deeper gleam. She sought the Sea Folk now as never before, drawn towards them like the tides to the moon.

Even before she glimpsed them, she felt her possibilities swell to the limitless horizon in their presence. She'd assumed Han had sent her to the Silent Sound because the shore was far enough away to escape the Oak Prince's clutches—but what if there were another reason to be here, tonight?

Great swathes of purpling cloud softened the darkness, and the ceaseless rhythm of the slow-rocking sea soothed Amber's skittering heart, and she waited at the shallows, wrapped in a reverence free from expectation.

The Maiden slid through the surface in silence, glistening water coursing the long tangles of hair contouring her body, her fish-pale skin glowing. Her ageless eyes shone with the wisdom of the moon. Her voice was as deep as the ocean and as sweet as the light dancing across it:

"Slivers of hope will always lie
Between fire and earth, wood, water and sky."

A shiver clutched Amber, not of fear, but of promise. The pieces were out there, and now she knew where—scattered amongst the elements of the Realm. Her quest was far from over.

The Maiden read the thanks in her eyes, and sank like a song beneath the surface again. Yet at her departure, Amber felt as though something vital and sustaining had left, too, tugged back into the diminishing tides and leaving her alone beneath a suddenly starless, cavernous sky.

Groggily, she wondered whether the Oak Prince had sparked something unnatural amidst his half of the gale, before Han had worked his own magic. She felt like she was burning up. Blotches bloomed disorienting atop her vision wherever she tried to focus her gaze; as though the fire were still imprinted through the lids of her mind's eyes. Racxen was out risking his life trying to ride the untameable. Ruby would bear the scars of her defiance all her days. The once invincible Centaur was fighting for the life of his forest. She had agreed to something so far beyond her ability it could be the death of her and the fever of it all threatened to claim her.

And yet, the swirling, tide-crusted sand anchored her and held her safely through the swimming night as she began to walk back. She had not come here to have her responsibilities absolved, only to find a way through them—and that had been granted. So, she continued with grateful steadiness over the windswept miles. The dune grass prickled beneath her toes and the hillocked, windswept fields still miles from the Meadows cleared her head, until at last the firefly twinkle of Fairymead welcomed her home.

As the night air cooled around her, Amber felt warmed through with the growing certainty that she knew her direction. Towards fire and earth, wood, water and sky, she reminded herself. The scattered remnants of the Selkie pelt had been cast by the Oak Prince to the mercy of the elements but now, she had a compass. She didn't know where exactly all those elements would be manifested but at least, she acknowledged with a shiver of triumph, hopefully in snatching pieces from the Goblin's cauldron she had got 'fire' out of the way.

Signs in the Soil

The still cave air enfolded Racxen completely, its soothing embrace cooling the Kelpie-fever in his mind as he padded a pilgrimage made many times before, his spirit expanding as the light from outside slipped away to remove the limits of vision. He knew he'd made the right choice in coming here to think, and he stood in silent gratitude within the soft darkness for a moment before lighting the familiar, ornate lantern that had stood witness here for years, to spill a warming glow upon the treasured scene he had sought solace and sanctuary with so many times before.

Yet, as his gaze flickered torch-like across the cavern's contents, Racxen froze as if, should he succeed in doing so quickly enough, he could stop everything spiralling further out of control. What he beheld was so unexpected that he didn't know how to proceed.

He had accessed the ancestors' cavern countless times; he knew the placement of each piece as automatically and unconsciously as he knew the events and unfoldings of tribal myth, for the artefacts contained within this sacred space held the collective memories and skills of the Arraheng people. One could always, without necessarily being able to discern each piece amongst the whole, gain comfort from knowing that knitted together they preserved and protected the wisdom and legacy of the entire tribe. Spending time down here, amongst the most treasured gifts from long dead loved ones, was akin to once more connecting with their spirits.

Yet now, here, something was wrong with the collection. Something was different, was intrusively, insurmountably changed. Nausea thrashed in Racxen's chest. Someone, or something, had disturbed the ancestors' gifts.

He stepped closer, and wonder flowed anew. Not disturbed. Added to…

"I hope it was okay to bring it here," Mugkafb blurted, appearing from a shadow and making Racxen start violently. "Only, I didn't know where else to put it to keep it safe."

He pointed to the pelt piece, nestled between heirloom earthenware like a seal pup curled in slumber.

Racxen stared at him in mute astonishment, as the horns blew to warn the tribe to stay below tonight, for safety. "How?" he managed in amazement.

"You're not the only hero in this story," his brother retorted proudly, grinning all over his face. "But that's a tale for another time," he added, suddenly serious. "If you want to get that to Amber tonight, you're going to have to race. I'll stay here, I promise. I'll guard the cavern."

Thunder reverberated deafeningly through the tunnels.

Racxen cast an urgent, thankful glance to his brother and deftly swept up the pelt piece. Tying it around his wrist, he headed towards the storm-broken night.

Time to defy the curfew.

Below and Beyond

Amber woke unevenly into indecipherable silence, feeling like she was falling. Memories of the Oak Prince's poison knotted around her. Half aware, she twisted fractiously amidst roiling waves of darkness, and sat up with her heart hammering before she was quite awake.

Drawing her gaze to the pelt, its mottled grey glowing buoyant and reassuring against the swimming darkness, she dragged her breathing back into a steady rhythm. It felt as though the rolls of sea had permeated her room, were diffusing through her skin. Her blood whooshed in her ears to the rhythm of the ocean, seeping through every pore, soaking her mind and drenching her senses, reminding her she had to return to the edge of the ocean. According to the Sea Maiden, it wasn't just to the Icefields that she must journey—but to the Icefields she must go as a start.

Throwing back the bedclothes, Amber flung away the tendrils of doubt like the drowning weeds they were. Let the Oak Prince cast his warnings where he would—he clearly didn't know how many better voices she had to listen to.

She swung her legs out of bed, into the cool darkness of potential, her grin widening as her resolve strengthened. It was about time she paid the dearest of these voices a visit—and midnight was a time better than most.

This place holds no fear, Amber promised herself, as the blanket of night rolled back to reveal its secrets and the marshland slurped and chirped and stirred. She had always delighted in visiting Arraterr. She felt a private, privileged thrill to be part of it, even if it had started just by association through Racxen. It thrummed with awe; every time she came was an initiation into the exotic.

And yet tonight, with all its darkness and depths, she wished that this unseen path, which she had trodden so many times until she knew it as well as the passage to her own front door, could feel a little less thrillingly strange and a little more easily familiar. She could almost hear Jasper berating her for celebrating the mystery, when right now she had to admit that he'd had a point about the necessity of attending to the mundane.

And yet her soul sang a song all of its own to find herself once again amongst the rich teeming of life which made, if not Arraterr hers, then at least her one of Arraterr's. Greeting its waters and mangroves in turn, she gladly let its welcome swirl away the taint of the Oak Prince as she found herself anointed with it cleansing, clinging mud as she trekked the squelching half-tracks towards the caves.

However much she was relishing the hike, Amber couldn't help casting a hopeful gaze beyond the lattice of marshways to the safety of the caves. They looked as far off as ever, the realisation slammed against her chest as she stared.

Much closer, lamp-eyes flashed in the gloaming, trickier than will o' wisps, and worse for leading you astray.

Goblins.

Her heart beat a frantic tattoo. She'd spent so long worrying about the Oak Prince, she'd forgotten about the accursed Goblins.

Who hadn't forgotten about her.

She refused to lower her eyes as the leader stalked towards her, even as the others fanned to cover every path of exit. Amber nudged a heel into the soft edge of the pool cautiously, feeling safer in the sinking clutches of the marsh than in the fell gaze of the Goblins. Yet the prospect of tracing the sprawling tangle of silver threading through the marshlands filled her with almost as cold a dread. The surface glimmered before her, more liquid mud than lake, opaquely refusing to yield either secrets or hazards, oiling itself against danger now that another crouched behind her reflected in a strange gleam.

"The swamps are treacherous, especially at night," the first Goblin whispered from the shadows, his strange lamp-eyes flashing against the marshlight. "One might presume yer've gone looking for trouble."

The confidence that had buzzed in Amber's chest drained away into the Goblin's sallow eyes.

"Don't worry, girl—it won't be my clutches around yer as yer die," the Goblin leered. "I'll take a step back before the swamp claims yer and the mud forces inside yer throat. There is but one way across, without being dragged down to your doom." Realisation gleamed like a stolen prize as he felt Amber stall. "Ah, but wait—only Arraheng know the way, I've been told. Yer think you're so close to him—but has he ever shown yer?"

Goblin truths are the foulest, and Amber felt this one seize with drowning terror. Racxen had never told her. Hope fled, escaping like the trapped bubbles squirming up and spitting from the swamp mud. But she still had one option that wasn't of the Goblin's choosing. Sodden moss clung anxiously around her bare toes, urging her into the embrace of the swamp and away from the Goblin's grasp.

Easing a tremor-clung foot backwards, Amber focused on her breathing, tried to flush away her fears into the swirling eddies as they took hold. She'd rather yield to the sucking cold than to the cliff-edge gaze of the Goblin. Yet each step took her deeper, clung to her more insistently. Danger gnawed with the chill, and she began gulping down air in preparation.

"Let's count the reasons why, shall we?" her pursuer hissed, stalking towards her. "Because he doesn't care enough. Because he never wanted you to know. Because you didn't mean enough to him—"

Racxen slid from the murky embrace of the swamp, marshwater sluicing from his hair and clothes. "Because," the Arraheng corrected, his voice beaconing through the dark, warm by Amber's ear, "it's not a journey I'd ever leave you to make alone."

As quickly as he'd slipped to the surface he dove, and Amber followed, gripping his hand and trusting him to lead her as surely as a Selkie. Together they powered through the concealing murk, leaving behind the Goblin chatter and trading it for the clear song of the streaming tunnelways beyond before bursting through the surface safe inside Arraterr.

"The paths will always open themselves before you as surely as they do for me," Racxen promised, his eyes glowing safe and sure in the darkness. "But I should have showed you these sooner, I'm sorry." Racxen's breath was soft at her ear as he waded beside her while they sloshed through the shallows, guiding her fingers through the water's opaque skin to explain.

Amber gasped in astonishment as her hand brushed the secrets carved into moss-slicked stone: a glyphic scrawl eons old spread like brail beneath Amber's touch, intimately acquainting her with a language beyond sight of reassurance and revelation which told her she'd never be lost again. She grinned as though finding hidden treasure, which she supposed she had. She stole a thankful glance at Racxen. He'd shared with her everything about this place. Amidst the midge-thick, scent-syrup air, it suddenly felt the most important place in the Realm, and disregarding the mud clung to her skin, she slipped her hand from Racxen's and wound both of hers in close embrace around him. "Thanks for rescuing me."

His eyes shone with molten-copper warmth. "I didn't need to rescue you—but I do need to show you something. Stay close."

Rain began to hiss down, blurring the boundaries of the Realm as they hurried towards the marsh caves. The darkness pressed intimately as the tunnel entrance opened before them and Racxen led her through into a low-ceilinged, firefly-warm grotto. Tongues of marshwater lapped like shadow against firelight as she stepped over the threshold, and Amber's breath caught in wonder as her gaze rested on what lay within, the shadows thrown warm and wild by the torchlight from the wall.

"Welcome to the cave of our ancestors," Racxen breathed, his shadow comfortingly solid against the floating dusk outside that made her eyes swim.

"We come here when in need of counsel, to remember the wisdom of those who once walked beneath the same stars that now watch over us. We cannot demand answers from those who have earned their sleep, but knowing that they confronted, and conquered, the same problems we now face offers comfort. Each member of the tribe, since first we were led to the caves, has designated a most beloved item of theirs to add to the ancestors' cave at their passing, and contemplating what was revered by our loved ones can evoke insight, for we all intend to leave the best of ourselves behind for those who come after."

Racxen spread his clawed hands in explanation. "I came here earlier to calm my thoughts. The grotto has become so full that it can at first appear strewn with inexplicable nostalgia—but it is so dear to me that the placement of the smallest offering is imprinted on my mind. And one item was new." A wry smile played across his lips. "Mayhap the spirits of the elders guided it to its safety; mayhap it simply floated in on the tide. Either way; it was easy to notice an unfamiliar, welcome switch of fur."

Amber took the piece with tentative, tender fingers. Something sparked in the air, warm and private, as Racxen passed it to her freely. The cave glow pressed, comforting, tantalising.

"All that is mine I give to you freely," he shrugged simply, his voice catching on his words and her closeness. The cave suddenly felt deliciously intimate. Its confines amplified every breath, every shift of skin against stone. He'd never felt so aware of the lack of space between them, as the rain outside built feverishly.

"I'm sorry this messed up our plans," Racxen admittedly helplessly, tugging a rolled blanket free from a rough-hewn shelf and spreading it before her as he watched the deluge sheet down to curtain off their shelter. "I know how desperately you want to finish the pelt, and I was supposed to be tracking the Kelpie."

Amber snuggled into the blanket and his arms, feeling the sense of security woven by both the cave's protection and Racxen's proximity cocoon her as she let a grin spread across her face, the shadows cast by the wall torch dancing against the low ceiling. She grinned, sure and steady. "But now there's no Selkie. No Kelpie."

"And more magic than ever." Racxen grinned back, his gaze clinging to her like Kelpie skin; more intimate than any touch and buoying her up like a Selkie—catching her thoughts in his night-shone eyes and keeping them safe and sacred. The air shimmered, alive and alight with the anticipation of what they had been awaiting all these months.

The night outside pressed above them, a hot, sticky blanket far too heavy to sleep beneath, as marsh insects thrummed their angst, impatient to reclaim the now stretched-tight sky for their own once more. Amber's heart clamoured as urgently in her chest, fluttering an ardent plea not to waste this night. Thunder broke raggedly, the storm refused to settle. And yet her soul felt anchored and serene; exactly where and how she wanted to be.

Entwined in Racxen's arms as they watched the storm, the claws he brushed gently along her back fired more electric than the lightning.

"This could last all night," Amber whispered, her smile widening as she tenderly shifted her body more intimately against his, brushing her lips against his.

"If you want it to," Racxen promised, kissing her softly and deeply, his need as great and his touch as tender as her own as he pulled her in closer, gentle and urgent, his eyes spilling starlight as her response mirrored his.

As they melted into each other, Amber felt like she was flying.

She'd expected the Realm to blur and fall away, but she hadn't expected the Prince's dartwing messenger to flutter obstinately into her vision at the same time.

"Curse you, Jasper!" Amber growled raggedly as she unfurled the Dartwing's message with shaking fingers and stared at it wretchedly. "We've been summoned to the Castle," she blurted helplessly, unable not to laugh at the ridiculousness of it. "They've sighted the Kelpie. It's been unleashed."

Racxen chuckled. "Lucky Kelpie."

Amber snorted with laughter, her gaze sticking to him as she sighed with longing, desire fighting with duty. And they both knew which they would have to choose tonight.

"Engo ro fash," Racxen promised, his kiss a soft balm despite his hardness. Even this was enough; to have her feel as she'd whispered to him that she felt, writhing and ready with him. He couldn't love her more than he did right now, but later he'd show her just how much that was. Whenever she wanted.

"Engo ro fash." Amber nodded, biting her lip and steadying her breathing. They'd have other times. She could wait. For him.

They locked eyes with each other grinning and gasping in one last full body embrace until, sinking into a final kiss, Racxen sprang back, and Amber after him, scrambling for their clothes and running together through the night once more.

Voices on the Wind

Pearl's thoughts rode the tumultuous wind that rattled against the window she had been drawn to opening. It was now being lashed fit to be torn off its hinges, and she couldn't help wondering whether the same fate would befall her mind.

In the background, Laksha moved like a painted shadow, but unease still twisted the Queen's heart as if she were alone. It did not feel so many seasons ago that a different voice carried upon the wind had spoken to her thusly—one that had thrilled her with ecstasy, instead of chilling her with fear. And yet, there had been danger even in allowing that—so could she really trust herself to make the right decision now, with this voice? The wind taunted and harried her—and yet she could not very well shut it out now.

Laksha slipped forward with a blanket; more to anchor her mistress in the safety of familiarity than merely to ward off the cold.

"It is nonsensical to conjure what one cannot control," Pearl was arguing doggedly, seemingly with the curtain, which was whipping fretfully in the gusting wind. "I might be able to summon it, but my skills end there. This will end in disaster."

Laksha fixed the clasp with deft fingers. "Yer Majesty? I know the hours Dragons keep, and if this were one of those times yer know I'd keep the fire stoked fer yer an' keep me questions to meself. But this ain't one o' those times, is it?"

Pearl looked her handmaiden squarely in the eye, and shook her head. "I've always been honest with you, Laksha," she promised.

"An' I've always been discreet fer the privilege," Laksha shrugged acceptingly, her voice honey over broken glass. She placed the blanket around her Queen's shoulders as she had so many times before: after nights on the Dragon plains, her first meetings at the Castle, more nights on the Dragon plains, where decisions were made and pledges offered. Laksha grinned. "None fits as a Goblin wi' secrets." And yet, for probably the first time in her life, the handmaiden looked uncertain. "But yer not talkin' about Dragons, this time, are yer?"

"Kelpies." The word shimmered like a jewel on Pearl's tongue, and for a moment her doubts seemed to fade. But she wrung her hands as reality crowded in. "I know not whether to trust the voice, nor whence its missive came, nor in whose interests it might prove," she admitted. "And so, I pace the corridors of my own castle," she noted ruefully in apology, smoothing a hand through her tangled hair as though she could stop the rest of the night unravelling.

"I would trust yer answer, whoever posed the question," Laksha offered readily.

A glimmer of her old smile flickered around the Queen's lips in response, before she sighed fretfully. "I fear the message has been carried by some fell spirit, and received sanctuary inside my mind."

Laksha's eyes rested as flints on the knowledge, considering it as seriously as Pearl had trusted she would.

"You have heard the rumours of the Oak Prince, have you not?" the Queen pressed. "How he worms into one's thoughts?"

She smiled weakly, ashamed, realising she had not voiced such fears to any one. "What is it about Goblins that makes one bare their soul before them?"

"Ah, but I use me powers fer good," Laksha promised, her throaty chuckle soothing. "Yer could give up yer kingdom an' return to the desert, an' I'd follow yer back to the wildening sands wi' no judgments an' fewer regrets."

Pearl looked into those strange eyes and saw the truth reflected in them. "Even if it is the Oak Prince's voice," she murmured, resting her brow upon the Goblin's, "I have so many reasons to heed it this one time. For my Kingdom, for my King—and for you. The wight warns of the Moonstruck Kelpie—so I find myself urged to summon it, as many wait to attempt to ride it. After all, without the Kelpie there can be no room for magic such as ours. I do not fear what is strange."

"Oak Prince or no, this decision sounds too closely aligned with yer soul ter be feared as strange," the Handmaiden agreed carefully.

"Then it is settled. I shall call to the Kelpie. I only hope I can handle what comes after." Pearl sighed, but whether from worry or release Laksha could not yet tell. So the Handmaiden spread a second blanket beneath the window, where the moon rays settled clearly despite the battering of elements outside, and purloined cushions from a shadowed cupboard, scattering them into a nest of sorts there in the corridor.

The Queen's eyes glittered mischievously as she curled her knees and spread her skirts, cosying into the scatterings. "I used to do this when I was small," she admitted, beckoning the Goblin down beside her. "I thought that if only I could make a good enough nest around me, stayed very still and concentrated exceptionally studiously, I might hatch into a Dragonling."

Laksha grinned and crouched. "I did similar in the dungeons. I used ter gather twigs an' things from the corners during labouring hours; and when the nights drew in I shaped an' shaped 'em. I thought if only I could place them in such a way as ter discern wings in the flicker of shadows, a Dragon might summon itself ter me." She sighed, not entirely melancholic. "The things we pretend."

"It worked, didn't it?" Pearl smiled gently. "You crafted your Dragon, and sent your soul upon its back to keep it safe. That's not pretending. That's making believe."

"An' I walked wi' Gorfang, an' you wi' Roanen." Laksha leaned back, the moonlight softening her rough skin. "Yer know I'd chase down the Kelpie for yer, don't yer? If not fer the fact that it would scent Goblin an' dive a hundred fathoms."

Pearl nodded peaceably, closing her eyes. "Do you want me to shut that window?"

Laksha listened to the wind lifting around the stones, tremulous and free, alluring and strange, ancient and eternal.

"No need, me Lady. We know which voices ter listen to."

"Jasper, have you considered that the Oak Prince might be luring us to conjure the Kelpie not for our own good, but for his?" The possibility coiled festeringly around Amber's chest.

"Let's just deal with one monster at a time," Jasper murmured. "I have no choice but to attempt the summoning, for it is the only hope for our people. I have to make this decision, so that they are spared from doing so for themselves."

His jaw tightened. "It cannot be denied that we are unleashing a volatile, uncontrollable and savagely bewitching predator. But you need to focus on your own quest now—for one day soon, there will be a reckoning."

"At Trickster's Gate," Amber murmured, remembering the Goblin's goad.

"At Trickster's Gate," the Prince acknowledged. "Yet, Amber, remember also: you are the only one the Oak Prince fears now but, when he comes after you, we will give him cause to fear us all."

Mid-Recö Maelstrom

As she and Racxen approached the castle, Amber's stomach knotted beneath the nauseous-looking sky. The Kelpie would come tonight; everyone was saying it. In response a gnawing fear had been trying to demand Amber's attention, squirming in her belly like a worm brought to the surface by rain as a possibility flexed, uneasy and undeniable in the tautly charged, pre-storm air. Racxen's eyes were gleaming with the thrill of the night, as though he were running free out there already. She felt ill that she couldn't protect him yet also, part of her barely dared acknowledge, it terrified her that she wasn't enough, that he was drawn to a temptation far greater than anything in her ken.

Catching her glance, Racxen twined his claws with her fingers. "I love everything about you," he promised. "Everything I know, everything I am still learning, and everything that remains yours alone and is an enigma to me. The part of your soul that knows the ecstasy of flight, and the part that survived being torn away from the sky. The part woven from everything you shared with your parents, and the part you have sewn for yourself since. The part that soars stitching the pelt in the silent reaches of the night, and the part that conjures what will come after. The parts of your soul forged from so many fragments I can never guess at as well as stories I am privileged to hear or walk beside you through.

"My soul may brush against those parts and offer its love and admiration and wonder but it will never know entirely—and it will never have to in order to love you. I will always honour what is not mine to know and protect your right to it, Amber. I do not need the Kelpie. That is why I must ride it; I know it must be done by someone who knows that they can and will return."

His lips pressed earth-cool against the storm-fevered sweat of her own, and she felt the steady beat of his pulse through her own skin. She cast her fears aside, treading them into the ground where they belonged. "I know it, and will remember," she whispered, the promise true.

Her hand firm and sure in Racxen's, she ducked gratefully into the castle's protection and stared out with him through the ancient windows to the wild, wired twilight fired in the distorted glow that precedes a tempest, trying to hold on to that calm within herself despite the gusting clouds of bickering as an argument with no clear answer worried at the huddled party already assembled.

"The Kelpie's nature is inherently fickle. It is not so much a creature of the sea, as a creature of the storm," the Prince insisted. "This of all nights will be auspicious for its summoning. And we can wait no longer."

The silence stretched, swollen with the anxieties of his audience.

"But we have been warned against it! The Oak Prince has guarded us for centuries, with our best interests at heart. It would be folly to trade his measured magic for the unhinged sorcery of such a wild creature, whom we have had no dealings with." Amber didn't recognise the speaker, but many murmured their agreement with his words.

"Each inhabitant of this Realm has their merit, not reliant upon any perceived value they purport to offer us," Jasper reasoned. "The Kelpie is no more dangerous than the Oak Prince—less so, I would argue—and the balance of the Realm has never been more precarious, the state of magic within it never more erratic. The stakes are higher now; we must rise to meet them."

"Even so." Yenna paced tightly. "Jasper, we Wolfren know what it is to risk our humanity every time we become our other selves," she pleaded frankly. "And we rely on magic to bring us back; we kindle it amidst our own souls. To work personal magic requires resilience, spare emotional capacity, impulse control, and an unwavering moral compass – it is because we can access those elements within ourselves that we can each conjure our versions of magic. What you're suggesting is so much larger. You've seen me struggle to return. You know what it takes, with the most comprehensive support in the Realm. It is a rare individual indeed who can jump into the floodwaters and return unchanged—if at all.

"Magic as leaches from the Kelpie has not been worked by any since the time of Sorcery. We have not assimilated it safely into our beings; it remains wild and unwieldy—magic from the great source. Amidst magic like this we may lose ourselves. It may engulf us, and never spit us out. It renders the Realm perilous indeed."

"You will survive this better than any of us, and are the beacon guiding my decision," Jasper murmured in acquiescence, his stern features softening.

He drew himself up to address the huddled crowd renewed. "Our Wolf Sister is right, and we must never forget it as the Goblins and others who lose themselves over to sorcery do. But I must be letting you all influence me more than I would admit, for I find myself in the undeniable position that I would rather tread a perilous realm in the thrall of enchantment than a treacherous one under the rule of one who would seek to dampen all such hope and outlaw all such ecstasy. I would rather live at the mercy of forces strong enough to shake my world for good or ill, than be forced to diminish behind the glass case of the Oak Prince's version of safety, and see all colour leeched from a greying Realm."

"And anyway." Jasper's eye took on a decidedly Centaur-like gleam, glimpsing Han watching approvingly from outside, his strong features sure and his hair streaming in the winds. "Dangerous is unsafe and unwise. But perilous smacks of adventure."

As the others exited, Yenna waited aside the tussocked hill as though she were standing atop a dune peak, tasting the wind and mapping the night, her gold-edged midnight veil streaming like a summoning banner behind her in the wind. Her watchful eyes glowed like muted beacons, and stopped Jasper in his tracks.

He joined her quietly, the white accents of his shirt luminous in the soft darkness as he waited for the words he knew she struggled with.

"It is not that I do not trust your judgement," the Wolf Sister warned finally. "It is that I am more cautious of the Kelpie than most. I have not yet learn whether I can join this hunt, or whether it would scent my wolf blood, and run amok. So, I am loath for you to face alone what I may not be able to help you through."

"Cannot help me through?" Jasper grinned, crookedly and calmly. "How do you think I learned that I can well afford to put my trust in the tempestuous?"

Her eyes sparkled as she read the warmth of his truth and he kissed her in the darkness.

The lash of the oncoming storm pulsed an uneasy rhythm against the battered windows, drawing out their predicament unbearably.

"Summoning the Kelpie is only the start, if someone who can accomplish it may be found," Han warned darkly. "It is what comes after that needs most vigilantly be guarded against. For those who fall under Kelpie-thrall behave as though moonstruck. The desire awoken by his call is more sustaining than the satisfaction: you will follow his cry beyond all passion and reason and, once upon its back, all motivation for returning to shore—even returning to the surface for so much as one more gulp of air—will slip from your mind like sloughed skin."

Amber felt her throat close and her heart skitter as though poison were seeping through her veins. Han didn't know that here amongst all those eagerly professing their intention of riding the Kelpie there was only one who, she knew in her bones, had a chance. Racxen's eyes were fixed on the coming storm, as though he were out there already. He was beyond listening to their doubts. All he could hear was hoofsteps and an ancient heartbeat approaching.

"Well, with all this I'm now starting to believe the Oak Prince," Jasper admitted, infuriated and ashamed. "There's no denying that there is a certain loss of control inherent in any magical condition. It renders our position fraught indeed."

"It is not losing control," Yenna reminded, steady after earlier. "It is accessing a part of our experience—a part of ourselves—that the Oak Prince can never reach. He is the one who will lose control: control over us because we will not need him, so long as we retain this part of ourselves. He wants to close off that part, make us less than all we are. Worse, he wants us to close it off ourselves out of misguided shame."

"And it wouldn't be just his kind of magic that we would lose," Racxen added, the calmness in his voice speaking of a decision already made. Amber wondered if anyone could hear it apart from her, as the Arraheng's gaze brushed hers in a reassurance that spoke straight to her heart, even as she feared for what he might face. "It would be the kind that pushes through the earth with the tendrils of new life. That skims blue fire atop the ocean and oxygenates the water. The kind that has enabled us to thrive despite everything that we've been through, and that one day will let us meet unafraid that which we cannot survive."

"It is our ability to endure, fragmented, that the Oak Prince fears," Amber agreed in solidarity, defending Racxen's chosen quest as fiercely as her own. "We owe it to ourselves to fight for it. It will be what defeats him."

Racxen's eyes glowed like embers in response, and she felt their warmth fire through her.

"So, we move ahead into this fool's errand with the Kelpie?" Jasper surmised, half enthused, half dismayed. "Marvellous."

"You love it," Yenna shushed, her eyes agleam.

Jasper smiled. "Mainly vicariously. But yes. I suppose I must. And whatever my personal views, I stand behind my people. I must find out how one conjures such a creature. If it is in my power, I shall summon this Kelpie for you even to my ruin."

"Actually, it might not be in your power, but in that of one of your own," Han reminded.

"Mother?"

"Who else?"

"No," Jasper warned. "I'm not having her dragged into this."

"Dragged? Even Roanen's been trying to talk her out of it."

A protesting growl of thunder rent the sky.

"Although, I fear, to no avail."

Pain pounded into her temples as the Queen hastened to document another complaint. Had the Realm changed so much? Beleaguered as she was becoming by so many accounts attacking magic, Pearl was not yet ready to cast off her own dearly held beliefs—wrought of memories which let her glimpse back to another time and place, and which whispered to her a promise that such freedom and purpose were not forever lost.

Frustration crushed against her heart as the door knocked again. If it was another complaint, Pearl decided, she would run off to the Dragon plains tonight, storm or no storm.

A glad cry escaped her lips to greet the Centaur figure waiting as she dragged her tired gaze from the papers. "It is well that you find me, Han," she admitted, eyes gleaming with purpose. "I wish I were out there giving rein to one duty instead of suffocating beneath my other in here." The Queen's features loosened into a determined smile.

"The Oak Prince has done enough damage to the Realm convincing everyone that magic drives people mad," the Centaur acknowledged passionately. "But he hasn't reckoned on those of us whom it keeps sane." He bowed his forelegs and grinned roguishly. "And we're forever at your service, your Majesty."

Pearl swept aside the wretched correspondence, relief flashing across her features as she hugged Han thankfully. "Then send word to my husband for me, for it's time to see if I can summon more than Dragons."

Summoning the Storm

The dissonance of metal charms clashed and clanged, jarring through the restless night. The stench of iron filled the air, cloying it with the tang of rust and blood.

The wind whirled into a dervish; the rain battered with unnatural force, thunder crashed spasmodically as if the whole Realm heaved and coughed in preparation for spewing forth the tempest-ridden spirit about to be summoned.

"This isn't mother," Jasper managed faintly. It was the explanation he could muster. "One cannot summon a Kelpie as one would a Dragon. It has burst its banks—as must any uncontainable force placed under unsustainable pressure."

In the archway of the castle, which offered the clearest view of the Realm beyond, the friends huddled against the uncanny ferocity of the storm, watching the trees outside rail and writhe like skeletons possessed. Silently they had gathered; however vital it was that the Kelpie be summoned, there was not one amongst the bravest in the Realm who would be foolhardy enough to walk abroad this night. And no one wanted to risk finding themselves unaccompanied when this storm broke.

Yenna alone remained calm; a statuesque stillness amidst the chaos. Ruby sat next to her, deathly pale but poised, her wounds echoed by the jagged scars of lightning knifing across the sky. Jasper crouched, subdued and sickened beside them, guilt churning in his gut at what he might have set into motion.

As thunder broke overhead, Rraarl's face tensed into a snarl he could no longer control and Amber knew he was being taken back to the night of his transformation. She shifted to stand beside him, guiding his hands to his chain to count the links.

Racxen stepped back quietly and carefully; aware of the effect the sight of his claws could have on the survivor of a Vetch attack in the throes of flashback. To the tracker, the stench of iron spoke a warning. *We should be in the caves. It tempts fate to be out on a night like this. Bearing witness counts for nothing if we cannot intervene.* He caught Amber's eye and felt a similar unease within her.

"This can't be the right way," she mumbled miserably, staring out into the storm. "What hope is a creature brought forth amidst so much fear? What hope has such a creature?"

"You have your quest; allow others to walk theirs. The Kelpie will not experience this the way we do," Jasper promised, his eyes sallow and Goblin-like in the whipping torchlight. "This is a language it speaks and recognises. It is a creature of the storm—what scares us excites it. Perhaps this is Mother's doing, after all."

"So you've no idea whether we can trust our own feelings, but you're presuming to interpret the Kelpie's?" Amber grimaced. And yet something amongst the clamouring dissonance and tuneless jarring sang a deeper, unifying note, easing her misgivings and urging her to join the wild dance. Could she not give up the struggle about whether to trust the Kelpie for a moment, and instead focus on trusting herself? Would that not be a stitching up of a gaping tear equal to what she sought to grant the Selkie through healing the pelt?

As it swept around her in a wordless chorus of primal belonging and bade her follow, her eyes found Racxen's. His gaze held hers, as sure as ever and twice as shining, before he sprang away into the storm-seized night, leaving the other challengers trailing.

Unbridled Magic

Her veils as fluid as shadow around her, Yenna passed undetected through the night. The night unrolled its scent-map around her, and she felt her stride loosen as she became attuned to her wolf senses.

Suddenly, the Realm shifted and began sluicing. An overwhelming awareness of the Kelpie poured against her in a deluge. The sound of hooves filled her mind; percussed through her chest. This would be a hunt like no other…

Yenna sank into a crouch, gouging her nails into the ground as she struggled to keep her skin from shifting. Her heart pounded like she was already in pursuit. Colours began to fade before her eyes; scents flooded instead. The salt-rust tang of blood coursing beneath equine skin sweet as meadowgrass bloomed fit to eclipse all else. She could sense it bodily—could almost taste it already. Yenna felt her mouth fill in readiness, and she spat convulsively in alarm. If the Kelpie came any closer, came into view even, she wasn't sure she'd be able to stop herself. She smeared mud across her face to drown the scent, but it pervaded everything: it filled the rain, the vapour in the air, the moisture in the ground…

Frantically, she clawed through her scarves for her bandana, drinking its scent in great gulps. The woodsmoke and spiced air of her desert home, the scent of parchment and pageantry that seemed to linger around Jasper, the lupine earthiness that sang of her packmates gradually overpowered and replaced the blood-quickening, saliva-inducing rush of scent spilling from the Kelpie. The pressure behind her eyes eased, and she saw with human vision again. She whimpered, and wondered if anyone had heard. Skin shifting was supposed to be a liberty, not a liability. She had always been able to control it. Until now.

Yenna adjusted her scarf and veil and pushed herself to her feet. "I withdraw from the Challenge," she murmured, to wherever the Kelpie had run on to. "I must keep you safe from me. But I warn you," she added in a soft growl, her golden eyes blazing in the night. "I will keep them safe from you also."

A shocking, keening cry, like a hawk in the throat of a horse, sawed through the air, to be heard by another also. Racing to gather the horses scattered by the grotesque alluring call, Naya stumbled to a halt aside the Lake in despair. All lay still now, as though in the grip of enchantment. Naya's steps wove a spell as bright as the gossamer path she trod through the kind of night spoken of in hushed tones, which lingers in the mind as a memory that light cannot burn away.

Time stretched as thinly as her nerves, the moonlight quivering atop the water's surface like the silver scales of a caught fish, warning anyone foolhardy enough to venture close, so deep and dark on a night like this, that they would become similarly ensnared. Oh yes, there was magic afoot tonight, she knew. The lake thrummed, alight and alive with it. But something else was stirring in the forest, billowing up in noxious spores as though once long dormant but now disturbed, spilling toxic and tempting on this knife-edge night. It frightened Naya more than the cry that tore the night now, wild and unhinged and seductive.

Her horses must have followed it. She plunged after the call, pacing the ragged lip of the lake, stumbling through the snagging vegetation, searching the depthless night. She knew she was sailing too close to the storm. Knew it, and sailed on regardless.

Hooves more than equine percussed the earth. Naya's heart tattooed amongst the undergrowth as she flattened herself into hiding.

"Han!" she hissed in relief, as the Centaur's unquestionable form burst through the trees. "I was afraid you were the Kelpie."

"At least you still are afraid," Han noted dryly, hugging her. "I fear the rest of the Realm is half moonstruck already. The Kelpie has been summoned, but no one has thought any further. This is an ill night indeed to be out."

"For you included," Naya warned, concern softening her hunted features.

Han shrugged confidently. "I am still the guardian of the forests," he promised proudly, determined. "And I need send a message through the Dryad network."

Naya nodded, hope rising. "I shall go to the horses that draw me more urgently than any Kelpie, and ensure their safety as well as I can my own," she promised. "We become forever responsible for what we have tamed, after all."

"Yet what about those we cannot tame?" mused the Centaur, watching the treacherous shadows dancing atop the lake's centre. "What is it that binds us to them?"

"We pledge not to lose them," Naya murmured. "Or ourselves."

"Those words I would follow across the Realm, even were they not yours," Han pledged approvingly. "I shall will them true, if it is in my power."

"And I will let them echo in my heart louder than any hooves I may hear," Naya promised with a grin, fading with purpose greater than fear into the shifting night.

Left alone in a forest that no longer felt like his own, Han shivered, flanks trembling at the bewitching touch of the fell mist clinging over the lake. Stamping his taut, equine nerves into the blurring mud, he broke into a gallop.

Whether she saw it with her eyes or in her heart Naya could not in honesty tell, but a single glimpse of the translucent glimmer which had turned the forest depths to starlight now flooded her mind until she could fix on nothing else.

She realised belatedly, as though through a fog, how close to the water's edge she had come. So much closer than before. But she wasn't scared like earlier. Now that she had stopped running, the only sound sawing through the night was her own ragged breath. She found she didn't want even her breathing to disturb this scene. The otherworldly tranquillity of the lake eclipsed all else; its surface glowed, thrummed, quivered until she wanted to drink it in—drown in it, even.

As though in response to her yearning, the Kelpie splintered the Realm with its voice: a savage, desperate cry; cavernous in its need and all-consuming in its beauty, shivering between ecstasy and terror and deafening her to all reason.

And then she saw it. The apparition trembled, as though sight alone could not contain it. Naya dropped to her knees as its vision filled her being, the rain sluicing the creature's strange power into her until it permeated her every pore and smeared away any sense that such a breach was best avoided…

It wasn't approaching the bank. It wanted to her to approach instead. It was giving her the choice.

She wouldn't have to go in tomorrow.

Yet even in her half-bewitched state, something in Naya stalled and regrouped.

She grappled to regain control of her breathing. If she could manage that, maybe she could win back her steps. But it felt like a betrayal. She didn't want to go back to the grey, to the claustrophobia. She wanted an endless ride through a night spiralling out forever.

But I'm already carving that for myself, she promised herself. *And on my own terms. I want Roanen. I want Seb. I want Taiko. I want my niece and nephew. I want my home, where I can write my poetry and paint, and dream, and ride until I'm gasping. I have this—in snatches, for now, but I am working towards my forever, and I will have it as I wish. But on my own terms.*

She pictured it all. Pictured it until it glowed. When she opened her eyes, at first the night breeze seemed to sigh with disappointment. Opening her eyes tore her uncomfortably from a too-vivid trance that couldn't sustain itself without depleting the dreamer. Everything felt empty. Too empty to ever be filled again.

She let herself cry; cry until she gulped and gasped and recognised her body again. And then, into the burning Kelpie-void, Naya allowed her breath, gathered her thoughts, and held onto her promises. The trees above knitted the Realm back together around her, rustling comfortingly and busily, jostling to accommodate her plans until she felt that both they and she were anchored in reality once more.

Steady within herself now, Naya stared into the oozing blackness until her eyes swam. She knew horses better than anyone, certainly better than the men who rode them for a living and lectured her. And horses' eyes didn't feel like this against her skin.

Naya broke into a run. She had to get to the Meadows. They had no idea what they had summoned—or how soon it would breach its banks. Or how strongly her heart called her back to the lakeside.

Sweat poured from the Centaur's flanks, so slickly he felt like he was bleeding. How had he managed to lose Naya, after speaking to the Dryads?

For the first time in his life, Han felt the claustrophobia of the obscuring forest, but he snorted, shaking out his hair stubbornly in an attempt to shrug off the net the Oak Prince was casting over the land. Han was not immune to the magics of the forest, but he was cursed if he was going to allow himself to be frightened by them. He had known the forest long before it had felt itself bent into submission, and if it proved still in his power he would rouse it once again. But for now, he knew, as the electric scent of the gathered storm lifted on the jostling winds curling through the tanglewood, mingling like the currents of a meeting estuary, the Kelpie had to be the priority.

Lifting his heels, Han charged away like a colt, closing the gap between himself and Fairymead. He only hoped he could intercept Naya before the Kelpie did.

The Centaur found Jasper on the castle grounds at Fairymead, his white shirt flickering in the gloaming like an ill-protected candle about to be snuffed out by the wrath of the gathering storm. An equine salt-tang scent hung heavily enough in the air, Han noted with a dry satisfaction as he approached, to rust any amount of iron contained in the monstrosity the Fairy Prince was ineptly brandishing.

"I don't know what you're fussing over," Jasper protested, as the Centaur eyed the bridle stonily. "It's not for you. But my people are safely inside the castle, and I must be prepared."

"Prepared for what it might do to you the moment you attempt to harness it?" The Centaur snorted his distaste. "You're chasing after the most volatile moon-summoned creature ever to walk this Realm, and you think you can subdue it with iron?"

The Prince shrugged uncertainly. "That's what the books say."

Han grimaced. "Clearly you're reading the wrong books. Join me, and you'll be ready after tonight to write your own—for the one you seek to tame may be your greatest ally if left wild."

Jasper stalled. "Or you may be recklessly romanticising, as is your wont. I must stay with my people, whatever dangers await."

Restlessness passed across the Centaur's brow, but he bowed in acquiescence. "And I will take my chances in the forest."

"The forest may as well be the lake, right now," Jasper returned, sharp with worry. "If anyone sees you, they'll mistake you. Or else, the night itself will rip you apart, if its pull on those in several minds is anything to go by. You're not limited to such perilous company as lingers out there, I hope you know," he added more quietly.

The Centaur's focus was caught on something wild and wilful gusting beyond the Prince's ken, weaving itself from the strands of discordant music strung from the Sea and the sky and the surf and yet, at those words, his attention grew fixed and firm upon his friend.

"I do," Han promised, as calm and stubborn as the Prince had ever seen him, all his tension dissipated into these moments, their truth coursing through him. "And it only might."

That same tantalising discord curled around other ears also. Racxen crouched beneath the barred windows of the castle, watching the jagged shadows of a Realm torn to pieces jitter like moths against the glass. He shivered in anticipatory sickness, lost in the shifting pattern coursed by the rain rippling in a grey sheen across the grassland threatening to turn the meadow to marsh. With the trail of hopefuls following him, he'd had no hope of tracking successfully. Yet.

He glanced across at Amber, knowing she out of all these companions shared what was straying through his mind. Frustration gnawed into him at the forced waiting, and yet all the time in the Realm could not hope to prepare him. Still, part of his soul yearned to be out in the sluicing rain, to feel its slick weight lend a second skin to his own and cloak him with its illusion this night. He needed to be out amongst so changeable a landscape after the stale monotony of being cooped in the castle.

And yet how could he speak against such things, in company offering him such vital protection? He needed it and was grateful, as much as he also needed the subtle play of dancing shadow, and the exploratory, curious lick of firelight to awaken his vision again for him to have any hope of tracking the one who would be unleashed amidst this storm.

Until Amber left for the Icefields he knew he would stay, for a tie more binding and ancient linked him to her; one he would surrender to more willingly and wildly than the voice urging him into the storm. The power and passion the night winds spoke of, building feverishly now, were nothing compared to what he and Amber had woven together. Whatever intoxication the night thrummed into his veins, hers would always whisper more deeply into his blood.

His heart tugged in his chest to see Amber waiting at the door, as though she were going to fling it open and risk her soul to ease his own.

"We can walk our own routes whilst sharing a path," she promised. "Instead of waiting, which could risk diminishing them both, perhaps we should start out, and interweave them as best we can. Whilst the road is destined to feel different beneath my feet and yours, that's what makes sharing it together such an experience," she murmured, her voice aglow with the potential of this strangest of nights. "Go on. Track what's tracking you."

Her heart glowed like a firefly, fierce and bright in the darkness, drenching his soul in a fierce, supported certainty.

Seeing in his eyes the thoughts written in the space between them, Amber kissed him softly, her lips wet with more than rain. "So I must to the wild wood, and you must to the wild waters." She grinned, just for now feeling lighter than the air, stronger than the storm. Steadier than any chasm they might have to cross.

"And if the search for it takes you to the Icefields, I will be the fire that warms you when you return," Racxen promised in a warm, soulful whisper. Amidst the storm, an unconquerable calm bloomed within him and he grinned, awed, his gaze tangling with Amber's as his claws intertwined with her fingers and their breath intermingled softly. Warmth curled around his heart. How he felt about the Kelpie was not dissimilar to how he felt about her; lured outside his own experience into another's to find something even greater together, pulled away from all certainty and yet rendered surer, bolder, happier than ever. "Because you are my wings."

Amber grinned back, her eyes and heart dancing with a spirit the storm could batter, but never break. "And you are my roots."

Racxen's eyes glowed with spilled moonlight as Amber jarred the door open and together they ducked into the sizzling rain.

Her heart afire amidst the blurring night, Amber let a slow smile bloom across her face as Racxen tucked his voice into her ear so only she could hear it and she allowed herself to linger at the contact, hidden as they were by the sluicing deluge.

"My shadow lies with yours 'til next we meet," he promised, his hands absorbing the contours of her body as they pressed together in embrace. "When I return, it will be to you. There's only one whose embrace I'd willingly drown in."

Another kiss, as cleansing and restorative as the rain and then he was gone, pressing through the night. Watching him go with a hope-calmed heart helped her own path settle firmer beneath her feet even as the Realm turned to mud and threatened to fall away.

The night rang with wild music as Racxen loosened his strides and ran with the shadows beneath the trees, following the twisting coil of silver thread cast by the moon through lichen-laced eaves before diving into a potent darkness as dense and deep as the lake itself. Here, amidst an ancient, pulsing darkness, his senses settled and expanded.

Thunder broke with a shuddering growl across the uncharted landscape, unable to dissipate the tension that clung in the air like a headache. Magic crackled across the waterlogged ground like fire atop spilt oil.

A stagnant, queasy scent pooled in the air, bleeding through the clean night from all directions. Racxen slowed in response, cold inevitability sinking into his stomach. It took a presence other than the Kelpie's to infect the Realm like this.

Sure enough, the furtive figures of three Goblins slunk in from the edge of vision, their eyes glinting like treacherous lanterns, approaching in hunting formation.

And if they were tracking the Kelpie, how could it be right that he was too?

"Yer never did tell me that what I did was wrong," a sickeningly recognisable Goblin mocked, closing the gap between them heart-stoppingly fast. "I doubt yer will now. Yer never were good at voicing such things. It was our King's favourite thing about yer."

"I have the words for it, now," Racxen warned. The fire that billowed in his blood insulated him from the chill insinuations of any stalking spectre. "And I've learned the words against it."

Opening his soul and his throat, Racxen summoned a wordless, haunting call.

Derision died on the Goblin's tongue as an eldritch, echoing cry returned from the Kelpie.

"I no longer need to put it into language to have it believed or healed," the Arraheng warned. "Neither do I fear any who lend me strength against you. I would lay my heart beneath the trampling hooves of the one I've summoned before I would chain it to die in your diminished, frightened world."

He thought he glimpsed real terror in the eyes of the Goblin as she considered his words. Racxen had no idea whether his cry had even been heard but, rid of any fear the Goblins could feast upon, he strode on unmolested.

The benevolent gaze of the moon replaced the glares prickling at his neck, and Racxen could breathe again. The earth coiled, tense and alert beneath his feet as he crept forward; the moon's gaze the only steadying influence amidst a darkness restless with possibilities. The night quivered, so alive that he could barely focus. How could he track the Kelpie through such a swamp of sensations? It was as though he had lost the ability to screen and discriminate between stimuli: the entire sensory experience threatened to overwhelm him. Perhaps these very moments were being conjured by the Kelpie as a smokescreen so he might pass through undetected.

Racxen slowed his pace, steady as a soothing heartbeat. Amidst a night of monsters, he would ensure the Kelpie had nothing to fear from his approach. It felt as though the mere possibility of the creature's presence had awakened a thrumming impatience throughout lake and land, unseating all certainty and upon unravelling every thread of the Realm's fabric—yet both Goblins and Oak Prince had reckoned without the intervention of this tracker. Racxen didn't drown in such sensations as this night spilled. He drank from them. Drenched and decided, the Arraheng stole away, at one with the forest. Was there any better way to court company with the Kelpie?

Of Stone and Shadow

Slipping away unseen from the chaos and cacophony, Amber ran with relish across the familiar open swathes of the meadows and away to wilder spaces yet. The unease planted by the Oak Prince had burrowed deep, yet with Racxen unreachable tonight there was someone else she desperately needed to see. So, she turned away from the lights of home and followed the warmth in her heart awhile, her journey easing the conflict of feelings railing behind her ribs.

The night expanded comfortingly as the companionable noises once drowned by the night's discord unfurled themselves around her, and her soul leapt with her footsteps in response to the harshening terrain for she knew she was getting close.

Amber took her bearings with shining eyes. Some denounced this corner of the Realm as bleak; this wind-wuthered ridge of both boundary and beckoning, where the wilderness spilled itself upon the meadows and mingled its strangeness with all that felt familiar—but it rang with her soul-call as much as with the imprint of the one she sought, and she clambered across the jutting teeth of scattered rocks amidst the tangled traces of weeds and wildflowers with a glad heart despite the austere severity of the rock-strewn landscape.

As Amber wandered now towards the curls of shadow spilling from the hill-hewn cave, her gaze drank in the yielding depths within. This time, she didn't worry about waiting for her vision to adjust to the darkness as she ducked inside, relishing instead the anticipatory knowledge of what the brief disorientation would melt into.

Her jaw fell slowly in appreciation as the blurring swathes of colour conjured by her shifting vision dispersed to reveal glistening pillars of layered flowstone towering away into the high darkness. She followed eagerly the dripping calcite fingers beckoning her deeper through the twisting tunnel, into a cavern gleaming with the fireside hues of dripstone drapery spilling like candlewax from the gnarled ceiling. Tiptoeing past milky stalagmites rising from the stillest of waters shimmering like a pool of melted copper in the gloaming, she could taste a familiar presence in the air. A cold, clean tang that combined eternity with vitality: Rraarl. Somewhere, amidst these swimming shadows, waited solid stone. She could feel the Gargoyle's attention shifting towards her; a tangible gaze both penetrating and reassuring, which kindled a warmth within her to defend against the chill smotherings that had clutched around her heart since the Oak Prince's invidious attentions. Here, in contrast, only the one she wished to find her knew of her coming, and she smiled in the secret-sharing darkness to know that even as she sensed him he, far more greatly attuned, must have been aware of her proximity from the moment she had strayed into his domain. And would have felt her living heat like a beacon even in pitchest black.

As though in answer, as her eyes adjusted to the gloom, Amber could discern the imposing silhouette of the Gargoyle crouched motionless in waiting, his hulking dark outline impressive against the flowing milky calcite. Amber made a mental note to maybe not bring Ruby down here.

He held still, as though loath to startle her. Like he ever could; as panicked as she had been by demons in both the distant and recent past, little made her feel safer than being in the presence of this man some called a monster.

I'D HOPED I COULD PUT ENOUGH DISTANCE BETWEEN MYSELF AND THE KELPIE HERE, the Gargoyle explained, in words she could just pick out in the dimness of the cavern. I HAVEN'T HEARD HORSES LIKE THAT SINCE THE WAR. BUT EVEN FROM THE LAKE, ITS HOOVES ECHO IN MY MIND AS WELL AS ACROSS THE MOUNTAINS. I DO NOT KNOW WHETHER IT IS ITS PROXIMITY OR THE LONELINESS WE INHABIT TOGETHER THAT HAUNTS ME MORE.

His ember eyes gleamed as that obsidian gaze fixed on her, as fierce and comforting as she remembered. His gaze stoked a warming fire within her as his ravaged face twisted into its familiar grimacing smile as he beheld her. YET SUCH FEARS FADE IN CERTAIN COMPANY, his fingers traced softly.

Amber grinned in return, a rush of memories flooding over her. "Well, you give me a reason to keep searching the shadows."

She crouched beside him companionably, the better to see his words. "Speaking of which, I've got myself tangled up in something. I've been warned against the 'Shadow-Armed Witness'. Does the name mean anything to you?"

Rraarl shook his head slowly, although she noted the muscles in his jaw bunch before he replied.

IT PAINS ME TO NOT KNOW HOW TO PROTECT YOU FROM THIS. YET MY IGNORANCE MEANS LITTLE—IT WAS A LONG TIME AFTER THE SEA BATTLE BEFORE I DARED AGAIN CONCERN MYSELF WITH THE LIVING, the Gargoyle admitted.

PERHAPS YOU SHOULD SEEK AUDIENCE, WHILE THE EYE OF THE REALM IS OTHERWISE TURNED, Rraarl contemplated. A WITNESS NEED NOT BE AN AGRESSOR. PERHAPS THEY ARE A SURVIVOR. A SUPPORTER.

As she had so many times before, Amber suddenly felt over-awed to be a trusted part of Rraarl's world. "No-one could teach me that better than you," she promised softly.

The Gargoyle grinned his sharp-toothed grin. DO NOT DOUBT YOURSELF, AMBER. THE SMALLEST LIGHT IS STRONGER THAN THE MOST SOLID OF SHADOWS. SHE CAN TRANSFORM THEM OR SEND THEM FLEEING AS SHE SEES FIT.

Amber stared at him, rendered speechless and safe to know that was the way he saw her, despite all the times he'd seen her terrified and vulnerable.

She wished she knew what to say in that moment to thank him as deeply as he deserved, but she knew she could serve him best by acting as she should. So, her mind made up she shrugged contentedly, confidence blooming with the flames of hope his words kindled. "Mayhap I shouldn't let his words frighten me. After all, how can I fear the shadows, when I found you amongst them?"

Those lava-amidst-obsidian eyes held her safe, stretching the moment as long as she needed. BUT THERE IS SOMETHING ELSE HURTING YOU. SOMETHING I WOULD HAVE YOU UNBURDENED FROM. WHICH I WILL HELP YOU WITH, IF I CAN. Those fierce eyes held no judgement; his words left her no question to answer.

Rraarl's hand hovered carefully over the ground, holding the silence as only a Gargoyle could. I HAD ONCE THOUGHT THAT NO WORDS COULD ENCOMPASS ALL I HAD LIVED THROUGH, he traced finally across the moon-splashed ground. BUT YOU MADE ME REALISE THAT TO THE RIGHT EAR, NO MEMORY IS UNVOICEABLE. THAT THE WORDS I ALREADY HAD WERE ENOUGH. I WILL LISTEN TO YOURS, he promised, WHENEVER YOU CHOOSE. AND UNTIL THEN, I WILL WAIT. WITHOUT EXPECTATION, WITHOUT PRESSURE, AND WITHOUT NEGLECT.

Met with such acceptance, Amber felt the chain of the unsaid loosen, and she knew that in the presence of her Gargoyle friend she could allow it to fall.

SPEAK WHAT HAPPENED, Rraarl reminded. I DON'T WANT THE WORDS HE'S TRIED TO FORCE INTO YOUR MOUTH. I WANT THE ONES YOU'VE CREATED, THAT SPILL FREELY FROM YOUR SOUL. I WILL HOLD WHAT THEY CONTAIN. I WON'T QUESTION WHAT THEY'VE COME FROM. AND I WILL TRUST THEIR TRUTH.

So, she leaned gratefully against his shoulder, yielded to his safety and voiced the unspeakable, the chill stone of his touch easing the feverish pain of her thoughts as she told him of the Oak Prince and his harassment, of the Goblins and their assault on Ruby.

"I hate what's been done to her," she whispered brokenly afterwards, the words themselves making her sick. "I hate what this world can contain."

YOU ARE ALLOWED TO BE ANGRY, the Gargoyle reminded, his ember eyes honest and ablaze, and yet also keeping their fire in containment.

"Here, maybe," Amber acknowledged, her grateful grin honest. "Out there, I'm not so sure."

THE WHAIL CAN BEAR YOUR SORROW, Rraarl promised. AND I CAN HOLD YOUR ANGER.

Crouched next to him, Amber began to feel like maybe she could hold her own. After all, Rraarl had taken all his anger—there was no shying from it—and metamorphosed it into something transformative instead of transgressive.

She grinned appreciatively. "I can see why they warned me you were dangerous," she chuckled wryly. "You make it easy to make decisions they convince me should be hard. I will go to the Shadow-Armed Witness. I can no longer hide my transgressions, or my intentions, from the Oak Prince."

The Gargoyle's eyes flared in recognition. WE WILL ALL HELP YOU SURVIVE THIS, he promised.

"You already have." Rock solid against the fickle clamour consuming the Realm in the Kelpie's wake, he had not only anchored her safely against the swarming dark, he had given her a reason to brave the madness once again.

The stalwart silhouette of the castle rose through the darkness as though braced against the night's hysteria. Solid proof of what she had returned to, Amber let it chase her fears away for now and took refuge gratefully behind the heavy oak door that groaned at her late entrance like a chastising parent ushering their wayward offspring back to safety.

Padding along the soft-candled veins of corridors she knew well enough to walk in her sleep, she found Jasper at his now customary place at the banqueting table, folded apologetically at one end of the ingot of gnarled, age-smoothed oak, as though embarrassed to be using such an archetypal piece for less than formal means.

Black locks flopped forward over a stern, haunted brow as he hunched in concentration over a hulking, cloth-bound tome; she dreaded to think how many others he'd scoured in vain at such an hour. Hers was not the only quest tightening a stranglehold on its participants, she reminded herself, chagrined, as she beheld him.

She unhooked a lantern from the wall to indicate her presence without intruding, and approached slowly in case the same flighty vigilance that had wound itself around her heart since the Kelpie's emergence had begun to seize in Jasper's chest also.

"I'm glad I found you," she offered him in reassurance, as defensive excuses flickered warily in his eyes. "I don't think anyone else can answer this question."

"And you think you come to the right scholar?" A brow rose archly, but his eyes told her of his gratitude.

"Well, you'd claim to be too busy to stop if I merely asked how you were. But I can always appeal to your arrogance," she retorted with a grin.

Snorting acquiescent laughter, Jasper sighed and pushed his book aside in resigned invitation. Meeting her gaze in the ebb and flow of the candlelight, he grew conscious of just how relieved he was to see her, of how thankful he was that she always seemed to see through his unfounded, instinctive avoidance. "I have locked myself away with this too long," he murmured. "What are you here to ask?"

"What do you know of the Goblins, since the fall of Thanatos?" Amber began, setting her lamp down and sitting beside Jasper, starting on safer grounds than the Oak Prince.

"As unsettling as their presence is, they have broken no laws, so there is little I can tell you," Jasper admitted. "I have to assume they have broken no word of your deeds to the Oak Prince."

It was Amber's turn to nod in gratitude, assimilating this new information amongst what she knew she had yet still to learn. Outside, the storm railed and rattled, fighting to intrude upon this fragile peace within.

"Then it is as good a time as any to do what I must." She couldn't avoid the abruptness, the fear, leaking into her voice.

The Prince raised a wary brow. "The Icefields? Now? I approve. It's probably safer than staying here."

"Not the Icefields, yet." Amber's gaze sought refuge in the horizon, but she brushed glances with him, knowing that despite his verbal fencing he would consider her veiled request as gravely as any high-council proposition.

"I need to return to the forest." She grimaced. "Rraarl thinks that's where the Shadow Armed Witness is."

Jasper held very still. "And you think the night when the whole Realm has gone mad is the time to do it? The time to walk into the very heart of the Oak Prince's territory and steal what he most desires even as he seeks it himself?"

"He won't be after it tonight; he'll be focussed on the Kelpie," Amber mumbled defensively. It had sounded a much more sensible idea in her head before she'd spoken it. "I have to try, Jasper. At least one piece has to be hidden in the forest, doesn't it? Every time I enter the woods, that accursed wight hounds me—so I cannot very well avoid the forest now in fear of the Kelpie if it's my best chance of avoiding the Oak Prince. Just, once I've been in the forest, I'm sure he'll know. I can't lead him back here. I'll have to just keep going until I find all the pieces—or he finds me first."

Jasper's glass-green eyes met hers. "And no-one here can know. I'll attend to it, Amber, with all due diligence," he promised, leaving much unsaid.

She couldn't tell him how grateful she was, so she squeezed his shoulder in thanks. "I'll try to come back safely."

The Prince sighed, worry etched deep into the lines of his face. "And I'll try to keep silent about it until you do."

Into the Wildwood Labyrinth

"I know you want to go straight to the Icefields, but it does make sense to find the forest piece first, before the Oak Prince's grip tightens beyond all hope," Jasper had suggested, heaving open the castle door bodily and speaking not a word of reprimand as the light spilling out swept restoratively over Amber and ushered her in from yet another too-late night. She'd had a suspicion that the Prince was in his own way trying to keep her out of the way of danger from the Kelpie, now that the Moon Lake Kelpie had breached its banks, and she had to acknowledge a sense of misgiving at heading abroad with the Realm in such turmoil—but as Jasper was possibly the last person in the Realm the Kelpie would let near him, she decided she could afford to leave him and continue her quest for the pelt.

Plus, she had to admit his advice made sense. Now that the Oak Prince knew of her intentions, he must have gathered at least some of the remaining pieces close to him. Her previous venture into the forest had come to nothing after her encounter with him, and she could no longer afford to wait. There was no denying the creeping expansion of the apparition's ever-deepening shadow, bleeding in from the outskirts of the woodland—she would have to reach the very centre of the forest this time, in the hope that any pelt piece had avoided his poison.

She needed to return to a place of another time, a place of ancient eaves and lengthening shadows—a time when light and dark and air and earth were closer met.

To the heart of the forest, where the trees were rumoured to be sentient still and where surely the soul of the forest held true. To the Wildwood Labyrinth: whence the Oak Prince had emerged—and where the Shadow-Armed Witness held sway.

Amber packed her haversack with practised ease, threw on her cloak and, with the sun encouragingly at her back, set out in high spirits. Skirting the sprawling marshland of Arraterr as they lay in glistening welcome, as dear to her as the brightest fields of Fairymead, she continued across the grasslands, her heart as open and at peace as the landscape, until she came to the feather-curve of trees brushing the edge of the forest.

Amber breathed carefully. It had been beneath these eaves that the Oak Prince had descended like choking smog, forcing his poison into her ears. But Han had been right: she didn't have to let it into her soul. She had a sudden vision of the Centaur reaching the Dryad network as he'd intended, whispering hope-surging words into brittle, long-resigned arboreal minds. If she could hold her nerve and reach the primeval heart within the forest, she had every hope of finding something wilder and more ancient than the Oak Prince. Somewhere he could claim no dominion over—and somewhere likelier than any to hide a pelt piece, for perhaps the Dryad network Han spoke of had swept it safe and sacred into the untamed tanglewood of the Wildwood Labyrinth where the sentient tree spirits could keep watch over it.

Amber considered cautiously. She couldn't just expect the forest to trust her, seeing as how the Oak Prince was the last to come after the pelt. The Dryads could shift at will and answered to none. There could be no guarantee that the way they revealed, if any, would be a safe one, but she'd rather trust their eldritch guidance a hundredfold than leave herself to the mercy of the Oak Prince's putrid whispers.

And so she ducked without fear into the sylvan verdure. It would be a long journey, but she basked in the inimitable patience of the ancient forest. Grass damp with morning dew pillowed the mist-touched ground. Sprouting fungi bunched around myriad gnarled trunks, like gesturing hands signalling the way. As if in encouragement, the leaves shivered deliciously in the breeze.

Amber grinned, unafraid. If she remembered correctly, the last time she'd got this lost it had turned out rather well.

For a long time, it was just her and the sound of her own footsteps padding as steadily and—given the lushness of the undergrowth—as softly as a calm heartbeat. Tiny forest noises reassured her, passing her like snatches of overheard conversation between old friends. The smell of lichen sank as deeply into her lungs as her feet did into the yielding moss. Tasting the damp earth on her tongue and feeling the cool shadows brush her skin, she journeyed as though wrapped in peace.

But uncertain hours later, that sense of safety slipped away like so much mud through her fingers as the canopy closed in above her with sluicing rain. Amber eyed with dread the heavy swathes of branches stabbing down from the sky as the Realm was shaken by gale-force gusts. She thought quickly. Infernal influences might be seizing hold, but beneath ancient boughs was no place to be in a storm, regardless of its beginnings. Orienting herself as best as she could, she pushed on towards what she hoped would be the edge of the forest. The false night of the storm fell swiftly, riding the drowning wave of knowledge that real darkness wasn't many hours away.

She gritted her teeth. The choice to come here had been hers. The responsibility to keep going certainly was. But the forest kept getting more and more impenetrable, whichever way she turned. She pushed onwards resolutely, her Realm shifting into a dense tangle of darkling wood, stripping her of all certainty of direction.

The hatching branches, crossed like interlacing fingers around her, blocked out the storm until the silence grew sinister. Amber took a steadying breath. She didn't have to get through unintimidated—she just had to get through.

I am in control of my choices. I fear no path, Amber reminded herself as she walked on, purposely draping her fear like a cobweb from the furthest tree and leaving it far behind her as she crept between unnaturally angled branches jointed like broken bones from wizened trunks. *I have water. I have food. I can make shelter. And I've navigated through darkness before.* Her mind curled, unsatisfied and unsteady, but her soul insisted. Amidst the deathly quiet, as the density of the canopy began to block out what little light there was left Amber sensed the forest restructuring itself around her for new purpose. She padded through silently, as cautious as a stalked animal.

The air clung with pungency: decay and something crawling out of decay, audacious and shocking. She crept forwards, overwhelmed. While this section of forest, thrumming with energy and teeming with life, felt eye-wateringly fertile, the very fecundity of the land seemed to belie a waiting menace. Beneath these eaves, dense enough that Amber couldn't help but imagine the tree limbs locking themselves together should they want to trap her, she could die hidden amongst a travesty of plenty and be greedily swallowed up to sate the vegetation's endless hunger. Even after her death, she imagined, the forest would not stop until a more primal and absolute victory had been gleaned, for she had encountered no other ecosystem waiting so readily to take such an active role in dismemberment and re-absorption. Fungi dripped from branches as dark and moist as decay; beetles crouched poised and as polished as death's heads to perform their post mortem service; twisted roots protruded above the ground in readiness, thirsty for what would remain of her body were she to succumb. Life slunk unseen and watchful all around her—nestled predatory and restless amongst the groves of ferns and saprophagous foliage, its richness as undeniable as the perverseness of its origins.

And yet she realised, with a sudden rush, that she was walking through it untouched. The sensation left her tingling with a sense of the numinous. She found herself feeling as though she were accompanied— escorted, rather than stalked. The forest was fearsome, but she need not be fearful. So much life was being sustained. She found herself thinking that if she were to die here, she would be returned to a kind of life faster than anywhere else in the Realm. And perhaps she would continue to sustain the life that supported her friends. It removed some of her fear, and she walked on unweighted.

She was approaching the nucleus of the deep forest, now. She could feel it. The muted roar of wind billowing through long-leafed limbs rushed like the sound of the distant ocean, the sway of the branches all around rocking her like the swell of the sea. Yet the vegetation pressed less intrusively here. Space drifted where once had fallen shadows, letting light glimpse in like a secret. Finally, the trees formed a clearing. Around one huge, draping arboreal presence.

Amber gasped. The shadow-armed witness. It had to be. For the solitary tree, if mere tree it could be called with its trunk clothed in shining, skin-like bark, the endless snaking grooves more complex than her own fingerprints, depicting a roadmap of a journey Amber wasn't sure it was within her power to navigate through a time she could no longer be sure still existed, rose in stoic splendour from the fecund earth. It drew the eye like a vortex; its finger-like branches reaching searchingly from canopy heights down to form aerial roots that dipped into the soft earth beneath, its clouds of drifting leaves forming a strange twilight territory in between.

Perhaps, everything should have smacked of danger. Instead, it put Amber in mind of the Fairy Ring, and she stole towards the tangle of branches trailing like the ancient limbs of a multi-legged, majestic monstrosity, draped in stately slumber.

Reluctant to enter the bough-shadowed ground for fear she would be transgressing some atavistic boundary—or else trespassing into a hunter's territory in a manner akin to straying between venomous tentacles – Amber inched forwards, scalp prickling as leaves brushed her head, like fingernails trailing through her hair from above. On her quickened breath she tasted moist earth churned by the probing of burrowing roots, and turned-over leaf mould that could have been fermenting for years. The air smelled of shadow, and something that maybe shouldn't be disturbed. She was reluctant to acknowledge the fevered worry that there could be more than vegetation rotting beneath the layers she was now disturbing.

And yet now she was through, unmolested. She almost gasped in relief at the cooling shade. A pounding in her head eased. She could breathe again. In here, it smelled of moss, and stillness. Of eternity and patience. The air held still, and rich, as if full of silent voices. This was a place of germination, of gestation. Surely the Oak Prince hadn't yet tainted it.

Tiny noises bubbled around her, like lung sections crackling and popping and breathing themselves back to life. Branches rearranged themselves around her like limbering hands, creaking as they unfurled for the first in a long, cramped time, amidst the rustle and ripple of aged leaves splaying to taste the air for residual messages.

Amber froze at the sound of a cracking twig outside, another Realm away that threatened to splinter her own.

Another crack. Another.

Bile rose as she glimpsed between the sheltering leaves the Oak Prince, snapping twig after twig as though he were breaking fingers.

And she was trapped inside—but, worse, what if she had trapped a Dryad with her?

Could she really be alone here, when her surroundings felt so sentient?

"Hello?" Amber whispered, barely louder than a thought and twice as pleading. "Please. I need your help."

The silence laughed back at her. What had she expected, that the tree would answer? She chewed her cheek to hide her annoyance at herself. Time to think up another plan.

Crack. Crack.

The ground shook as though the entire forest were disassembling and remaking itself around her.

Branches reached out to her, and stories of people being enveloped by sorcery-ridden trees and trapped inside for all eternity skittered against her mind, her thoughts clamouring to distance themselves from her and escape, but something bade her stand her ground. As the tips of the branches neared, close enough to skewer her should they chose, Amber realised they were trembling, and she stood perfectly still in an attempt to ease their nerves. No longer fearful, she smiled as the leaves quivered over her, building a picture of the Fairy and taking her measure in a fervent, paper-soft reading Amber wished she could interpret.

Twigs tapped across every part of her skin, like the feet of dartwings, and finger-like branches clutched, disbelieving and urgent, towards her as a grandmother stumbling across the desert reaches out towards a child the wheeling vultures have not yet seen, in an effort to save another when she fears her own time is already near ending.

A frantic rustle of leaves shushed her into silence, and Amber held her breath, held in the sheltering arms of the Dryad, as the Oak Prince stalked closer.

"Give up the child, hag." The Oak Prince's command slapped like a branch across her face, but at his burr-scratched voice, the wizened branches curled protectively round Amber like the long-neglected fingernails of an old woman. "I seek a penance for her transgression. By way of a challenge."

In her ancient cocoon, Amber laid a hand aside the gnarled trunk, the bark as papery and fragile as aged skin. "I thank you for the kindness you have shown me. I have no wish for you to endanger yourself on my account." Her voice sounded dry and airless, as though it could barely pierce through such claustrophobic terror, but Amber had to complete the words that fear had earlier closed off. "His fight is with me, for I seek to reunite an ill man with his skin, and the Oak Prince has thrown the pieces to the wind."

An incensed hiss had taken hold of the Dryad at the mention of the Oak Prince, but at Amber's reference to the pelt, her leaves rustled secretively, an excited shiver running through enlivened branches. With the creaking of old bones, a knot in the trunk widened into a fissure from which slid forth a gleaming pile of pelt, slipping to the ground like a glistening newborn.

"Thank you," Amber whispered, overawed, gathering up the swatch of fur. It was a whole armful, drowsing against her chest like a sleepy seal pup. She slipped it around her shoulders gently, in the hope that it would feel well balanced and securely carried.

She turned to the Dryad, hope rising. "I will accept his challenge, if not his penance," Amber promised, murmuring into dry leaves that smelled of crumbling age and yet the scent of something warm and nourishing. She barely dared breathe the words for fear of how close she now felt the Oak Prince. "I will not allow him to blanch these forests of your kind, but I must ask you to relinquish me, before you are drawn into a fight that need not be yours."

The Dryad stilled at her words, and the blustering of the Oak Prince penetrated Amber's haven for a moment.

"The balance must be restored," he was railing. "None can be allowed to live in both Realms; the old ways would crumble to dust. The Selkies cannot be permitted to share both land and sea, the Kelpie cannot be seen to listen to a creature of the swamp—and that abomination you shelter from me, old wretch, has destabilised the order more than any. She throws away her only connection to the source, and purports to find it under a hundred different guises! But I have been here since the Age of Ages began and I will not see magic diluted thus."

His disgust dripped like rain through the leaves, but Amber let it roll from her instead of absorb into her. "I do not flee for my own sake," she whispered urgently to the Dryad. "Yet I must complete this pelt, ere he learns I have all the pieces. You hear why I must go, when you hear how he rants."

A whistle of air like an indrawn breath whooshed around Amber, branches cracking and snapping and leaves whipping in their haste as at the Dryad's rustled command the forest reformed before Amber's eyes into an arboreal stairwell reaching towards a cloud-flung azure sky untouched by the tension below.

"Hasten, young one," the Dryad wheezed. "My strength is not what it was, and the Oak Prince has the vigour of a sapling. But I will not leave him time to follow you."

Taking the branches at as close to a running climb as she could manage, the moment Amber started scrambling skyward through the Dryad's branches, more stretched before her, snatching themselves away from her heels at the exact moment her weight was no longer upon them, their movements expertly and swiftly replicated rippingly by each further bough in turn. The speed dizzied her, the altitude taunting her with the achievement of an elevation never again reached since that fateful night between the boulders when she had lost all chance of flight forever.

And yet the heights spun past her now as dizzyingly as they had once, and the recognition gasped like fire in her chest and thrummed in her veins as she fled through the treetops, for she was in charge of her path and her body and she was part of this great well of magic and wonder that let her fly through the Realm even now. Her own energy propelled her onwards and the hands of Dryads thrust her further, the sky blooming ever on until branch-spread hands bent towards the ground once more to soften her descent—

Skidding breathlessly, Amber kissed her hands and ran fingers upstretched to thank as many Dryads as she could reach as they laughingly rustled their acknowledgment and creakingly stretched tall again as though they had never moved from a single position.

She dared not stop but behind her, Amber thought she heard a contented sigh on the breeze that ruffled brittle leaves with new life, and she blew a kiss back on the wind for the oldest, original Dryad.

"The balance will be restored at your expense!" roared the voice of ages behind her through the victorious trees. "Your doom awaits at—!"

But bustling leaves shushed the threat, and it faded from her mind as, safely alone once more, Amber slowed her flat-out pace, blew on her hands still stinging and smarting from the bark-burn, and unwound the largest pelt piece she had found from about her shoulders.

Her blood chilled to behold the steaming offering in her hands. As proud and as grateful as she was, cold sweat broke on her brow as her gaze fell upon her now pitiful-seeming boon, bought as it had been at a price that would make a Goblin rub his hands with glee. The piece the Dryad had nursed so carefully, and for which she had incurred the wrath of the most fickle, treacherous enemy she had yet encountered: the very trickster the Goblins themselves seeking to ally themselves with and supplicate themselves before, might be the biggest she'd yet found—but it was too small to complete the pelt. She had no option but to keep searching. There had to be at least one more piece remaining out there.

As she formed the thought, a cold dread sank upon her like the murk of chilling fog that had descended with the Oak Prince's presence. And yet, as she stepped forwards with purpose, both lifted, and she couldn't help but notice how all their boughs were stretched towards the North.

The Unquenching Well

"But there's nowhere else to try, Jasper. It has to be the Icefields."

On the pretext of examining the book in front of her, Jasper sat down quietly next to Amber. "I know," he conceded, his eyes flicking from the tome to brush her exhausted gaze, gathering her unspoken anxieties safely into his own eyes. "And I know you'll have the Song Weaver to help you, but with your quest looking likely to take you places we cannot reach you no matter how savagely we may wish to before the end, I just wanted to be sure you have enough to come back for. You do know you'll always have us, for what it's worth?"

Amber smiled, overwhelmed and relieved. "It's worth everything. And I'll do my best to remember."

The Prince smiled his most serious smile. "I'll do my best to remind you."

"I have reminders of my own for you, child." The Nymph swept through the castle hall like a Northern blizzard, but Amber couldn't help but feel warmed, although she half-glared at Jasper, who squeezed her shoulder warmly. "Well, it's not like I can call your mother on you."

"Your Prince is right to be wary, for the Icefields are not to be attempted until all other options have been exhausted," Zaralathaar began. "There are water bodies to search other than the lake and sea. A pelt piece may be revealed in any one of them, and I must caution: they each have their hazards. Yet you might try drawing from the Unquenching Well."

"Are you sure?" Jasper asked, turning to the Nymph. "Given whom you're asking this of?"

"Water is my element. I am rarely mistaken in relation to it," Zaralathaar reminded in chill rebuke. "Yet beware," the Nymph murmured into the chastened silence. "This well quenches some thirsts and awakens others."

Jasper shivered. "That does sound like the kind of thing we're looking for."

"Looking does not prove you are willing to find it," the Nymph warned. "Make yourselves as ready as you are able, for this is not a journey I can take with you. I'm not asking you to fly there, girl," the Nymph reminded with a touch of her usual crispness, as Amber balked slightly. "Yet let me provide my guidance; for though I cannot walk through this darkness with you, I would have you trust me to illuminate the path a little further with my knowledge, until you are ready to walk on undaunted alone."

Amber swallowed. "I don't think I'll ever be ready for that."

"Heavy fears, for someone who's brought a Selkie pelt back to the edge of life," the Nymph dismissed as though it were nonsense, her irreverence a sunbeam through the chill-damp fog of the Fairy's anxiety.

"Realms shift and realign all the time, Amber. This one will go on without me, and so shall you. You are discovering and awakening sides of yourself that have lain dormant; knit them into your soul and you will remain secure in yourself whatever comes. A patchwork skin enables you to shift into anything you need to be. It doesn't make you belong any less—quite the opposite, for you will always have a home, and a place. You have the gift of transformation; you are a child of all the elements, Amber—not just the one you were born into. And so, although you might not feel yourself ready, my child, you will find yourself more capable than you ever believed." A rare smile touched the Water Nymph's lips. "More so than I first believed, I grant you."

Amber's smile swelled to her lips in response. "Then I will grant you my best attempt, as I always have."

"A well that awakens thirst?" Jasper sputtered, as soon as Zaralathaar had exited. "No wonder people are convinced that magic is perverse." The Prince rubbed his stinging eyes tiredly and turned to Amber. "What do you want to do about this? Considering the Nymph hasn't even told us where it is."

Amber grinned, unperturbed. "Getting lost is the first step to finding something worthwhile, right?"

"The site must be there to be found," the Prince endorsed with a shrug. "Perhaps what you draw from it is up to you."

Amber grinned, hope blossoming. "Then I must follow if I can. For, even if it doesn't hold a pelt piece, the Well might still help revive Hydd. The scraps of fur are drying; I fear they could die. Perhaps if I could douse them in the Well…"

"You could not then avoid the waters touching you also," Jasper protested, his face clenched grim and pale.

"But I need something to return life to the pelt," she shushed. "Jasper, I'm not going to drink from it."

"What if you didn't need to drink from it? What if a touch was all it took? You really think you could restrain yourself?"

Amber grimaced, thinking. "I'm not sure I'd have to."

"Not sure you'd have to dip the pelt?" the Prince attempted to clarify, worriedly glimpsing the look in Amber's eyes. "Or not sure you'd have to stop yourself trying anything further?"

"I'm sure I preferred it when you were refusing to help," Amber grumbled pointedly, but she squeezed his shoulder in farewell as she slipped past him into the waiting night.

"I suppose one of us should try to check where this will lead," Jasper sighed to empty air, as begrudgingly proud as he was resigned. Dragging another tome from the shelf he began to pore through it, and was still reading when morning sunlight streamed.

With the pelt pieces bundled firmly into her haversack, Amber strode into deepening moss-drenched shadows beneath the bark-skin touch of ancient boughs, following with eager steps the course of a riverbank which bucked and plunged as energetically as any Centaur. Water had to lead to the well, right?

When it started to rain, she was not at all sure that it was a sign to turn back. Instead, she pressed through the ever-more verdant vegetation, heedfully now that the bank had begun to slope unevenly down, and inched along the piling mud, more to find some sort of sign than shelter. Before Amber's wishful eyes the lush ferns seemed to adopt the sweeping curves of seal-like flippers, and she chose to take that as an affirmation until, parting unidentifiable fronds after slithering increasingly mud-smeared along the wending curve of the riverside, Amber was rewarded with the sight of the well sliding into vision as smoothly as a seal breaking the surface to breathe.

Squinting against the driving rain, Amber crept forward reverently. The captive water swirled its secrets beguilingly, rich with algae and alluringly deep—but her heart plummeted to behold the sheer drop which guarded them, for the surface of the water shone so far below as to render the smoothness of the flanking well shaft as deadly a deterrent as any foul scheme the Oak Prince could have constructed.

A shiver of intrigue brushed Amber's spine. Why had the Selkies designed it thus?

She let the endless patterns of diffuse light scattering across the surface with the bouncing rain tickle at ideas. Maybe the well was the site of a transformation ritual, like a phocidaean version of the Presentation of the Gems. Perhaps here each Selkie donned their pelt for the first time, slipped beneath the skin of the water, and travelled an aqueous path unseen from the surface, which one had to trust to be there before the way would be revealed.

Amber chewed her lip. So it was with all metamorphoses—this particular format might be unfamiliar to her, but surely was no more fearful than risking a fall when you first chanced trusting your wings and your self. It commanded no less respect, and could summon no greater horror.

All further thought drained away like fading hope as the woods grew dark and still and dangerous behind her, the presence of the Oak Prince gathering like a sickness in the trees. Storm clouds pressed intrusively overhead, looming like voyeuristic ghosts to witness her victimhood.

"What is it to be?" Fetid words dripped wickedly, snagging on the undergrowth. "Save yourself—or save the skin?"

The well winked and shushed behind her, with the furtive light of a hope that could remain both concealed and clung to a little longer.

Amber's thoughts flickered as she shuffled towards the concealed rim of the well, stumbling towards it as though to merely distance herself from the voice. She'd prove the Oak Prince wrong, she risked promising, taking in the anxiously waiting depths rippling beneath as her heels scuffed the curving stone. She hadn't thrown away her only connection to the source. She just wasn't confined to one any longer.

As she clutched the pelt protectively to her chest, it felt heavier now—not a drowning weight, but more a muscular potential. It shivered with the buoyant salt-smell of the live sea; all open waves and tumbling surf. She tensed like a seal before a dive. She wouldn't surrender the skin to the Oak Prince. But could it find its way home if the wight seized her?

Time to find out. The lurch as she plummeted was slapped away by the sting of the surface, and she was sinking already, engulfed by the hungry, urgent chill of the water. Gulping a lungful of air, Amber plunged her head back down and thrust through the membrane of the surface, powering deeper and deeper, towards where the shadows and sunlight danced indecipherably far below, twisting into a tunnel that promised escape.

But she couldn't dive far enough. She couldn't reach the urgent allure of the rift gaping beneath. Her connection was lost, after all. The way was shut to her. Again she tried as the water squeezed at her chest and pressed into her eyes while she tugged her limbs through the swirls of salt. She might have become a better swimmer these seasons past, but the claustrophobia of failure began to strangle that away. She felt the sapping shadow of the Oak Prince's presence dragging against her back, and dared not look back lest he see her fear.

Bearing witness to her efforts far above the pelt floated, flapping in agitation on the surface, a sacrificial mother refusing to dive while her newborn remained in danger.

Laughter echoed from the bank. "That carcass will not save you, Fairy. I will claim two skins for my own before dawn breaks."

Amber shut her eyes in horror. To come this far, only to die flailing in the shallows—

Yet, as her conviction trembled, crushed beneath the iron squeeze of her lungs, the pelt rippled as though alive beside her, buoyant and bubbling with oxygen.

This is for you, Hydd, Amber vowed, and as she pulled the headpiece over her face the flippers and sides curled protectively around her, gifting her their strength and speed even as the muzzle offered its breath.

Her lungs swelled as never before and Amber felt the pure sweet stream of oxygen thrumming through this new-borrowed body, at once more ancient and—she feared—more alive than her own.

The remainder of the swim flashed by as she thrilled through the water tunnel in a blur, her soul attuning itself to a new, pulsing language of swell and pull, of green and blue, of depth and eternity; previously undreamt sights glowed afire through the gaze of another who saw the Realm more wondrously than she and from whom she pledged to learn to adjust her own view.

Gleaming memories would return later, skipping fleetingly through her mind like silvering fish jumping atop a sunlit ocean, but all at once and too soon the womb-warm water was gone. Amber's webbed hands now grappled fearfully through a savage, storm-seized sea of incomprehensible depth and dominance. The fur around her locked in her breath and buoyancy, blocking out terror for now, and yet she must make for the far, jagged shore, where the pelt could no longer protect her.

The winds above screamed like cautioning Harpies, but she had no choice. As she broke the membrane of the surface and sloughed herself upon the rasping shore, the precious droplets of another Realm leached from Amber as she peeled off a skin that was never hers and never would be again, and she shivered and shivered and shivered, bereft less from the cold and more from the feeling that she might have peeled away something of herself too, so vulnerable and confused did she feel with just the vestiges of those strange, familiar memories jostling with her own now that she sprawled as if birthed onto the savage, scouring sands.

The cold seeped into her, pulling heat and thought irreparably out of her, until she didn't have to bother with either worries or warmth. And yet, memories skittered about her like sprites, refusing to leave, refusing to let her lie. Was this what she had been doing with her quests, Amber wondered disjointedly. Crowding in memories, so that they could stitch her together when reality threatened to pull her apart?

With a last effort, Amber drew the pelt around her like a cocoon, and collapsed into sleep.

By Night and By Sea

The gaping vistas of her surroundings ignited a hallucinatory night, dreams squirming and shifting before seeping reality could intrude too harshly, until Amber found herself standing atop a screaming cliff edge, poised to leap.

Ice slivers dug anxious fingers towards her heart as her faith let slip its grasp and her reason began to dissipate. The flight would be intoxicating, certainly—but what about the fall?

"What makes you so sure that the fall is inevitable?" retaliated the Water Nymph, incongruously and unarguably here for real now. The surrounding ice glistened like a second skin as Zaralaathar stood before the Fairy, every inch as at home here as in the sea she had once walked from, not allowing herself to look back. "Do you not believe that you deserve to fly?"

"Zaralathaar?" Amber sat bolt upright, barely trusting her own returning vision, shoving back the frost-crisped skin she'd bundled around herself. Waking from such a dream wrenched more painfully than the smacking cold, but as Amber held still, she found the Nymph's message remained crystallised as though hovering in the chill, holding air, as well as in her mind.

"Have a little faith, child, as well as a little sense," Amber told herself aloud, as though the Water Nymph truly were here to guide her. She rolled up the pelt and hobbled onto frozen feet. The curl of a smile brushed her lips as lightly as the dusting of frost atop these lonely swathes. "Trust your own wisdom. You have made your preparations. You are ready for the Icefields."

The Icefields? Amber echoed, in the privacy of her own mind. Her blood slowed to think of them, as though their deathly grasp were already stretching across the miles towards her. The deadlands, the spiritlands: the lands legend told had been formed of crystallised magic and now clung perilously to the very edges of the northernmost point of the Realm, which people said would one day break into a thousand shards and fall away into nothing, and begin the long descent of the Realm back into the void…

And yet it was somewhere she ached to visit. After all, she'd survived thus far. But she wasn't far enough yet. It took her a moment to soak up the magnitude of her surroundings, for she was standing—shakily—on the brink of the loneliest shore she had yet witnessed: a thin, tenuous expanse ripped apart by jagged edges and sheared away by the ravages of the most arctic of elements.

The cold slapped her and stung her, rendering her paper-thin as the wind whiplashed and whimpered, howling in ecstasy and fear, taunting and tempting her, challenging her to show how she would stand in its stead. It promised to scour clean her wounds—but at what price? It would take the strongest of souls to remain sturdy beneath those raking tongues of wind.

Staring out into the cataclysmically gaping vista, Amber felt its emptiness turn her inside out until she felt not just alone, but almost unmade.

But she wasn't going to stay here, stranded on this spit of land she found herself beached upon, so alien and hostile that it could have been another Realm entirely. She had to find the Song Weaver. So, she drew her unfocused gaze away from the limitless terror of the horizon and towards the manageable steps in front of her. Rising winds wrapped possessively around her as she started walking, blurring grey horizontal swathes into vertical, and she knew she wouldn't survive out here, for long, if she stayed on her own.

Scrambling across the skin-scuffing gravel, the cold engulfed her like a fever absolute and overwhelming, but through the snowstorm she followed the shifting shoreline until she finally reached its point and the blizzard sank, as spent as she was. In the aching silence the landscape opened up again, at its own form of peace, and Amber felt her breathing settle in response. Her gaze tracked from the torn-paper foam-flecked sea at her feet, to the glimmering pearls of icebergs afire far off beneath the setting sun. The vision rose so blisteringly beautiful that she wasn't sure whether her mind had conjured it out of relief.

Taking the measure of her surroundings, Amber wrapped the pelt around her more tightly and advanced as closely as she dared towards the treacherous, biting sea.

You've found the threshold, her heart realised. *Your journey starts now.*

Adrenaline flooded with misgivings washed through her as she considered her next move. "Song Weaver?"

Her voice whipped away on the wind, too small for this vastness.

Only the voice of the sea answered, leaving Amber staring out across the ocean until her eyes streamed. Foreboding growled in her chest until it clamoured as loudly as the shrieking winds. She dared not risk inching further, for the land fell abruptly away into a fathomless grey that chopped and thrashed hungrily. So she waited, with faith, crouched against the spitting surf as she squinted and sang, in case she could be heard.

The sea ebbed and flowed endlessly around her, the stirring of waves conjuring ambiguous impressions that shifted and swirled into untold monsters, but Amber let all illusion flow past unhindered and unheeded, needing to be ready for the one glimpse she had journeyed here for.

A heaving bulk more real and solid than anything madness could conjure eclipsed any trick her mind could play, and Amber rocked back on her heels with a gladdening cry.

Waves sluiced in a great crash and the depths parted aside the gnarled bowhead, hot breath spewing into ice dust as in a great billowing cloud of impact the leviathan burst through the gleaming skin of water.

"You must leave the shore to cross the ocean, brave one." The Song Weaver's words hung oily and intimate in the frozen air. "But, after all, you have shown great skill in shifting between skins." She presented her own, waiting for Amber to climb on.

"Are you sure?" Amber stared, in awe and disbelief, overwhelmed as the Whail hovered gently beside her, holding still despite the battering combers. She felt as though the waves had slammed into her already, and were inexorably dragging her away from shore and safety. She'd never felt so validated, nor so exposed, in her life. How could she survive the crossing, in this weather, even on the back of the Whail? The glacial water would kill her in moments. The ocean stretched as bleak and savage and hopeless as her chances. Amber gritted her teeth, unnerved beyond admitting. "Won't I die?"

"Eventually, little skin-sewer, as we all do," the Whail hummed throatily. "But when that moment comes, you will look back on this day, and remember when you lived." Her voice was as sonorous as blood singing through veins.

Something stirred within Amber at the Song Weaver's words, warming her through like a cloak that couldn't be torn away. She could do this. She could do this, she wasn't alone, and she would return from it.

Gasping fitfully as the sea's tongue lashed at her, Amber reached through the spray to trace the warm, leathery rubber of the Song Weaver's skin, and eased herself gently onto the Whail's barnacle-gnarled back. Great cuffing palms of solid sea jarred against her as she sprawled for purchase, the green ribbed waters slapping around her impatiently, breathlessly cold and deep.

Amber breathed in bellows against the fear and freeze. Her salt-raw fingers slipped as she tried to cling on, so she resorted to hugging the Song Weaver's broad, furrowed back with outstretched arms and sprawled legs. As the Whail moved off, keeping carefully at the surface for all its thrashing foam, Amber felt as though the whole Realm were churning. Spray stung blindingly in her eyes and the wind whipped against her fit to tear not only the pelt from her, but also her own skin.

As her panic grew, the shore was getting smaller. Real terror reared up, flaying away reason and hope with every lash of the pitiless wind amidst the sluicing waves as she realised that it would, instead of some impossible, grandiose foe, be the unending, interminable cold which would take her at the end—an end that could not be far, for her teeth ached with it, her skin burned with it, her limbs shuddered with it. It was the kind of insidious, inescapable cold that you could drown in, deeper than the churning, death-grey sea as it picked soul and skin apart. She could feel it claiming her.

Impossibly, a throbbing heat rose to claim supremacy: Amber felt the Whail's skin yield, sticky and warm and melding. It felt as though first her hands and then every surface against the Whail's skin were sinking through into her lifesaving layer of blubber and she felt, incredibly, the steady, thrumming beat of the Song Weaver's heart throbbing deep below her own chest.

As her mind floundered to believe it, she realised that the wind's battering against her back was easing into a dulled, distanced clatter, and with a warm pressure squelching across her legs and along her back, she felt herself sealed away from the worst of the pain and cold as the Whail's skin reformed around her.

Spluttering against crash after crash of wave, Amber clenched her eyes shut desperately, but she had left her fear somewhere outside of this blood-and-body cocoon. On some primal level, she knew she would survive this now. She dared not flinch for fear of hurting the Whail, who was protecting her in so breathtakingly intimate a manner, but as her thoughts drifted away as though compelled by enchantment, the last thing she remembered thinking was what if this journey took so long that she could not escape after?

Yet the thrumming warmth beneath her chest lulled her with an ancient rhythm, and incongruously, with the wind howling against her and yet held so safe and wet and warm, Amber felt herself drift toward a strange sleep.

Glaciers groaned ponderously like slumbering whales easing into waking and, as she opened her eyes, Amber grew sure she was sleeping still. Or was she passing into another Realm? Blue-gleaming icebergs lit a luminous darkness; passing like mighty ships aside the Song Weaver as she surged with her charge through an ice-strewn night. The ocean heaved as though to vomit, weird lights danced in agitation across a sky that seemed more like an upside down sea, and the waves had turned into grasping hands seeking to pull Amber from her cetacean sanctuary.

The wind's voice lifted into a fevered moan as the Whail slowed, beaching herself ponderously and with great care onto a black sand spit. Bereft, Amber felt herself peel away from the Song-Weaver's generous body. For several heartbeats amongst the dragging tide she let a gut-wrenching sorrow wash over her with the knowledge that she was no longer melded to something far greater than herself.

"You are, skin-sewer," the great boom of the Whail resounded in her soul. "You always will be. That is why you must go."

"I must leave?" Amber spluttered, awash with devastation.

"No. You must go on," the Whail reassured, her sonorous voice full of peace and promise.

Flailing with the fear that the bond she had grown so quickly and utterly used to was now severed as though it had never been, Amber balked at the enormity of the task ahead. But going on is part of keeping the memory alive, she promised herself. I'll polish it like a gem to guide me through, and it will become part of the kernel of my soul that will change me for the better, for all time. And she saw in the deep, smile-wrinkled eye of the Whail that her choice was a good one.

And so, she kissed the Song Weaver goodbye peaceably, and gifted her tears gladly to the ocean to watch her go.

Pushing through the contractions of water pulsing against a jagged shore, Amber birthed herself upon the berg-strewn, ice-carved bank with a huge sputtering breath.

She was no longer scared of the Oak Prince; she was no longer scared of the Kelpie. She barely remembered them. All that mattered now in this dangerous, sucking dark was the land—and she could barely remember that either. She couldn't even stand. For strokes of the tide uncounted she lay as though limbless, the landscape stretching as empty and barren as her mind; scraped clean and tossed from the storm. Slabs of ice protruded from the storm-smoothed coast, sublime and untouchable, afire beneath the pale moon.

But, as slowly as lichen-wrapped stones tumbled bristling past her across the bleak swathes of wind-scoured shore, Amber's thoughts gathered themselves, herded by those icy sentinels, to congregate around her soul. She tried to speak; an abrasive bark rasped from her throat. Half her mind dared wonder whether she had turned into a Selkie herself. She called out again, weak but stronger. To stay soundless in this vast emptiness felt dangerous—as though one could fade away entirely. So, she kept calling, hoarsely.

As the feeble echoes scudded outwards, pulsing scattered clicks probed in response. Amber felt relief warm her. She was still of some mortal form, at least; she felt it being mapped out. There was proof that she was still here. Proof she realised she needed, right now. She tried to sound a thank you, but her pitiful attempt scraped itself away into the sand.

A chattering of seal-like chirps flurried in encouragement of her efforts. In, out, their rhythm reminded her. She gasped, and gasped again.

A guttural boom resounded as though summoned by the chirruping swell of urgency conversing around her, and a tusked monstrosity both grotesque and glorious hauled itself a length up the shore, shingle rattling with its lumbering progress. *Shh-thwack.* The pulse jarred life back into Amber's chest. *Shh-thwack.*

She pulled herself up on her elbows, and stared and stared, hope packing itself around her like blubber. What she had initially seen as a desolate wasteland was crowded with seals of all descriptions—lugging themselves eagerly and laboriously towards her, their monumental efforts through an alien environment putting her to shame. They packed themselves in around her; wobbling with blubber and steaming with generous warmth, sealing out the desolate howl of the racing wind and closing a healing heat around her.

Amber smiled to realise that the pelt was surrounded by its own kind again. But as the company pressed and snuggled, she wasn't sure they'd even noticed it. They'd simply found a lost, frozen soul, and responded. Their humphings and grumphings washed over her in a nurturing murmur, soothing away the cavernous silence and her insignificance within. Amber had never felt belonging like it.

"Thank you," she murmured peaceably and, like a moonbeam sliding over storm-stilled waters, the words slipped easily, returning her voice. Her companions, so far away from any civilization, might not be Selkies, but they had saved her—and to do so they had needed to be none other than themselves. Perhaps, out here, her own self would expand to fill requirement too. With that realisation, she felt herself slip towards sleep like a pup slithering from an iceberg into welcoming waters.

Northern Nights

The wind-scoured stones were singing with someone else's footsteps, as Amber woke into a disorientating night. She stank of something visceral, akin to blood and fat and life, and it took her exhausted mind a moment to remember why.

"Ye've reached it, then. The last shore a'fore th' Icefields," a gruff voice introduced itself, shouting over the gale. "The Nymph said ye'd do it by ye'self. But ye' dinnae need tae start it entirely alone."

Amber took his webbed, furred hand readily in hers, taking in a frost-clung vision at once ephemeral and earthly; a weathered figure so bedecked in furs that she couldn't work out, initially, whether he was a man or animal or something else entirely. Even in her ice-slowed state she knew he must be a Selkie in man form. His pelt was worn like an all-enveloping hooded cloak, but his was not the sleek garment of the Selkies at the Sound. His was rougher, thicker. Wilder.

"Dinnae let this place consume ye. Ye have tae stay separate, tae want tae survive," the elder warned, hauling a blanket across her shoulders as his whistled words sent the seals ambling amiably to a camouflaged distance again, knowing their work had been done. "Th' icescape main tempt, or i' main teach ye that. It is a place o' fiercer magic than anywhere else in th' Realm—but there is nought so fierce as seal-warmth, ye ken, as ye found ye' sel' tonight. Still, it is raw, elemental—it cannae be reasoned with, nur diluted. Its experience cannae be found in any other land—for both ill an' good. Perhaps ye have tae come here, tae realise ye want tae go back haem after all."

"I can't go back yet," Amber promised. "I have to find the pieces to fix the pelt of one of your kind." The strange truths he spoke stirred her, and yet she barely dared speak, lest she send the hallucination fleeing. Surely he could not be truly here and real.

"Real enough tae help," the Selkie man insisted, his seabird-grey eyes glinting beneath thickset brows crowned by the heavy mantle of fur that gowned him like a shaman.

Amber grinned, although the exposure ached in her teeth. "I accept your help with all gratitude." Then she faltered. Staring over the expansive vista, Amber had never felt so tiny. "But I fear I can offer little in return." The wind tore into her, ripping her open. The vastness of the landscape reduced her to a speck. She straightened miserably. "I'm no use to you. I can't fly."

"In the blizzards tha' seize each hour, nur can anyain," the elder replied, unmoved.

Amber grimaced wretchedly. "And I basically can't swim."

"In such frigid seas, nur can anyain."

"And I can't really run."

"On this ice, nur can anyain."

Dismissing her panic, Amber took a milder breath, and tried again. "So, what can I do?"

"Tha's the better question," the Selkie approved. "The air that chokes me welcomes ye."

Amber let his words swirl and thaw beneath her skin. Could it be true? Could she skinbreathe, without flying?

"Th' frost precedes th' thaw," the strange man promised, and she saw nestled in his eyes the same gem-like spark of magic radiating from the dancing skylights; the same magic that fires Renë to stir after Restë and keeps hope gestating through darkness before it can break through and survive newborn.

"Th' earth main close in an' lie dormant first," the Selkie continued, watching her closely. "It is in th' iciest grip tha' germination an' restoration can occur. Mayhap those are also the conditions needer fur yer transformation: a descent intae heavy braw an' endless mirk, afore th' slow push tae light an' air."

Amber shivered and gulped mechanically. She felt like her skin had been peeled away by both the sea and his words, leaving her vulnerable and receptive. She heard the ocean's endless, hypnotic roar as a far off, lulling murmur—a reminder that she had not only passed through a portal, but also in doing so passed a sort of test.

She sucked a careful breath, although inhaling the brittle air felt like inviting clouds of glass dust down into her lungs. As the sea continued its incessant onslaught upon a shore it could engulf but never consume, Amber realised that it hadn't consumed her, either. The realisation gave her courage. Clad in Hydd's almost blood-warm fur, continuing felt not just imperative, but almost possible.

The elder watched her shrewdly. "Ye were born tae th' limitless air, an' birthed mere nights ago intae th' boundless brine," he mused, his voice as gravelled as the shore. "Whit is tae stop ye returnin' again, an' becomin' a bairn o' th' air once more? A skin main be shed, ere the threshold is crossed, an' shed it ye have—yet ye have nae been left withoot. Ye hae grown anither. Ye need more than yer ain skin here, but yer ain will save you in th' morn—for oot in these savage stretches can be found a piece o' pelt infused wi' the sky itself, if yer nerve holds true."

Strange flames crackled behind him as though summoned by sorcery; the dancing tongues of green and blue flames streaked eerie and exultant in a reflection of the rippling curtains of eldritch light whipping across the sky. "Until then rest, an' tak yer energy frae th' fire—fur tomorrow, ye main stand, whether ye wish tae return haem o' journey onwards."

As Amber pulled herself gratefully towards the blaze, sensation stabbed painfully back into her limbs, and she flinched at the reawakened agony. She closed her eyes, and the lights still danced beneath her lids.

"I thought I'd be alone, out here," she confessed thickly, ashamed. It was too cold even to speak fully. With each breath the air froze achingly against her teeth and deep inside her lungs.

The Selkie's eyes were hidden and hooded. "Helpers are the most extraordinary shapeshifters o' all," he impressed. "Ye can find them in limitless forms, if ye determine tae look."

Amber thought not only of Racxen and Ruby and her friends, but of everyone her life had been touched by: Finsbury, the Leaf People, the seals of the shore. "Always," she pledged, and she wriggled closer to the lifegiving, frost-thawing flames, feeling as limbless as a seal.

"Ah willnae be here forever," he murmured, flaring the fire with all the colours of the sky as Amber slipped into a slumber wrought of sudden safety. "But I will be here lang enaw. An' when ah hae left, gang on alone in good heart."

Amber mumbled her thanks peaceably, half dreaming already. The night faded rapidly beneath her lids, melting into a healing thaw, but an abiding memory etched itself into her mind and remained long after: that stooping figure, ancient and time-riddled as the ice, befurred and unbowed, stoking a fire that cast her fears to the scattering lights dancing above and swept her spirit down into its warmth, safe despite the swirling snow.

Learning to Breathe

The probing fingers of a glacial wind snaked across the rock-strewn shore to prod Amber awake with a perverse insistence. Although snow glinted eerily beneath the permadusk, the warmth wrought last night still smouldered in her core and the remnants of the fire she'd slept by still flickered obstinately. She rose with a sense of a slate having been wiped clean and, wrapping the pelt around her like a shield, she strode alone into the disorientating whiteness with a steady heart.

Hours later, the preternatural gloaming finally lifted away into the cleanest dawn she'd ever witnessed, and sharp sunlight doused the ice in a cold pink fire as if the dull surface of the years had been scoured away to reveal a clear way into a gleaming future, the blistering, clarity-inducing cold stripped away all nonessential thought until only a keen awareness of certain truths remained.

The Selkie elder was gone, leaving in his wake a landscape wilder and more desolate. But this new isolation felt not only inescapable, but also possibility-expanding. As she left behind the ragged shore, before her squinting, sleep-stuck eyes the true, uninterrupted Icefields glided into view, arresting and formidable, knifing across a horizon as pale as a Renë sunrise strewn with jagged glaciers alight with the gleam of newly cut glass. Surely in such a pristine environment a stray swatch of pelt would be easy to spot. And yet the elder had claimed it needed to be infused with the sky. Hadn't he noticed she had no wings?

Amber straightened. She would focus on the part of his prophecy that she knew was in her power to uphold: her nerve. With the sky aflame in the dawnrise behind her and the sea illuminated as though its waves were crested with golden foil, she started walking, the reflections glowing in her eyes.

The frigid air clung with a metallic, scalpel-sharp tang. It was so clean she almost felt she tainted it just by breathing. Yet the morning seemed to stretch calm in the knowledge of having overcome last night and, as icecap after icecap blurred together, Amber even found herself getting used to the cold.

A strange quietude rang across the expanse, wrung through with the eldritch voices of the wind. It soothed her wrought senses, and Amber gathered herself in the restorative solitude and settled into a flowing pace, staring out as if with new eyes onto a new Realm. The tired grey of the tumultuous shore had been gusted away to reveal a pristine depth of whiteness Amber had never before encountered. It made her eyes hurt. It almost made her soul hurt. But it was a cleansing pain; a sloughing of old hurts and limitations she had not realised she had still been carrying. The emptiness of the land gaped like a rough-edged wound, and everything about it cut her open—perhaps so old hurts could be healed.

Even so, not even the tiniest swatch of shadow, let alone fur, crept forth to reveal itself or even grant visual sanctuary from the glare of endless ice. As the day wore on, Amber's eyes streamed from the inescapable, blistering brightness until she longed bodily for the merciful darkness within the caves of Arraterr. She wrapped her sash around her eyes, grateful for the shield the loose weave provided as it softened her view with its veil. It helped to realise that while this environment was wilder and more ungovernable than any, she still had control over how she let it affect her. With only the sound of her own footsteps to focus on amidst the visceral, unhinging quiet that thrummed through her core as though threatening to reduce her body to atoms and tear her mind to shreds of cloud, she had to fight consciously and unrelentingly for that control.

Out here, in such an environment as defied delineation or demarcation, she had to maintain her boundaries to keep a sense of her self. So, as she breathed the scouring air, she focused on the roar of her lungs, recognising by the warmth of her breath frosting in front of her mouth that she could in this way, if for a second, warm even the limitless expanse of the Icefields. Holding on to the revelation like a mantra, Amber found she could walk steady and unsullied amongst the abyss of silence, until the unhinging humming in her ears sank into a hush of memory and could no longer hurt or hinder her.

And so, alone with her thoughts and the ripped-open landscape, Amber trekked the desolate plains, confronting the peculiarly primal fear that such vastness would consume her. In such a landscape, anything could be possible. In such a landscape, it might just have to be.

Filling her, yet scouring her out, with nothing to anchor but nothing to fetter her either, the icescape offered a unique vessel: perhaps the best container in the Realm for such cavernous an emptiness as she sometimes feared hollowed inside her. Here, she didn't have to avoid it. She could inhabit it without it destroying her. And if she could leave it here, Amber chanced to wonder, caught in the strange, chill web of the place, perhaps she could stop its inward seep towards her organs. Or, perhaps she could carry something of the Icefields inside her and stop it herself.

It was supremely unsettling, being in the presence—indeed, at the mercy—of a landscape so unquestionably indifferent to her survival. And yet, perversely, it felt liberating in equal measure, because she was in no way indebted to it. In the face of such dispassion, her destiny lay, irrevocably and indisputably, in her own hands. There could be no 'what ifs' to haunt her as there always had been on occasions ending in rescue or intervention; no fear of whether she could cope with something worse than the current circumstance, because out here was the very worst. The spectre of utter abandonment and aloneness could be met and found to be an adversary of conquerable size who could be persuaded to spill their secrets upon the bone-white canvas.

And so, something inside her sang to be amongst it for, however many years she might have to put in with Sarin, these memories would keep her safe. They would keep part of her separate from the suffocating tangle, and remind her that having traversed this, she no longer need fear any road she might later take.

But the comfort of such thoughts tore away seconds later as the wind's companionable murmuring whipped itself suddenly into inconsolable hysteria and Amber's hard-earned steadiness splintered as the thousand-mile icescape blurred into a threshing whiteout.

Cocooning herself within the pelt, Amber's Realm shrank close as she struggled on blinded, retreating into her core where warmth still clung weak but vital like a faint heartbeat, while the rage battered from outside. Battered, but did not breach.

Breathing was getting harder; the icy, dusty air scratched in her throat and filled her lungs with every mouthful, until she was coughing like some pitiful, choking Dragon. She couldn't ignore the truth that not even the Selkie elder had dared trespass into these reaches of the ice.

How much further could she struggle? It felt as though the rest of the Realm had been erased entirely, blasted into nothingness by the blizzard. She felt as though the snowstorm had already fixed its claws into her; she felt her heart sputter and clutch, as if it were freezing over, and her lungs heaved with each breath of frigid air until she gasped as if drowning.

The coldness of the air clutched its way down her throat and stabbed into her chest—the kind of coldness that was so pure it was painful, so sterile it could kill. But only if she stopped. So she stumbled on, footstep by fumbling footstep, the Icefields seeming to ring now with a thunderous, chastening quiet beyond the screaming of the gale—the sound of the death that waited beyond, or mayhap the relief that waited beyond that.

Before she could succumb to such fatalistic musings, the cold gouged into her anew like welcome teeth reawakening within her the urge to fight, to live. But at some belated point, the realisation that she was no longer shivering brushed her consciousness with the unease of impending frostbite; and she realised the cold had sealed off, as if surgically, the parts of her that could bring themselves to care. Not for the first time in her life, she wondered if her dedication to a quest would kill her before it saved anyone else.

The wind howled its derision and the emptiness hurt just a little more. So, she gathered Racxen's love close to warm her through, conjured Mugkafb's chatter to her ears to quicken her mind, invoked Rraarl's stoic perseverance to stave off the slowing pain of ice, and summoned Jasper's barked commands keep moving despite every screaming urge to the contrary.

On, you fool, he insisted, his command cutting through the shrieking winds, and she heeded his imagined voice; her stumbling progress a tremulous candle snatched just out of reach and refusing to be snuffed. Yet instead of abating, the blizzard's fervour increased and grappled to consume her. Ravenous winds stole her breath at every step, screaming incessantly, louder than the Vetches. Yet, what really stabbed fear into her was the note of abandon in their voices. They weren't threatening her—they were calling her, tempting her.

On she staggered, utterly blind, almost bereft, until she feared the blizzard would tear her from the Realm itself. Her eyes streamed, and panic clutched with crushing pain around her chest as she felt like she was truly choking.

And then, the stinging air slapping into her skin was enough. She took a newborn breath, full of wonder, her skin tingling. Her chest didn't hurt. The air around her was suddenly sufficient. It filled her, picked her up and carried her. Her lungs no longer burned; her throat no longer closed in wheezing desperation. It felt like she was in the sky again, at one with the air. Tears streamed from her eyes afresh as she felt the oxygen stream through her skin.

Skinbreathing. She was skinbreathing, instead of lung-breathing. The ultimate achievement reached at the pinnacle of flying—which she'd never experienced before and had assumed she never would.

She didn't need her eyes any more. She could breathe. She lay down in the savage snow and laughed with the relief of it all. She could breathe! She sucked and sucked, draining deep draughts of sweet air until she felt like she could float away.

But she had an anchor. The pelt. She would find the sky piece. Wondering if some kind of ice-drawn fever were seizing her mind as well as devouring her body, she tore off one glove with her teeth, and crawled along, stubbing her frozen fingers through the biting, blinding snow. A spirited-away, detached part of her mind railed a warning that she would pay in pain once she was back in the warmth, but she swatted it away, buzzing with the rapture of feeling well.

Ice sharp as glass raked against her clutching fingers for attempts uncounted until her breath caught in exhilaration for, billowing in front of her with heart-stopping suddenness, snatched a ripple of what could only be the pelt, caught writhing in the blizzard like a creature in agony. Instinctively, Amber scooped it into an embrace, tucking it inside her layered cloaks, beneath Hydd's pelt and against the warmth of her skin. Stooping low to protect herself and her precious charge from the battering force of the squall, she stumbled back across the miles until all at once the storm stilled. Amber unpeeled herself from the ice shakily, still clutching the newest swatch of fur. The piece was so large that she could feel the weight of her task lifting with its presence, and her head spun to recollect all she had just encountered and achieved.

"Creature o' th' air," promised a familiar voice with deep satisfaction, as the Selkie elder materialised in front of her like some kind of elemental frost-creature. Gulping down air as though it were pristine water, Amber felt like she was taking the first breaths of a new life as she worked out how to use her lungs again, and she burst into exhilarated tears and hugged the elder, overwhelmed that he had come here to witness her re-emergence. "How did you know I'd find the pelt there?" she managed.

"Ah conjured it here fur safe keepin'. Yet times changed, an' ah couldnae gang back."

Amber stared at him. "You made the same choice as Zaralathaar."

His calm Selkie eyes met her curious gaze. "Tha' 's a name ah remember frae younger days."

Amber grinned. "Then you should make your own journey, back across the sea."

"Mebbe." The smile melted across his face like sunlight, before he sent a sterner glance back towards the far sea. "Yet cast yer focus fur now tae yer ain journey: fur now ye main return tae meet th' Ook Prince's challenge; an' do so in his ain element."

Amber's blood thrummed with the oxygen coursing through her veins. "No matter. I carry mine with me now," she promised him, with a sure and heady smile.

The elder nodded approvingly, settling a furred hand upon her shoulder, and Amber breathed deeply. The coursing winds buzzed through her, thrumming in her veins, making her feel as though her feet would never touch the ground again. Now the wind's voice was a shriek of ecstasy; the vast expanse stretching before her in a liberating summons to adventure. "I've thrived amidst the freeze," she admitted, grinning dizzily. "I trust it's given me the strength to survive the thaw."

"It's nae goin' backwards, tae return changed," the elder promised with a snow-twinkled smile. As she set off, he swept his cloaks around him and became a seal once more, bearing liquid-eyed witness to the Fairy until the distance claimed her.

A pale and watery dawn slid across the horizon like a wavering blue flame, but Amber strode into it as steadily as a ship slides towards a far yet certain shore. Gurgles echoed all around, as though the meltwater rivers were clearing their throats and shaking debris free from the land.

Numbed, cramped, and yet renewed, Amber felt herself similarly cleansed. After all, she had returned to herself. She had skinbreathed. The memory billowed, gusting her to dizzying heights until elation reverberated through every fibre of her being. This was what she had to follow. Anything that made her feel like this had to be the right path. What a journey it had been... and yet: a pang akin to physical pain spread to realise that her odyssey was not yet over. The elder had been right. Getting here was one thing. The real test lay in bringing herself back...

Staring out and breathing deeply, Amber let the icescape flood into her one more time. This incredible environment was not only as austere and chastening as the Water Nymph, but also as life-affirmingly awakening.

I can return home, she promised herself, *if I can return to this. And for this, I would return in a heartbeat.* Amber grinned, a lightness of heart gracing her, and she pushed on, for now unafraid. She had learned not only to follow this feeling, but to carry it with her as well. And she would let it carry her all the way back home.

Turning the Tide

The wind gusted, fractious and discontent and ill at ease, as Yenna stared out over the shifting ocean twisting far below. The feathers gracing her bow shivered as she nocked a darkwood arrow with practised ease and adjusted its load carefully.

Jasper squinted into the storm. "This is going to need to be the shot of the season, even coming from you."

Yenna arched a brow. "I might need you to be the voice of reason, but I never promised to thank you for it."

Jasper shrugged good-naturedly. "I'll always be here for you, whether you thank me or not." He graced her with one of those rare smiles reserved for her and for how she made him feel. Seeing the surety in his eyes Yenna raised her bow confidently, drawing back the string with her hair billowing like flame, her form still and poised and watchful, calm amongst the battering conflict thrashing amongst the elements beyond.

Jasper was still gazing at her in an admiration tinged with wonder when the forest-felling shadow spilled onto theirs, and he instinctively closed the gap between him and the Wolf Sister.

"Some actions must be completed regardless of audience," Yenna warned with a low growl, her golden eyes blazing as they locked on the approaching wight. "Stall him for me, my love."

"I thought it was beasts who transformed into princes," the apparition sneered, drifting obscenely close—and right into firing range.

"Clearly, you're not from around here," Jasper warned readily in return. "Our 'beasts' are beautiful just as they are, and it is they who inspire transformation, not the other way around."

"For a leader of wolves, she is a woman of few words," the wight mocked, his eyes travelling Yenna licentiously as she kept poised, bowstring taut. Waiting. Waiting. "And fewer actions, I'll wager."

Sucking a breath, Yenna loosed the arrow, felt it thrum electric through the air.

It whooshed harmlessly through the wisp-formed Oak Prince and skimmed into the shallows far below.

As the Oak Prince hooted in derision, the Wolf Sister lowered her bow calmly, nodding in tight satisfaction. "What makes you think that wasn't part of the plan? After all, I wouldn't tell you. Being a woman of few words."

Those cavernous eyes narrowed dangerously. "A message. You passed a message to the sea." He plummeted with all the force of a lightning-struck bough, but a Selkie form was already parting the waves far below, as swift and sure as a dream, and sinking untouchable and untraceable.

Watching the wake of its progress companionably with the Wolf Sister, Jasper turned to kiss her. "You never cease to surprise me."

Yenna's eyes glowed with a fierce warmth. "I know what it is to struggle to shed one skin and inhabit another, and you've always brought me back. Now we need to do the same for Amber."

Singing Against the Squall

No word from the Whail. It could only mean one thing: that Amber was out there bearing what he should be carrying while he, cursed against asking for help, floundered on the shore powerless in this weakened state to sway the course.

Through the open doors of the castle, the north wind reached its icy tongue towards Hydd, callously eager. He wondered if it could taste his fear as he could taste its threat of snow. Once, to him, snow had been an earth- and air-dweller's problem. His people would have been safe in the deeps, swimming beneath such hurtful things, or would have been nestled fatly together, drawing comfort from the shared warmth of bodies, immune to the pain of the wind raging above. The wrench of being so cruelly dislocated from those consolations cut him more keenly than the cold.

But such hurts were nothing compared to hers, out there. So, instead of fleeing, he held fast and bore out the pain of those who feared his presence was a desperate omen even though he tried to help. How could he blame them, when he feared the same of himself? What could he, his health failing without his skin, do? *Ye're still a Selkie*, he promised himself. *Ye'll bear witness, an' contain what ye see so tha' it disnae break her boundaries, even if it is th' only thing ye have tae offer. An' first, ye main convince th' others tae join ye.*

Breathing the scent of the winds flurrying around him, reading the air currents like those of the sea, Hydd stood poised before the gale, staring out towards the Icefields and the path that Amber had taken on his behalf. He had been trapped for so long not being able to ask it, and she hadn't even needed him to.

Ye're oot there findin' mah sool, Hydd pledged, hot tears sprouting like whiskers against his face despite the frigid air. *Ah'll find a way tae guide yers home; ah swear it.* After all, he might have left himself open to having his soul stolen from him, he reminded himself with a shiver. But Amber had already had to engineer the kind of soul that none could steal.

Abruptly the night lurched, and he had to stumble back inside and seek the cloistered oblivion of dark halls. In his fevered state he knew he had not long to survive without his pelt. Longing for it sent him frantic; he half thought of throwing himself into the sea and letting it sweep him to oblivion. It took all his strength to let the urge surf away instead, carried by the waves to deeper, further water where it couldn't drag him down. *The fight will nae always be sae fierce,* he forced himself to mouth. *It is nae okay noo, but it will be again. The currents might sweep ye awa', but they cannae droon ye. Nae if ye keep yer energy yer ain instead o' throwin' it sacrificially tae the storm. Ye've got tae keep yerself afloat, afore ye can strike fo' the shore.*

Blearily re-orientating himself to the pull of the ocean, Hydd stumbled drunkenly through the hall, only to find the Fairy Prince bolting the doors and dragging bars across the window.

"Bide! We cannae leave her alone!" Hydd cried. "Tae shut out th' storm on this night is tae bolt her frae our hearts—"

"Stop talking nonsense, man, and help me with the beams," Jasper interrupted curtly.

"Nae—we main stan' vigil!" Hydd pleaded. "That is our side o' the magic—"

"No!" Jasper spat back angrily. "A vigil achieves nothing. You're the reason she's out there in all of this. We're not listening to you any more. There's no sense in us assuaging your guilt by endangering ourselves out of some misplaced primitive notion that it can change anything. It's too far to fly, and you can't swim. All I can do is keep the rest of my people safe. That means everyone—including you. No-one goes outside."

The door banged angrily behind him, accentuating the taut silence remaining.

"Ach, ye've ne'er been caught in the throes o' a curse," Hydd growled weakly, feeling the last of his strength threaten to leave him. It would be so much easier to obey, to simply find some warm corner of the castle to curl up in and crash into unconsciousness. But he had to help. Even though it required more of Amber's companions than one ravaged Selkie. If only they could just—

"I believe you," whispered Mugkafb, emerging from the shadows, his worried eyes as large as the pools of darkness his tremulous torch couldn't quite disperse.

"Really?" Hydd murmured in relief, his voice cracking like stone beneath the incessant weight of the waves.

"I might not have once had magic, like you," Mugkafb admitted, drawing himself up grandly. "But I know something of how it should be done."

Hydd's green eyes shone like seaglass worn smooth. "We main sing her back, afore she gets lost i' the brine," the Selkie warned. "Everyone plans fur th' journey—few prepare fur the return."

Racxen appeared at his side in an instant, spilling from the shadows as though they couldn't contain him. "To bring her back, we would follow you anywhere. Lead us."

The night stretched perilously, its hope gossamer-thin but tenacious.

Racxen's watchful eyes took their rest on the soft, settling darkness. All the practical steps, he had taken. Now, he let his mind drift into the other, less defined reaches at the far edge of the Realm, for to find Amber might mean delving into a Realm truly other. And there were steps that could be taken for that too—to push out the fear, to cultivate courage, to maintain the poised readiness of mind necessary for this next watch.

Beside him, he sensed the calm focus of the Selkie. Hydd's attention bobbed unperturbed upon the storm thrashing its torments before them. The Arraheng felt his own soul crouch tense and coiled in comparison to the smooth flow of his companion's beside him. He resolved to absorb and learn.

"Ah can watch," Hydd reassured him, his voice soothing, like the insistent burble of water over rock. "And tha' has its place. But ye can track."

The knot in his chest eased then. Racxen let his sight drift inwards: tendrils of memory signposted the way, and all the while he trained his vision on the firefly-bright vision of Amber, out of view but never out of reach from his heart...

Refocusing on the outside Realm, a burnished gleam seemed to flit across the waves, star-dusting the anxious sea until it was anointed with calm. "I know where she is," Racxen gasped, his soul settling and stirring. "And I'm going to need your help."

The ocean lashed and shrieked its warning; fearsome already and still far away, Amber couldn't help but acknowledge grimly. Surely to attempt the crossing now would mean death. And yet could she afford to wait exposed to this terrifying nothingness, when night raced towards her as deadly as the storm itself?

Stirring song spliced the screaming winds, and Amber knew she must be close, for these were the voices of Selkies from earlier, lifting and bracing and swirling in time with the ethereal lights as their wordless song summoned her through the formless, endless dark.

She couldn't see them yet, though, and a dangerous thought swirled inside her. She could stay here. The Selkies wouldn't find her. She could let the inevitable take its course. Relinquish control, responsibility. Anything else was too hard. Numb with exhaustion, she felt the death-grip of the whiteout slide into a fearful, interminable clutch around her heart. With a similar creeping certainty, she knew she would soon not be able to take one step further. Death lay before and behind, creeping closer from all sides.

And yet Amber lifted her storm-stamped heart and her blizzard-torn eyes. One more step towards a friend, towards sanctuary, was a different matter. That journey she could take faltering, falling and fading; towards voices she trusted more than her own when she was alone in the dark – and who would tell her different than her beleaguered mind could right now. When she reached them.

And a few steps were all it took, for a row of seals advanced towards her, their reassuring bulks wobbling like warming candlelight, steaming in ripples across the featureless ice, hope glowing in halos around them as though reaffirming the landscape as a place of living.

Radiating an ease that belied their familiarity with ushering lost and frightened souls, the seals approached to guide her into safe harbour and beyond.

They sang to her soul and yet it almost physically pained Amber to follow them, for they traced the shore—and the shore was the threshold she must cross, must battle through, to return home. Home, across a chasmic rift—she feared in this state she would never be strong enough to survive the passage.

And yet the seals made no move to send her away. "Ye hae journeyed here—now receive whit will be provided wi'out askin'," a voice murmured, as comfortingly as fat greasing chapped lips, and Amber rubbed her storm-squinted eyes, for she could have sworn the words came from a seal.

She grinned. Maybe they did: she found herself enclosed in an assemblage of furred women busying comfortably amidst their pinnipedian companions, radiating impervious warmth amidst the catastrophic weather raging outside the circle.

A ladleful of steaming, saliva-inducing broth nudged Amber's lips, and she thanked the women earnestly, gulping it down gratefully. Life seemed to work its way down through her gullet into her core again.

"Things can be asked fur here which might nae seem possible in mair pressured an' claustrophobic reaches," another woman joined comfortingly. "Once ye hae survived here, ye will carry within ye a fire stoked sae weel that nane will be able tae snuff it oot. Th' Ain Prince? He would nae last half a tide here! Tha' kind o' fire would burn him tae kindlin'!"

"A shoreline guarded by fat auld women an' he dare nae show his face," another barked with raucous, encouraging laughter.
Amber joined in their laughter with delight. "Are you Selkies too?"

"Aye, lass. We are th' ones who prepare. The ones who keep watch. The ones who guide th' ships an' souls tae shore—an' away, when they are ready."

"An' we shall keep th' way open fur ye, fur as lang as we are able."

Selkie after Selkie professed their warming promises to Amber, refusing to leave her to the false mercy of oblivion. Their strong hands softened her fall and caught her, their words re-found her voice, their blankets reforged her boundaries, and their morsels of food reawakened her cavernous needs. In order to survive the self-dissolving North she had melded with the Icefields; sunk herself into them so that they could no longer hurt. Now, with gentle insistence, the Selkie Wives in all their kindness were insisting that it might, for a short while during healing, have to hurt after all.

Lightheaded and disorientated, Amber bowed to the Selkie Wives' wisdom as they peeled her out of her rapturous state, little by little; just as one cannot plunge a frostbitten limb into hot water.

"An emptiness once numbed can be filled, if ye dare find it ag'in," one of the women was encouraging. "Let this place heal ye up, nae hollow ye oot. It might be bigger, but ye are stronger. Eat."

Amber hugged her back tightly, feeling her fears dissipate into comfort. Seeing the Selkie wives, fat and sustained and resilient, warm against the raging blizzard, was suddenly the most reassuring and hopeful scene she could have ever hoped stumble upon. These women weren't just surviving in this ice-splintered environment. They were thriving. And they were suggesting she could too.

Confidence began to nestle, quiet and secure in her chest, tucking itself surely beneath her ribs. Against the constant, subtle nourishment of the sea, the skeletal Oak Prince had no chance of competing.

Earlier, her hunger had cast itself upon the rocks; torn itself to shreds amongst the ripping winds. Something deep within her hadn't felt safe enough to eat. And yet now, watching the Selkie Wives go about their calm, capable business, Amber felt surrounded by a strength closer allied to survival than any carved of denial and deprivation: the strength gleaned from allowing oneself to heal and be helped. And so she surrendered in relief as the Selkie women nurtured and sustained her with such grace that she began to wonder whether she could in time learn to nurture and sustain herself…

"Main ye starve yerself? Would ye be any less worthy, any less strong, wi' a little mair flesh tae cushion yer bones; a little mair fat tae protect yer organs; a little mair muscle tae support yer limbs; a little more fuel tae propel yer journey?" The Selkies, in the kindest possible way, weren't giving up.

"Yer body is a' much a part o' ye as yer mind, Fairy," another urged, her liquid eyes deep and searching, holding the calmness of the eternal sea. "Ye cannae survive on air alone. The sea's composition is very much like blood—particularly after such a journey, ye nae doubt feel it pulsin' through yer pores, spreading through ye like a current. Let into yer body the sustenance offered freely by the brine an' the earth, as easily as you do the sky. Eat. Rest. Share warmth. These are strengths th' Ain Prince dis nae have access tae. We can make them his undoin'."

Amber took their offerings with cautious reverence, swilling the soup awkwardly with her tongue as she relearnt her mouth. The broth soothed her lacerated throat and reignited a thawing heart. Everything of hers had suffered neglect these past days, for her quest had exerted a savage toll. Yet ensconced amidst the Selkies, that tightness loosened and eating began to feel, if not natural, at least possible again.

They were still with her when dusk began to swim. Amber felt ashamed to admit her dependence upon the kindly Selkie Wives, but they had no qualms about demonstrating their equanimity as wholeheartedly as they had promised it. Amber began to feel, in her bones and blood, as though she could survive after this; she could leave soon and still be okay.

And so, an overnight later, which felt like a new lifetime, Amber crouched on a Selkie-watched shore, deliberately sacrificing her dearly won warmth to the deathly hunger of the ice-strewn sea as she scrambled atop the Whail once more and gasped against the sickening throbs of pain seizing her as the cold reclaimed her flesh. To bypass these trials would be to diminish the worth of her final triumph, she tried to tell herself, and yet right now the grim discomfort of being soaked through, salt-sored and bone-hollowingly freezing overrode all else.

She clung desperately to the life-preserving folds of the Song Weaver's generous body. The shivering had returned; her own body was seized fit to shake her apart. To have been returned to the warmth of life, only to be torn from the safety of its grasp again and have to brave the raging sea once more was almost more than she could bear. But for Hydd, she must, and it was easier to do for another than for herself. Her resolve remained, to brave the dark, frigid waters one last time. But would her strength?

The Song Weaver pulsed through the deepening night like oxygen through blood. So disorientated grew Amber that she began to fear she was being absorbed either by the Whail or the water itself. The heartbeat that pumped against her body deafened her own. The whale was keeping her body safe; she knew that more than she knew her own mind now. But her soul was being scattered. Darkness swamped everything; her vision, her direction, her memory. A cold, stealing darkness that threatened to spin her apart strand by strand.

"Amber!" A voice spooled out like a thread on the wind, thin and fragile.

"Amber!" Another. But these weren't the voices of the Icefields, strong as those had been.

"Amber!" These were of Earth, of Sea, of Wood, of Air…

"Amber!" These were voices she knew—and they weren't to guide her across.

"Amber!" These were voices to bring her back—

Distorted by the water but unerring in their power, the songs and shouts of her friends dismantled the distance as the Whail shifted course towards them.

But the sounds began to wobble away. Not the songs, but her ability to focus on them, Amber realised, her mind flailing and frightened at the threshold. She was just so very tired, and it was too much to ask of them, who couldn't see her yet.

And then Racxen's lantern shone, like a firefly, as it winked through the shifting shades of the fickle, storm-blown night, and suddenly her Realm expanded so that it was more than dark and drowning depths. It included a shore—a shore within reach, lined by friends ready to help.

A spew of spray heralded Amber's return into the Realm of air as the Song Weaver threw her huge bulk free from the constraints of the sea and curved in a great arcing crash as she breached in greeting, sending joyous waves running to meet the rescuers waiting in the shallows.

Disorientated after so long on the sea, Amber fixed the vision in her mind and fixed her course accordingly in her soul. Letting her vision expand with her mind, she knew she'd make it home. Another lantern bobbed, and another, across the lurching vastness she must cross. Skittering and jumping, flickering but never fading, their flames formed a steady barrier against the marauding dark: a stretch of beacons guiding her in.

Mugkafb felt as though his chest were breaking apart, as if every slap from the ocean were stripping away his skin. He barely had breath left to snatch air amidst the frothing surf, and yet he clung to the song like a barnacle to a rock through the storm, spilling it from himself until he couldn't recall which language he had even used, pleading with the sea to give back his friend until he glimpsed the callus-crowned brow of the leviathan breach the surface as though in answer. Mugkafb threw himself from the weed-clung rock, his friends barraging after him.

Racxen reached her first; the second word from his lips after gulping her name was to thank the Song Weaver for returning her across half a Realm away. Deftly, he ran his palm along the squeaky-smooth, rubbery contours of the Whail's skin, and at her sonorous agreement hooked his claws carefully at the enfolding flaps still half-encasing Amber. Though once protecting, they now risked trapping her, until in a sudden, inside-out wave of nausea that dissolved into the flooding chill of the ocean and the solid, steadying warmth of being wrapped in her friend's arms, she was back with them, separated from the Whail once more.

Amber stumbled as her limbs grieved for the one who had supported her so intimately, but her friends formed her skeleton and she wrapped her arms around the Song Weaver steadily, bowing her head against the noduled snout of the Whail. She heard her purr a deep song of recognition and farewell. With her tears of thanks adding to the salt of the sea, with Racxen's arms strongly around her and with her friends' comfort at her back, Amber stumbled finally from the ocean towards a shore of blankets and torches and sweet foods, until she felt the strange suction of her journey fall harmlessly away into the sea whence it came.

"I'm home," she murmured.

"No offence, but you're in no fit state to go anywhere but the rec hall," the Prince pronounced. "You're not home yet."

"I know," Amber growled pre-emptively as she stumbled to greet Jasper. "I look an unspeakable mess." She was too elated and exhausted to care.

The Prince smiled, considering, and calmly enfolded her shivering form into his white-shirted arms. "Mayhap. But you also look like you at your best, Amber. So I trust you'll be fine."

Beneath Moonstruck Waters

"You left me sleeping, and he's gone out there?" The rain drummed frantic fingers against the sodden ground beyond as Amber stared haunted from the rec hall bed into the relentless deluge outside, unable to be soothed until she could read some sort of sign that Racxen was okay. He didn't have to be here, but he had to be safe.

"I've got to help him." She broke away from the tangle of sheets and blankets and paced miserably, fraying Jasper's already fraught nerves.

"No—you want to help him," the Prince corrected, as soothingly as he could. "Like you want to find the remaining pelt pieces, which Racxen has gone out to find for you. I understand your fears, I truly do. But Amber, it's nearly dark. You can't possibly go out; none of us can, who do not possess the skills and abilities that enable one to meet the gaze of a Kelpie without losing their mind; and mounting one without allowing, or—dare I say—encouraging, it to carry one into the lake only to be dragged down into the depths. And, no offence, but I literally cannot think of anyone I would trust less on that account. And secondly, when it comes to Racxen," Jasper continued smoothly before Amber could break in with an indignant response, "that fool would give you a piece of his own skin if it meant you being able to finish your coat. If you ask me, he'll already have found the last fragment."

The Prince watched Amber stare out into the uneasy twilight, as if she thought that by watching his steps she could guard them.

"Good point," she admitted. Then she grinned, as fractious as the storm-torn, darkening sky. "Although not good enough to convince me to stay away."

Despite the warning sky, leadened after the torrential rain, Racxen luxuriated in feeling the soft earth beneath his feet cushioning his steps; its shifting nuances grounding him, centring him, bidding him focus elsewhere than on the difficulties and dangers ahead. So much of the quest so far had forced him to maintain diurnal hours, but if he were to have any hope of intercepting the Kelpie, he knew he needed to reacquaint himself with the night. And, with any luck, it might acquaint him with a pelt piece to further Amber's quest while she healed.

And so he had set out, instinctively shunning the grotesque stain of artificial light spilled by those gathering to pursue the Kelpie. He headed instead for the vast swathes of moonlit wilderness where the night stretched precious and limitless.

Racxen breathed deeply, letting his senses expand in attunement with the stretching darkness of a Realm slipped free from the chains of daylight. Everything felt softer and more secret, more exposed and more sacred. He began to relax in a way he hadn't noticed he'd been missing these past weeks amidst the constant knot of misgiving entangled by the sinister, ever-watching presence of the Oak Prince and the unrelenting fatigue of what the wight had put Amber through. Being unable to stop it had eaten away at him.

But with Amber safely returned and curled in sanctuary, Racxen allowed himself these moments. The darkness settled and steadied him, reconnected him with an earth-deep strength as he pushed on through the night.

The bells were still ringing out past midnight, to signal that the Kelpie had not yet been caught. The usually serene lakeside was a cacophony of beaters and whoopers, and Racxen wondered if the Genie had been right and the Realm had truly become moonstruck. He was glad that Amber was not here to see Fairymead descend to such madness, and it was with relief that he fled the clamour of voices and whistles and sought refuge following the tributaries that twisted and stretched out from the lake instead. Surely the Kelpie would be avoiding the main body of water and the din that surrounded it?

To run with a such a creature; so fast, so strong, so free—what a ride to share... As he padded reverently along unseen paths, Racxen felt his boyhood dreams rear up, long since quashed with the responsibilities of being a tracker.

On an intake of breath, the Kelpie appeared: shocking in its suddenness, startling in its silence. The Arraheng barely had time to wonder whether it had been his thoughts that had summoned it before the Kelpie's presence overwhelmed him. Racxen's skin tingled as though clutched in the grip of fever and he staggered unseeing, unable to focus as the night itself shuddered and convulsed as though in the grip of an enchantment too wild to be contained by the senses.

All else faded as his whole being latched onto the one sure sight before him: fluid, wild and coursing water, the Kelpie seemed to pour into his soul as it turned towards Racxen. Even limping along the rough-torn track it was magnificent. Yet the once proudly arched neck slumped tiredly, and the glistening flanks were drying. Only a restless, slanted eye that seemed to burn somehow deeper than its socket betrayed that here was not a horse of the earth. The creature stared; its gaze a challenge that no one had mentioned, its breath bellowing brokenly beneath pale ribs jutting from a sluicing coat.

The night waited, storm-laden and electric. Of course the Kelpie wanted to be ridden. Why else had it come?

"Those are my hopes I'm hearing, not your own answer," Racxen whispered in apology. "You cannot tell me yes. You will never need to tell me no."

The Arraheng approached unassumingly, and when the Kelpie neither shied nor postured, laid a hand aside its steaming neck. Its wet coat seemed to cling to the Arraheng's skin, tempting him to mount. As he bowed his head to rest his brow against the Kelpie's shoulder, Racxen felt its fur yield stickily, hungrily. He felt his own heartbeat thrill in time with the throb of that salt-flushed blood pulsing beyond the thinnest of barriers.

"I do not wish to ride you beyond endurance," Racxen murmured, ashamed. "This is not what I signed up for. I release you from your bond if it is in my power to do so, and beg you return to the waters to heal."

At his words, muscles bunched alarmingly in the Kelpie's stretching neck as with a hacking, frightening cough it regurgitated what Racxen was initially convinced would prove to be the remnants of its last rider, and it spat a throatful of slimy, pelleted fur onto the sodden floor. A strange chill traced the Arraheng's spine. This wasn't the half-digested remains of prey—this was the final piece of the Selkie's pelt. The Kelpie must have swallowed it to prevent it falling into fearsome hands.

Racxen bowed his head and, locking eyes to ascertain its agreement, crouched to retrieve the boon.

The Kelpie threw back its head, flinging out a mane that coursed water anew, its chilling cry of release issuing throatily behind un-equine teeth. For a moment Racxen felt its strange joy, and his heart surged to share in the ecstasy of a creature he would never again lay eyes upon, let alone share such an experience with.

But these moments were enough, as he stood silently on the bank amidst the tangle of yearning branches, watching wistfully as the Kelpie disappeared in a riot of thrashing water at the centre of the Lake—half-tempted to follow, but wholly sure that with the Kelpie running free and his own heart pounding in an echo of its hooves, magic would never fade from the Realm.

Uncounted moments later, a twig snapped and Racxen turned elated, half expecting the Kelpie's return. What he didn't expect was to see Jasper staring at him, ashen-faced.

"I'm sure you had your reasons," the Prince managed tightly. "But I hope you realise what you've done. And I am not going to be the one to explain this to my father."

The Seventh Soul

It was almost seal-size now, the pelt. Amber's routine had to be honed. Many things had to be sacrificed. *Prioritised,* she reminded herself. *This is a choice—my own at that—and I'm never going to have this opportunity or this privilege again.* Everything superfluous went.

And so the nights found her, each after each, in calm and in anguish. Sometimes, in the quietness of the late hours when the darkness of her room cuddled round her comfortingly, she would take out the pelt and curl up and sew it, hoping with all her heart that the sense of home long since torn from the Selkie might be infused back into it. And sometimes, on the nights when her mind buzzed and her heart skipped, she would wrap the pelt up under her cloak and take it down to the sea, and sit on the rocks—which was, she soon realised, not half as romantic and twice as uncomfortable as she had presumed—and sew until her hands grew numb, in the hope that the coat would become as flecked with freedom as it was rapidly becoming with sea spray.

As though in recognition of her closeness to completing the quest and the shrinking hours he had to ensnare her, the Oak Prince was becoming more insistent in his attempts to worm his way into the twilight at the edge of her consciousness. Yet with each thwarted attempt, Amber's resistance and resilience grew.

"You've left it too late to either dissuade me or disrupt my course," she warned in a high-spirited growl before the wight could even begin his latest onslaught tonight. "So, throw down your judgement where you will—it will find no lodging here." Her conviction crowded out the insipid, insidious presence until her reality left no room for him, and she felt the once sure Oak Prince dissipate until she was alone once more. She had enough good in her Realm to displace him just for now—and just for now was all she needed.

It felt as though nine tenths of the night must have passed before Amber let slip the needle from her cramping fingers and lifted the completed pelt with a surge of welling triumph that lifted her soul higher than all four winds of the Realm.

She'd done it. It didn't feel real—and yet she knew she would remember this feeling for all time. The relief that coursed through her crashed like a tumbling wave: she'd feared it would unseat her when it came, but instead it broke her anchor. She found herself floating in the exhilaration of all she had created and achieved, letting her horizon expand to surpass everything that she had once felt herself limited to. Past setbacks were rendered transient and insignificant. Her moment stretched until it encompassed everything she needed to hold on to for the future. She bathed in it, swam in it, felt as though she could fly forever on its updraft. It would always be hers and it would always be true. And she could always access it, from here on out.

Amber breathed more freely than ever before. It was time. The night outside her window lay calm, as if all its tension had eased with the culmination of her efforts. Amber, however, felt suddenly as though all its previous agitation had been washed into her. Now, after all, was the moment of truth. Re-making the pelt was one thing. Revealing it was another.

Amber let her gaze rest on the pelt for just a moment longer. It had never been hers to keep, but it had been in her care for a while. Its creation had awoken her, sustained her, reimagined her. Now its completion left her open, exposed. Her soul lay wrapped within its folds, ready to be stamped on to defend the pelt itself. Could she send it into the Realm and remain intact herself? She had never felt so vulnerable.

Or yet, so liberated. The joy and compulsion of it thrummed in her. How could she stop now? How could she hold it back? It would never grow greater than herself if she never let it live beyond herself—she must set it free, and there was only one way to do that…

I lived it and breathed it, she reminded herself. *But I only began it, and now it must continue. It must go to whom it was always destined for.* The rightness of what she must now do—and a restlessness to put herself to the test—tugged at her heart, urging her steps onwards again. There stretched before her a final gauntlet left to run: down to the sea, past the Oak Prince no doubt waiting. But the prospect beyond calmed the unease within her wrought by that insufferable wight; Amber knew, just as she had rashly foretold the Water Nymph, that the battle must play out now upon such shores as Zaralathaar had once turned her back on for the good of all people. It was in water magic and her own that she herself must now place her trust.

"A wild call, but a clear call," Amber promised the night as she gathered her precious full-limbed cargo to her chest and slipped out beneath the stars.

Though the chill of night still clung, dawn birds stirred in the quietude and proclaimed a delighted chorus as she ran past. Amber felt a sudden flush of kinship at their tiny, glorious testimony. Heart trembling, blood firing, dizzy with elation until she felt equally vulnerable and invincible, she cut through the forest—no longer fearful of the swallowing quiet or the ambiguous shadows. The trees were awakening, unfurling after the rain, and the darkness that had once blurred every conviction now obscured every doubt. The impressionistic depths held her, helped her, kept her from being swept away beneath the weight of what she must still accomplish.

So Amber ran on, spirits undampened. The current sweeping through the Realm might not be under her control, but she could surf it with the best. As she scudded down to the shore, the knowledge that she could finally help Hydd sustained her as surely as the pelt would revive the Selkie. She no longer needed to see the way, for she held it within her.

Shining sea spilled sudden silver beyond the dark arms of the forest, but Amber wasn't out of the woods yet. As abruptly as the passing of a cloud overhead the atmosphere changed; a suffocating veil rose to douse the bright stars and strangle the spacious breath of the trees, as the Oak Prince loomed to invade the sacred quiet.

Amber threw herself between branches and over tangled roots, tucking the pelt clumsily out of sight beneath her cloak and hoping desperately that she'd only been sensed, not seen. She couldn't let herself stop. Against her pumping breath, claustrophobia squeezed nauseatingly, bleeding into the horrible sensation of something holding its breath and tensing still and taut and ready. With sickening certainty, Amber understood the fatal change. Now that the pelt had been completed, her fraught relationship with the Oak Prince had splintered. The predator had tired of playing with the prey. There would be no more threats, no more empty words. His next blow wouldn't taunt, as it so often had, the better to analyse her weaknesses and wear her down. There was no need of that any more. The imperative now was simply to kill. And she was by far the easiest target—Hydd would become whole again, whereas she was destined to remain broken.

"I might not be whole," Amber muttered in final promise to the brave trees curling protectively around her, standing firm amongst the cursed darkness the wight had cast. "But I can be well." She thought of Hydd, and clutched the pelt more tightly. "And one of us will be both. Tonight."

Overhead, a shadow passed like a storm as the Oak Prince shivered in rage.

He had underestimated the wingless one.

And all the Realm would bear witness to his retribution.

Skidding across the sand, Amber flung herself towards the surf like a Sea Maiden reunited with the ocean. The shallows rolled and swirled as though conjuring life at her feet, and the depths beyond drew her hypnotically. Surely here was the place to reach Hydd?

Amber stared out, drawing strength from the mesmeric waves as openly and freely as she drank in the healing taste of the wild, ocean-crossed winds. This felt right. It felt like it was going to work. Yet fear cramped her fingers more severely than the cold as a savage memory seized. 'A death upon the sands', the Oak Prince had warned. What if she couldn't save Hydd?

What if she couldn't save herself? The prospect thrashed suddenly, cavernous and terrible.

But what if you can? asked the mist, rippling a banner of summons as dawn rose like a promise over the pale glass of a calm sea

And so Amber strode into the surf, drawn as if entranced. Her footsteps trod surely; this was of her making, this magic. The ink-glossed water swelled and slurped around her, glinting spellbindingly as though with some latent primordial force beginning to waken. She sent her voice out to it, not to summon a lost being, but to ask a friend to hear her.

The waves sighed and soothed with the steadiness of a rising and falling breath. As her voice drifted atop the sun-lustred surface, Amber stood and stared, her vision swimming in the expanse of sky above the sea as the wind blew spray against her hair. It felt so long ago that she had first made her pledge to Hydd. Would he heed the call? Had he ever actually believed in her enough to listen out for it?

Amber waited at the threshold, swathed in a silence thick with hope.

"Ah always kenned that she who walks 'tween Realms would lead me haem." Hydd's voice arrived as quietly as his footsteps as he approached, his skin looking so pale amongst the shadows of this place that he almost glowed. She'd never seen him shiver before, but now he was convulsively trembling. Amber felt a similar tremor grip her as she waded towards him, seized in the urgency of this moment towards which everything had been staggering and which even now just before the completion still trembled.

She gritted her teeth against the panic that her best might not be good enough as she relinquished the pelt, her fingers seizing with the cold as she clutched her work. She grinned lopsidedly in embarrassment. She'd wanted it to look magnificent for him; for it to reflect the hours of work, the tiniest detail of effort; all the frustration and joy and surging triumph she had felt completing it. But it just looked like a bedraggled sealskin.

"My friend Yenna is a Wolf Sister," Amber blurted in anxious explanation. "She tends something precious which transcends her transformation and keeps her safe in the in-between. I hope this pelt can do the same. I hope it protects your soul when you shift between skins. I know it means more for you—but for what it's worth, it meant everything to me."

She flushed as he took it with shaking hands, and averted her eyes as he ran his cold, searching fingers over her work: the part of him that once was broken and that he had trusted her to heal.

"This will always be a part of who ye are, tae," he whispered. "Naught can diminish tha'; nae the completion, nae the handin' o'er. Amber, I will forever be in yer debt."

She returned his gaze, buoyant and sure and calm, steady in the face of the gravity and meaning of the moment. A smile flicked across her mind as she wondered whether she had, through working so closely with the skin, inherited something of a Selkie's ability to witness, to bear out, to sit with and accept without having to deflect. Yet Hydd's eyes told her that her efforts had instead activated something she had held inside her all along.

She found she was able to grin, bow her head in thanks, and neither refuse the complement nor shy from its intimation.

Yet, mindful that what would come next might be too intimate a moment to have an audience, Amber turned to leave.

"Bide," his lilting voice asked shakily, suddenly sounding far younger than his ravaged frame or grizzled coat. So she stayed, watching the black waters eddy mysteriously as she heard first the rustle of clothes onto rock and finally the whisper of fur over skin.

His groan of release washed through her and the surface of the sea began to shudder, as though realising one long estranged was about to come home. As Amber looked up, it brought tears to her eyes to witness the fur that as patches in her hands had looked so separate, so dead, now flowing as if alive across his form as he stood half-shapen, the remainder of the pelt hanging at his waist. He didn't look lost, or frightened, or fragile. Not any more. He looked astonishing. He looked himself.

"In returnin' mah skin an' mah soul, ye hae restored mah power." Hydd's voice shivered huskily, and Amber realised suddenly how little he had been permitted to reveal of himself while under the curse. The waves sounded muted, as though the ocean's breath had become quick and shallow. Against the impressionistic haze of sky-night, the Selkie's outline seemed more a vortex than a shadow.

"I can heal one o' yer hurts, if ye wish." His voice slid as safe and soothing as it always had. "Only once, but my debt tae ye is boundless an' my heart is ready."

There in the darkness she felt the power radiating from him, lapping softly at her heart. Whispering promises she never expected to be offered.

"You know that's not why I did this." Amber breathed carefully, clutched with a certain coldness around the site of her wing stubs. The lack of sensation still, even now, provoked pain. And yet, her body was no longer the enemy. It had more than carried her; it had orchestrated her survival thus far. It had awakened her to possibilities she'd never known lay within her reach. Beneath Racxen's touch, the whole of her came alive enough to eclipse all sense of lack that dared still sometimes haunt her— and alone, clutched in the fell embrace of the Icefields, she had skinbreathed, wings or none. Her feelings settled, and she thought suddenly of another.

"Ask Ruby, instead," she responded with certainty, handing him the bracelet to scent. "And, if she wishes, make your offer."

Hydd smiled a daybreak smile as he breathed it in, and his promise danced like sunlight upon the curling sea.

A smile bloomed in Amber's heart too, for she could feel the waves of belonging and completion washing through Hydd and radiating from him now that he was one with his skin, and she rejoiced on his behalf. Yet something in her own chest pained her, for she was ashamed to admit that she wanted some of that sensation too. So often since losing her wings, she had felt like she was noting everything distractedly, observing longingly but no longer able to fully connect.

The Selkie's response flowed as soothingly as the sea. "D' ye nae recognise tha', amidst the ashes o' that mirk time, ye hae forged a deeper connection atween the Realm an' its beloved inhabitants than ye ha' ever experienced afore? Ye hae been buildin' on it e'er since. Abody main journey a long way tae come haem, an' ye hae travelled far." His gaze rested on her, searching and gentle. "Yer journey's end is nae within my sight, but ye ken where tae go tae find yerself, Amber—so anywhere ye find yerself is yer haem, fur ye feel sure o' yer ain skin."

Amber nodded slowly, taking courage from his gaze. He was right: she did. She really did. Hydd wasn't questioning her choice; he was giving it solemnity. A chance to solidify. Travelling further suddenly lost its fear.

"Pledge me one thing." Hydd's soft Selkie eyes missed nothing, she realised as she nodded.

"Dinnae furget. Wear yer ain skin proudly. It will be important, afore th' end."

Amber remembered her imminent rendezvous with the Oak Prince and shivered. But she gathered her courage. "Soul-heartedly."

"Stoatin," Hydd approved. Velvet webbing curled around Amber's fingers as the Selkie took her hand in his. "Dinnae fear the next steps, Am. Ye hae sae much power in ye, sae much magic. An' if ye find ye'sel' needin' remindin', ye need nae stride out somewhere alone an' far away. Come tae the Selkie shore," he reminded softly. "Ye are already welcome. An' there are still wild places, which hold pockets o' whit might be called magic, if we but dare tae name it so. In any of those places, call my name, an' ah will come fur ye."

Her heart swelled in gratitude, and yet she felt unworthy of such an offer. "But I'm not a Selkie."

Hydd watched her calmly, his liquid eyes accepting. "Ye hae sewn mah skin back together. Whit would happen if ye chose tae trust that yers is flawless exactly as it is?"

Amber couldn't answer that. "I'll miss you," she mumbled awkwardly instead. "I'll miss your chill hands, and your quiet voice, and the fact your molten eyes hold a peace the Oak Prince hasn't been able to shatter and a hope he'll never snuff out."

Hydd's eyes swam with the wisdom of the oceans. "Our folk dinnae hae words fur gratitude as deep as mine fur ye, which ah hold as closely as ye held mah skin tae yers," he admitted softly. "Selkies share a gaze, an' all is communicated. But the words we do hae hold their ain power, an' in the realm o' magic, ah can grant this: in times far frae now when ye hae need o' such a thing to hae faith in, remember: One spared tae the brine is three spared tae the land." His eyes shone with a magic chill and strange and sure.

What they had shared shimmered through Amber sacredly, aching and healing, awakening and satiating as she considered his awe-stirring words. She yearned to know how he could speak of such things with such confidence. Yet his serenity enveloped her so steadily and unswervingly, like an incoming Renë tide, that she felt no need to question his prophecy, even should it later come to naught.

In response, Hydd smiled his empathic, oceanic smile, and with webbed, furred fingers tugged a ragged, skin-soft edge carefully from his pelt, and tied the piece around her wrist.

"I don't understand," Amber's voice wobbled uncertainly, although her heart flushed with gratitude. "Don't you need this?"

"Ye will, later."

Amber's eyes narrowed in worry. "Do you mean I'll understand—or I'll need it?"

Those memorable eyes gleamed reassuringly from a now whiskered face as he slipped his skin across. Without being able to look back and note the particular moment it had finally happened, Amber saw that he was changed entirely.

As his soulful eyes looked into hers she laid a hand on him, and he lifted his muzzle to taste the sea breeze. He felt like a strange kind of wet dog, fat and firm and sleek and warm. And he felt like he radiated happiness. *I'm part of that,* she rejoiced silently, her grin stretching like the folds of that most comfortable of skins. *I will always be part of that, no matter what happens next.*

"What now?" she found herself asking, now that he couldn't answer.

"Many things are found a' th' edge," she heard the echo of his voice slither away between the rocks as he hauled himself towards the sea. "Journey there, an' seek that which ye cannae ask fur."

A thrill of fear snaked to realise Hydd was right. The quest was far from over: there was still the Oak Prince and the matter of the Kelpie to contend with.

And yet as she walked back, the sea and the sun clung to her, reminding her of what she had already accomplished. The coolness of the damp, crusting sands forged a second skin atop her sea-raw limbs, and she returned home with salt-air-infused lungs and a steadied heart, prepared for the next challenge.

Fighting with Water

"Racxen!" Amber reached him just as he was about to enter the castle. "You're not doing this alone." Her mouth was mud and urgency as she kissed him. "I stand by your decisions as wholeheartedly as my own. I trust you as much as I have ever shown you and more. I'm coming with you."

Racxen grinned at her wonderingly, as though he feared that her being here was just some trick of the marshlight, so she kissed him again.

"I thought I could do this quietly, and spare you the anxiety," he acquiesced gratefully. "But the entire Selkie clan is on the shore and, it feels like, half the Realm is with them. With you here, I can go through with this. I can tell Morgan, and bear what comes after."

The Arraheng took strength from Amber's steadying hand, slipped inside his. He hadn't felt so trapped since that night of bargaining with Thanatos. This time, as then, he'd felt so sure he had been doing the right thing. And yet now, to have his news broken across the Realm like a storm cloud that could no longer bear its load, risked unseating him more violently than the Kelpie ever could.

The night had stilled, but the wind that whispered in from the sea was still shivering in trepidation. *Fear strips your senses*, his tracker instinct reminded. *Stand firm.*

With Amber at his side, that was easier to do. Next to him, her silhouette felt as solid as a Gargoyle's. *What I did was right*, he promised himself, as softly and surely as her shadow. *I will bear its consequences undaunted.*

Amber squeezed his hand tighter. And unafraid.

"I will see you on the shore," Racxen promised, his resolve set. His mind took refuge with the waves. Like Amber, they hadn't abandoned him. They hadn't changed their steady, calming breath. The news hadn't broken them. They would be here when he came back.

With a final strengthening, sealing kiss, he strode into the castle.

Nerves strung taut, Amber paced towards the shoreline. She was beyond thrilled with Hydd's reunion, but it seemed incongruous that the

Selkies were already celebrating, when so much remained at stake. She sighed the uncharitable thought away—they had no way of knowing Racxen's choice, and they deserved their joy wholeheartedly.

Still, her knowledge would shatter their illusions, so she felt too guilty to join them. She took refuge in Jasper's company, finding him loitering similarly awkward and away from the revelry, and together they waited.

The Arraheng returned sheened in sweat. He looked as sick as if he had taken an audience with the Goblin King, instead of Jasper's own father.

"What happened?" the Prince blurted, feeling sick in turn as Amber wrapped him in a hug.

After returning her embrace, Racxen dragged his claws through his hair and turned to Jasper. "Reading all your books, you might have known this," he admonished weakly. "What do Kelpies do with their prey?"

Jasper stalled. "Eat them. Don't they?"

Racxen sighed. "In all the books you've ever read, have you encountered a carnivorous horse?"

Jasper's blood ran cold. "What are you saying? What do they do?"

"They desire you to ride them, because they need you to touch them, so their skin can begin to fuse with yours." Racxen waited for Jasper to realise what he meant, but the Prince looked blank. Racxen growled in frustration. "They steal your skin. You've seen how fluid they are. They don't have a proper skin of their own. They rely on the skins of those who touch them for protection. It's a kind of symbiosis."

Jasper looked decidedly green. "Not a very mutually beneficial one."

Racxen's heart thumped in recognition. "But for a time, they offer what the Realm's inhabitants most desire: a merging, a union, a dissolution of barriers and boundaries."

"So they steal their rider's skin; I get the picture," Jasper assured him hurriedly. "But what if the Kelpie did... acquire... a new skin? How would that help the Oak Prince?"

"For a time, after the merging, the new skin is loose and vulnerable. Easy to steal from the Kelpie's own back."

Jasper felt sick. "So, you're saying because Amber thwarted his plan to steal Hydd's skin, he wanted to highjack the Kelpie's attempt to steal another? What now? He's running out of options."

Racxen nodded, exhausted. "If he'd managed to take the Kelpie's new skin, he'd have been able to draw magic from it to sustain his own. And I can only think of one other being, of similar power, who merges her skin."

"The Song Weaver," Amber finished in horror. "He's going to come after her."

Jasper sank his head into his hands. "So, we have to find a way of protecting her. And after all this, there was never any truth to our only hope of protecting the Fountain? Of protecting ourselves?"

"Perhaps there was, or perhaps there was not," Racxen dismissed. "None of us would countenance the sacrifice of an endangered animal for any boon—potential or proven. Most likely, it was just another lie spun by the Oak Prince in the hope we would collude with his plan." The Arraheng watched the Fairy King and his Horse Master advisor approach the shore from the castle, Magnus clearly trying to carry on a conversation Morgan considered long over.

"The Moonstruck Lake Kelpie is gone." The Horse Master's warning rose angrily as he reached the waiting crowd clustering anxiously like moths around a diminishing flame. "With the Fountain sorely endangered, we are all in mortal peril. The time has come, sire, when we must fight fire with fire—"

They all stopped and stared, as through the sea mist the Selkie man whose skin Amber had re-sewn emerged from the shallows, the water streaming from his pelt and a crown the colour of sand gracing his head.

The sea shone with his power, the waves flowing into green-gold enchantment and glittering to rival the encroaching domination of the forest. "You have not yet run out of water," Hydd reminded them, an enigmatic smile lingering upon his pale, pelagic face. A strange, sure glow shone from his viridescent eyes as he stepped into the Nymph's place.

Sea Fever

That night, her soul was still singing from joining the tribe in their celebration of Racxen's choice with the Kelpie when Amber stood at the doorway of her own home once again, sleep impossible, her senses thrumming and her soul both settled and stimulated. She had sewn the pelt, and the rightful bearer to whom she had glad-heartedly returned it was, with his power restored, proving an Enchanter to match Zaralaathar herself. His youthful energy offered a perfect complement to the age-honed skill of the Water Nymph, and their forces combined were conjuring magic anew to the Realm without forcing the involvement of the Kelpie, thus turning the tide against a struggle the Selkie had for so long been forced to watch impotently from the sidelines. In this knowledge, and with the Kelpie safe as well, even as the Oak Prince swept his unknowable trials ever closer Amber felt buoyed atop a success-swollen sea.

And so, drawn by a pull she could neither resist nor understand, she let herself run down to the shore, for even now the heave and crash of the oceans buzzed in her veins, thrumming a fierce joy that burned its course through her blood. She had done it! She might not be the best seamstress or the bravest soul in the Realm but, whatever might happen after, she had made this happen and had survived thus far. That was something to be proud of; she pledged to remember it always. So, for tonight, she would let herself bask in the glow of the strange delight brought in on the tide in the wake of Hydd's return and cavort amongst the glittering waves.

As the shore slipped into view, Amber heard the ocean sigh like the release of a long-held breath. Its steady, rhythmic flow soothed her frantic pulse and realigned her off-kilter emotions. The inky depths before her held no fear, cresting instead a sparkle that dared her to hope for the future as the sea mists slithered in as though Kelpie-summoned; drenching and intoxicating and promising to shield the night from the glare of morning for a few hours longer as she ran down to greet the sea.

The sandcrust sprang gritty and cool beneath her feet, slowing her fevered steps.

Close she padded, and yet the deep urged her closer. Strange echoes of light coursed across the surf as the sea's fingers played lightly against the shore, speaking to Amber in a language she could neither define nor resist. And so she found herself, disoriented yet certain, at a new threshold, with the disinhibited howls of the wind tugging at her throat and the drunken waters surging and sloshing around her feet.

The sea pounded its ancient rhythm, complicated and contradictory, against the rocks. Amber couldn't work out whether it was drumming a warning or a summons, as it threshed the night into a strange kind of fever; a fever she felt herself caught in.

She had half let herself imagine, swept up in the power of the night, that the sea had called only to her, but she found herself relieved to glimpse a stalwart, equine silhouette striding solidly amidst the shifting tides towards her. Amber grinned in the darkness, and hailed the Centaur gladly. Han made anything feel normal enough—and magical enough—to handle.

"Tempestuous night," Han offered gently, stronger than the conflicting storm of currents tugging around her.

"It's the honour Hydd deserves," Amber agreed, wistful and proud, her grin flowing like water. "The entire ocean is welcoming him back. I want to be part of that for him, but it's hard to enter the sea just yet," she admitted, embarrassed at the revelation. "I can't feel calm. Too much is still at stake."

"Much still is," Han recognised. "But so much freedom, so much peace, has been won back also. You have been part of that—the revelry is yours, too."

Amber's soul ached to know his words were true and yet she felt an old fear squirm, risen painfully close to the surface with her skin rubbed raw in the wake of all that had happened and in the knowledge that she still had to face the Oak Prince. "I'm prouder than ever to have handed back the pelt, but I feel like I'm less, without it to do," Amber managed. "The wight told me not to hand it back. He warned me that it would feel like I was dying."

The green light of the forest shone agleam in Han's eyes as the Centaur stood strong and steaming in the shallows beside her. "Maybe he doesn't know what being reborn feels like."

Amber let his words sink deeper than her own fear had settled, and she threw her last doubts to the sea for the waves to dash. "I'd better show him," she admitted with a decisive grin, stamping her fears into the sand and letting the sea lift her. "I can't wait forever for these clouds to break."

Han smiled back, understanding. "Time to dance beneath the storm."

She ran with him into the surf, the wet sands sinking and supporting in equal measure, urging them onwards with all the abandon of the magic-flung night until Han was rearing and bucking like a colt in the shallows and Amber was breathless with excitement, the waves lifting and swaying her, carrying her in a timeless dance of grace and power. She was sure she could hear the sweet song of the Sea Maidens surging around her.

A heartsoaring cry beyond the purest of songs splintered the ocean into myriad scattering swells, for in amongst them danced an equine soul wilder and more ecstatic than even Han's: the Kelpie was here. In amongst them, transforming the water into a vessel of ecstasy, it moved like a creature from another time, binding magic back into the water and infusing the revellers equally.

Watching the Kelpie rear and cavort through the waves, Amber felt enveloped in a depthless longing that seemed to need no other home but to partake of this moment. The Kelpie was free and, in the knowledge she had done her all for Hydd and seen it good enough, something in her was free as well.

"Ye're allowed tae need both, ye ken." Hydd surfaced in Selkie form, sea-slicked and breathless and webbed with magic. "The Realm abune an' the Realm beneath—they balance, nae negate, each other. The brine will ne'er turn its back on ye, Am. Ye need nae bide away."

She hugged him in thanks, his sleek, soaking skin doggish and warm, as muscular as the rippling ocean. "You owe me nothing."

"Aye, tha's how it is wi' friends," Hydd pronounced in deep satisfaction, his sea-glass gaze lingering on hers. He gestured further along the shore, and bid her see.

Amber gasped in delight. Weaving amongst the heaving waters of the shallows rolled dozens of Selkies. Spilling like ink through their element, they jostled and spun and barked in tumbling ecstasy through the waves, welcoming the Realm's inhabitants in as Wolfren, Fairies, Arraheng gathered, drawn by the sacred pull of this night.

With one unified voice, the Selkies invited them closer, bid them be not afraid.

Amber's grin split open on an influx of joy. She might not be able to survive the Oak Prince. But these moments, right here and now, gem-cut and gleaming, held all eternity. And with enough of them gathered, clutched tightly to her chest so they could never be stolen, she knew she could face that wight.

And so she threw herself into the night as though it would never end. She ran through the surf with the Selkies, enjoying the anointment of its foam brushing her face, plunging beneath the liquid night of the ocean and letting her heart surge with the waves. She heard the glorious calls of sea birds reverberate knowingly around her as she revelled in the wildness and the wonder while the wind yowled its recognition to her.

Awe descended, both peeling her open and blanketing her in comfort. Somehow, the Realm was still vast and unknowable—and, somehow, the awareness settled her spirit as much as it buoyed her soul. She was a child of all this. This couldn't possibly break her—instead it would continue to define her, mould her, lift her spirit as it had once lifted her wings. And on it, her entire spirit could fly.

She had to bring Racxen here, she realised suddenly. He deserved to be out in this more than anyone. And there was no one she'd rather spin this wild dance of joy with, or run atop the dishevelled tide beside.

She let the next wave catch her and sweep her back to the silver-edged shore and, with her fear sloughed away by the sea, she left her doubts and uncertainties to sink into the mud behind her, until only the serenity instilled by this night lingered, clinging like salt to her drying skin. She strode from the water with a lighter mind—and a sea-drawn soul washed through with magic.

The sand settled solidly beneath her feet now, as did her plan. Amidst the spirit-settling, mind-clearing space of the shore, the muted roar of the ocean resounding like a bloodrush behind her in her ears. It grew curiously easier to orient herself. With an encouraging wind at her back and the sea air singing in her lungs, Amber turned for home. Letting her thoughts turn to what she had yet to accomplish didn't seem so dangerous now, when she had these moments behind her and seeing Racxen ahead.

Yet where the shore met the meadow-sward, Jasper stood, at once a pale candle ghost upon the dry shore and a guardian at the cross roads, holding back as though trying not to intrude.

"It's not enough though, is it?" Amber murmured, the weight she'd so recently managed to cast off making a desperate clawed grab for her ankles. It was almost a relief to see the Prince, not least because he looked serious enough that she need not pretend she could cope with more than she could, and in relinquishing some of that effort she could redistribute her energy where it was better needed. But more than that, his stoicism steadied her, and she knew, just as she knew he would watch to keep her safe and deny himself such revels, that she would brave any storm to ease his burden. Preferably without telling him.

"The celebrations were timely, and they lifted my heart to witness—but I'm afraid not, how things now stand, for they appear to have hastened the Oak Prince's plans," Jasper pronounced warily, offering Amber his dry cloak. "After all, we must remember, it seems his motivation has always been his self-assumed duty to tend the balance of life. Which might not, at first hearing, sound evil," he added, unable to stave the repugnance from his voice. "To prune off the weak and refocus energy, in a magic-leached Realm, where it has the best chance of surviving has a certain pragmatism, as a theory. But it cannot be countenanced in life, for followed to its terrifying and logical conclusion it would assign death to some, when all deserve life and protection. Your Selkie friend was the epitome of what that wight was trying to erase. And then with Racxen re-writing the rulebook for the Kelpie—well, you're messing with forces beyond your control and comprehension. And once again you've dragged the rest of us behind with you."

It was with considerable relief that Amber realised the Prince was smiling dryly instead of glaring at her.

"Once again, you'll learn to live with it," she retorted, grinning, lightheaded with the storm dance and lack of sleep.

Jasper rolled his eyes. "You know what you're doing, exactly?" he pressed.

Amber shrugged brightly. "No, but I've got a vague, half-formed kind of an idea, and that's enough to run with for now."

Jasper huffed. "Just like old times, then."

Amber grinned. "As ever, though, I am indebted to your advice and support more than I tell you. I need to be ready, because you're right: it wasn't the Kelpie the Oak Prince feared most," she admitted. "It was the Selkie. The Kelpie gifted the final pelt piece, but Hydd was the heir to the Fountain."

"So you've restored one prince to full glory, and robbed another of his final chance at a skin," Jasper warned. "There is going to be a reckoning."

Amber nodded grimly. "At Trickster's Gate."

And yet, she strode from the water with a lighter mind and a surer soul. Doused in the sluicing embrace of the sea, Amber's salt-drying skin felt suddenly a closer, better fit. She no longer felt like a part of her was tearing away and being left in the sea, when she returned to dry land. She felt like a part of the sea was coming with her.

The Oak Prince was waiting in the forest. Well, she'd bring the whole Realm.

Wolf's Eye Vigil

Yenna couldn't bring herself to join the revelry in the surf, instead standing still and stalwart atop the cliff above. The coast seemed to be safe, but the Wolf Sister had long ago learnt to trust her instincts. Her friends had earned their celebrations, but it would not have felt right to leave them unguarded.

The Oak Prince surged towards the sands, as erratic and unhinged as a gathering squall. But his volatile mind was centred for once, for it had deadly purpose to settle itself upon: with the Kelpie and the Selkie Lord both returned to the storm and the sea and the source of their power, it was time for a new sacrifice to be torn from the ocean. And so the forest he left behind quailed and trembled in his wake.

As her friends revelled in the pull of the ocean below, Ruby spun her own song of triumph amidst the darting clouds above, letting the cold air skin the outside of her and peel away everything superfluous until it felt like there was only her soul left: cleansed and clarified and flowing through an endless sea of stars, come alive anew amidst the battering elements as though she were blood and the sky a body.

She let her surroundings blur into the flight, feeling her Realm both expand and narrow as everything regrouped into a unique focus; every obstacle stripped away by a speed-borrowed sense of the transience of all she was witnessing and experiencing, the mist-muted smears of earthen colours daubed far below the only proof that she was still anchored to the Realm beneath instead of streaming through an eternity entirely hers alone.

Ruby breathed more steadily now, although her core fizzed and burned as though she were scattering away into bubbles to become part of every sector of the Realm. This was why she loved flying—not for the proof of her own impermanence, of course, but for a reminder of how everything mattered even more so because of it.

Including everything down there, from the lantern-scattered shore of the Southern Sands to the empty, dark curve of the Silent Sound far beyond, left abandoned and vulnerable amidst the celebrations. That lightless, overlooked emptiness called to her. Suddenly wishing it to know it wasn't alone, Ruby banked sharply towards it, gathering speed.

She had never flown so far at night, but her heart guided her wings beyond all logical knowing. She unerringly followed the shore-flung crests of white glowing aside the swathes of grey-swept sea, and the curve of stone-toothed jaws heralding the closest edge of the Silent Sound jutted proudly offshore to lead her down. Preparing for the descent, Ruby squinted down through the streaming winds and mapped the desolate shorescape reflected back to her with a fierce joy as if the place were possessed with spirit. She felt her own soul swell in response to realise that here was somewhere powerful and pure, which refused to be beautiful. Perhaps it was the perfect place for her this night, and she let herself drift closer, feeling as though she were being drawn, caught in the sea's current even as she swept through the sky.

But then she flared her wings in amazement, snapping from her descent and treading air awkwardly in astonishment, thoughts whirling as altitude yielded to the clarity of the lower reaches and the strangest sight greeted her wondering eyes.

Tangled, luminous webbing sprawled through the shallows of the Sound; whole trailing mats of the stuff, drifting by the shore. Almost like a membrane between sea and land.

Could such a membrane prove protective?

What had begun as the instinctive, singular response of a compassionate heart, bloomed now into a vital, coherent plan. Ruby had an idea. And Amber wasn't the only one who could sew.

Amber's soul lifted as the warm spiced scent of smoke curling on the air from the Wolfren camp reached her across the sands. Her head spun with lack of sleep, and yet on this of all nights she felt like she could last forever and so, unable to find Racxen or Ruby, she'd sought out the Wolf Sister.

"Jasper's attempting to research this figure from the annals of antiquity, and I will return to join him now my watch is over," Yenna reassured the Fairy as she embraced her warmly in greeting, her eyes as fierce as the storm clouds darkening the approaching horizon. Enveloped in the Wolf Sister's presence, Amber could almost forget that she would soon have to stand alone before her foe.

"If you must meet with him, we can at least arm you with knowledge, and even the Prince of Fairymead had to admit the Library Vaults of Loban are still the most comprehensive." When Yenna smiled, her canines showed, although her voice softened in concern, for she knew upon which fears Amber's mind would be dwelling.

"I have long had to pit myself against those who would kill off the wolf or woman within me, so I know what it is to have someone seek to rob me of my own coat," Yenna admitted quietly. "I will not let anyone tear yours from you, not least after you've given one back to another." The Wolf Sister spoke so blazingly that it warmed Amber's heart. If Yenna believed it, Amber was prepared to too.

"Yet, before the Wildwood, there may be one other arena we have to face him on," the Wolf Sister cautioned. "Ruby came here, to warn me. She's been spending a lot of time with the Selkies, for one obvious reason in particular, and she reminded me that the Selkie Lord is not the Seal Folk's—nor the Realm's—only protector. So, until he reaches his full power under the tutelage of the Water Nymph, he is not the one who poses the greatest threat to the Oak Prince."

Amber's breath caught. "But the Song Weaver is?"

"Your Song Weaver is their Sea Mother. And now that the Selkie Lord's strength is returning, the Oak Prince has only the smallest of windows within which to strike. Ruby fears he will attack the Song Weaver."

Revulsion rose like bile in Amber's throat. "Because of her accommodating skin. We have to—"

Something about Yenna's poise silenced the Fairy, and she held both her tongue and her breath, taking her lead from the Wolf Sister.

The wind gusted fretfully, as if knowing its companions stood now between two worlds on the cusp between danger and relief, as the Oak Prince's voice stole towards them like poison ivy.

"Let it happen, Wolf Witch. The Sea Witch is dangerous; there is no place for her in the new Realm. Imagine a Realm without the hurts and griefs she carries around. It will be better for you. Less volatile. Less messy. Less unpredictable." The words clouded—suffocating, disorienting, and draining.

Yenna let her fingers creep to the frayed edges of the bandana she had worn since girlhood; a tattered link unimpressive to an onlooker no doubt, but one which had allowed her soul time and again to be plucked from obscurity and danger by the mouths of her brethren and the hands of her friends. She clutched the sand-clung, time-crumpled fabric now, counted most dear amongst all her meagre possessions.

Her golden eyes glowered proudly in the direction of the sibilant, insufferable voice. "So what you're saying is: I would simply be less."

Silence gaped like a wound around them; but it was one struck against the wight, Amber reminded herself. She knew the Wolf Sister needed her silence more than her speech right now, and so she refused to be drawn into something she could not extricate herself from without endangering her friend. As surreptitiously as she could, Amber inched just slightly closer to her instead.

"The 'magic' you rely on is sorcery," the Oak Prince wheedled, changing tack. "It will ruin you, rip you apart. You are as children playing with fire; you need defending from yourselves. You lack restraint. I can see you seek freedom, but you deserve protection as well. I can grant you both."

"I require neither your limitation nor your liberation," Yenna corrected, golden eyes afire with all the power of the borderless sands. "I don't need to buy your brand of freedom. I carve my own."

"Brave words, standing with the skinless one." Menace dripped anew from that dead-breath voice.

"I stand with whom I choose, wood-wight, and my skin is not such that you can flay it from my back and cast its pieces to the wind," Yenna warned with a growl. "It took me many seasons to wear it with pride, yet both sides of me are as entwined as blood amongst flesh, and sinew between bones. I would rather die than be forced to surrender half of what I am. I can live richly; I can live poorly. But I must live freely. And remember this, for I am not in the mood to allow you to forget: I will fight with all the fury of both woman and wolf any that would seek to tear half my soul from me—and that is nothing compared to what I will do if you threaten my friends."

It was all Amber could do not to punch the air as the spectre faded.

Yenna squeezed her hand, understanding.

"Mark: this battle is not destined to be settled on the dusty plains this time, half-mind. There are fights that have not come to you yet, while you grovel and fret over this one." A faint impression of a sharp-edged figure, swathed in leaves, reared before fading.

A flicker of uncertainty invaded those steady eyes, and Yenna growled a muttered challenge of her own to the now-empty air. "Whichever arena you choose, my teeth will grind your branches so small that your memory will be lost to both story and song, scattered beneath the sands of my kingdom," she spat.

For all her friend's bravado, Amber could feel the outrage thrumming in Yenna's threatened soul. "You have given me peace, and I would give it back to you if I could," she soothed, once she could trust that they were alone. "It's not you he's accosted, and demanded to meet in challenge, after all," she grinned. It was easier to be strong for her friends than it was for herself.

Yenna was still bristling. "Why not?"

Amber shivered. "Probably because he's not in the habit of losing."

Yenna's temper doused instantly. "We will arm you, to the extent that we are able," she promised, golden eyes sincere and glowing. "We will come with you, as far as we can, and we will stand by you in any way possible. You will not be unprepared when you stride out before the Gate."

Amber was careful to keep her breathing steady. "That was close, though. It's not safe for you to be around me."

"A lone wolf is no wolf," Yenna shushed cheerfully. "We must turn our minds away from angst and towards action," she reassured, her golden eyes distant as her mind raced. "The Song Weaver's skin is as generous as her spirit, and we have a chance now of defending her. But we must make haste, for the sea is not yet safe."

Breathless after her flight, Ruby hastened to the shining shallows and the draping strands swirling adrift beneath the water's surface.

They had to be magic, intuition urged her. Sea magic. Cast off from the Kelpie, from Hydd's transformation, even. They glowed life-green, like the eyes of the Selkie. *You fool*, Ruby warned herself, brimming with a hope that felt at moments like these felt more akin to despair. *You're in even deeper than he is.*

She huffed a steadying breath. *But this isn't just for him, so get on with it.*

The strands swayed like tentacles, staying her hand.

"The Oak Prince underestimated the Kelpie, it seems," the Genie murmured, conjured on moon-glanced reflections scudding atop glistening water and joining the Fairy's gaze. "It is the storm personified. Magic made tangible. The strands trailing from the Kelpie's neck? Magic. The phosphorescence glittering in the heaving waves of his wake? The very same. And the sea is a thrumming cauldron, brimming with potential, for it to have been cast into."

His potent voice enveloped her like a wreath. "And such a woman for it to have been cast before."

Ruby wrinkled her nose uncertainly as she dipped a hand in and the strands tangled amongst her trailing fingers. They felt gloopy and peculiar. Far more... visceral than she had imagined. "They're kind of gross."

"Gross, or surprising?" the Genie countered probingly, without judgement. "What are you surprised by? Its nature—or the fact it does not repulse you?"

Ruby shivered at the chill touch of the sea, which was wrapping gentle fingers around her upper arm as she reached in further. "You ask a lot of questions. I don't have many answers."

The Genie settled, as still and watchful as a cloud. "A lot of questions for a lot at stake: an entire age, in fact. But for you, Ruby Rhodonite, I have a lot of time. And, I suspect, you may have the one answer you need."

"Fair enough," Ruby grinned, rising to the challenge. "The Song Weaver needs me, so I wish to use the strands of magic, if I can."

The Genie swelled proudly. "Told you."

Ruby sniffed, to conceal her pride. She swirled her hand above the strands, and they reached towards her in unison. "Why are they responding to me?" she asked curiously.

The Genie gestured expansively. "They are a manifestation of one of the most potent forms of energy you will ever be privileged to access," he offered. "I think they respond to you, because you are not afraid."

Ruby smiled thoughtfully, trailing her fingers around them. "Maybe they are not afraid of what I have in mind."

The Genie beamed. "Hopefully that, too. They cannot be hurt, but they require gentleness."

Ruby nodded. Letting her eyes and mind settle, she lightly peeled a slippery, strangely viscous strand from the damp-shining rock, and meditatively pulled it into a thread.

She rolled it between her fingers and considered. "It feels weird."

"Indubitably," acknowledged the Genie calmingly. "But does it feel wrong?"

Ruby grinned. "It feels workable." She twirled and coiled a couple of the strands. But there were so many of them... "It's no less scary. But it's a good sight clearer," she admitted. "And that's a start."

"I'll gather you as many helpers as I can. You have some time, at least," the Genie reminded encouragingly. "This place seems to stretch it out. The sands are so still. And the water here is dark and deep."

Ruby nodded thankfully, her hands already full. She barely looked up from her task, although the light in her eyes gleamed brighter than the swirling sea.

Amber sat bolt upright, her grin spreading like the visit of a welcome dream after too long a night. She'd fallen into an exhausted sleep, drained by trying to think how to protect the Song Weaver. But now, she stared out into a darkness newly wakened with potential, drinking in the sensation of listening to the steady heartbeat of approaching footsteps she'd recognise anywhere as Racxen's.

Their signal tapped against her window, as welcome as his touch against her skin, as soothing as his words against her soul. She wrenched the window open eagerly, feeling her soul both settle and soar in his presence as Racxen climbed in with a breathless grin and a swift kiss. "Sorry to wake you." His skin glistened like a Knight of the sea, slick beneath her touch. "But we must go down to the sea again."

In the luminous darkness her gaze locked with Racxen's in a joy-drenched stare that neither could tear themselves from, drawn by the same pounding, soaring delight.

"On her flight, and with a seamstress's vision, Ruby saw what we could not," Racxen half explained, eyes dancing. "Even the most clear-sighted need support—and I can think of none better than yours. Her plan requires many hands."

Amber could tell he was holding a joyous secret, and to run side by side with him she needed no further bidding. Her answering look mirrored Racxen's own, full of trust and meaning, and he could tell she was relishing the return to their old days, when they could run together instead of in fear.

"To the sea, to the sea! Where the white horses roam and the darkness shall flee!" he invoked in remembrance, grinning.

Amber kissed him swiftly, and grabbed her cloak. "Over rock, over stone; over all fear and shadow—"

"On to bright waters—and hope for tomorrow!"

Together they sprang for the open night, racing through the blue-lit expanse beneath the high free stars towards the shore.

Amber and Racxen scrambled down the bank, the tumbling stones clacking an urgent warning as they skidded fast as an avalanche amidst the companions' rushed descent.

The sky and sea sang wild music together on which Amber let herself soar. "The storm, the Kelpie; those fevers are nothing to being close with you," Racxen promised, the softest of shadows beside her; his claws cool and steady between her fingers, solid against the strangeness of the night and the tug of the water's fickle embrace. "I know the Oak Prince would have us fear this wild magic, but the strongest storm cannot unseat us. And I'd love to dance beneath it with you."

Her heart overflowing as she kissed him in response, Amber felt she could run forever on his words.

But they'd reached the shore already. The sea clamoured urgently as it slid into view, slurping and sighing and trying its new strength, craning to see what was happening beyond as two new pairs of footsteps rounded its edge.

Amidst all the hurry, Amber stopped, and stared in hushed awe. All along the moon-blanched shore curled Selkie men and women, weaving eerily glowing seaweed-like strands into a living web pulsing with light.

At the centre of the enterprise crouched Ruby, unknotting a section, her bright hair falling unheeded over her eyes as she grappled with the net-like structure.

"Sorry, Am," Ruby grinned as she looked up, elbow-deep in viscous green. "But sewing one coat does not the best seamstress in the Realm make. Check out what we're doing. The Selkies will fill you in."

Strands of Hope

"And this is going to save the Song Weaver?" The bizarre structure drew Jasper's gaze like the shore draws the sea; for all along the tideline stretched garish, gelatinous lengths washed from the depths, strung through with viscous, softly pulsing globules of energy.

And there, amongst it all, crouched Ruby, as at-home as he'd ever seen her.

Yet amongst what, exactly? He'd approached to find out.

"Jasper, if you're not going to get your hands dirty, at least stay out of the moonlight. I can't weave if you're going to cast a shadow on my hands."

"Wouldn't dream of it," the Prince appeased, sidestepping neatly. "I'm merely offering a spare pair. Direct me as you will."

He rolled up his shirtsleeves, and Ruby grinned in apology. "I love you for it, but I've got this covered. The Genie is gathering helpers to join me. What I most need you to do is keep watch. The Oak Prince will be after us. He wants to kill the Song Weaver and take her skin, and we're going to protect her."

The solemnity of Jasper's response warmed Ruby. If he was prepared to believe in the necessity of her work, and in her ability, she was prepared to trust him with what she knew. "These are strands of magic," she murmured, as though talking about the most natural thing in the Realm; and really, Jasper supposed, chastened, she was right. "It forms such filaments when endangered; the better to cling to its surroundings instead of becoming washed away," she continued, holding it up to show him. "Everyone talks about magic leaching from the Realm—but it's still here, it's just been cast adrift in the recent turmoil."

Jasper examined the strands dripping from Ruby's hands with ambivalent fascination. Draped passively in front of him they intrigued him, but he couldn't help comparing them to parasites seeking a host.

"So much magic has been discharged recently—great lines of it are drifting through the ocean and becoming beached upon the shore. If we harness it, we can protect the Whail," Ruby insisted steadily, her voice cutting short Jasper's none-too-admirable thoughts.

"Of course." Jasper wriggled, endeavouring to distance himself from his own discomfort. "Perhaps you could instruct me further, that I may know better," he admitted simply, as his eyes rested again on the odd streaks, trying to decipher his feelings about them. He couldn't decide whether they reminded him more of a sticky, trailing net—or of overstretched, outreaching hands.

"The strands retain a certain magical residue," Ruby offered, understanding, as her hands continued their deft work. "But it requires connection with a living being for that potential to be fulfilled—for magic to happen. It is when you touch it, so to speak, that you have a hand in its curtailment or continuation. Depending on your choice it will either discharge harmlessly, ending with you, never to live again—or if you fashion yourself as a conduit, it will channel itself through your actions, and resonate forever more."

She smiled acceptingly. "The Selkies here say that the strands of magic are like fibres of cardiac muscle; if they are not knitted together into part of a greater system, their responses are fated to remain uncoordinated and erratic. But when combined with the right energy, they can sustain the workings of a heart. So, the magic needs us as much as we need it."

Jasper nodded thoughtfully. "Can it be harnessed?" he asked, encouraged by Ruby's calm acceptance and obvious competence. "Or does it ensnare?"

"Both," Ruby returned. The Prince marvelled at her assuredness and found himself accepting it without question. "It isn't sentient in the way we would traditionally understand, and I don't expect its true nature will ever fully be understood. But, from what I've learnt with the Selkies, I think that it drifts in a kind of dormancy until it finds a suitable host. The relationship that develops thereafter can be symbiotic—or possessive."

Ruby grew silent, letting her words settle. She cast the Prince an honest glance, her challenge held within. "Does this knowledge make you more or less inclined to save this 'sorcery', as a certain wight would call it?"

Jasper considered. He recalled a similar moment, so many seasons ago now, when one of Yenna's pack-sisters had asked him whether he would shout for her in times of need. The realisation aligned magic with a wild animal in his mind: it deserved to be saved for its own intrinsic worth, not to have its safety held to ransom on account of its perceived usefulness or malleability.

The Prince looked out across the waters. "Mayhap our survival depends on our response not to what we can bend to our will, but to what we cannot."

He smiled wryly. "Talking of which, here comes Amber. I will take my leave, and keep watch as you asked."

Ruby waved her thanks and hailed Amber.

"Racxen and I have been learning what to do from the Selkies—we didn't want to disturb you," Amber apologised quickly, her face flushed with the night. "But I did want to congratulate you. This is amazing."

Ruby grinned, shaking back her hair from her face. "The Oak Prince left the strands discarded as waste—they're not grand enough for him to either notice or fear. But they're threads of magic. Think what they could do knitted back together."

Amber beamed fondly, plaiting her friend's hair loosely to stop it from falling into her eyes again. Only Ruby would consider what they could do, instead of what whoever found them could do. Magic was in the perfect hands.

"At first, I just thought knitting the strands back together was simply the right thing to do; that it might repair some of the Oak Prince's destruction," Ruby shrugged, weaving deftly. "That was enough of a reason, and I figured that if there was another benefit, it would reveal itself in time. But as soon as I laced my fingers amongst the strands, I felt their power and knew what to do: if we drape them in blankets across the Song Weaver, or perhaps even simply lay them along the shore, they will form a barrier the Oak Prince, with his dry-earth devilment, cannot breach. And we will have defended the Whail as she has always protected us."

Amber felt tears prickle with relief as well as pride. Something to love; something to work at; something to hope for. Ruby had all three.

Crouching beside her readily, Amber spread her hands. With a thankful grin, Ruby introduced the slippery threads to her waiting fingers.

One Selkie alone had not joined the project. Hydd, stumbling tentatively along the shore in the hesitant manner of one long dislocated from all he desired and now steps from being reunited, watched the shimmer of the growing blanket tracing the tideline. His hands still shook too much. His coordination was not sufficiently regained to be of use to them yet. His clan were all there—and amongst them crouched another figure. A figure who had shone through this waking twilight of strange days like a beacon guiding between shore and sea. Ruby.

Gone now were the adornments and affectations she had layered herself with as though fearing her own skin were not enough. Now the wind and water were raw upon her hair and fingers, her face infused with the glow of the elements and her own drive.

Right now, she only had eyes for the blankets and the Selkies who wove them—and in that moment Hydd knew his eyes would never look elsewhere.

With scuffed-raw, salt-stung fingers, Amber clung grimly to each slipping thread as she ineptly fought to emulate some semblance of the skill with which Ruby wove and tied in the ebbing light and tide. She would not let go; she would not leave until Ruby gave the word. This task garnered as much urgency as any desperate quest, holding at its core not the defeat of one so-called sorcerer—but the safety of another.

She willed her fingers not to seize around the fear that all she could give wouldn't be enough. If it could have helped, she would have been tempted to prostrate herself before the Goblin King as Racxen once had, but she knew that would have made it worse in Ruby's eyes, not better. Ruby wouldn't have wanted her there, hurting herself as though that could heal anything. She wanted her here—to stay when the Selkie sewers had dwindled away after she had sent them home. She couldn't bear to see their hands, webbed and unused to the work, reddened and excoriated.

Of course, Ruby had tried to send Amber home too; but only in a manner that Amber had no problem deflecting and that Ruby had no interest in upholding. So they sat now together on the rocky shore, companionably cursing at the difficulty of it all even as their eyes shone with the ocean and the challenge, while the salt-sour smell of the sea, drifting its own scent of magic as though to help with their task, settled solidly between them lulling and urging in equal measure like the ebb and flow of the tide.

Amber wasn't about to question the motives of the friend who had walked through Goblinfire for her, so she paused in solidarity and anticipation as Ruby stopped fretfully and glanced to the tempestuous sky.

"I just hope we're in time. Tie yours off, Am. We need to start carrying them down for the Song Weaver, before the Oak Prince gets here. I've sent Jasper to keep watch, but it can't be much longer."

Amber gazed at the wet-gleamed, near-finished mantles shining with all the promise and power of the ocean revitalised, and she stalled. She'd brave the Icefields twice over for Ruby, but this felt too intimate a triumph to infringe upon. "I'm not worthy of this though, Rube. This is your doing."

Ruby shook her head. "I know what it is to lose my own skin, but you know what it is to mend and carry someone else's. Not just Hydd's—mine too. Together we are going to help the great spirit who has not only borne both our sufferings when we feared they would stretch beyond the endurance of our souls, but who has also, unseen and unsupported, provided the same service for most of the Realm at some point. What we are doing is nothing to what she has done—but by everything good in this Realm, we shall do it yet."

Amber's heart thrummed to Ruby's words, and a smile of pride and promise split her face as she redoubled her efforts. She could feel in her chest that this would work. It was the Whail's kind of magic—of course it would work for her. And Ruby was a force to be reckoned with, side by side with a re-pelaged Selkie or standing alone.

"You two are going to make the most astonishing pair," Amber added in wonder, almost shyly, as she saw Ruby's eyes flit momentarily to find a certain figure on the shore. "When you take the throne beside Hydd."

Ruby's eyes danced with gratitude at her friend's approval, before glinting with a spark of her own. "As a wise woman once said: 'mayhap not today, though'," she noted archly, her eyes agleam with her plan. "My heart and hands are full already, and any kind of future relies on me finishing this first."

"On us finishing this first," Amber reminded warmly, and Ruby smiled as she stretched out her fingers.

"Well, in that case, victory is inevitable," she retorted mischievously. "Race you!"

Together, blankets flying like banners, they scrambled down to the sea.

Running back to warn them of the Oak Prince descending along the ocean-line like an impending storm, Jasper skidded in the face of the incongruous, incredible sight that greeted him as he alighted on the sands. "What are you doing?" he managed weakly. "You don't have time! The Oak Prince is nearly upon us."

Ruby and Amber, Racxen and Yenna, and several more Arraheng and Wolfren, were wading through the shallows, hauling with them shining net-like blankets that glittered with the phosphorescence of the swirling tides through the concealing darkness.

"But the Song Weaver is not safe and the sea is not protected," Yenna reminded, wilfully disregarding her beloved's warning. "To abandon our posts now would ruin everything we have so far achieved with the Selkie and Kelpie. And, in answer to your question: we're wreaking havoc," she added in a quick, appeasing promise, a light agleam in her golden eyes. "By creating magic."

Amidst the surf, the Whail's protruding back glistened like black ink. Patches of her body shone with woven armaments as though she were growing a new skin from the blankets that mantled her. She was rumbling in continuous, sonorous gratitude to the helpers around her, but a savage, thunderous growl suddenly drowned her music.

"He is here!" Yenna emitted a Wolfren bark of warning and, although her voice rang strongly, a disjointing fear rippled less as a wave and more as the disparate, fleeing rhythm that threatens to fibrillate a beleaguered heart.

The Song Weaver began to flop back into deeper water with great beleaguered sighs, as though by distancing herself she could protect these small beings around her from the danger.

"But we haven't finished!" Ruby hissed, her numb fingers frantic. "We've got to get the rest of these pieces out to her; the Selkies aren't wearing their skins, to keep them safe; and I can't swim, my wings would slow me down too much—"

"You're not the only one here," Amber admonished with a grin, striding deeper, a wild thought dancing on the waves.

As though in collusion, Hydd surfaced a second later, parting the obsidian depths in a swirl of molten night. Amber's heart swelled to see him in his element thus. "Plus, there's one Selkie who's never going to be parted from his skin again."

Racxen approached next, to wait reassuringly at Ruby's side. "And, as Amber will tell you, I'm never one to stay out of the water—or away from the wild things."

Ruby stared at each of them, in overawed gratitude.

"You've done enough," Amber reminded her firmly.

"And you three haven't?" Ruby retorted faintly.

"Hold oot upon the shore, an' we'll make it through th' brine," Hydd promised.

"Aye," Ruby grinned, risking a glance to the Oak Prince, who was still scouring the sands instead of the surf, not risking to think they might yet dare dance amongst the waves. "Ah can do tha'."

They shared a blazing glance before turning away, afire with shared purpose.

"Come," urged Hydd to Amber, taking an end of the next blanket in his teeth after sending Racxen on with another. "Th' Ook Prince disnae wish ye tae be as comfortable here as ye were once in air. Bu' he disnae realise tha' ye hae nae lost a haem—ye've gained several. The brine thrashes tae see ye trapped sae. Come intae the haem that cleaves tae ye now."

And so, she bundled a blanket as closely to her as she had Hydd's pelt so recently, and followed that seaglass stare away from the macabre heat of the Oak Prince's advance and into the living, chill embrace of the slow-breathing sea.

Hydd flowed like a watery shadow beside her. His presence buoyed and anchored her in equal measure as readily as if he steered her hand in hand. His steadiness amidst the confusion of waves helped Amber find her own rhythm as she kicked through the yielding cold and immersed herself in this new realm, towing the blanket behind her.

The sea vibrated as though in ancient song, a deep hum of approval as if the sea itself were purring, as Amber caught up with Hydd and Racxen and together they swept their weavings across the Whail's great bulk, the waves jostling them to make haste. "I will speak with you again, ere long we part," the Song Weaver throated. Amber felt it in her chest even as the water slapped about her ears as she headed back to the shore for the next blanket, flanked comfortingly by Racxen and Hydd.

The wind cut against her hungrily as she stumbled onto the sands again and felt the land-swept fear slap against her more strongly than the sea.

"We need more time!" Ruby squeaked in panic, the ocean squirming with her fear and the blankets bucking with the roil of the waves. "We need a distraction—"

"Cast your eyes to the living waters, deadwood demon! Those you seek to destroy do not stand alone!"

"That Genie knows who to call in a tight spot," Jasper muttered disbelievingly as he turned. "Zaralathaar herself!"

Amber's heart bloomed with a warming chill to hear the Water Nymph's familiar ringing tones, and she spun in awe to stand in proud witness as the waves parted, tamed at the aging Princess's voice, to trail in her wake as she strode from them, her dress clinging like the scales that used to adorn her body, her hair streaming like the Kelpie's mane.

"Cast your fire," Lady Zaralathaar warned dismissively, "and I will quench it with a glance."

Amber couldn't stop staring at the Water Nymph. She seemed to shine with the pure, cold light of the moon itself. Her presence drew the power of the tides to her fingertips. Her eyes flashed like living ice. Amber had never felt so relieved to witness someone so frightening, hadn't felt so safe and scared all at once since Rraarl had thrown himself over her as the Arkhan vaults had collapsed as the Venom-spitters attacked in the library ruins.

"You are fading from this Realm, witch!" The Oak Prince bristled and raged, his anguish the sound of dying forests whipped to a frenzy until their branches scream and break. "How can you believe yourself worthy to stand against me?"

"I am both death and its defiance," Zaralathaar thundered in response, her voice ringing with the kind of strength the Oak Prince would never possess. "What fear can you hold for me?" She flung the challenge as contemptuously to the deadwood Dryad as she would to a young stripling. Amber grinned to hear it.

Yet the air shivered with foreboding, as if the Oak Prince were threatening to break the fabric of the Realm. "You are quicker than you once were, Zaralathaar, to come to the aid of those who would falter alone," he hissed, low and dangerous. "Yet who will stand with a dying woman? Let us see what influence you still possess, here before the end."

Amber felt clutched with real pain. The Water Nymph allowed few to glimpse the constant and wretchedly deep loneliness she had become accustomed to since she had turned her back on the sea to watch over the Realm's inhabitants.

"I own the element in which this Realm stands," the Nymph rallied, steel in her gaze and ice dripping from her tongue. "That is all I need."

"It might be all you need, my lady. But it is not all you have," Amber blurted. "Standing with you, for all time, is the sky above."

Racxen nodded quickly, understanding. "The earth below, also."

"The fire within," Yenna pledged next.

"The wood surrounding," Han added.

"And th' brine beyon'," Hydd finished, sealing their vows.

The Nymph had never been one to voice gratitude openly, and yet amidst her silence her companions stood firm; knowing they would willingly walk through fire for this woman carved of ice.

"I have stared into the hollow eye of death," the Nymph concluded, a deep-held, faint-heard warmth glowing in her voice like magma beneath a glacier. "It taught me many things, and patience was not one of them. Step back, or endure the ignominy of subjugation by a woman so old that the most ancient Dryads of this land have branches less brittle than her bones."

"Done!" Ruby breathed victoriously from the shallows, tying off and breaking the final thread as the last blanket slid away between her fingers like a fish sensing freedom as it's lowered into the water for release.

"Underestimate not the power of beings unafraid to stand in their element," the Nymph finished haughtily, sweeping away as though the Fairy's signal had been pure coincidence.

The apparition's attention snapped back to Amber. Her heart bloomed a fierce relief, for here was a chance to keep his focus on her—and away from Ruby and the others with the Song Weaver further down the bay. Still, her resolve tremored as his worm-words writhed.

"I came to save you," the Oak Prince wheedled, sawing into her vulnerability. For all the Realm he sounded like a beloved grandfather, worn down by care. He had come so far out of his element, risked so much, for children who never appreciated what he had sacrificed...

Amber felt her heart contract in shame, but even as she realised it, her soul railed at his attempt to manipulate her compassion. It had been a wild night indeed for entering the water and yet, in a heady rush of certainty, she knew she needed to again. The predator in the water held no fear for her. The predator of the forest, she would deal with here and now. The pain seared shriekingly into her as she made her choice and strode back into waves. The ice of their fingers felt safer than the burn of his touch.

"You'll catch your death," the Oak Prince hissed. "You shy from me to cavort in this den of monsters?"

Amber strode undaunted through the surf, her breath puffing mechanically against the pain and her steps dancing to the solemn, untameable rhythm of the sea.

"Yes. And you don't get to take that choice away from me," she warned, her voice steady, as hypnotic and potent as the swirling waves. "I have as much right to be contradictory, and changeable, as anyone, without it eliciting the kind of judgement you seek to pass upon me. We will never tame the Kelpie—whether for you, or for ourselves. Should his depths, which you seek to drain, become lost, we would lose something immeasurable and irreplaceable.

"As you so frequently seek to warn me, I am perfectly aware that he is the wild. But the difference between you and I," Amber warned, giddy on knowing her own heart amidst the touch of the free night, "is you want to tame it. I want to run with it. You are mistaken in your endeavour to turn me from him, sir. He is not fear. He is the numinous awe that I chase. That sustains me. Follow me if you dare, for I go into his Realm with no fear of losing my way home."

The Oak Prince stopped. Amber couldn't tell if there really was something in her words, or if he was merely dragging out her death.But in rallying himself the Oak Prince broke his attention away from Amber for just a moment—and his gaze fell upon the others further along the shore, weaving strands that could no longer survive unnoticed.

A deathly chill descended as the Oak Prince approached, until even the sea, which had until now been fretful with life and urgency, seemed to still in its terror. Amber hastened through the sloshing surf to stand once more with her friends.

Malevolent, inhuman eyes flared as the apparition's disdainful gaze brushed the blanketed strands. "They won't hurt me," he hissed.

"They're not meant for you," Ruby sniffed.

"And they're not intended to hurt." Racxen swept the next bundle easily over his shoulders and wading into the shallows with it, shaking out the glowing lengths until they billowed in the gusting breeze and settled discarded at the surface.

No, the Oak Prince corrected himself ashenly. *Not discarded. Offered…*

The shallows shifted into bubbling ink as the Whail spumed a great breath and nudged the blankets—mere scraps alongside her bulk—until they tangled with the trailing rags the litter of whelps had tried to make. The reason behind it seemed nonsensical; pure sentimentality, and yet the Oak Prince shivered to sense it: deep, unusual magic, like a change of season stirring prematurely. Those scraps spun in the Whail's wake like a stream of stars. She shone with phosphorescence. She shone with hope. Restë blackened in his eyes. Armour. They were making her armour. Out of discarded sorcery.

Racxen passed a reverent hand across the Song Weaver's rubbery skin, now laced more with magic than with scars. The gentle power emanating from her caught in his breath, and he knew right then that if the Oak Prince tried anything upon these shores, they would all stand with her against him no matter the consequences.

The Oak Prince grew storm-cloud sullen as he realised what was happening. They were protecting the Whail. His final option. The creature that he hadn't bothered to consider; that no-one dared acknowledge; that everyone trained themselves not to see, for fear of facing what she protected them from: these runts had not only faced up to her presence and proven brave enough to hold her gaze—but they were even defending her. His luck had run out.

The apparition darkened, thunder-like. The full weight of his terrible gaze fell on Amber, even as her friends pressed closer in solidarity.

"No more games. I have learned all I need from you. Next time, the dance will be beneath my eaves. And to my tune. Your doom awaits at Trickster's Gate."

The apparition's words hung in the chill air long after he had departed.

"'Your doom awaits at Trickster's Gate'," Jasper murmured in sudden realisation. "It's not as direct a threat as we feared. We thought he'd wait for you there. But it's the site of his final chance at transformation—his final chance to claim a skin. From someone in the Wildwood Labyrinth."

"From the Dryad." The knowledge settled putridly in Amber's stomach. "Her skin enveloped me, hid the pelt from the Oak Prince himself. Hers is exactly the kind of skin he is looking for. And it's my fault. I put her in danger," Amber finished, her voice strangely hollow. She wanted so much to return home and hole up and hide. To claim she had done her part and any more would be too much. And yet, the safety of her friends remained at stake.

"It's not your fault—the Goblins told him, remember?" Jasper insisted helplessly. "And it's not your fight. Why do you always have to involve yourself like this?" But Amber's gaze had slipped into the distance, as though she were already planning to leave them. Jasper felt himself tense.

"Because I know what to do about it. On my own. I can't bring an army. I have to outsmart him, and he cannot suspect." Her decision was made, and what use would preparation be, for a journey that could only end one way? Surely, it could only be made alone and without ceremony.

So Amber readjusted her cloak, and started walking.

Flotsam and Jetsam

"There's a reason why I walked away from you all," Amber snuffled. "You weren't supposed to see me crying like this."

"The brine is awash wi' tears uncountable," Hydd rejoined peaceably, "an' yet 't'will outlive us all."

Amber nodded, her breath pure on her tongue once more now that the crippling convulsions of her sobs had eased with the ebbing tide of her emotion. She should have known that her friends wouldn't have left her. There were some hints they collectively remained stubbornly blind to, after all this time, and Hydd was rapidly assimilating himself into that collective.

"Th' others hae gang fur help, as will I, an' Racxen will stay," the Selkie promised. "Ye dinnae hae tae do this, ye ken." His wise seal eyes seemed to hold her tears for a moment.

"It's because none of you would ever ask me to, that I will always decide to," Amber admitted, her grin watery but sure. And calm now, truly, lulled by her friends and the knowledge that this was for them.

So, she stared out towards the forest, her eyes ready and gaping. "I'm not dead yet. Let's meet what's next."

"Whatever may happen after, what's next is of your choosing." Shade shifted into solid form as Racxen slipped into view from the darkness beneath the trees, the soft shadow of his liquid silhouette pure solace as Hydd, understanding, took his leave.

Amber's relief at his coming, when she had feared nothing could help, trembled through her to know that she wasn't alone even now, and she twined her fingers through his claws as though she'd never let go. Racxen guided her to a cave tucked inside the tanglewood, his steps as light as if it were any other night and any other shelter; as though time enough remained. And she learned that it did in truth for, leaning back to back in a companionable silence, listening to the gentle night-noises by the light of the moon, they passed a treasured night.

And, because he didn't demand that she try to sleep, but instead settled in close beside her, his scent mingling in the air between them, slowing her breath and easing the frantic racing of her heart as he enfolded her completely with his arms and body, cocooned softly and knowing safety, Amber slept.

She woke without immediately knowing why. The nameless knowledge she couldn't escape pressed, trying to suffocate, and yet Racxen's presence and embrace had forged a castle around her that no fear could penetrate. So she lay for a moment, letting the memory of his closeness imprint itself deep within the memory of her skin, her blood, her bone.

Then she slid out from beneath the touch she never wanted to leave, with a soft, fierce kiss and a whispered promise that she would return, and crept outside.

In case it proved to be the last time, amidst the Realm's permission of silence Amber let the moonlight splash her skin until it began to thaw the ice of fear that had crystallised again as she stood alone with what she must do. She stared into the waiting swathe of trees, aglow with myriad hues of the forest at night.

Amongst it all, viridescent eyes shone.

Amber stared, hope unshackled. "Hydd? You came back!"

"Selkies ne'er forget tae come back, nae matter the distance atween," Hydd promised. He grinned self-effacingly. "Tha's how I lost mah pelt i' the first place."

Amber squeezed his hand warmly, and managed a smile in return. "Perhaps it is how you got it back, also." She shivered suddenly. "Might need you to piece me back together too, at this rate. I'd better go before I start crying my eyes out again."

"Waves cannae damage water," Hydd promised. "The brine will survive the strongest storm—an' so will ye. Ye can be hurting, an' healing, an' whole, all at the same time. Ye're mair than good enough, exactly as ye are—an' what ye're becomin' will astound even ye." The Selkie's voice washed as soothingly as the tide.

"And before you do—go, I mean, not cry—" Stumbling over the words as he approached, Jasper gestured to the others and Amber's breath caught in her chest as her friends stepped forward from beneath the trees, each with an offering: King Morgan's cloak to replace her own, the Prince's Gem from Jasper, a carved amulet from Racxen, a threaded ring from

Ruby, his own precious chalk once more from Mugkafb, a forest-woven circlet from Han, a bandana from Yenna, even a feather for her hair from Tanzan, who had appeared amongst them as suddenly as a nomadic Dragon-friend was wont to do. Finally, Amber's fingers strayed to the strip of his own pelt that Hydd had bound around her wrist.

"Wear them," Mugkafb advised solemnly. "No-one sends their best friend into battle without a talisman. And, well, you have lots of friends, so you'll have lots of talismans."

Amber hugged him. "I feel safer already," she promised, meaning it.

Her friends stepped forward, as though to dress her with intimate care. Amber let their attentions settle deeply into her, in reverent silence save for her whispered words of thankfulness. Each piece fired a piercing, grateful warmth, as though her friends had peeled off pieces of their own skin to patch hers, worn as it had been willingly by restoring another's. As Rraarl silently slipped his chain across her shoulders, however, her tears threatened to slide.

THANKS TO YOU, I FEEL SAFE WITHOUT IT, the Gargoyle promised, his words placed careful and considered upon the scuffed ground. YOU HELPED ME DEVELOP THE KIND OF STRENGTH I NEED NO CHAIN FOR.

Laying a hand aside his stone shoulder, she accepted gratefully.

As Racxen approached next, she saw with a fresh pang of love the tears on his cheek, and she hugged him, wanting to ease his pain more dearly even than she wished to banish her own.

The Arraheng released a shuddering breath as she buried her face against his. "I'm not crying," he promised with resolve. "I'm a rock." He pressed a knuckle hurriedly into the corners of his eyes as he turned slightly, still holding her. "Which cries sometimes," he admitted with a shaky grin, embarrassed.

Amber leant companionably against his shoulder. "That's my favourite kind," she promised comfortably, wrapping her arms more closely around him and wishing they never need part from these precious moments.

"Trust what we have," Racxen murmured, his breath warm amongst her hair. "The Oak Prince will test you; he will try you—but what will remain true are the dreams we breathed as we lay together beneath the stars, the promises we whispered in the pre-dawn softness under a shared blanket, the pledges we made and held amidst the rebuilding of the Realm, and the sacred moments savoured with only the moon as witness. Nothing he can do or say can erase them, nor waver my love for you." He twined his claws with her fingers, drinking in her gaze with his own.

"You've sewn another's skin back together," He reminded her, his words so soft now that they were hers alone. "And standing in nothing but your own, you are the most awe-inspiring sight I've ever beheld. You are the equal of everything in this forest, this Realm. You are not of one part, as most of us are. You are of all of it. The Oak Prince has nothing on you."

"The strength you give me to walk away now is matched only by my desire to return to you," Amber promised whisperingly as she brushed her lips against his and stepped back shakily. "I will always return to you—but I must now into the forest, to be swallowed up in leaves that blow away." She breathed a tentative idea around the words as she strode on, possibilities afire as she let her fingers curl protectively around the many talismans her friends had gifted her. Perhaps, just perhaps, there was hope.

Yet the truth gathered inescapably, bearing down upon her with all the potency of a brewing storm. Beneath the ancient eaves, the shadows lengthened, as a predator approached his prey.

And behind her, the trees pressed closer.

At Trickster's Gate

With dust flurrying hot-temperedly in the wake of her footsteps and dry leaves bristling irritably at the audacity of her presence, Amber strode through the ravaged remains of the forest that foreshadowed Trickster's Gate.

Swarming images of her friends protectively before her eyes, Amber fought back the fell visions oozing through the undergrowth in the wake of the Oak Prince as his chill, smothering twilight descended to snuff out the sun and all hope of rescue or release.

She refused to let his sorcery be the unhinging of her. She had borne the cavernous silence of the Icefields, and heard her own song rise in response inside her, so the Oak Prince didn't know what he was dealing with if he thought such things could unsettle, let alone unseat her.

Yet she advanced in vigilant silence, time itching along her spine like sweat, for this silence, in contrast, claimed a ruptured absence, bearing witness to the sullying of a once sacred landscape.

"You were so fixated upon keeping the Selkie Prince from his skin," Amber bellowed, flinging her challenge into the forest. "I wonder if you dare risk your own, here at the end? I wonder if you understand why I offer my own, in defence of his? I wonder if you realise how it proves the existence of a magic we don't need your Greenwood Court for?"

With the pricking of a dozen needles atop her scalp, she braced herself against the swirling onslaught of skin-slicing leaves flurrying into familiar form as the wrath of the Oak Prince descended in full force.

"You have no idea what you are proposing. I need a skin—and a skin I will take. "You must know that you cannot hope to stand against me, damaged as you are." The Oak Prince's gaze lingered disease-like upon her wing stumps as his savage eyes materialised at the centre of the apparition. "You are broken."

"Yet stronger than you are whole," Amber warned steadily. "So don't taint the air with your tongue." Against the bewitchment holding the forest frozen in oppression, her voice sounded pitiful even to her. But her words were her own and still under her control, and they gave her courage.

She stood before the Oak Prince unafraid. It was not so long ago, after all, that she had stood at the brink of the threshing, chopping tides of ice and sea and had borne their wild, tumultuous thrum inside her soul; coursed their soaring pulse within her blood. In learning to integrate with them, melding with their strengths and incorporating their power into her own, she had reformed and reaffirmed her own boundaries. And she would not let them now be breached.

"You think you can end this, on your own?" the wood wight murmured in his scalding-hiss voice. "Something changed, when you patched that shameful rag of skin."

Amber's response was a smile he couldn't steal, for his words might be spores of malice, but she wouldn't let them settle here. "Perhaps, in healing someone else's wounds, I have come to terms with my own, and opened myself to experiences which have filled the remaining void so completely that they twine between the gaping spaces in my soul, to snugly guard the gap through which your toxicity could once seep," she warned brightly.

"Brave words indeed." The Oak Prince's eyes narrowed dangerously. "Yet who will heal the healer, I wonder, once I have finished with you?"

She bristled at his presumption, but refused to let him tie her tongue. "Whatever wounds may come, I can withstand them. For I have healed another's hurts," Amber acknowledged, sacred knowledge gleaming in her eyes. "And also, I have accepted my own. A process no less arduous, in its own way. And no less transformative."

"You speak well of transformation, wingless one." The mocking words dripped leisurely, his voice a shard of ice drawn along her spine beneath her cloak, and she fought hard not to shiver. "For it is over a skin that we now fight."

"My Prince knows the old ways and tomes," Amber warned back, undaunted. "He told me you set yourself more in thrall to a bargain than will any Goblin. And so, I offer you one now: my skin against yours. Last standing survives."

Those soulless eyes glowed dangerously as the Oak Prince's leering visage shifted more clearly into view amongst the foliage, and in response the branches around Amber shuddered as though itching to rip her apart.

"You don't have much of a skin." The voice crackled with the dreadful force of dying seasons. "This will not take long."

"To chance becoming more, one must risk becoming less," Amber reasoned steadily, although fear squirmed in her gut. "And I have these." Cold sweat broke on Amber's skin as she touched the first amulet. This was moving too fast; what was she thinking? "They're what my skin is made of. Pieces of who I have been. Who I am. Who I'll always be."

Blood-berry red gleamed amongst the decaying green. "This I can work with."

Amber's heart tattooed fit to surge from her chest.

"Take them off," the voice warned.

Amber's blood grew chill in her veins. Each piece felt burned against her; the last remnants of life in this dire place.

"One condition," she bargained, stalling, her frantic plan flailing half-formed amidst her desperately racing thoughts. "You are a spirit of the old ways. You know that magic—" the word on such sorcery caught in her throat like a betrayal "—is only as potent, only as binding, as the energy exchanged. As you said, I have no armour. These are all I have, more layers of self than anything else. I will remove them one at a time—but," she added firmly, before her voice and resolve could both abandon her, "as you have lain down your side of the bargain, I will put forth mine. For each layer I remove, you will remove one also. That way the balance will be maintained. That way the power will be magnified."

"Agreed." His eyes gleamed so lustily they made her feel sick.

Drawing a steadying breath that didn't work, Amber peeled Yenna's bandana from around her neck. Her throat felt horribly exposed as she cast it slowly aside. It fluttered away, caught on the gusting wind, and for a moment Amber let herself imagine that it might find its way back to its owner, and the Wolf Sister would find a friend's scent mingled with her own to remember her by, once this was all over.

Any comfort that idea could afford was torn asunder by the splintering scene before her. True to his infernal word the Oak Prince, with a disquieting crackling, snapping sound as though some unholy fire were ripping through his boughs, had stripped away a layer of his own bark, and was now looking distinctly more Requë than Recö. His leaves browned and curled, his branches thinning as he turned in challenge to her, his every aspect now more brittle and angular, honed tight with a predator's skill at waiting.

As the hideous turn-taking continued, and Amber let drop Morgan's cloak from her shoulders, Mugkafb's chalk from her pocket, Jasper's Gem from her hand, Ruby's ring from her finger, Hydd's pelt scrap from around her wrist, Tanzan's feather from her hair and Rraarl's chain from about her waist, the Oak Prince with every turn grew more skeletal. His leaves fell to a pile on the floor, his branches became twisted and brittle.

Amber's heart sputtered weakly as she felt her fingers clutch her final amulet: Racxen's carven tracker sigil, which hung around her neck on a cord.

She refused to look at the apparition before her until she had forced her breathing to keep within her measure. Racxen had released the Moonstruck Lake Kelpie. The Selkie Lord had his skin back, and had pledged of his own volition to maintain the Fountain. Now was not a bad time to die, surrounded by close-knit pieces from everyone she held dear.

Thanks to them, she had known all the love she could ever have needed. Thanks to them, surviving this far was enough, for her brief years blazed in her mind like a thousand of the best. And the memories—ah, the memories! She would hold them close, until the Oak Prince had finished and she herself was but a memory in her turn.

Her heart stabbed afresh with the love coursing through her veins and pulsing in her fingers as she clutched Racxen's amulet tightly. Amber let this final talisman fall, lifted her gaze one last time to the Oak Prince, and resolved not to lower her eyes.

"Tell them I tried, okay?" she whispered, in case the matronly old Dryad who had tried so hard to help could somehow still hear her.

Something fired in Amber and she set her jaw. A final drenching gulp of her surroundings, a final mouthful of the sweet clean air that was still sustaining her and then, to the Oak Prince, she muttered more in challenge than resignation: "Your turn."

His savage eyes flashed faintly, embedded in the almost petrified trunk, before a whistling sigh of rushing wind enveloped the Oak Prince's now wintry form.

It was so unexpected that Amber almost fell backwards, but she knew with an urgent certainty that she had to bear witness. Squinting through the lashing gusts she saw a raw and terrible change, as the whirlwind contorted branching limbs and threshed away bark skin.

And yet, as the last remaining leaves were stripped away, the constrictive, gnarled trunk cage and skeletal branches split open, releasing bud-burst blossoms of renewal. The death-clutched horror of moments ago spilled into memory as pristine tendrils reached out in bloom and a harmless cloud of greenest leaves billowed, swirling tightly and dissipating on the remaining Renë breeze in fragrant confetti.

"I diminish: you are free to pass." She almost missed the rustling breath, easing away on the cleansing wind, that finally whispered: "I will never have a skin."

Amber gathered her wits, and her breath. "There will always be room in this Realm for the skinless, the vulnerable," she promised. "If you have learned anything else from stalking us, have you not learned that skins cannot be stolen—but they can be mended in more ways than there will ever be means of damaging them?"

The fain wisp of a smile. "Perhaps you are right. Perhaps I can start again." New shoots reached out hopefully, tender and tentative.

Amber, exhausted, found the strength to smile back. "If you are willing to be more flexible, as your remaining skin now is, I'm sure many will help you grow one."

A sigh of release, and he was gone, leaving in his absence a reawakening forest shaking itself free from his shackles. Amber rubbed sweat from her eyes weakly and staggered back, staring up in wonder as the arboreal prison he had wrought retracted itself from around her, letting in space and sunlight. She stared in stunned relief at her friends assembled in the dappled clearing beyond. Shakily, she stooped to retrieve the precious fragments of the patchwork armour which, having saved her life in its disintegration, now lay spread and scattered.

As she gathered them to her again, she held each to her chest in gratitude. Yet one eluded her. She felt herself grow frantic.

"Racxen, I can't find your amulet. It's your sigil; your tracker mark—"

"The mark of a tracker is that you never give up searching for the one you hold dearest in all the Realm." Racxen, with a smile, guided her to her feet and pulled her close. "And I found you again, didn't I? So all is well. Engo ro fash." His breath was warm on her hair. "Even could we never be together again, I would track you beyond the ties of this Realm to keep you safe, and be your second shadow so you knew you were not alone."

Amber grinned. "And I thought that was just my overactive imagination."

Racxen returned her grin, kissing her softly as his arms slipped around her to hold her close and safe, his voice warm and private. "Say the word, and we'll turn any imaginings you wish into memories."

Memories already shared flooded beneath his gaze, and Amber grinned unashamedly, her breath quickening at the thought. "I'll remind you of that, later," she promised.

She breathed deeply, and looked back round at her friends in appreciation. "But just being here with all of you, after everything, means the Realm to me. It's everything I'll ever need."

Racxen kissed her softly in agreement, and as the dawn stretched luxuriously around them, all pink sky and silence, Amber leant companionably against Rraarl's shoulder, hugged Mugkafb, clutched hands with Jasper, shared a blazing glance with Yenna, stroked Ruby's hair.

The early sunrays traced along her back, their golden fingers as gentle as Racxen's claws, and she lost and found herself in his gaze as together with her friends she watched the sky unfurl over a Realm at peace once more.

"Ah ha' ne'er seen somaine so bonnie as when ye were tyin' the strands into nets on the beach tae defend the Song Weaver," Hydd admitted to a guarded, but intrigued, Ruby. His quiet voice was honest as he tried out the caressing words tentatively, as though trying on a new pelt as wondrous as the one he'd so recently been reacquainted with. "I offer this not tae change wha' I'd ne'er think needed fixin'—but from the wish tae ease a reminder o' a pain that should ne'er hae been wrought and disnae hae tae be borne."

His eyes burned and trembled, uncertain as to how his next words might be construed. "The return o' mah powers ha' granted me a certain, finite, ability: o' healin'. Ah offered it tae another first, as I knew ye would hae wanted. So, this gift, if ye desire it, comes from someain who knows ye better than I, an' who stood their ground more firmly than mah insistence."

Ruby's eyes filled with tears at the realisation. "Oh, Amber."

Hydd nodded gently. "What d'ye say, lass? I can fade tha' scar, if ye wish."

"I'm not sure if I'd say this if I didn't have the option," Ruby admitted raggedly, chewing the possibility. "But, I'm not entirely sure I need you to, any more," she said finally. A part of her was surprised by how easily calm welled up inside her now, despite holding the gaze of a man she'd always expected would make her go weak. Instead, he had helped her reconnect with her own inimitable strength.

She grinned, her voice steady and sure. "After all, the Realm is full of strange and wondrous beings—it can stretch to one more. If you can be my scarred hero, I can be yours."

Hydd grinned in turn, his sharp seal teeth gleaming, his smile dancing on weather-chapped lips like sunlight glimmering atop a post-storm sea. Ruby wondered light-headedly where the courage to talk with him like this had come from. She'd been so used to talking herself down with men. Or, she corrected herself, at first in embarrassment but then smirking mischievously: with Sardonyx and Carnelian, which, of course, was a completely different experience to talking with men.

Hydd strode into the shallows and turned back to her, raw and half changed and uncertain. "This isnae too weird fur ye?"

"Anything that makes you more you, is good by me." Hearing the weight the words pressed on his soul, Ruby answered softly and sincerely. Then she giggled, light as air and just as strong. "But don't forget: I've woven real magic upon these shores. For all you know, you might not be weird enough."

So she stood and watched, saw his transformation complete, and ran into the surf to join him exactly as he was, her laughter mingling with his joyous barks.

Upon New Sands

Torchlight flowed across the cave walls as Racxen worked swirling rich earthen hues into endless patterns, etched through with gouges and riverlets carved by his claws.

He looked up and grinned at Amber's approach. "I won't be late for the party. I wouldn't miss it for the Realm," he promised. "I just realised there was one more thing left I needed to do. To reset the balance." He wiped a smear of clay from his brow with the back of his hand. "Legend tells that for anything taken from the ancestors' cavern, something must be given back. The old stories whisper that everything in this cavern will have its day of use. I have no way of knowing how or when that will be, but I want this piece—and myself—to be ready. After all, I have no intention of letting this be our final quest together."

"That's a pledge I think it's safe to make," Amber promised, her vow written large in her broad grin, relieved to know he felt the same way. "May I?"

At Racxen's nod, she stepped beside him, wondering at the way the fluid shapes, the merging symbols and figures, seemed to climb through the clay every time she shifted her gaze. "Wow."

Racxen smiled in thanks, scooping a mound, smoothing it with his palms and working it with a claw. "You're not going to ask me what it will become?"

"It's your vision; I would gladly guard its secrets," Amber reassured him warmly. "I'll meet you out there."

Amber let her feet guide her to the shore again, let the sea's tongue lick away the ardour and anxiety of the past. With the angst of recent times washed away, she felt so light she could almost be floating on those sparkling waves.

Happiness bubbled as she stared out across the endless ocean, watching the tides heave and pull, iridescent in the morning glow as the seals slapped and rolled as though conjured anew wherever sunlit spray struck salty foam.

Towards her rippled a sleek, mottled seal-form as supple and unbreakable as willow: every fluid line and curve a celebration radiating transformational power. She waved eagerly, a grin splitting her face as she laughed with Hydd's joy and her own.

Amber's smile caught slightly as she saw Ruby. "He told me he could heal you."

But Ruby grinned fit to rival a Goblin. "That's a lot to hang on one person. But he loves me, which is a start and, knowing that, I can help myself heal."

Amber hugged her best friend proudly, thrilled, and watched her stare out wistfully towards the Selkie Lord again.

"Are you going to be okay?" she pressed softly, slipping her arm round Ruby. "I know he'll be spending a lot of time at the Basin, but he won't be gone forever."

Ruby shrugged brightly. "You know me. If he's not eerie and unobtainable, I'm not interested."

"He's not eerie," Amber protested with a grin. Then she shoulder-nudged Ruby affectionately. "Royal, though. Told you you'd find your Prince."

"You will see him again, and often enough," a familiar, formidable voice promised. "His presence is a comfort to an old woman, as is the fact he will do well," Zaralathaar prophesised. "He is not, after all, the most impetuous youngster I have ever had the troublesome fortune to encounter." The Nymph's clear grey eyes shone with an ancient brightness as if a weight were now lifted. "Don't stop meddling, child."

Amber bowed to her, awed and astounded.

"I went back to the water," Zaralathaar explained, as though it were the simplest thing of all time. Perhaps it was. "I cast the Gem to where it would. To whomever might need it."

"That might be us, in the not so distant future," Jasper admitted worriedly, with a quick bow to the Nymph to apologise for interrupting. "The Oak Prince was right in a perverse way, after all. We've chosen to adapt, rather than die out gracefully. The real fight is yet to come. Even with the Selkie Lord's power, the Fountain won't last forever. When that fails, we must be ready: to fight for our lives and for our futures."

"We're more ready than ever—haven't we just proved that?" Amber shushed, her eyes as agleam with the joy of the sea as they were shining with the steadiness of the vast, restored forest.

"You've proved it," Racxen corrected, padding over and slipping his arms around her. Their eyes sparked as though the rest of the Realm had stepped back for a moment, and the warmth of his smile melted her. Amber couldn't stop her grin from widening as she realised that they'd finally have time to spend together. Uninterrupted.

"I'm inclined to agree," the Water Nymph interrupted pointedly, with a clearwater smile. "The writing on it gave Hydd hope, when he stumbled to the shore on the eve of the attack they wrought upon him."

A shiver ran through Amber to hear of it. "That's how he found me?"

"No. It's why he trusted you."

Amber smiled, her gaze swelling contentedly with the sea. "He helped me learn to trust myself, too. And he wasn't the only one. Promise me something? Don't you stop meddling either."

The Nymph's eyes shone like aged ice. "I know you will find your way, child, when I am not here. Yet take care, for the Realm is changing. Paths once clear have tangled into labyrinths. Even the elements we once trusted implicitly fall now towards turmoil. There are rumours in the desert that the rains themselves will one day fail—or even the light itself." Then a light lifted in her own eyes. "But they say also that my days are short—yet here I am, feeling better than in a long time. All days deserve to be lived as well as they can be, and I intend to spend at least a hundred more basking in happiness. Do not fear, child. This Realm will always hold far more adventure than angst."

Amber hugged her. "We will do everything we can to further both your investigation, and your happiness." The grin of affirmation Amber shared with her companions was full of fellowship and confidence, for in the light of all they had achieved, the tangled paths ahead glowed enticingly, promising to welcome her back beneath their boughs. "And we will always be here to help you choose adventure."

About the Author

As a qualified Occupational Therapist with a Master of Arts in Psychoanalysis and experience working in a variety of psychiatric settings, Laura is especially passionate about using writing and other creative pursuits therapeutically to help children, teens, and adults cope with and recover from mental illness and trauma. A steadfast believer in the value of fantasy as a nurturing space and safe escape, she draws inspiration from everywhere wild and magical and seeks to both celebrate and inspire the indomitable nature of the human spirit through her writing.

Printed in Great Britain
by Amazon

29511343R00158